SUNNY SKIES AND SUMMER KISSES

ELIZA J SCOTT

Storm
PUBLISHING

Ebook ISBN: 978-1-83700-365-5
Paperback ISBN: 978-1-83700-366-2

Cover design: Rose Cooper
Cover images: Shutterstock

Published by Storm Publishing.
For further information, visit:
www.stormpublishing.co

For my family xxx

ONE

THE THIRD SATURDAY IN MARCH

'Penny for them, Noushka.' Kitty hitched the bulging washing basket higher on her hip, sending a sock tumbling from the pile.

'Hmm?' Anoushka had been leaning against the Aga, gnawing at a hangnail for the last ten minutes, her mind in turmoil. She pulled her gaze from the flagstone floor to see her step-mum smiling at her as she made her way across the sun-filled kitchen. Ethel, the family's black Labrador, looked up from her slumber and blinked sleepily, while Mabel jumped up from her cosy spot, curled up in the crook of Eth's tummy, and trotted over. The little cocker spaniel scooped up the stray sock, her golden tail swishing busily.

'Everything okay?' Kitty popped the basket on the worktop and bent to retrieve the sock. 'Thank you, Mabes, I think I'll have that.' Though she was smiling, the flicker of concern on her step-mum's face didn't escape Anoushka's notice.

'Yeah, everything's fine; I was just thinking about...' Anoushka stopped herself, biting down on her words before they came rushing out, anxiety squirming in her stomach. Right now, the last thing she needed was to share her feelings with Kitty, whose compassionate disposition had a happy knack of making it the easiest thing in the world to pour your heart out. One look from those gentle brown eyes was all it took before, whoosh, out they'd come in a torrent. Kitty always knew the right words to make you feel better, how to chase your worries away. Well, until recently, that is. And with Damon, Anoushka's boyfriend of the last eighteen months, due in half an hour, now wasn't the time for one of *those* conversations. She needed to face him with a clear head, without the influence of her family – or their opinions – ringing in her ears. Not that they'd ever try to force their views on her, but this had to be her decision, and hers alone. She was twenty-two years old, for goodness' sake.

Anoushka drew in a deep breath. 'Just lost in my thoughts, that's all.' She gave what she hoped was a convincing smile as she lifted her mug of tea to her mouth.

'You don't say.' Kitty laughed. The pause that followed suggested her step-mum was choosing her next words carefully; there'd been more than enough disagreements whenever Damon's name cropped up these days to make everyone wary. It didn't sit easy with Anoushka.

'If there's any more tea in that pot, I wouldn't mind grabbing a cuppa; I've had an idea for what to get your dad 'for his birthday and I'd like to run it by you while he's out... if that's okay?'

'No problem; I'll get another mug. Damon's not due 'til two-thirty, so....' Her voice tailed off and she flicked her thick, flaxen, mermaid plait over her shoulder. Though she'd tried to sound breezy, she could still sense the weight of her step-mum's gaze on her as she padded over to the mug cupboard.

'Righty-ho, I'll just get this washing on; I'll be with you in two ticks.' Kitty flashed a quick smile before disappearing into the utility room. If her body language was anything to go by, it was evident she too was mindful of treading gently, of being careful to skirt around the subject – or rather, the *person* – who had been the catalyst to so many arguments that had rocked the usually calm Cartwright family equilibrium.

Ughh! She needed to get Damon out of her head right now if she was going to have a comfortable conversation with Kitty. But with what she had looming ahead of her that afternoon, it wasn't going to be easy. A feeling of dread pooled in her stomach.

The sound of the washing machine filling with water pulled Anoushka back into the moment. She released a slow sigh. Jeez, since when had her life got so complicated? She glanced around the room. With its low-beamed ceiling, stout mullioned windows and thick, uneven walls, the kitchen was the epitome of cosiness and countryside charm with the aroma of hearty home-cooking imbued in its very fabric. Her heart lifted every time she stepped through the door of the quaint, traditional longhouse with its heavily thatched roof that put her in mind of a fringe desperately in need of a trim. Her thoughts wandered back to when she and her dad first moved into Oak Tree Farm five years earlier, joining Kitty and her two children, Lucas and Lily. As an exuberant teenager, Anoushka's mind hadn't been in turmoil then, it had been brimming with unbridled enthusiasm and optimism for their future together as a family. A proper family, at last! It was no exaggeration to say she'd been deliriously happy. Her greatest wish had come true when her dad had finally got together with Kitty. The pair had been childhood sweethearts until Kitty had been lured away by the uber confident Dan Bennett who, despite everyone's warnings, she'd ended up marrying. Though Anoushka wasn't in possession of all the facts, she'd gleaned enough snippets of information to know that her step-mum had endured several years of mind games and controlling behaviour throughout her marriage at the hands of her ex-husband. She'd only stuck it out for the sake of her children, until it had started to affect them too. "Gaslighting" was a word that had been bandied about regularly when Dan's name had cropped up in the conversations she'd overheard between Kitty and her best friends, Molly and Violet. And, rather worryingly, it had become increasingly familiar; they could almost have been talking about Damon.

'Phew! Sorry that took so long; lots of pockets to check for the dreaded paper hankies and hair bobbles.' Kitty flopped down opposite Anoushka at the scrubbed pine table. 'So,' she said, picking up the teapot and filling her mug, 'you don't need me to tell you how tricky your dad is to buy for.'

Thoughts of Damon scurried away. 'Too right!' Anoushka laughed and rolled her ice-blue eyes. 'He's been absolutely no help whenever I've asked if he needs anything; at this rate, he's in serious danger of getting nothing more exciting than socks from me.'

'Well, he always needs those.' Kitty giggled. 'Anyway, after racking my brains for something inspiring to get him I was flicking through the *Heather and Dale* and spotted this.' She pushed the small moorland magazine – filled with a mix of adverts placed by local businesses, articles on local history, nature and anything else the editor, Freya Ingleby, thought would be of interest to its readers – over to Anoushka. It was open on a full-page advertisement for fly-fishing lessons at Danskelfe, the nearest village to Lytell Stangdale. 'He and Jimby have been talking about having a go at fishing for a while now, and I was wondering if I should book a lesson for the pair of them. What do you think?'

'I think it sounds like a great idea, especially if Jimby goes with him; they'll have a right good laugh together.' Anoushka scanned the advert, thinking it would be good for her dad to try his hand at something new; he worked long hours as a much-in-demand local joiner, not that he ever grumbled about it.

'Mmm. That's what I thought, so long as Jimby doesn't end up in the lake, that is. You know what he's like, he can't seem to walk down the road without having some kind of mishap,' Kitty said with another giggle.

'Don't I just.' Anoushka couldn't help but chuckle at the thought. Only last week Kitty's accident-prone older brother had ended up headfirst in the local pond trying to rescue a stray cat from the huge willow tree whose branches reached across the water. News of his dousing had travelled like wildfire around the village and he'd been ribbed mercilessly in the local pub ever since.

'Seriously though, I think it's a fab idea; Dad'll love it.' Anoushka closed the magazine and passed it back to Kitty. 'Maybe I could get him a book on fishing to go with it.'

'Good idea,' said Kitty, nodding her approval.

Talk of her dad's birthday had helped dissipate the awkward air of earlier, leaving the two women comfortable in one another's company once more. It was a blessed relief for Anoushka to feel the tension slip away from her body for a moment.

'Well, that's sorted then; I'll call the number this afternoon and get a gift voucher organised.' Kitty patted the cover, a beam spreading across her pretty elfin features.

'And you're sure we can't tempt you to join us help celebrate his birthday meal? You can bring Damon if you like. It's just going to be at the Sunne. I've booked a table for one of Bea's legendary curry nights. I'm sure she wouldn't mind adding an extra seat... or two... the usual folk will be there...' The caution threaded through Kitty's last sentence was tangible. Her step-mum didn't need to say whenever Damon was involved in any of their get-togethers the atmosphere was always fraught.

'Erm, I'm not sure... I'll have to check.' And just like that, the tension sprang back. More and more recently, Damon's name had a knack of triggering that. Only now, Anoushka could understand why. She appreciated Kitty's kind-hearted gesture, but she still didn't feel ready to tell her of her intentions to break up with Damon just in case things didn't go to plan. Anoushka desperately wanted to join her family at the Sunne but, equally, she didn't want Damon there. She hated being in such a dilemma. Much as he professed to despise family get-togethers and did all he could to avoid them, Anoushka knew from experience that Damon would kick off if he wasn't invited to her dad's birthday celebrations. Big time. And it wasn't as if she could keep it from him and go on her own since she always spent the weekend at his place in York. Wriggling out of that would take some doing and the potential trouble that would ensue didn't bear thinking about. And, besides, she'd already let slip that her dad's birthday was coming up and that

Kitty was planning a meal to celebrate. Anoushka also knew, even if she invited Damon, he'd whinge and moan about how he didn't want to go, making the run-up to it hell. She wouldn't put it past him to try to talk her out of going too. It wouldn't be the first time, she thought wearily. But if he did join them... *Ughh.* That didn't bear thinking about. True, Bea might not mind adding a seat or two to their table, but Anoushka wasn't convinced her dad would be overjoyed if she rocked up with Damon; nor would "the usual folk" for that matter. There really wasn't an easy option.

Anoushka released a sigh. The more she thought about it, and much as she'd love to be there celebrating with him, the last thing she wanted was to wreck her dad's birthday get-together if she hadn't managed to end her relationship with Damon by then. If she was honest with herself, she knew she'd be on tenterhooks the whole time, worried that Damon would say something offensive, or mock village life as he seemed to take pleasure in every time he was in their presence. It would make her gabble, like it usually did, with Damon pulling her up about it later, making her feel foolish. Just like the last time he'd joined them.

'Was there any need for the way you were talking non-stop over the meal?' he'd said disapprovingly when they'd joined her family and their friends for Sunday dinner at the Sunne.

'What do you mean?' she'd asked, well-aware of what he was referring to; she'd been conscious of it herself but hadn't been able to stop.

'You know full well what I mean, the way your mouth went into overdrive whenever I spoke. It was as if you were trying to diminish what I'd said. In future, I'd prefer it if you tried to keep yourself under control. You should've seen the way everyone was looking at you.'

Anoushka's cheeks had burnt crimson as his words sank in, embarrassed at making a fool of herself in front of the people she'd known all her life. She cringed at the memory.

In truth, everyone had felt sorry for her, knowing that Damon's mocking, arrogant comments were making her squirm with discomfort, and that she'd been merely attempting damage limitation, hoping that no one would pull him up or challenge him. Anoushka had heard later that her step-mum's cousin, Molly, had found it particularly difficult to rein in her naturally outspoken nature. Her infamous "death stares", however, hadn't gone unnoticed.

'That Molly's so full of herself,' Damon had said later. 'Like we care what she thinks; she should keep her narrow-minded, parochial opinion to herself. And I don't know who she thinks she is, dishing out filthy looks the way she does. She may look like Kitty, but that's where the similarity ends. Her bloke Camm deserves a medal for putting up with a witch like her.'

'Molly's lovely; she's been a good friend to my mum,' Anoushka had said, feeling nettled at his criticism.

'Pfft! Really?'

'Yeah, really. And she's had a tough time of it, what with her losing her husband, Pip, so young.'

'Still doesn't change my opinion of her,' he'd said coldly.

He didn't know it at the time, but he'd had a lucky escape from one of Molly's savage tongue lashings thanks to pleading looks from Kitty who hadn't wanted things to escalate for Anoushka's sake.

It didn't help that only the other evening, Anoushka had overheard her dad and step-mum talking about Damon. She recalled the mix of annoyance and sadness that had swirled around inside her at their words.

'Honest, Kitty, I don't know how much longer I'm going to be able to sit back and watch what he's doing to our Noushka. Flippin' 'eck, I'm not a violent man, but I've got this overwhelming urge to knock that sneering expression right off the arrogant little twerp's face. What he's done to our daughter; how he's changed her. She always used to be so carefree and bubbly, always smiling and laughing, but now...'

'Listen, Oll, I totally understand how you're feeling, but you've got to promise me you won't go doing anything like that. You'll just be playing into his hands, and you'll run the risk of pushing

Anoushka closer to him, which is the last thing we want,' Kitty had said, her voice full of concern.

Ollie had spat out a noisy breath. 'I never thought Noushka would fall for someone like him; he reminds me of that monster you used to be married to. I can't bear to think about her going through the same sort of thing you did.'

'Same here, which is why you need to listen to me when I tell you not to act in haste. I know it feels counter-intuitive, but please trust me on this.'

'I know. Doesn't stop me from thinking he's the last person I want with us all when we're celebrating my birthday; if he didn't come, it'd give her some time to enjoy herself with us. I'll have to sit on my hands to stop myself from throttling the little prat. Urghh! God help him if he comes out with any of his cocky one-liners.'

'If you don't invite him, it'll make things far worse for Noushka, and you don't want that. You're just going to have to bite your tongue if he chooses to come – for Noushka's sake.'

Ollie had heaved a sigh. 'I know, love, but it doesn't make it any easier.'

Anoushka had never heard her dad sound so angry. The conversation had made her heart ache, and thinking of it today had helped galvanize her decision to break-up with Damon. There was no way she was going to give him the chance to ruin her dad's birthday meal. She silently hoped she'd find the right moment to break it to him. Thought of being free of him gave her an overwhelming sense of relief; she'd be able to look forward to celebrating her dad's birthday with their family and friends without having to worry about Damon putting a spanner in the works and making snidey remarks, or trying to talk her out of going. But she'd keep her plans for the split to herself for now – just in case the conversation with Damon didn't go the way she hoped.

Kitty hesitated a moment, as if mulling something over before she spoke to Anoushka. 'There's a whisper Gabe Dublin will still be here.'

A prickle of annoyance ran across Anoushka's shoulders; why did Kitty have to go and mention him?

'Really?' she said, deliberately trying to sound uninterested. She disliked being drawn into conversation about him, especially by her family. His presence was another good reason not to mention the meal at the Sunne to Damon; Gabe was a regular there and Damon couldn't stand the man. Though he appeared to be the only person she knew who felt that way.

'You never know,' said Kitty, 'Gabe might give an impromptu performance at the pub like he did at Jimby and Vi's Christmas party. That'd definitely be worth joining us for, Noushka. We're so lucky he does things like that.'

Rather frustratingly, Gabe Dublin's handsome face, wearing one of his ready smiles, floated into her mind. Her heart gave an unexpected lilt.

The twenty-eight-year-old indie-rock singer hailed from Southern Ireland and had an affable, down-to-earth nature and self-deprecating sense of humour that belied his status as an internationally successful musician. He couldn't be more different to Damon if he tried. He'd become a regular visitor to the area in recent years, with an open invitation to stay at Danskelfe Castle – the family seat of the titled Hammondely family. He was best friends with Sim – who'd also recently become the new drummer in Gabe's band – and Sim's wife, Lady Carolyn. Gabe had become such a familiar face, locals no longer batted an eyelid when he was about. And it was no secret to Anoushka's family that he'd had fallen for her hook, line and sinker when he'd first set eyes on her. It had been at the wedding of local GP, Zander Gillespie and his bride Livvie, that had taken place at the castle a couple of Christmases back. Since then, Gabe had asked Anoushka out several times. 'I suppose I still can't tempt you to ditch the po-faced, suited fella and let me take you out on a date?' he'd asked a couple of months ago, his expression hopeful. But he'd been disappointed when she'd very kindly, and not a little bashfully, turned him down. Despite her string of refusals, he hadn't seemed to lose the hope that he'd win Anoushka round one day. And the newly installed recording studio located in a renovated barn in the grounds of Danskelfe Castle now offered him the perfect excuse to head back to the windswept corner of the North Yorkshire Moors whenever he wanted. But, thus far, and despite finding herself liking him enormously, Anoushka had remained resolutely immune to his charms. Which was exactly how she intended it to remain. The last thing she needed was to break up with Damon and immediately throw herself into the arms of someone else. Particularly someone who spent a great deal of time in the media spotlight.

Frowning, Anoushka pushed Gabe out of her mind, flicking Kitty a look. 'I'm not sure I'll be a—' Before she could finish, the sound of a car horn blasted impatiently from outside, making both women jump.

'Oh, my goodness! That frightened the life out of me.' Kitty's hand flew to her chest, her eyes wide. Ethel and Mabel shot up, barking and looking around, their ears cocked as they trotted around the room.

Anoushka leapt to her feet. 'That'll be Damon,' she said, panic flooding her body. She glanced up at the clock on the wall; it was two thirty-five. 'Oh, flippin' heck, I'm late! I'd best dash.'

'Blimey, I wish he'd just knock on the door like everyone else.'

'Yeah, you're not the only one.' Anoushka sighed, grabbing her bag and coat from the hooks by the door and rushing out. 'See you later, Mum.'

'See you later, lovey,' said Kitty quietly while Ethel and Mabel looked on with interest.

TWO

Anoushka pushed her arms into the sleeves of her khaki utility jacket as she raced down the garden path, her long, slender legs making short work of it. She flung the gate open to see Damon in the driver's seat of his new car, its glossy red bodywork gleaming in the spring sunshine. His face was set and he was drumming his fingers impatiently on the steering wheel. *Ughh!* Her heart sank; punctuality was an obsession of his – one of many, she'd come to learn to her detriment. She'd had enough experience to know this didn't bode well. The thought that it hardly mattered with the news she was about to deliver as soon as they got away from the village flitted through her mind, triggering a squeeze of anxiety in her stomach.

'Hi there, Noushka,' said a soft voice in a familiar Southern Irish accent that could melt chocolate.

She turned quickly, flicking her plait from the collar of her jacket, to see the very man Kitty had just mentioned: Gabe Dublin. Her heart leapt, her worries momentarily skittering away. He was looking achingly handsome in his faded jeans and denim jacket, his white T-shirt setting off the tan he'd acquired from a recent trip to sunny climes. He was smiling in his familiar easy manner, his chocolate-brown eyes crinkling at the corners. In his hand was a red dog lead, at the end of which a lanky black Labrador with rather large paws and a swishing tail was pulling towards Anoushka.

'Oh, hi, Gabe,' she said, aware of Damon's eyes boring into her like a couple of laser beams. The young Labrador sniffed at the legs of her skinny jeans with great interest, no doubt intrigued by the scent of Ethel and Mabel.

'Off somewhere nice?' Gabe asked, his lopsided smile widening and making mischief with her insides, adding to the cocktail of emotions already whirling round her stomach.

'Er, no ... I mean, I'm just going for a drive with Damon.' She hooked her bag over her shoulder. The timing couldn't have been worse.

'Right.' He nodded, his smile briefly falling. 'Well, I'm just taking this wee rascal for a walk and popping into the village shop to grab some essentials.' His velvety accent had a way of making even the most mundane of sentences sound delicious to her ears.

'It's a good day for a walk on the moors; we don't get many like this in March.' She smiled, conscious of Damon watching her every expression. She felt torn between not wanting to appear rude to Gabe but not wanting Damon to be able to accuse her of being too friendly – or worse, flirting, which was his latest obsession – and keeping him waiting, adding to the already difficult situation she was heading into.

'You're right there.' Gabe's eyes twinkled and she felt the warmth of a blush colour her cheeks.

'And who is this gorgeous rascal then?' In a bid to hide her embarrassment, she bent to the Labrador who was looking up at her with friendly eyes. She offered her hand for him to sniff, which he did excitedly, swiping his tongue over her fingers.

'Ah, let me introduce you to the very naughty Bob. I've only had him for a few days; got him from a rescue centre over by Middleton-le-Moors. I'm told he found himself there because of his mischievous ways and fondness for chewing shoes, but I took one look at him and "boom" that was it, I just had to bring him home with me.'

'Well, hello, Very Naughty Bob.' She scratched between the young Labrador's ears and he wagged his tail appreciatively. 'I can see why your dad here couldn't resist you, but you don't look naughty to me, you look adorable.'

'And doesn't he know it?' Gabe beamed at her. 'And I should add I use the word "naughty" jokingly; he's just full of high spirits, that's all. Not unlike a teenage boy actually. And, so far, I'm pleased to report I'm still in possession of all my footwear,' he said, making Anoushka giggle.

'That's good to hear.'

He bent to pat Bob, his head inches away from hers, treating her to a waft of his fresh, spicy cologne. She inhaled deeply, the fragrance releasing a flurry of butterflies in her stomach, making her blushes deepen; she was heading into dangerous territory.

Anoushka pulled herself up, Gabe following her lead. Though she was an athletic five-feet-ten, being a broad-shouldered six-feet, and built like a barn door, made him seem so much bigger than her. 'Will you be in the pub tonight?' he asked, his eyes locking on hers.

'Oh, well, I'm not sure.' That would very much depend on how her talk with Damon panned out. She gave a small smile, the butterflies dispersing and anxiety taking their place. From the corner of her eye she'd seen Damon wind his window down; she hoped he hadn't caught any of the conversation, she knew he'd jump on the opportunity to twist and distort her words. 'Right, well, I'd best head off,' she said with an apologetic shrug. 'See you later.'

'Oh, okay.' Gabe's smile faltered. 'Maybe see you at the Sunne.'

'Mayb—' The peace of the village was shattered by another long blast of a car horn. Both Anoushka and Gabe started. Bob barked, looking about him in alarm.

'Jaysus, what the—?' Gabe said, puffing out his cheeks. 'Who does that around here?' His eyes slid over to the car. 'Ah. Your man does that.'

Anoushka felt her face burn with embarrassment once more. 'Yeah, it's... erm, it's Damon.'

'So I see. Didn't recognise the car at first.'

'It's new.' She paused. 'He doesn't like to be kept waiting.' She gave a small roll of her eyes. 'I'm late.'

Gabe hitched up his eyebrows. 'Right.' He leaned in closer, lowering his voice. 'Not sure it warranted that little display of impatience.'

'Sorry.' She winced, her voice barely above a whisper. She wished the ground would open up and swallow her.

'Hey, no need for you to apologise. Tell him from me you're worth waiting for,' he said softly, holding her gaze as he went to walk away, pulling gently on Bob's lead. 'Catch you later, Noushka.'

'Yeah, see you later.' She drew in a deep breath, releasing it slowly, and made her way over to Damon's car, her heart racing with trepidation. *Oh my days! Did Gabe really just say I'm worth waiting for?* But now wasn't the time to dwell on that. *Did Damon hear him say it?* She hoped not.

'Hi,' she said as she settled into the passenger seat, taking in the aroma of newly valeted car, the vehicle immaculate as ever. Tension bloomed in the air, and her breathing became shallow as she braced herself for the onslaught. She risked a sideways look at him as she fastened her seatbelt. He was staring straight ahead, his jaw clenched, a muscled twitching at his temple. There were no two ways about it, he was seething. Anoushka groaned inwardly.

Everything about Damon was precise, from the way he dressed – always in the same order every day: neatly folded and ironed boxer shorts, socks (neatly folded too), shirt, then trousers – to the way he styled his hair – no more than three weeks between trips to the barbers' – to the way he ran his life. He was the antithesis of Gabe who was laid-back and easy-going, and didn't seem to mind having scuff marks on his trainers or holes in his jeans. And, judging from the way his hair sometimes curled on his collar, going an extra month before getting his hair cut was no big deal as far as he was concerned.

'I see you're happy to keep me waiting again.' Damon turned slowly, his dark hair slicked back and groomed to perfection. He pinned her with his gaze, impatience oozing from every pore. 'I told you I'd be here at two-thirty on the dot, which I was.'

'Sorry.' She swallowed, her chest heaving. 'I was talking to Kitty about my dad's birthday and lost track of time.'

He didn't appear to hear her. 'And what was that display about?' He ran his tongue over his teeth in the way he always did when he was angry. 'What made you feel the need to make a fool of me with that arrogant tosser?'

'How did I make a fool of you with Gabe? I was only saying hello; it would've been rude to ignore him.' She resisted the urge to say Gabe wasn't the arrogant tosser around here. In fact, she hadn't seen Gabe behave any way other than relaxed and unassuming.

Damon nodded slowly, his eyes cold and hard. 'Looked like you were saying more than hello to me, flicking your plait around, giggling like some silly, starstruck schoolgirl. Don't you realise how ridiculous your behaviour is?'

Why did it always have to be like this? She felt the sting of tears and quickly blinked them back. The last thing she needed was an argument on the doorstep of her home in full view of the locals in the village. 'I'm really sorry, Damon. I tried to end the conversation as quickly as I could, and besides, it's not like we have to be anywhere for a particular time.'

'That's not the point; you know how important punctuality is to me. If I say I'm going to be somewhere at a certain time, I'm there on the dot and I expect to be afforded the same courtesy by the people in my life, particularly my girlfriend. Shame she's not inclined to be of the same mindset.' He spoke in the unnervingly calm tone Anoushka had grown to dread.

She leant her head back against the headrest and puffed out her cheeks. She hated this kind of conflict with Damon, it made her feel sick to her stomach. But at least it served to do one thing: prove to her how she'd made the right decision. He was in a bad mood already; surely her news couldn't make it any worse?

'I've already apologised, Damon. I don't have control over who walks by my home; I didn't expect to have to make conversation with anyone when I stepped out onto the path, but it's done now.'

For a moment he looked confused; she'd wrong-footed him. This wasn't her usual reaction where she'd try to appease him and do all she could to bring him out of his dark mood, apologising profusely, promising to never do it again. He was silent for a moment, scraping his teeth over his bottom lip. 'I don't know what's got into you today but you're acting oddly. It doesn't suit you.'

She was thinking of a suitable reply when their attention was drawn to a familiar four-wheel drive pulling up on the road in front of them. They watched as Kitty's cousin, Molly, climbed out, the breeze ruffling her chocolate-brown curls. Spotting Anoushka she smiled and gave her a quick wave. Anoushka's good friend Kristy, who was Molly's son Ben's girlfriend, was in the driver's seat. The young woman beamed at seeing her, waving happily.

Anoushka mustered a smile and waved back, hoping her expression didn't betray the anxiety that gripped her body.

'Ughh! More flaming yokels. Get me out of this depressing little backwater.' Damon pushed the car into gear and sped off, Anoushka's head bumping against the headrest as he did so.

THREE

Damon was driving way too fast to be safe on the twisting country roads of Great Stangdale but Anoushka was loath to give him the satisfaction of asking him to slow down. Experience had taught her he'd do exactly the opposite, relishing making her feel uncomfortable, scaring her. So she girded her loins and kept quiet.

As she watched the countryside whizz by, one thought loomed large in her mind: she wouldn't have to tolerate this for much longer, though the anticipation of delivering the news that they were finished, that she'd had enough, set the nerves jangling in her stomach. The previous night, when she'd been lying awake, she'd considered telling him over the phone, but had decided against it. Knowing Damon, that wouldn't be the end of it; he'd have the brass neck to turn up at her home, thinking she hadn't meant it, convinced he could talk her round. She didn't want that drama for her family. No, there was no alternative but for her to break it to him face-to-face, and well away from Lytell Stangdale. Worry had kept sleep at bay well into the early hours. And now the moment was drawing closer, she was beginning to have serious misgivings, scared of how he would react.

'What the—!' Damon swerved to avoid one of the Danks's

hefted sheep that had trotted out in front of the car. Anoushka gasped, gripping onto her seat, her heart thudding at the near miss.

'Brainless animal!' he said, his ill humour showing no sign of abating.

How had she put up with him for so long?

They were heading to Middleton-le-Moors, a quaint Georgian market town ten miles away. The plan had been to have a mooch around the tasteful shops there before going for a drink in one of the pubs, then finishing up at his place in York. Unless, of course, things had changed and Damon had decided not to head that way. Thanks to his capricious moods, it wouldn't be the first time he'd changed their plans without deigning to tell Anoushka. As they drove on, she was still trying to work out where would be best to broach the conversation – *was* there a good place to tell someone you were breaking up with them? – and she was growing increasingly twitchy about it. She'd need to find somewhere quiet and discreet where there'd be no one to stare when he lost his rag – which he inevitably would – but, on the other hand, she was keen to do it out in the open, with other people around, just in case. One thing she knew for certain, she needed to break the news to him before they got to York. She didn't want to be stuck at his apartment, with him ranting at her. A shiver ran up her spine at that thought. Middleton-le-Moors would be the best spot, being not too far from her home. The scenic path that led to Middleton Hall School popped into her mind. It was a route popular with dog walkers and runners; there'd be plenty of people around without it being overly busy. She'd tell him there. When she'd got the deed over with, she'd call home and ask if someone could come and collect her. She knew they'd be only too happy to help, especially when they heard the reason why.

Anoushka heaved an inward sigh of relief, glad to have got that sorted in her mind.

But, as they zoomed along the country lanes, tiny seeds of doubt started germinating in her conscience. Before she knew it, old habits had kicked in and her mind had started reaching for ways to soften his mood. Was she being too hasty in wanting to break up with him? Was their relationship really that bad? Should she give him another chance? No! A strong voice suddenly piped up. Stick to your guns! He's a controlling bully and he'll never make you happy. She took another steadying breath, getting a blast of sense once more; she wouldn't be sorry to say goodbye to the stress and strife that came with her relationship with Damon. It had been tearing her in two, not to mention the negative effect it was having on her relationship with her family. She reminded herself she'd had more arguments with her dad and Kitty in the last few months than she could ever remember, bickering and bitterness becoming a regular feature. She felt riddled with guilt. In recent weeks, playing back the arguments she'd had with her family over and over in her mind, she'd begun to realise that right from the start, Damon had criticised every aspect of her life, trying to mould her into somebody different; somebody she didn't want to be. He seemed to be insanely jealous of her closeness with her dad, struggling to understand that's what sixteen years of it pretty much just being the two of them had created. She adored her dad – he was her hero – and now that love and affection had been extended to Kitty and her new siblings too. There was no way she was going to let Damon damage her bond with them. Nor anyone, for that matter. Her family meant everything to her.

She slid her gaze warily across to Damon to see his jaw clenched, his neatly manicured fingers gripping tightly onto the steering wheel. Her spirits took a sudden nosedive; he still hadn't finished punishing her for today's "misdemeanours".

As they drove on, he was forced to ease up on the accelerator when they came up behind a tractor trundling its way along. Anoushka recognised it as belonging to the Campions from Camplin House Farm, and from the looks of it, it was Bill bouncing along in the driver's seat.

'Flaming farmer yakkers! Talk about inconsiderate.' Damon slammed his palms angrily against the steering wheel. 'Just because they've got plenty of time on their hands, doesn't mean the rest of us have.' He exhaled noisily. 'For effing chrissake! Doesn't he have an accelerator or even the decency to pull in and let me pass?'

Anoushka was tempted to correct him; plenty of time on their hands was the last thing farmers had. But she sat quiet instead, his angry mood filling her mind with reminders of the times he'd made her feel bad about herself. Of how he always somehow managed to turn everything around and make her the one in the wrong, souring her happiness. Kitty's recent warning started ringing in her ears, dispersing the niggling doubts she'd been having about breaking up with him. 'I know you won't be able to see it yourself, lovey, but we can; he's playing mind games with you, mental gymnastics. I know how it happens; I've been there with Dan, don't forget. Before long, you won't be able to recognise yourself. Just please, *please* listen to those that love you, and be careful.' At the time, Anoushka had dismissed Kitty's advice as being way off the mark and had snappily told her so. She cringed as she recalled it. But now, looking back, she had to concede her step-mum had a point.

Oh, jeez. How had she got herself into this mess?

Damon Swales was Anoushka's first serious boyfriend, and there'd been no hint of his capricious moods and controlling ways when she'd first met him; he'd been all charm and smiles and flattery. It was while she was studying Drama and Dance at university in York that they'd first met. She'd got a weekend job as a dance teacher at a studio and they'd got talking when he'd collected his young niece who was a student there. He'd confessed later he'd made up a reason to get chatting to her and had been thrilled when she'd agreed to go out for a drink with him a couple of weeks later. On their first date, he'd arrived at her student house armed with a huge, elaborate bouquet and box of expensive chocolates which had been romantic, if not a little overwhelming.

Though he was only older than her by five years, the age gap could easily be double that. He was the manager of a call centre, and seemed so sophisticated compared to boys Anoushka's age. Added to that, he was attractive and charismatic, and he made her laugh; she'd found it an irresistible combination.

It hadn't taken long for them to become an item, Anoushka spending all of her spare time with him, staying over at his apartment in York. She'd been too swept up by his seemingly endless supply of romantic gestures – trips on the river in his friend's boat, sipping champagne with him feeding her plump, sweet strawberries, dining by candlelight on the balcony of his apartment, whisking her off for impromptu nights away in fancy hotels – to notice how his insidiously controlling personality had infiltrated their relationship.

It wasn't until she'd moved back home after finishing her degree that she'd been able to sense that things weren't right. One Sunday, after much pleading from Anoushka who'd been worried Kitty would be hurt if he refused yet another invitation, Damon had reluctantly accompanied her back to Lytell Stangdale. She'd been keen to properly introduce him to her family, sure they'd love him just as much as she did. But she'd been disappointed, and a not a little angry, to find they didn't seem quite so taken with him. She'd done her best to ignore how he'd held court over one of Kitty's delicious afternoon teas at the kitchen table of Oak Tree Farm, boasting about his achievements, belittling Ollie's "small town business" as he'd called it, mocking Jimby's profession as a blacksmith. 'Is there really still a need for them?' he'd said with a snigger, adding, 'I suppose there probably is in the back end of nowhere.' The glances exchanged between her dad and Kitty had nettled her. At other points in the conversation his charm offensive had been in overdrive but she could see it hadn't sat well with Kitty whose reserved nature had clearly felt uncomfortable with the lashings of compliments Damon had layered upon her. 'Beautiful and an amazing cook too; not difficult to see why Ollie fell for you, Kitts,' he'd said making Kitty visibly squirm, her face flushing. His overfamiliar use of her step-mum's nickname had made Anoushka cringe.

Later, when Damon had left, and Anoushka was sitting on the sofa in the living room with thirteen-year-old Lily stretched out beside her, her stepsister had asked, 'Noushka, why do you like Damon?'

'Why do I like him?' Anoushka's brow had creased at such an odd question. 'I like him for lots of reasons. Why do you ask, Lil?'

'Hmm. Just wondered, that's all.' Lily hadn't taken her eyes away from the TV screen.

'Do you like him, Lils?' Anoushka had asked warily.

A long pause had followed as Lily considered her answer. 'Well… he's *okay*, I *suppose*. He's, kind of… not the sort of boyfriend I thought you'd have.'

'Oh? What kind of boyfriend did you think I'd have then?'

Lily had scrunched up her face. 'Well… sort of… nice… like Gabe—'

'Damon's a prat,' seventeen-year-old Lucas had said, walking into the room, bringing the smell of fresh air with him. He'd been playing football in the garden with Ollie and little sister, Lottie. 'He really fancies himself. And I can't stand the way he talks to you and takes the mickey out of Ollie and Uncle Jimby. He's a right dickhead.'

'Lucas!' said Kitty, who'd been passing by the door.

'Well, he is. Gabe's *way* cooler and he's mint at football.'

'I agree with Lukes, Gabe is *way* cooler, and he talks to us like he's interested, unlike Damon,' Lily had said, stealing a look at Anoushka.

'Well, I think that's really unkind. You haven't given him a chance.' Anoushka had felt hurt by their words. But something deep inside her knew they were right.

She couldn't pinpoint when he'd changed, when the acts of control had started to creep in; it had all been so gradual. Damon had skilfully operated below the radar. His criticism had been so subtle at first she'd hardly noticed, before slowly becoming more blatantly passive-aggressive, spiteful even. 'Why do you dress like that?' he'd asked one day. 'Don't you think you'd look better in something more sophisticated? More flattering? I'm not saying you look *tarty* per se… but maybe you could do with toning it down a bit, look less *flirtatious*?'

'You think I look flirtatious?' she'd asked, shocked. It certainly hadn't been the look she'd set out to achieve; she'd just thought she dressed like the other girls her age. Granted, some of the skirts and dresses she wore did show a little more leg than they would on her friends, but that's because she was so tall in comparison. And it wasn't as if the skirts were that short anyway. She'd been comfortable with her style until then and certainly wouldn't have described it as tarty or flirtatious. The next thing she knew, he'd started to buy her clothes that were more befitting of a woman twice her age, sulking if she didn't wear them, accusing her of not being grateful for his "thoughtful" gifts. That had led to direct accusations of flirting with other men.

'I've seen the way you go on with that tall lad, flicking your hair around and fluttering your eyelashes at him,' he'd said one afternoon when he'd met her after a dance class at the studio in York.

'Who?' she'd asked incredulously.

'You know *exactly* who I mean – unless you behave that way with every man you come into contact with – the one with the Scottish accent who always seems to be hanging around you. Can't keep his hands off you.'

'What? You can't mean Jamie, surely?'

'That's him.' His eyes had narrowed. 'Jamie.'

Anoushka had shaken her head vehemently. 'You've got it so wrong; I don't flirt with Jamie. He's a mate and he's certainly not interested in me. And besides, he's tactile with everyone.'

Damon had snorted. 'Yeah, right. And you expect me to believe that when I've seen the way the pair of you carry on with each other.'

She'd turned to him, exasperated. 'Damon, you've got to believe me! You're way off the mark. There's nothing going on between Jamie and me. He's in a relationship with Felix. He's gay.'

Her reply had rendered him speechless for once.

Later, he'd criticised her decision to stay in Lytell Stangdale after finishing her degree, rather than move permanently to York. 'Why would you choose a stagnant place in the sticks, where everyone knows your business, over a bustling city with everything you need on your doorstep?' he'd said, his top lip curling in disgust.

He'd been working on her to move in with him and had expected her to cave.

'Because Lytell Stangdale has everything *I* need,' she'd said. 'And besides, York's not that far away.'

Ever since she was a young, dance-crazy girl Anoushka had set her heart on starting her own dance school in the village where she'd grown up. And since she'd returned home, she'd tested the water by running twice-weekly dance classes for local children in the village hall, offering ballet, tap and disco – Saturday mornings and Wednesdays after school, which had been the only regularly available slots the much-in-demand venue could offer. The plan had been to start off small and see how things went. She boosted her earnings by helping out at Romantique Designs, the wedding dress design company her step-mum and Violet owned.

That had been nine months ago. She'd been in her element and was pleased to find it quickly became a roaring success, with parents asking if she'd consider running classes for older students too. And when other locals had started making enquiries about dancing classes for themselves, she thought she'd burst with excitement. 'I quite like the idea of doing a bit of ballroom, lovey,' Little Mary had said. 'Aye, pet, and I wouldn't mind shaking my booty to a bit of that disco stuff,' Big Mary had said in her lilting Wearside accent, giving a shake of her hips when the pair had stopped Anoushka outside the village shop one morning. It had warmed her heart and had meant the next stage of her plan could be put into action far sooner than she'd anticipated: to find a suitable premises to have her own studio, enabling her to run as many classes as possible.

Her excitement hadn't lasted long once she'd shared her news with Damon over drinks one night at a bar in York.

'And I always thought you had ambition, Anoushka. Drive. Just goes to show how wrong I was,' he'd said with a snort, throwing cold water over her happiness.

'I do! That's been my dream for as long as I can remember and it's about to become a reality! I'm over the moon. I love spending time in the city, but I'm a country girl at heart, and I've made no secret of the fact I've always wanted to have my own dance school back home. And I know I could make a decent living out of it too.'

'Depends what you call decent.'

'Decent enough to make me happy. And I intend to start out at my new studio looking professional. I'm going to get some branding done, set up an online dancewear shop; advertise properly. My mum's friend, Vi, used to have a really successful PR business and she said she'd help with promotion. There aren't any other dance classes for miles around back home. We always had to trek over to Middleton-le-Moors which isn't ideal in the winter months; my dad used to have to do lift sharing with other parents. It was a heck of a commitment.'

'I don't suppose you've thought there might be a reason there aren't any other dance classes for miles? As in, no one's interested,' he'd said, in a tone that suggested she was stupid.

Anoushka had bitten down on her anger. It wasn't worth argu-ing; Damon always had to be right. He never backed down. Ever.

'I guess you can take the bumpkin out of the countryside, but you can't take the countryside out of the bumpkin.' He'd chuckled, amused at his own observation.

Reliving it all, Anoushka could hardly believe she'd put up with his unreasonable, bullying behaviour for so long. She cursed inwardly. *Ughh! What have I been thinking?* If one of her friends had told her their boyfriend behaved in such a way, she'd have no qualms in telling them to kick his backside right out of their life. Which made it difficult to understand why she hadn't applied that advice to herself.

FIVE

'There's no need to sulk.' Damon's words pulled her back to the present as the car climbed the precipitous lane leading to Great Stangdale Rigg. Anoushka gazed out of the window and sighed. Normally, she'd drink in the glorious panorama the vantage point afforded them, where the road wrapped around the valley of Great Stangdale, dividing it from the villages of Danskelfe and Arkleby that nestled in their own broad valleys. But today, her vision was hampered by her jittering stomach and a clutch of negative feelings, and her eyes merely skimmed over the cluster of thatched cottages where smoke curled up and out of squat stone chimneys.

'I'm not sulking.' *I'm absolutely seething!* Her nostrils flared and she clenched her jaw in a bid to keep her anger from spilling over.

'Yes, you are; I can tell,' he said, reaching across and taking her plait from between her fingers, holding it up between his forefinger and thumb. 'And I thought we'd agreed you were going to get this cut.'

'*We* hadn't agreed anything of the sort,' she said. 'Careful!' Her heart lurched and she gripped onto her seat when he narrowly avoided one of the many sheer drops down the side of the bank.

His head swung back to the road as he righted the vehicle.

'Calm down, I've got everything under control. And I distinctly remember us having a conversation about it only last week and you agreed to make an appointment at the hairdressers. You can't tell me you've forgotten already?' They'd reached the top of the incline and were heading along a comparatively straight stretch. He turned to look at her again.

'I haven't forgotten. It's not every day I get told my hair's like "some childish fairy princess" that I should've "grown out of years ago".'

'That's not what I said.'

'It's exactly what you said. And that I should get rid of the "silly, baby blonde" – which might I point out is actually my natural colour – and get some lowlights put in so I'd look my age.'

She sensed Damon tense beside her. He started drumming his fingers on the steering wheel, running his tongue over his teeth. 'You know I've only got your best interests at heart. My advice is well meant, but as usual, you choose to twist it around; throw it in my face.' He exhaled noisily. 'After all, everyone knows it's not a good look for a woman in her twenties to have her hair like a ten-year-old little girl. I'm actually being kind by telling you that. And you shouldn't use it to flirt with other men, flicking it around at any opportunity. Makes you look ridiculous and immature.'

Ughh! Here we go. She shook her head and bit down on her reply, ignoring his attempts at goading her. She wasn't going to play into his hands today.

Doing all she could to stem her building anger, she turned to look out of the window again, spotting Brogan striding across the moor, her rich, red hair glowing in the sunshine, a gaggle of dogs in tow. Brogan ran her dog-walking business – Pond Farm Pooches – from her home at a smallholding named Pond Farm just out of the village. The sight of her friend triggered a surge of relief and an overwhelming need to talk to her. Over recent weeks, Anoushka had been confiding in her and their friend Kristy more and more about the mounting misgivings she had of her relationship with Damon. On the last occasion, they'd listened quietly, both wearing expressions of disbelief. 'Let me put it this way, Noushka, what would you do if Lily started going out with a boy who treated her like that? What would you say to her?' Kristy had asked, her striking blue eyes shining fiercely.

Her words had made Anoushka sit up and pay attention; she hadn't thought of it that way. 'I'd tell her to dump him as quickly as possible. Then I'd want to get my hands on him and throttle the living daylights out of him.' Her hackles had risen at the very thought.

'Exactly. And now you know how your parents feel. And me too for that matter,' Kristy had said, flicking her glossy black hair over her shoulder.

'Same here,' Brogan had said. 'You need to get out of that relationship before it's too late, Noushka.'

Now, back in the present, sitting beside an increasingly agitated Damon, Anoushka's mind tugged at the conversation again, and was soon joined by the things Kitty had told her about her own experiences. It would seem, to Anoushka's way of thinking, that all the people closest to her, those who loved her, were worried about her and shared the same view of Damon, had the same advice to give about him. They couldn't all be wrong, could they?

With her heart pounding, she scrunched up her eyes as the car shot along the rigg road, bouncing over potholes, thoughts piling up in her mind. Why was she still with him when he'd been making her feel so miserable and down, and had almost succeeded in driving a wedge between her and her family and friends? *Because he's skilful at pushing you into a poky, dark corner and making you feel absolutely rubbish about yourself*, a little voice said. *And then, just at the right moment, he pulls you back, talking you round, making you doubt yourself, which is exactly how Kitty had described her experience with Dan.*

She felt the mist in her mind lifting, her toxic relationship with Damon suddenly glaringly clear, revealing all its ugliness. She licked her lips, her mouth dry, as she drew all her courage together. Before she knew it, she was shouting, 'Stop the car!'

'What?' Damon's head shot round, his top lip curled in disbelief.

'I want you to stop the car!' Her heart was hammering hard against her ribcage. Was she actually doing this?

'Are you mad?'

'No! Yes! No! I can't do this anymore, Damon.' She couldn't wait a moment longer; she had to tell him now. Had to get it over and done with.

'What are you talking about? Can't do what?'

'Stop the car, Damon!' Adrenalin surged around her body and a feeling of utter fearlessness took over.

'But we're in the middle of nowhere.'

'To you maybe, but to me it's just a couple of miles from home and within easy walking distance.' Her chest was heaving, her pulse whooshing in her ears.

'Have you gone crazy?'

'If you don't slow down, I'll jump out.' Anoushka called his bluff, reaching for the door handle; he'd do anything rather than risk her causing damage to his precious car.

Damon brought the vehicle to an abrupt halt, pulling on the handbrake as he turned to look at her, his face distorted with disbelief. 'So are you going to tell me what's got into you? You're behaving like a mad woman.'

She took a fortifying breath, swallowing hard to steady her nerves. She could hardly believe what was about to spill from her mouth. 'We're done, Damon. We're not right for each other. That's it.' She shrugged. 'It's taken me a long time to realise it, but I have now—'

'*What?*' He glared at her, his face blanching as he pushed his fingers into his hair.

'You heard what I said.' Her stomach was churning, a feeling of nausea rising at the back of her throat.

'You can't seriously be telling me we're over?'

She nodded. 'Yes, I am.' This felt seriously surreal.

'You're crazy. You don't know what you're talking about.' He laughed scornfully.

'I think you'll find I know exactly what I'm talking about. We're over, Damon, we shouldn't have lasted this long; I'm amazed we have. I don't want to be with you anymore and now I just want to get out of the car and walk home. I need some fresh air.' She went to open the door but he grabbed her arm.

'I don't know what's gotten into you, but I daresay it's got something to do with that family of yours pouring poison into your ears. They've never liked me. But let me tell you this, you've been batting way above your league going out with me. Everyone knows that – your country bumpkin family included, that's why they don't like me; they're intimidated by my success, by my lifestyle.'

Anoushka stopped herself from snorting with disbelief just in time; it wouldn't help to infuriate him any more right now. She listened in silence, aware of her heart leaping wildly in her chest. There was so much she wanted to say to him, but now wasn't the time; she needed to get away from him as quickly as possible without inflaming his anger any further.

'You'll be crawling back when you've come to your senses.' He let go of her arm and she scrambled out of the car. 'But don't think I'll want you then. You've blown it!' He revved the engine angrily and she looked back to see him shooting off along the road with a roar, giving her a final reminder of just what a turkey he was.

SIX

Anoushka strode towards the bridle path that led down to Lytell Stangdale, checking her mobile as she went. She'd had a text from Kristy asking if she was okay; she'd obviously picked up on Anoushka's anxiety earlier. With her hands shaking thanks to the adrenalin that was still pumping around her body, she fired off a quick reply, telling her friend she was fine and that she'd fill her in on everything later. She could only imagine Kristy's response.

She slid her phone into the back pocket of her jeans, her eyes landing on Brogan. Cupping her hands around her mouth, she shouted, 'Brogan!' The breeze, always strong up on the rigg, whipped her words away as soon as they left her mouth. A brace of nearby pheasants flew off, cackling vociferously at being disturbed while a handful of rabbits shot off in all directions, their white tails bobbing amongst the brown foliage of the heather. She tried again, only louder this time. 'Brogan!'

Brogan turned to look in her direction and Anoushka waved. 'Wait up.' Anoushka hurried towards her friend who started heading back up the track. The path was muddy in parts and she was glad she'd opted for her sturdy biker boots rather than the white plimsolls she'd almost worn.

Soon, the two friends were face-to-face, both short of breath and rosy-cheeked. The four panting black Labradors, who all knew Anoushka well, greeted her enthusiastically, pink tongues lolling from their mouths.

'You okay?' Brogan asked, giving a concerned smile.

'I'm fine... well, I am now.' The fresh air was making Anoushka's cheeks sting. Wayward strands of hair had escaped from her plait and were now blowing around her face. She swiped them away with her fingertips and gave a watery smile.

Brogan frowned. 'Well, that sounds ominous. Want to join me walking these renegades? You can tell me all about what's been troubling you.' Her expression brightened. 'And you can join me for a cuppa after if you like? I picked up some of Lucy's chocolate-dipped flapjacks from the village shop; freshly baked this morning.'

'Sounds good.' Anoushka was reluctant to head straight home and to the questions that would follow her early return. She bent to ruffle the ears of Zander and Livvie Gillespie's Labrador. 'Now then, Alf, you're a lovely lad, aren't you?' Alf wagged his tail happily. 'Here, let me take a couple of leads,' she said to Brogan.

'You can have Alf, but watch Murphy, he's a horror for pulling.'

The walk over and done with, the two friends were sitting at the table in the warmth of the little kitchen at Pond Farm, the dogs having been deposited in the extension just off it, where they were now curled up, sleeping contentedly. Brogan would drop them off at their respective homes later, after her chat with Anoushka.

Brogan released a low whistle when Anoushka had finished sharing her experiences with Damon. She'd told her everything this time – no more holding back thanks to some misplaced loyalty to him. And though she'd cried as she was telling her, they weren't tears of regret, they were overwhelming tears of relief.

'Wowzers! I always thought he was a prat, but he sounds like a right controlling dickhead,' Brogan said.

'Yeah, I can see that now... well, I kind of could before, but not all the time. I kept trying to ignore it, telling myself it was me who was wrong... and he wasn't always that bad; he could be really charming sometimes.' She sniffed, wiping away her tears.

'Yeah, all part of his master plan, I reckon. And from what I can gather, you probably kept doubting yourself because that's exactly what Damon wanted. It's how people like him operate.' Brogan picked up a chunk of her chocolate-dipped flapjack and popped it into her mouth, chewing slowly.

Anoushka nodded. 'Hmm. You're probably right.' It always felt good to talk to Broge. Though her friend had only lived in the area for a few years, having moved to help her grandparents with the running of the smallholding, the two young women had struck-up a friendship quickly. Both had down-to-earth personalities and a love of the outdoors, in particular, the North Yorkshire Moors. Kristy, who knew Brogan from Skeltwick where they both hailed from, was from the same mould too, and the three young women had developed a tight friendship.

'Being in a relationship with him was becoming exhausting.' Anoushka huffed out a weary sigh.

'Sounds like it. And the jerk's not worth shedding another tear over – or wrecking your mascara for. Here, you're starting to look like a zombie with all that black smudged under your eyes.' Brogan grinned, passing her a box of tissues.

'Thanks.' Anoushka laughed as she started wiping the smears away.

'And you know what? The pompous prat was punching way above his weight, going out with you; Kristy thinks so too. I reckon it's why he felt the need to keep putting you down.' A hint of anger had crept into Brogan voice.

'I'm not so sure about you're right about him punching above—'

'Stop right there!' Brogan held her hand up. 'I so am, and I'll bet me and Kristy aren't the only ones who think that; I'd put money on it. Listen, chick, I hate seeing what he's done to you, chipping away at your self-confidence. You've got a fun, bubbly personality – or, at least you did have, until that weasel got his claws into you and began to snuff it out. You need to be your own person, not be ruled by some insecure, sociopathic bully. You're gorgeous, and have hair to die for, which makes me wonder why the heck he wanted you to lop it off.' She shook her head in disbelief. 'You were so right to ditch that loser.'

'Wow! So you're on the fence then, Broge,' Anoushka said, slightly stunned by the vehemence of her friend's opinion. Though she'd been growing increasingly aware that Brogan wasn't crazy about Damon – like so many other people she knew – it would seem her friend had been holding back on voicing her true thoughts. Until now.

'I'm only saying it because you're my best friend and I love you. That's all.'

'And I appreciate that,' Anoushka said, meaning it.

'There's a name for it, you know. What he does.' Brogan ceased chewing and frowned.

'There is?'

'Mm-hm.' Brogan nodded. It's on the tip of my tongue... um... gas... Gaslighting! That's it! That's what they call it when people behave like him, with all their mind games.'

There was that word again. *Gaslighting*.

'You're not the first person to have said that.'

Brogan snorted. 'Is there any wonder? And I can't believe you actually caught the slimeball scrolling through your phone.'

Anoushka licked her finger and pressed it onto a crumb of flapjack, popping it into her mouth. 'Yeah, it was a bit of a shock; he must've watched me type my password in – he denied it though.'

'What a weasel.' Brogan looked across at Anoushka and they both laughed. 'Bet he was livid when you switched to one with facial recognition.'

'He was; his reaction was way out of proportion. Accused me of having something to hide.' Anoushka tensed at the memory; he'd gone absolutely ballistic and she'd ended up a sobbing mess.

'Seriously? Is he for real?"

'I know. I can see how bad it looks now.' She was actually

beginning to feel quite foolish for sticking with him for so long, never mind defending him to everyone.

'I'm just glad you realised before it was too late.' Brogan sounded suddenly serious, making Anoushka feel acutely aware of how close she'd come to being trapped in a relationship like the one Kitty had had with her ex-husband. The thought sent a shiver running through her.

'Yeah, me too.'

'Makes you wonder how someone becomes like that, I mean, I don't suppose Damon was born that way. Surely something must've happened to have made him like that.' Brogan looked thoughtful.

Brogan had a good point, thought Anoushka. 'I reckon you're right, and I'd say his dad probably had something to do with it.'

'Really?'

Anoushka nodded and went on to share the only time she'd ever met Damon's father.

It had been a Saturday afternoon and she and Damon had been returning to his apartment after having a leisurely lunch in the city. Damon was just pushing the key into the lock of the main door when a sharp voice behind them, demanding to know where they'd been, made them turn. Damon had been flustered to see his father standing there. The angry expression on his face was almost sinister. He'd turned up unannounced, expecting Damon to be home and was furious to find him out. He'd waited over two hours for him to return, and all that time his temper had been stewing away.

Once inside, things had been little better, with Damon's father Eric picking and criticising his son's every move, mocking him to Anoushka, encouraging her to join in, which she managed to avoid, though not without some difficulty. Eric seemed to be getting a huge power-trip out of belittling Damon who appeared to have shrunk in his father's presence. The situation had made her feel dreadfully uncomfortable, and had left Damon subdued and snappier than usual for days after.

'Well, that explains a heck of a lot, though it doesn't excuse it, mind. And my opinion of Damon still remains the same; you're still way better off without him,' Brogan said firmly.

'I agree. I still can't believe how good it feels to be free of him. I know it might sound bonkers, but the sheer relief has made me feel so much... lighter, for want of a better word.' She looked at her friend and laughed.

'It doesn't sound bonkers at all. So...' Brogan, laughed too, a mischievous twinkle appearing in her eyes. '...dare I ask, where this leaves things with a certain drop-dead gorgeous, Irish singer?'

'No! You dare not! No way! Don't even go there!' Anoushka's heart leapt at the thought of Gabe. 'I intend to have some time being single. Actually, make that a *very long* time. Nope, actually, let's make it a *lifetime*. The last thing I need is to get involved with anyone, least of all someone whose life is under the media spotlight, not to mention the great, long list of glamorous exes he has to his name. No, that's so not for me.' Her mind might be saying that, but her heart was telling her a whole different story if the way it upped its speed when she was around him was anything to go by. It had been that way right from the start, but her head had point-blank refused to listen. And, somewhere along the line, she'd ended up with Damon.

'I'm not so sure the "someone" you refer to would agree.' Brogan gave a cheeky waggle of her eyebrows, making Anoushka giggle.

'Well, I'm afraid he doesn't have much choice. It'd be a case out of the frying pan and into the fire.'

'Yes, but what a sizzling-hot fire it would be with gorgeous Gabe and his flames of passion. It'd be worth it even if it didn't last.'

'You're wicked.'

'Given half the chance,' Brogan said, and they hooted with laughter.

SEVEN

Just over an hour later, Anoushka was making her way along the track towards Lytell Stangdale, still feeling as if a great weight had been lifted from her shoulders. Yes, her emotions were a little raw, but now there was no trace of the ball of tension that had taken up residence in her stomach when she'd left the house earlier that afternoon. It spoke volumes; she hadn't expected to feel so free, for her soul to feel so much lighter as quickly as this. Breaking up with Damon had been, without question, the right thing to do. Her only regret was that she hadn't done it sooner.

She strode on, her mind now clear to savour the early signs of a moorland spring; lapwings dipping and diving over the heather, their distinctive "peewit" cries interspersed with the shrill call of the curlews. Above, the blue sky stretched out like a sheet of sun-bleached linen, punctuated by fluffy white clouds idling their way along. The air was filled with the pungent aroma of slurry, thanks to Molly's partner, Camm, over at Withrin Hill Farm who was spreading fertilizer over one of their fields, the muted hum of his tractor reverberating around the dale – the smell of slurry was something else Damon hated about the countryside.

In the distance, Anoushka spotted a lone walker heading towards her, a black Labrador trotting along jauntily beside him.

Her heart gave a sudden lilt. She'd recognise those broad shoulders and that easy lope anywhere: Gabe Dublin.

Before long, he was standing in front of her. 'Well, hello there, Noushka. It's good to see you again, though aren't you heading in the wrong direction?' He flashed his trademark smile. 'Thought you were headed over to Middleton,' he said as Bob pulled on his lead, eager to get to her.

'Change of plan,' she said, smiling back, bending to fuss Bob whose tail was wagging so hard you could beat eggs with it.

'Ah, sure.' Gabe nodded, his smile faltering as his eyes ran over her face, taking in the tell-tale signs she'd been crying. 'And are you okay?' he asked softly.

She nodded. 'I'm fine, thanks.' She didn't feel ready to tell him about Damon. 'Just fancied some fresh air, I've got a few things I need to straighten out in my mind.'

He paused a moment as if contemplating her words. 'Right.' He pushed his smile back up. 'Well, if you ever you need to talk, you know where I am. My sisters tell me I'm a pretty good listener; I've a willing ear. Having five of them – that's sisters, not ears – I've done a whole load of listening in my time, I can tell you.' His smile widened; he was clearly trying to lighten the moment, make her feel better.

'Thanks, Gabe. I'll bear that in mind.' She couldn't help but chuckle at his joke.

'I'll be sticking around for a couple of weeks, so just holler if you need me.'

Holler if you need me. At this very moment, the thought that she very much needed him burst into her mind, taking her completely by surprise. To feel his arms around her, feel the warmth of being pressed against his chest. She felt her cheeks flame. *What are you thinking, woman?* She glanced at the floor, hoping he hadn't noticed. *Best keep those wayward thoughts to yourself.* She was aware of him looking at her but kept her eyes rooted very firmly to a small puddle on the path.

'And if it's that fecking eejit that's got you all upset, then he doesn't deserve you, that's all I can say.' He sounded suddenly angry.

She shook her head. 'It's not... I'm fine... it's just... just a bad day. I've got a bit of a headache, that's all. I'll be right as rain after my walk.' She wasn't lying about the headache that was now squeezing at her temples.

'Okay.' He didn't look convinced.

'I'd best get home,' she said, giving him a quick smile.

'I meant what I said, Noushka. I'm here for you if you need me.' He reached across and touched her arm, the simple gesture creating a frisson between them she hadn't expected, nor was she ready to deal with.

'Oh!' Their eyes locked for a moment and she quickly looked away. *Don't even go there!* 'Right, well, I'll see you later. Bye, Bob.' She bent to pat the Labrador before slipping by Gabe and making her way along the track.

'Bye, Noushka,' Gabe said softly, watching her as she went.

'What is going on with me?' she said out loud when Gabe was well out of earshot. She rubbed her face briskly. 'Why am I even feeling this way about Gabe when I've only just broken up with Damon not five-minutes since?' *Well, apart from the obvious, i.e. he's drop-dead gorgeous, has a fabulous personality and is kind to the old ladies in the village. Not to mention the way his jeans hug that cute backside of his. Oh, and the fact that you're well suited and you might just be a teensy-weensy bit in love with him. Simple. As. That,* said a little voice. 'Arghh! I'm not listening!' she said, upping her pace and making her way back to the village. But pushing the annoying little voice out of her mind was proving easier said than done.

Anoushka found Kitty taking down washing from the line in the back garden of Oak Tree Farm.

'Hi, Mum.'

Kitty turned, surprised. 'Oh, hi, lovey!' She paused, a pair of jeans in her hands, her brows drawing together. 'Everything okay?'

Anoushka nodded, swallowing down the emotions that had suddenly rushed to the surface. 'Need a hand?' She started unpegging the washing, throwing it into the basket, aware of her stepmum watching her.

'Er... yes, thanks, that'd be good. I'll have to bring it in now the smell of slurry's in the air, it'll make everything stink otherwise. I'll pop it on the clothes airer in the kitchen, it'll be all right there.' Kitty folded the jeans, concerned eyes on her stepdaughter. 'You sure everything's all right, chick?'

Anoushka sucked in a breath, her bottom lip wobbling. 'It's over, Mum. Me and Damon... I've broken up with him.' A tear plopped onto her cheek and made its way slowly down to her chin. She brushed it away.

'Oh, sweetheart, come here.' Kitty dropped the jeans into the washing basket and wrapped her arms around Anoushka, squeezing her tight. In the warm embrace, Anoushka let the tears flow.

'I don't know why I'm crying; I feel so much better for breaking up with him. It's just...'

'I know, it'll be the relief, my love. I remember feeling that way when I knew it was finally over with me and Dan.' Kitty pressed a kiss into Anoushka's hair. 'But you'll feel better soon, I promise.'

Anoushka raised her head, her face flushed with tears. She sniffed, wiping under her nose with the back of her hand. 'Yeah. The relief's enormous; I don't regret it for a minute.'

'Good.' Kitty smiled, giving Anoushka's arms a rub. 'Tell you what, how about I make us a killer hot chocolate? I'm talking minimarshmallows, grated chocolate, whipped cream and a great big chocolate flake. The works. The perfect remedy for sore hearts in my book. And there's some shortbread cooling in the kitchen, it'll be perfect for dunking. Complete sugar overload. Sound good? Oh, and in case you don't know, calories don't count on a Saturday afternoon.' Kitty grinned, giving Anoushka a playful nudge with her elbow.

'Sounds perfect,' Anoushka said with a snotty laugh, nudging her step-mum back.

The kitchen was filled with the comforting aroma of home-baking, which had the almost immediate effect of bringing Anoushka's tension levels right down. She pulled out a chair at the table, watching while Kitty got to work on the hot chocolate, filling a pan with milk and setting it on the Aga hotplate. It dawned on her the house was quiet and there was no sign of the dogs, which was unusual since both kids and dogs would usually loiter in the kitchen expectantly when Kitty had been baking.

'Where is everyone?'

'Your dad's taken the kids and the hounds to the beach over at Micklewick Bay so we've got the house to ourselves.'

'Oh, yeah, course.' She vaguely remembered her dad saying something about a trip to the beach that afternoon. She smiled, remembering how excited she used to get at the prospect of a visit to the seaside.

It wasn't long before the delicious scent of chocolate joined that of the shortbread and before she knew it, Kitty had placed a chunky mug of chocolatey deliciousness in front of her, tiny marsh-mallows spilling onto the table. 'There you go, flower' she said, sliding a plate with chocolate flakes and shortbread towards her. 'Tuck in.'

'Thanks, Mum.'

The pair sat in silence, Kitty nibbling on a slice of buttery shortbread, Anoushka absently popping marshmallows into her mouth.

Kitty was the first to speak. 'I'll understand if you don't want to talk about it – and I'm certainly not pushing you – but I want you to know that I'm here and happy to listen if or whenever you feel the need to. And I won't judge you; none of us will.' Kitty reached across and squeezed Anoushka's hand.

Anoushka looked up, meeting the gaze of those gentle, kind

eyes. She felt a sudden rush of love for this warm-hearted woman she was able to call her mum. Looking at the cheerful person Kitty was today, it was hard to believe she'd experienced such dreadful psychological bullying at the hands of Dan Bennet; that she'd been able to move on and build a happy life for herself, and Lucas and Lily. On the outside, Kitty was soft and gentle, but Anoushka guessed she must have a hidden inner strength for her to have been able to leave such a man. She had to have. Lord knows, she'd found it hard enough to break away from Damon, and he hadn't been half as bad as Dan Bennet. The feeling of love suddenly turned to anger at what Dan must have doled out to Kitty throughout their marriage; Anoushka was aware she didn't know the half of it. Her step-mum may be oblivious to the fact, but she'd been a bastion of hope to Anoushka on more than one occasion towards the end of her relationship with Damon.

'Thanks, Mum.' She squeezed Kitty's hand back, recalling how she'd bitten her head off just the other night, telling her to keep her nose out and that her opinion wasn't welcome. She cringed at the memory. 'But, first off, I want to apologise for how I've been over the last few months. I know I've been defensive and moody and difficult at times. It must've—'

'There's no need to apologise, lovey. I totally understand. Your dad and me, well, to be completely honest, we've been worried about you. We knew things weren't right, and, I mean, with Damon not wanting to even come into the house... well... it's not as if we've ever been unpleasant to him; we always tried to make him feel welcome.' She heaved a sigh. 'I'm just relieved it's over; your dad will be too.'

Anoushka winced. 'I know, there was no excuse for Damon's behaviour, I can see that now; I could at the time, actually, but just kept telling myself he wasn't being rude, that it must've been me doing something to make him act that way. Burying my head in the sand, I suppose. I took my frustration out on you and Dad and neither of you deserved it. I'm sorry, Mum.'

'Hey, no more apologies, Noushka. Okay?'

'Okay.'

'Hopefully you can now see how Damon's behaviour is classic gaslighting; making you feel like you were in the wrong. I know exactly how men like him operate.' Kitty's face darkened. 'You've no need to explain his actions to me, and you don't need to beat yourself up over being upset about him; you'd been with him a good while and you can't turn your feelings on and off like a tap. It was exactly the same for me with Dan. And even though your dad and me don't know all of the details of what happened in your relationship with Damon, we could see just what a negative influence he was having on you. Honestly, chick, we've been so worried about you; it was the same for my family when I was with Dan – our Jimby was ready to throttle him. It takes a while for you to see it for yourself. And I can say categorically, that for both of us, breaking up with such controlling bullies – which is exactly what they are – was the right thing to do.'

'I know, and I hate the thought of you going through what you did.'

'Don't worry about me, that's well and truly in the past now. It was how he was affecting Lukes and Lils that gave me the motivation I needed to get away. But look at us now. We've never been as happy as we are with you and your dad. Not forgetting how blessed we've been with little Lottie.' She gave a broad smile that stretched all the way to her eyes.

Anoushka couldn't help but smile back. 'And Dad and me have never been as happy as we have been with you and Lukes and Lils, and little Lottie too.' She took a sip of her drink, savouring the rich, creamy flavour, happiness filling her chest. 'Mmm. And you really do make the best hot chocolate; maybe that's got something to do with it.'

'You could be right.' Kitty giggled.

Anoushka sighed, the urge to share her time with Damon suddenly overwhelming. 'I think I'm ready to tell you about what happened with Damon, if that's okay? As long as it's not going to upset you, Mum, or resurrect horrible memories of Dan. I think I just need to get it out of me, then it's all over and done with and I can move on.'

'That's fine with me, lovey. And don't worry about me getting upset about Dan; all the ghosts of my marriage to him have been well and truly exorcised; he doesn't get to me like that anymore. Mind, I can't guarantee that I won't want to kick Damon up the backside though, but I'm happy to sit quiet and just listen. Once I'd left Dan, I told Moll and Vi everything; it felt better to get it out, felt liberating. He took up too much space in my head until then, so I get where you're coming from.'

Kitty's words resonated with Anoushka; it was exactly the reason she needed to tell her. Yes, she'd told Brogan, and Kristy knew bits, but sharing it with her family was a whole different thing. And, once she'd done it, she knew she'd be free to move on.

She sucked in a fortifying breath and raised her eyes to Kitty's. 'Right then, here goes...'

EIGHT

'So you can see why I'm done with love for the foreseeable.' Anoushka flopped back in her chair, savouring the inexorable feeling of relief.

'You mustn't let your experience with Damon taint your view of it, lovey. You're only young; just think of your time with him as nothing more than a bump in the road, an irritating blip.'

An irritating blip. How he'd hate to be referred to as that, thought Anoushka. But, right now, it's exactly how she needed to think of him. By squashing him into a manageable size, it would help weaken the power he had over her as far as her mind was concerned. There must be no going back. And as for opening herself up to love again... *Pfft! Hell would freeze over before that ever happened.*

Anoushka met Kitty's gaze. 'That may be so, but the way I'm feeling at the moment...'

'I totally get why you feel that way, chick, but, trust me, something like this will make you stronger; make you appreciate what real love feels like.' Kitty smiled at her. 'And you will find it, when the time's right for you. And you most certainly won't be in any doubt about it, I can promise you that.'

Anoushka puffed out her cheeks and released a slow breath.

'When... *if*, I ever find myself in a relationship again – and it's a very big *if* – I want what you and Dad have. At the risk of sounding mega-cheesy, it's more than simply *love*, it's... it's... it's hard to put into words... but I want what I see when you two look at each other, just the way you are together; it's like you're meant to be. Like you love each other so totally... Ughh! Jeez! I'm making a right pig's backside of describing it, but if, as you say, I'll know it if I ever get to feel it for myself, only *then* will I consider it.' She looked at Kitty intently. 'After Damon, and how close I came to being swallowed up in a toxic relationship with him, there's no way I'm settling for anything less.'

'And I can't blame you for that, chick.'

'But in all honesty, it's never gonna happen.'

'Just try not to build your walls too high, flower, it's—'

In the next moment, the front door flew open and a gaggle of kids and dogs tumbled into the house, the smell of the beach clinging to their clothes, laughter and high spirits filling the room. Ethel and Mabel raced over to their bowls in the utility room, checking first for food, then noisily lapping at water before flopping down on their beds, exhausted. Ollie followed up behind an exuberant Lucas, Lily and Lottie, his dark-blond hair windswept, his hands full of bags and plastic spades. His smile fell as his eyes loitered on his eldest daughter before flicking over to Kitty questioningly.

'Woah! It smells lush in here! You been baking, Mum?' asked Lucas as he kicked off his wellies, his face glowing from his time on the beach. He'd had a recent growing-spurt and though his shoulders were starting to broaden, he'd gone tall and gangly. And he always had a raging appetite.

'I have, lovey, there's some shortbread here. Might be a good idea to wash your hands before you dive in though.'

'Yep, will do.'

'Thought you were going to York, Noushka,' said Ollie, concern in his voice.

'Change of plan, Dad.'

'Oh?' he headed over to Kitty, kissing her full on the lips as he always did when he came home. 'All right?'

'Fine thanks,' Kitty replied. 'Did you have a good time?' She beamed up at him.

'Aye, we did.' He smiled down at her before turning his gaze back to Anoushka.

'You okay, Noushka?' Lucas had finished his perfunctory hand wash and was reaching across the table for a piece of shortbread.

'I am now, Lukes.' She smiled at her half-brother.

'What d'you mean you are now?' asked Lily, her golden corkscrew curls sitting wildly around her face. Her smile dropped as she studied Anoushka. 'You look like you've been crying.'

'I'm fine, Lils. Honest.'

'Noushka! We've got some *real-life* pirate treasure! Look!' Four-year-old Lottie scampered over to her, gripping firmly onto the bucket in her chubby hand. 'See! And we've got some crabs' legs, loads of sea glass and look at these *fablious* shells! If you listen in the big ones, you can hear the sea!'

'Oh, wow, Lottie! That's amazing.' Anoushka pulled her half-sister close to her and pressed a kiss to her chubby cheek.

'So, where's Damon?' asked Ollie, glancing between Anoushka and Kitty.

Anoushka swallowed, her heart suddenly thudding. 'We've broken up, Dad. We're finished.'

'Oh, right.' He ran his hand over his head. 'And are you okay about it? You seem fine, by the way.'

'I am, in fact I've just been telling Mum how I can't believe how much better I feel now it's over with him.'

'Thank the Lord for that.' Relief washed over Ollie's face.

Anoushka smiled. 'I'll let Mum fill you in on it all, but I'm just so glad he's out of my life.'

'Me too,' said Lucas through a mouthful of shortbread, spraying crumbs everywhere. 'He was a right twa—'

'Thank you, Lukes,' said Kitty, silencing her son just in time.

'We get the message, but little ears and all...' She nodded towards Lottie who was engrossed in the treasures in her bucket.

'Well, he was.'

'I agree,' said Lily. 'I'm glad you're not with him anymore; he took away your smiles, Noushka, and you always used to smile all the time, and laugh.'

'I know, Lils, and I'm sorry about that. I promise to smile more often now.' She reached for Lily's hand, looking up at her, smiling as if to prove her point. 'Anyway, I was wondering if you fancied a manicure? It's been ages since we had a girly session.' Beauty nights and manicures were something Anoushka and Lily had regularly enjoyed until Damon had taken a grip and they'd eventually petered out.

'Really? That would be totally awesome!' said Lily. 'Can I try that blue, sparkly nail varnish you bought the other week?'

'Course you can.'

'Cool!' Lily beamed at her, her large brown eyes so like her mum's.

'Me too,' said Lottie. 'Can I have pink sparkles? And will you put my hair in a mermalade plait like yours? I want to look like a sea princess.'

Anoushka giggled. 'Of course, Lotts. How about I go and get "Noushka's Beauty Parlour" set up while you two grab a drink and some shortbread? I'll give you a shout when I'm ready.'

'Yay!' Lottie jumped up and down, spilling the treasures from her bucket.

Anoushka sat back a moment, her heart filling with the love she had for her blended family, the feeling of contentment and security it gave her. The look of relief her dad and her step-mum exchanged didn't escape her.

'So does this mean you're going to start dating Gabe?' asked Lucas, still chomping.

'No, Lukes, it certainly does not! I'm not dating anyone ever again. I'm going to spend the rest of my life as an old maid, living at home forever so I can look after you lot.'

'That right, Noushka?' asked her dad, an amused grin on his face.

She got to her feet, shaking her head good-naturedly as more knowing looks were exchanged between her parents. 'Yes! End of!' she said, laughing.

'You're seriously gonna smash Gabe's heart to bits, Noushka. I mean, we can all see he fancies you summat rotten.' Lucas flashed her a cheeky grin.

'Yeah, everyone knows he's totes in love with you,' said Lily. 'And he's *so* adorable.'

'Okay! Enough!' Anoushka rolled her eyes, smiling. 'You're making him sound like a Labrador puppy,' she said, before hot-footing it upstairs to her bedroom.

It felt good to be back in the fold of her flock again; that she'd come so close to turning her back on them didn't bear thinking about.

As she busied herself setting out her collection of nail varnishes, her conversation with Kitty rolled into her mind. Getting everything off her chest had been an inexorable relief; Kitty seemed to know just the right things to say, no doubt because of her own experiences. Anoushka very much doubted her birth mother would have given such sage advice.

NINE

Kitty was the only mother-figure Anoushka had ever known, her biological mother having walked out on her when she was just two months old. She was the product of a brief but stormy romance her dad had had with Nataliya Shishkin; a half-Romany, half-Russian trapeze artist he'd met when the circus had come to Middleton-le-Moors. She'd spotted him drowning his sorrows in a pub, fresh from his split from Kitty, and, with alarming speed, had insinuated her way into his life. In a matter of weeks, Nataliya had found herself pregnant, and her feet lodged, very firmly, under the table at Rose Cottage.

Their relationship hadn't been easy, and things had soured quickly once Anoushka was born, with Nataliya seeming almost resentful of her role as a mother. It appeared to highlight the fact that being tied down to one spot just wasn't in her DNA and the urge to move on, to pick up where she'd left off with her old life-style, proved too irresistible a pull to ignore. One evening, Ollie returned home from work to find a note on the table and little Anoushka sobbing inconsolably in her crib. Nataliya had gone, declaring what everyone had been able to see: motherhood wasn't for her. She'd stated in no uncertain terms Ollie wasn't to attempt to find her; nothing could tempt her back. Not even news of little

Anoushka. Unable to comprehend how she could walk out on their angelic little daughter, he'd ignored her warnings and searched for her, but it had proved futile; Nataliya was nowhere to be found. And so, at the grand old age of twenty-one, his life as a single parent began.

Whenever Anoushka had asked about her mother, Ollie had been at great pains to spare her feelings, explaining the situation as kindly as possible, telling her Nataliya had left, not because she didn't love Anoushka, but because she'd struggled to adjust to her new lifestyle; putting down roots had been hard when she'd spent her whole life travelling the world. He'd also told her Nataliya had left her with Ollie, knowing he would be able to offer their daughter a more secure, stable life with his close-knit family in Lytell Stangdale. 'She loved you so much, and she only wanted what was best for you, sweetheart,' he'd told a ten-year-old Anoushka. There might not have been a grain of truth in what he'd told his daughter, but his words had gone some tiny way to assuaging the hurt she felt at her mum walking out on her.

A quiet and unassuming man, Ollie had done a commendable job of being both mum and dad to Anoushka. It hadn't been easy but he'd promised himself he'd do whatever he could to ensure she'd never feel like she was missing out by not having a mum around. And, with the help of his parents, he'd pretty much been able to keep that promise. 'You can't miss what you've never had" was a reply Anoushka regularly gave when friends had asked how it felt to grow up not knowing her mum.

Despite juggling single-parenthood with a full-time job as the local joiner, he'd always made sure she got to her numerous dance classes over at Middleton-le-Moors, not to mention the swimming lessons at the pool there, along with all the usual childhood commitments that were thrown at him. He'd never once felt it a burden. Anoushka was the apple of his eye and, in turn, she adored him. He'd watched her blossom into a confident, bubbly young woman of whom he was inordinately proud.

It hadn't always been easy though, especially when the teenage years beckoned and Anoushka had pushed at her boundaries. The pair still chuckled about the time when, aged fourteen, she'd wanted to dye her waist-long, golden hair a shocking shade of bright blue with pink streaks. Ollie had been horrified and she'd hounded him relentlessly.

'Please, Dad! *Please*! I can't believe you won't let me. You're being so unreasonable! Jacey's mum's going to let her dye *her* hair bright green.'

'It's still a no, Noushka.'

'But why not?'

'Because, for a start, you've got beautiful hair and if you dye it some crazy colour, there's a risk you'll ruin it; there'll be no going back when you're bored of it. And secondly, you know what the school rules say about outrageous hair colours; you'd be expelled as soon as the teachers clapped eyes on you. So it's still a no, I'm afraid.'

'That's so unfair. Jacey's got blonde hair too, and her mum doesn't have a problem with her dying her hair bright green.' Anoushka's eyes had blazed with outrage.

'Well, that's up to her. I'm not Jacey's mum,' Ollie had said, patiently.

'Ughh! Too right you're not her! She's fun. You're mean and boring!' She'd stamped her foot and flounced off to her bedroom, slamming the door for good measure.

The argument had burnt itself out over the course of a couple of days, by which time Anoushka had completely gone off the idea of dying her hair and moved onto her next project: getting her dad to agree to more piercings in her ears. And it transpired that Jacey's mum had taken the same stance as Ollie on the hair dye situation; there was no way she'd agree to anything so drastic either.

Their – usually – peaceful existence had been rocked when, out of the blue, Nataliya had turned up when Anoushka was almost sixteen. But rather than the young girl being in raptures at finally getting to meet her mum who'd only ever been some elusive, mysterious beauty conjured up by her imagination, it had been a crashing disappointment. There'd been no invisible bond that had transcended time or distance, and no overwhelming rush of love on either part. And there'd been no gushing apologies from Nataliya, nor hot tears shed in regret of their lost years together. Instead, a great, yawning chasm had stretched out between them, growing wider by the day. Nataliya had been full of angry recriminations, blaming Ollie for their lack of contact. 'But we didn't disappear, Nataliya,' he'd said. 'We're still living in the same house. You could've got in touch any time you wanted.' She'd batted his words away scornfully. It was clear she hadn't changed one bit. During her stay, she resumed her cold and selfish behaviour, treating Ollie like a doormat with her diva ways. It was just as it had been during her earlier time in the village.

It had made Anoushka's blood boil and she'd found herself wishing the woman would pack her bags and leave as quickly as she'd arrived.

That day came when it had become clear to Nataliya that she wasn't going to be able to pick up where she'd left off with the ease she'd anticipated. In the end, she'd flounced out of Rose Cottage in a cloud of distaste.

Though she was relieved, Anoushka hadn't been able to lie to herself, despite the secure and warm homelife her dad had created, it was as if her mother had twisted the knife when she'd packed her bags and walked out of their lives for a second time. Anoushka was hurt that she hadn't been enough. Again. Her way of numbing the pain was to tell herself Nataliya's leaving was no loss, and, if she'd been in possession of the full facts, she'd have known she was absolutely justified in thinking that. Nataliya had returned to benefit herself and not out of any kind of maternal loyalty or regret. She'd been caught stealing by one of her fellow performers from the circus and needed to lie low for a while. Lytell Stangdale had offered the perfect hiding place; she'd only every planned to stick around until she'd sucked everything she could out of Ollie, before disappearing once more.

With Nataliya and her accompanying drama hightailing it out

of the village, the dust had settled and the easy atmosphere returned to the Cartwright household. And it had left Anoushka free – and even more determined – to concentrate on a spot of matchmaking for her dad and the newly-divorced Kitty Bennett. She'd got an inkling he'd been growing close to his childhood sweetheart, which was something she'd been keen to encourage. She'd always thought if she could ever choose a mum, Kitty would be perfect for the role. With her kind nature and gentle temperament, she was a female version of her dad. Plus, she was about as far removed from the frosty and brittle Nataliya as was possible, which suited Anoushka just fine.

The day that Anoushka had been so desperate for finally arrived when Ollie married Kitty, becoming stepdad to Lucas and Lily. Finding herself part of a bigger family dynamic and moving into Kitty's home at Oak Tree Farm, Anoushka couldn't have been happier. The two families had knitted together quickly, with baby Lottie arriving the following year, making them complete. A happy, patchwork family. Her new home had brimmed with laughter and noise, and Anoushka savoured every moment. She'd never forget how Kitty's eyes had shone with happy tears the first time Anoushka had called her "Mum". Of course, there were the inevitable glitches along the way, particularly in the early days when there were squabbles over time spent in the bathroom – according to Lucas, Anoushka hogged it and – worse still! – she left all her beauty products lying around, and, heaven forbid, a bra! 'Ughh! Bloomin' lasses and all their weird stuff!' he'd said, complaining to Ollie who'd given him a sympathetic pat on the back. What to watch on TV regularly triggered minor disagreements too, as did who took the last slice of cake or shortbread – Lucas and his burgeoning appetite was the most frequent culprit, though he'd always vociferously deny it.

This new family dynamic, fortified with love and kindness, became the blueprint Anoushka wanted for her own future. The bar had been set high, which made her wonder how on earth she'd managed to get it so horribly wrong with Damon.

But now, looking back from this vantage point and the clarity it afforded, she could actually see when things had begun to change between them. It had been after they'd shared a bottle of wine one evening at Damon's apartment and she'd found the story of how she'd grown up without her mum spilling out. With the alcohol loosening her tongue, Anoushka had confessed how, despite having a brilliant childhood, filled with happy memories, her mum abandoning her had left a tiny relic of hurt she couldn't ever imagine going away. Of how she'd sometimes had nightmares about her dad leaving her too and she'd find herself all alone in the world. She wasn't usually one for baring her soul, particularly about her mother, and she'd regretted it almost instantly, but Damon had listened, offering soothing words, telling her she had him now and how all he wanted was to make her happy. At the time she'd had no reason not to believe him. But it hadn't taken long for his cold, manipulative side to pounce, subtly at first, and in such little dribs and drabs she'd brushed it off, blaming herself for misunderstanding or reading him wrong. Only now Anoushka could see how she hadn't been to blame. He'd skilfully tapped his way into her insecurities as a way of getting to her, of undermining her and chipping away at her confidence. He was a skilled manipulator, and being young and naïve meant she was easy prey, and the reason it had taken her so long to come to her senses.

TEN

After days of unseasonably warm sunshine, Anoushka opened her bedroom curtains on Thursday morning to see rain slanting against the window, clouds sitting low in a gloomy sky. It did nothing to dispel the buoyant feeling that still ran through her. It was hard to believe it had been a whole five days since she'd broken up with Damon. She'd been relieved to find he'd left her alone that first night; the radio silence had been a blessed relief. But the following day, he'd hounded her relentlessly, bombarding her with a gut-churning amount of phone calls, voicemails, text messages and DMs, just as she'd expected he would. They'd been calm at first, cool almost, asking her to contact him, telling her he might consider taking her back. '*He* might consider taking *me* back,' she'd said to herself, incredulous. 'Well, that's never going to happen, buster.' When it became clear she was ignoring him, it hadn't taken long for his familiar, bullying tone to kick in. It sounded almost sinister to her ears now.

By mid-afternoon, she'd decided to delete his messages as soon as they arrived, not even bothering to open them, but he'd kept up such a sustained assault on her phone, she'd been forced to turned it off. 'You can't let him influence whether you use your phone or not, Noushka,' her dad said. 'That's simply putting power back into his hands, albeit indirectly. What if your friends have been trying to get in touch? Wouldn't it be easier just to block his number?' Which is exactly what she did. It had been a huge relief. And though it had silenced him for now, something in Anoushka's bones told her she hadn't heard the last of him.

It was hard for her to comprehend that towards the end of their relationship he'd even started dropping hints that he was considering proposing to her. Dangling them like they were tempting gifts. Who did he think he was? The thought of being trapped in a marriage to a man like him made her blood run cold.

Since their break-up, Anoushka had kept a low profile in the village – news travelled fast on the moorland grapevine and she wasn't ready to discuss her newfound single status with the locals just yet. She'd kept her interactions to a minimum at her mid-week dance class, holding back from getting involved in conversations with the parents as they'd dropped their children off. It wasn't that she was too upset to go out and face the world, it was just she was still feeling a little frayed around the edges. She needed time for the dust to settle; to recalibrate. After all, the spectre of Damon wasn't going to relinquish its grip that easily.

Over the last few days, she'd relished spending time in the cocoon of her family home, totally unencumbered by his influence, laughing and chatting with her siblings – little Lottie really did give the best squidgy cuddles – and helping Kitty in the kitchen. And now she'd had time to sit down and consider what she'd experienced at the hands of such a manipulative man, Anoushka was able to see it from the perspective of her family and friends. From this new vantage point, she'd been able to understand why they'd been so worried, understand why they'd tried to warn her.

'You couldn't see it for yourself, 'cos you were too close, chick,' Kitty had said. 'But, put it this way, how would you feel if it was Lily who was going out with someone like that? You'd be able to see very clearly what was happening, and you'd be worried sick. That's what it was like for us watching you.'

Hadn't Kristy said the very same thing? The thought had made Anoushka's hackles rise. If she'd needed any further convincing that splitting up with Damon was the right thing to do, it was her step-mum and Kristy's analogy. She promised herself she'd never let it happen again. And, for that matter, she was going to make damned sure it never happened to her younger sisters either.

Though she'd been keeping herself to herself, it hadn't stopped Anoushka from venturing up onto the moors, savouring some head-clearing walks. She'd always found being out in the fresh air made her problems and worries seem smaller, more manageable. And Anoushka had been a fresh air fiend as far back as she could remember, whether it be setting up pretend dance classes in her back garden when she was a little girl, heading out to the moors with her friends or going on bracing dog walks. Lytell Stangdale had been a wonderful place to grow up, where she'd felt safe, secure and happy, with the people she loved most close to hand. Life had never been dull; there were always plenty of activities and groups to get involved in, from yoga to pottery painting to computer classes. But the one thing it had always lacked was a dance school. Which, to her mind, was the perfect reason for her to stay in the place she loved and open her own dance studio. There was only one problem: finding a suitable location. Damon's mocking retort when she'd shared her plans with him still rankled in her ears. It had made her all the more determined to fulfil her dreams.

She'd had the house to herself that morning and had spent it ringing around, hoping that someone local would have the solution to her problems, that there'd be some barn sitting empty and ripe for conversion. But she'd had no luck. With a headache brewing at the back of her eyes, she peered out of the window to see the rain had given way to bright spring sunshine, wispy white clouds replacing the dour grey sky of earlier. The urge to head outdoors suddenly beckoned her. In the next moment, she'd thrown on her jacket, pulled on her wellies and headed out of the door.

The earthy scent of damp vegetation rose from the ground as

she made her way up the grassy track to the rigg, the air cool and fresh. She sucked in a deep breath, relieved to find her headache was loosening its grip.

She'd just reached the summit of Great Stangdale Rigg, panting and puffing with the exertion, when she spotted Gabe. He was gazing out over the rugged landscape, taking in the sweeping view of the dale, the gentle breeze ruffling his hair. He had one hand stuffed in his pocket, the other holding Bob's lead. The Labrador was sniffing around busily, stopping when he spotted Anoushka, wagging his tail enthusiastically.

Curious as to what had attracted Bob's attention, Gabe turned, his face breaking into a wide smile. 'Hi, Noushka,' he said, his voice as warm as summer sunshine, triggering a flutter in her stomach.

'Hi there, Gabe.' She smiled back, feeling suddenly shy. She hoped her cheeks were sufficiently rosy from the walk for him not to notice the blush that now warmed them.

'It's another grand day,' he said.

'It is,' she said, tucking her hair behind her ears.

Bob pulled towards her on his lead, whimpering excitedly. 'Hello, there Bob.' She bent to smooth the Labrador's ears.

'You'll have a friend for life there if you keep doing that,' Gabe said, chuckling.

'So I see.' She giggled as Bob closed his eyes, savouring the attention.

'And you've no canine rascals with you then?'

'Not today, no. Eth and Mabes are with Dad, keeping him company in his workshop; they do that sometimes.'

'Ah, right.' He nodded and a beat passed. 'You feeling okay now?'

She knew he was referring to the last time she'd seen him, just after she'd broken up with Damon when her eyes were red-rimmed and puffy and her mascara was round her chin.

'Yeah, much better, thanks.' She stood up straight, squinting in the sunshine.

'That's good.' Gabe's dark eyes roved over her face. 'Don't suppose you'd mind if me and Bob walked along with you?'

'Not at all, I'd be glad of the company.' And in truth, she was, though she ignored the little voice that said, '*I'd be thrilled.*'

'I've left my car in the village; I popped in at the Post Office and thought it was too nice a day not to get a leg-stretch up here. Bob didn't argue.'

'I'll bet he didn't.' She chuckled.

They ambled along, chatting and laughing away, Gabe telling her how Lady Caro's mother, Lady Davinia, had got rather drunk the previous evening and had collided with a suit of armour on her way to bed at Danskelfe Castle. She'd sent it clattering to the ancient flagstone floor, hurling angry accusations that it had accosted her.

'Honest, she may be a bit sour-faced—'

'A *bit* sour-faced?' Noushka said, giggling.

'Okay then, she may be extremely sour-faced, but she can be absolutely hilarious without meaning to be, especially when she's fluthered.'

'Fluthered?'

'Ah, sorry, it's Irish for being very drunk.' He grinned at her. 'She's rather partial to the odd gin and tonic.'

'From what I've heard, she gets "fluthered" quite often.'

'You wouldn't be wrong there. Anyway, she was talking to this suit of armour as if she'd run into a real person and not a load of old metal. He adopted a squiffy, cut-glass English accent. '"I'm going to shue the bottom off you, you beashtly fiend! You won't get away with thish".'

He had Anoushka in hysterics. It felt so good to let go like that; to have a real belly laugh. It was liberating, and something she hadn't done much of while she'd been with Damon.

'That must've been so funny to see, but how on earth did you keep a straight face?' she asked when she finally stopped laughing.

'Trust me, it was hilarious, but I didn't dare for the life of me make eye contact with anyone else, or I'd have lost it completely. Hats off to Lord Danskelfe who managed to keep it together while he helped her to her bedroom. Doesn't bear thinking about if he'd dared to show he thought it was funny.' He feigned a shudder at the thought. 'Poor fella.'

'I can imagine.' Anoushka had seen for herself how scathing Lady Davinia could be when someone annoyed her.

They ambled on, the conversation flowing easily. Gabe told her more about his sisters, recounting tales of how it had been growing up in such an exuberant household, and the mischief the six of them had created for their patient, long-suffering parents. 'It was the girls who were the naughtiest, especially our Saoirse – she's a couple of years older than me and was a right little rascal. Whereas I lived up to my name and was an absolute angel – well, mostly,' he said, with a mischievous twinkle in his eyes. 'Clodagh was a real bossy-britches – still is actually – while Grainne and Roisin where a right pair of tomboys, always getting into scrapes. Mairead was the quietest; gave the least bother, she always had her head in a book. Apart from the time she thought it'd be hilarious to fill my guitar with water. That didn't go down well at all, I can tell you.'

Anoushka's face was aching, she'd been laughing so hard. She couldn't remember a time when she'd felt so relaxed, and had, tentatively at first, allowed herself the indulgence of enjoying Gabe's company. It didn't mean they were anything more than friends, she told herself. He was easy to be around, made no demands of her, didn't make her feel like she was doing something wrong, or that his mood would snap and he'd become suddenly angry. There was no trace of the stress that had lurked whenever she was with Damon. She hadn't realised until now that her body had been on high alert around him, adrenalin primed, ready to surge at a moment's notice. There was no wonder she'd felt exhausted. Damon had sapped away her energy and her happiness. And there was no wonder the feeling of relief at being free of him was so great.

It felt good to share anecdotes of her own family with Gabe too, the most recent one being how they'd lost little Lottie and had spent ages hunting around the house and the garden, only to find her curled up, sleeping soundly with Ethel and Mabel in their basket in the utility room. 'She looked so cute, snuggled up with them, my parents didn't have the heart to move her.'

Gabe's ensuing hoots of laughter warmed her heart. She hadn't shared that particular story with Damon, knowing his reaction would have been very different. He considered pets in the house to be unhygienic. Hearing that Lottie had actually ventured into the dogs' bed would have been met with disgust and disapproval in equal measure and he'd have lectured her about it for ages after. He wouldn't have seen it for the sweet story her family thought it was.

'So, can I ask how things are going with your dance classes? Are you still holding them in the village hall?' Gabe asked as they moseyed down the stony track that led to Fower Yatts Lane.

It was the easiest thing in the world, walking along and talking to him like this. No one would ever guess as to his fame and success, and she'd never seen a hint of arrogance or starry behaviour; he always seemed perfectly happy to blend into the background, act like he was one of the locals. And he always sounded genuinely interested in what she had to say; there was never any need to brace herself in anticipation of negative comments, ridiculing her decisions, mocking her, like there had been with Damon. It was easy to forget Gabe's fame, and all its implications, up here on the moortop. She felt completely at ease with him. In fact, today, she found her spirits soaring, felt a welcome lightness in her heart. In truth, if she was completely honest with herself, she'd say she was really rather enjoying being in his company.

'Hmm. They're going really well, but I'm desperate to find somewhere permanent to set up my own studio. I've just spent the morning trying to find something suitable but had no luck. It's okay in the village hall, but it really limits how many classes I can run.' She went on to explain how Kitty and Jimby had an old stone outbuilding they thought might be suitable for conversion into a studio – as part of the trust their parents had left them, the pair owned various properties in the village together with the land associated with Oak Tree Farm. On closer inspection, it had turned out to be impractical for a whole variety of reasons. Anoushka had felt utterly disappointed.

'It's a shame you hadn't got in there quick when the new units came up for rent at the castle's old estate offices. I daresay they would've been ideal; some of them are pretty big.'

Anoushka pulled a regretful face. 'I know; they were snapped up before I had the chance. I'm just keeping my fingers crossed something comes up soon.'

'I'm sure it will; I'll keep my ear to the ground for you.' He smiled across at her.

'Thank you.'

'And can I just say, I think it's great you want to set up a studio here; it'll be another great resource on the doorstep of the surrounding villages; something else to attract families to settle here rather than having them head for the towns. It'll help stop the little cottages from being turned into holiday homes, standing empty for months of the year like so many places in the countryside.'

'Thanks.' Anoushka turned to him and smiled, a feeling of warmth rushing through her. It surprised her how happy it made her that they were on the same wavelength. 'That's one of the reasons I want to do it here. Plus I've seen the way Mum and Vi's wedding dress business is thriving. Even though it's off the beaten track, they get clients travelling for miles to have one of their designs. Their success proves it's possible to make a go of things out here. And Lady Caro renovating the old estate offices is brilliant in helping support that.' She paused. 'Plus, I like the idea of having my own business; being independent, not having to rely on anyone else.' Her time with Damon had galvanized that view, making her more determined than ever never to be beholden to anyone. She knew he would eventually have worn her down, made her give up her dreams of having her own dance studio, yet somehow making her believe it was what she wanted. It sent a shiver running through her.

Gabe nodded, absorbing her words. 'I get that. And have you got a name for it? This shiny, new dance studio?'

Just then, a rabbit darted out of the undergrowth, stopping Bob in his tracks. He stood frozen, one paw raised off the ground in a classic gundog pose as he watched its white bobtail disappear into the heather.

'Rabbit take you by surprise, did it, fella?' Gabe chuckled. 'And, I have to say, I'm liking that stance; you definitely look the part.' Bob looked up, wagging his tail before resuming his nose-to-the-floor investigation. Gabe turned back to Anoushka. 'Where were we? Oh, yeah, you were about to tell me the name of your dance studio.'

She went on to tell him how, after racking her brains, she'd come up with a whole tranche of ideas, from A.R.C. School of Dance – 'A.R.C. are my initials.' – to Moorland Dance Studios, which she felt sounded too rural. 'I don't want people thinking I just offer country dancing or folk dancing lessons,' she said with a chuckle. 'And with the A.R.C. option, there's the slight problem of the way it sounds if you say it quickly. 'A.R.C,' she said, by way of demonstration. 'Sounds a bit too much like "arsey" for my liking; I'm not so sure "Arsey Dance Studios" would attract many pupils.'

Gabe gave a great roar of laughter. 'Fair point. Though I, for one, would be intrigued to find out what a course of "Arsey" country-dancing lessons had in store,' he said, making her giggle.

'I'm not so sure I'd get many takers. Anyway, I finally settled on Danskelfe School of Dance. I figured even if I don't get a place in Danskelfe, my studios will still be close enough for it to make sense. Plus, I thought sharing a name with the local castle might add a certain kudos to my dance school.'

'I can see the logic in that. And I think it's the perfect name; sounds very professional.' He smiled across at her.

'Thank you,' Anoushka said, doing her best to ignore the ripple of something delicious his smile had sent rushing around inside her.

'So, can I ask what does the "R" in your initials stand for?'

'Rose; it stands for Rose,' she said. 'It was my dad's choice. He tells a rather corny story that it's because he thought I looked like a little rosebud when I was first born, so thought Rose would be the perfect middle name. Anoushka was my birth mother's choice.' She felt suddenly self-conscious sharing this personal detail with Gabe.

'Rose,' Gabe said, softly. 'Rose.' He repeated himself as if delighting in the sound. He turned to her. 'That's a beautiful name; it suits you. So, I guess it's official, you're a genuine English Rose.'

Her heart fluttered and she felt her face grow warm with another blush. She fixed her attention to the ground as they negotiated a steep stretch of the path. 'Oh, I'm not so sure about that. Anyway, how's the recording going?' Time to get the focus well and truly off her!

'It's going grand, thanks. Written a whole load of songs too. This place inspires me beyond belief. It's captured my heart like nowhere else ever has.'

Anoushka couldn't help but steal a glance at him, cursing herself when she caught his eye. 'Yeah, it's a pretty special place,' she said, trying to ignore the somersault in her stomach.

'It is. Makes it harder to leave; makes me dread going back on the road. I've only got another week here, then I need to head back down to London, got to prepare for the tour; s'just a small one, a few dates around the UK, but...'

Anoushka got the feeling the "but" carried a lot of weight. She waited for him to finish his sentence, his mind clearly mulling over something.

He came to a halt, rubbing his hand across the back of his neck as he gazed out at the view that took in the thatched rooftops of Lytell Stangdale. They looked achingly cosy in the last of the day's sunshine. 'Man, I love this place.'

'Yeah, me too.' Anoushka stopped beside him, aware of the rise and fall of his chest. It wasn't difficult to tune into his thoughts. But, much as she was enjoying spending time with him like this, she didn't want to go down that route today. Didn't want to see the look in his eyes when she turned down another date. She nibbled on her lip as she searched her mind for something to say that would divert his attention. 'So, you say you've written loads of new songs.'

'I have, yeah.' He looked thoughtful for a moment. 'It's funny, but I'm actually getting more pleasure from songwriting than performing these days. Probably because I get to spend more time here.' He turned to her with a look that was so loaded, she found herself having to turn away, conscious of his heavy sigh.

Anoushka was thankful when the thrum of Pete Welford's quad bike over at Tinkel Bottom Farm drew their attention as it reverberated around the dale. They looked on to see him making his way across the field at the foot of his land, scattering his flock of sheep that were now bleating noisily. Bob looked on with interest.

'The fields'll be filled with lambs soon,' she said, keen to move their conversation on. 'I always think they look like they're made of little pipe-cleaners with their skinny, wobbly legs.'

'That's a pretty good description,' Gabe said, laughing softly.

Anoushka met his gaze. He was standing close. The thought that his face wasn't just handsome, it was kind too, his eyes gentle, entered her mind, sending a ripple up her spine. Despite her reservations, it would be oh-so-easy to let herself fall for him. She was gripped by the sudden longing to know what it would feel liked to have his arms wrapped around her, the stubble of his chin against her skin. Her heart was thudding hard as his eyes travelled to her mouth, lingering as a frisson crackled between them. It was intoxicating.

'Noushka,' Gabe said, his voice no more than a whisper.

The revs of the quad bike came crashing into her thoughts. She blinked, pulling herself back. Their moment was shattered in an instant. *What am I doing?*

Her heart was pounding. 'Oh... erm... was that a spot of rain I felt?' She held out her hand as if checking for more. 'I reckon it's probably time to head home,' she said as she started hurrying down the track.

'Er, yeah, I guess you're right.' Gabe's voice was heavy with disappointment, adding guilt to the myriad emotions currently swirling around inside her.

Ughh! Why does life have to be so complicated?

Awkwardness still lingered between them when they reached Gabe's car. He popped Bob into the back and turned to Anoushka. 'Thanks for letting us walk with you. I enjoyed our chat.'

'Me too.'

'And I'll be sure to keep a lookout for any suitable dance studio locations.' He grinned at her, brushing his hair from his face.

'Thanks, I appreciate that.' She smiled back at him.

He bent and kissed her cheek, taking her by surprise. She gasped. 'Oh!'

'That's just in case I don't get to see you before I leave for London.'

She could feel her face growing hot. 'Well... um... good luck. Hope the tour goes well – if I don't see you before, that is.'

He climbed into his car and she watched him drive off, her hand going to where his lips had delivered that kiss. Her emotions were in a whirl as she headed towards Oak Tree Farm. She knew her mind had strayed into dangerous territory for a moment back there. They'd nearly kissed! It had shocked her; happening before she'd had chance to think about it. Thank goodness she'd pulled herself up in time. There was no way that was going to happen. No way was she going to cross that boundary with Gabe, for a whole host of reasons. For one thing, what she was feeling right now she could, very firmly, put down to rebound. Nothing more. If she'd succumbed to those feelings, she'd just be using him and that wouldn't be fair. He was a decent, kind man, and the last thing she wanted to do was mess him about. Not that he'd be heartbroken, she told herself. Yes, he'd been asking her out on and off for the last few years, but she was certain her appeal was just because she kept saying no; her refusals didn't seem to be causing him any heartbreak – for which she was glad. And besides, there were plenty of girls who'd be more than happy to fill her shoes. If his extensive list of exes was anything to go by, he wouldn't be single for long.

ELEVEN

It was Saturday evening, just before seven-thirty – a whole week since her break-up with Damon. It had gone by in a flash, and was untainted by a single moment of regret. Anoushka was making her way along the age-worn sandstone trod to The Sunne Inne. The sunny afternoon of earlier had given way to a clear and frosty evening. Above, the inky-black sky was peppered with millions of twinkling stars, while pale moonlight poured over the village. Woodsmoke curled down from the squat chimneys, lingering in the crisp evening air. She pulled her gloves from the pockets of her cropped, rose-pink duffel coat and pushed her fingers into them. It wasn't far to the pub from her house, but the cold was surprisingly biting.

Brogan had called that afternoon with a suggestion of a night out at the Sunne. 'It'll do you good to get out, chick, rather than sitting at home, stewing over Mr Dickhead,' she'd said. 'Say, seven-thirty? Kristy's coming too, Ben's dropping her off before heading over to his mates but she won't be there 'til around eight-ish. We're overdue a good old laugh together.' Brogan's tone suggested she'd brook no argument

Anoushka's heart had sunk at the time; she'd had another morning making fruitless phone calls, trying to find somewhere suitable for her dance studio. It had left her in no mood for socializing. And besides, she'd already talked herself into an evening in front of the telly followed by a long bubble-bath and an early night. But Brogan wasn't to be deterred and had badgered Anoushka until she'd agreed.

'You need to get out, Noushka, before you get into the habit of staying at home the whole time. Don't let that loser do that to you. The sooner you get back to your old self and old routines, the better for you.' Alongside her dog-walking business, Brogan worked part-time behind the bar of the Sunne, and had managed to wangle the night off, knowing that her friend could probably do with a girls' night out and having her mind occupied by a good old chinwag.

Anoushka's family had been vocal in their encouragement too. 'It might not feel like it now, but it'll do you the world of good, lovey,' Kitty had said.

'Aye, and you'll be glad you've gone,' said her dad.

Finally convinced, Anoushka had swapped her comfy loungewear for a pair of skinny jeans and a snuggly, duck-egg blue jumper. Freeing her hair from its plait, she tied it into a low ponytail, leaving loose tendrils around her face. And, after a quick freshen-up of her barely-there make-up, she decided she was good to go.

As she continued along the path a ping from her bag signalled the arrival of a text. She fished out her phone to see a message from Brogan.

> Hi Noushka, really sorry, running late. Wilf's been rolling in fox poo!!! Stinks something shocking!! Need to bathe the little monster. Will get there asap Bxxx

Anoushka chuckled to herself. Brogan's black Labrador was an adorable softie, but he'd developed a terrible penchant for rolling in anything undesirable he encountered – the more disgusting, the better – and regularly needed bathing because of it. She fired a quick text back.

Hi Broge, no worries. Good old Wilf! Hope you get him smelling sweeter soon! See you when you land A xxx

She couldn't help but smile as she pressed send.

Anoushka paused, toying briefly with the idea of heading back home, waiting 'til she'd got word from Brogan that she was at the pub, but quickly talked herself out of it; she was almost there, after all.

A moment later, she pushed open the heavy oak door of the Sunne. A familiar wave of warmth rushed at her, immediately lifting her spirits thanks to the gentle burble of chatter and the mouth-watering aroma of landlady, Bea Latimer's, delicious home-cooking. It was regularly said that the pub welcomed you in like an old friend and Anoushka couldn't argue with that this evening. With its thick, uneven walls and age-darkened oak beams, it oozed charm. Indeed, it had recently been described as a "delightful gem" and the "epitome of country style" by a columnist in a national magazine who'd waxed lyrical about it, declaring they couldn't wait to return. Bea's former incarnation as an interior designer was evident throughout the place, from the soft furnishings in colours that reflected the shades of the surrounding moorland, to the hand-forged light fittings (courtesy of Jimby), whose mellow light cast a gentle glow around the room. The open fire blazed away merrily, as it did each day, in the vast inglenook fireplace.

Feeling uncharacteristically nervous, Anoushka scanned the room, a little squirm of anxiety making itself known in her stomach. She knew her time with Damon had given her confidence a dent but she really didn't want to have to explain about him to others; she didn't relish people asking questions. She spotted a slew of familiar faces including a huddle of local farmers no doubt discussing the latest prices livestock was getting at the mart over in Middleton-le-Moors. She headed towards the sturdy oak bar where the polished brass handles of the beer pumps gleamed back at her. Portia, the landlord and landlady's daughter, had just finished pouring a glass of wine for Ella Welford – another of Kitty's relations. She was standing at the bar with her boyfriend, Joss Campion, while landlord, Jonty, whose half-moon spectacles were perched precariously on the end of his generous nose, was deep in conversation with local farmer John Danks.

'Hello, darling, what can I get you?' asked Portia in her cut-glass accent that stood out against the broad North Yorkshire vowels that burbled around the room. Her welcoming smile went some way to calming Anoushka's nerves. Like her mother, Bea, she was effortlessly stylish. Tonight, she was wearing a cream silk shirt over faux leather jeans, her long blonde hair hanging in an impossibly glossy curtain down her back.

'Hi, Porsh, can I get a bottle of Pinot and three glasses, please?' Anoushka asked, returning Portia's smile.

'You can indeed.' Portia regularly helped out behind the bar when she was visiting her parents and by all accounts was happy to stand in for Brogan this evening.

'Hiya, Noushka,' said Ella, her tone friendly. 'How's things?'

'Good, thanks, Ells. You?'

'Not bad.'

'Now then, Noushka.' Joss leaned around Ella and smiled at her.

'We don't usually see you in here on a Saturday night; I thought the bustle of York always beckoned.' Ella reached for her glass of wine, taking a sip, oblivious to the dread her words had triggered in her friend.

Anoushka tensed. She knew Ella wasn't being nosy, but questions like this were the very reason she hadn't been keen to venture out tonight; she wasn't ready to explain how she'd broken up with Damon. And besides, he'd occupied way too much of her headspace recently, tonight she wanted to push him well and truly out of her mind. She caught Portia's eye; Portia would know why Brogan wanted to swap her shift, not that Anoushka minded, the young woman had a kind heart and wasn't in the least bit gossipy.

Portia flashed her a sympathetic look. 'Ah, well, York's loss is our gain,' she said. 'I, for one, am delighted you're here, darling. I haven't seen you for an age; we've got lots to catch up on.'

'Yeah, I don't think I've seen you here since Christmas.'

'That would be right,' said Portia. 'And I gather you're meeting up with Brogan and Kristy this evening; I might pop over and join you later, if I have a spare minute, that is.'

'That'd be good.' Anoushka gave her a grateful smile. 'Kristy should be here just after eight, and Brogan's just texted me to say she's running late, apparently Wilf's been up to mischief, rolling in the dreaded fox poo.' She scrunched up her nose.

'Oh, no! Poor Brogan,' said Ella.

'Ughh! How ghastly! Nomad and Scruff did that last time I took them on a walk, little horrors,' Portia said of her parents' rescue dogs. 'I've never smelt anything like it. Took forever to get rid of the pong.'

'Yeah, rolling in yucky stuff's a favourite pastime of Mabel and Ethel if they get the chance – the smellier the better; they can't seem to get enough.' Anoushka chuckled. 'Anyway, I think I'll go and snaffle that table by the window before someone else grabs it.' She reached for the tray Portia had set up for her with three glasses and the wine in an ice bucket. 'See you folks later.'

'Will do, darling. Have fun.' Portia beamed a smile at her.

Anoushka had been sitting at the table for a good ten minutes, savouring the warmth belted out by the chunky, vintage radiator that sat beneath the window, when the door opened, admitting a chilly blast of air. She ceased scrolling through social media on her mobile and looked up to see Lady Carolyn Hammondely and her husband, Sim, bustling into the room. Her heart gave an unexpected flutter when Gabe followed up behind with Bob on a short lead. She hadn't factored in seeing him here tonight.

She quickly looked away, directing her attention to her phone once more, hoping he hadn't spotted her, willing her heart to be still. The last thing she wanted was for Brogan and Kristy to land and find her mid-conversation with Gabe; they'd put two and two together and come up with a whole load of something that was way off the mark. She could only imagine the resultant teasing; it would drive her potty!

A few moments later, she sensed a presence beside her, the familiar, spicy scent of cologne that could only belong to one person. Feeling her heart rate crank up several notches, she looked up to see Gabe smiling down at her, his eyes dancing happily. Bob, who'd been busy sniffing the carpet, lunged towards her, pushing his head into her lap, his tail wagging excitedly.

'Well, hello there, Bob.' She laughed at his enthusiastic greeting, smoothing his velvety brow which only served to make him wag his tail even harder. 'And hi, Gabe,' she said, looking up at him.

'Hi there, Noushka.' He brushed back his floppy fringe, his velvety tones sending a delicious ripple up her spine. 'You on your own?' His gaze fell to the three wine glasses. 'Durr. Stupid question, please ignore it. I'm an eejit.' He laughed. 'You're clearly not on your own.'

'I'm just waiting for Brogan and Kristy; they're running late.'

'Ah, I see.'

She smiled up at him, not knowing what else to say.

'Mind if Bob and I join you for a minute? We'll skedaddle when your pals get here; I've no intention of getting in the way and taking over your evening.' He flashed another smile, this one unleashing a host of butterflies in her stomach. She wasn't ready to deal with those this evening – nor the reason behind them.

'Course, help yourself.' She pushed her phone back into her bag and he placed his pint down on the table, before instructing Bob to sit, which the young Labrador obediently did, all the while watching his dad with eager eyes. 'Good, lad,' Gabe said as he slipped off his navy peacoat and hung it on the back of the chair opposite Anoushka. 'So, then, what's the craic?' he asked as he sat down. 'There must be a shedload since I last saw you a whole two days ago.' He flashed her a disarming smile. 'I know what a hotbed of activity it is round here.'

'Hmm, I'm not so sure about that.' Anoushka grinned. 'Not unless you include the news that Hugh Heifer's gone and got himself a new cow.'

Gabe nodded solemnly. 'Well, that's what I'd call very big news. Though I reckon it would've caused more of a stir if you'd told me he'd got himself a pair of new wellies; I'd call that headline-grabbing.' He pulled a mock serious face, making her giggle.

'Well, I think we both know that's never going to happen, though I had heard a rumour he'd stuck a new pair of soles on the ones he's been wearing – when I say "new", I mean he's taken the soles off an old pair of his son John's, and stuck them on his.'

'Ah, that's what I like to hear. Lytell Stangdale at the cutting-edge of upcycling and doing its bit for the planet. Good old Hugh, he's a great character.' The smile he gave melted her heart a little.

'He's that all right.' She really wished those dratted butterflies in her stomach would settle themselves, they were annoyingly distracting. Doing all she could to ignore them she asked, 'Anyway, how are things with you? How're the preparations for the tour going?'

'Yeah, they're going fine.'

Bob slid to the floor with a harumph.

She noted Gabe's smile had fallen, his voice lacking its usual enthusiasm.

'How long will you be away for?'

'Couple of months; I'm hoping to be back here in June; sure it won't come soon enough.' He held her gaze. He didn't need to ask, "Will things be different between us by then? Will you be ready to go out with me?" – those soft brown eyes of his said it all.

Feeling the colour rise in her cheeks, Anoushka quickly looked away, turning her attention to Bob. 'And what will you do with Bob while you're away?'

On hearing his name, Bob scrabbled to his feet, two large eyes peering over the table, his tail swishing over the carpet. Gabe caught Anoushka's eye and they both laughed.

'Ah, you're so cute, Bob.' She gave the Labrador's ears a quick ruffle.

'Caro's very kindly offered to Bob-sit for me, which is good of her. Can't be bad, can it, fella? Doggy bed-and-breakfast in a castle, eh? You'd best make sure you don't get all snooty with the rest of us while I'm away.' Enjoying the attention, Bob pushed his head into Gabe's lap, blinking up at him. 'He's promised me he'll stay well away from shoes, especially Lady Davinia's. Perish the thought he gets his paws on one of hers. She'd have him thrown into the dungeons before he could say, "It wasn't me, it was Lord Danskelfe!"' He pulled a face of mock horror, making Anoushka giggle.

'Hmm. I can't imagine she'd take it too well.' Lady Davinia Hammondely may have softened in recent years, but there were still moments when she forgot herself and the sour-faced dragon of her former years returned. Chewed designer shoes would bring about such an occasion, of that Anoushka was certain.

'No, neither can I.'

They both laughed and her eyes fell to her glass of Pinot Grigio, the contents suddenly fascinating.

A few moments followed before Gabe spoke. 'It's been good to see you smiling again, Noushka, see that sparkle return to your eyes.'

She felt her heart leap. How on earth did she reply to that? She drew in a steadying breath. 'It feels good to smile again,' she said, her eyes tentatively reaching his. It was true; there was no point pretending she didn't know what he meant, or ignoring it.

'And I meant what I said when I saw you last Saturday, if you ever need to talk, I'm more than happy to listen. I promise not to judge or pass comment; I'll just be an impartial ear for you when you need to let off steam. Well, maybe impartial's not the right word if it involves that eejit, but you know what I mean.'

She felt a smile pull at her mouth. 'Thanks, Gabe, that's really kind, but I think I'll be okay. I'm feeling much better now.' The way he was looking at her made her heart give another lilt and before she knew what was happening, she found herself wondering what it would feel like to have his lips pressed against hers. They looked soft and warm and— *Get that thought right out of your head!* She snatched up her glass and took a quick sip of her wine before looking away, glad that the lighting was dim and would, hopefully, hide the blush she could feel creeping up her face. How could she be feeling this way so soon after Damon?

A moment later, she felt a flood of relief as Brogan bustled into the pub and headed over to them, the frosty air lingering on her clothes. 'Brrr! It's bloomin' freezing out there. Sorry I'm late, Noushka. Hi, Gabe.' She unwound her scarf and plonked herself down on the seat next to her friend, bending to fuss Bob who was enormously pleased to see her if the tail wagging was anything to go by. 'And hi there, lovely lad.'

'Ah, the Bobster'll take all of the "lovely lad" business you care to dish out, won't you, young man?' Gabe delivered a resounding pat to the Labrador's rump.

Anoushka turned to Brogan. 'Dare I ask, how's Wilf?'

'Ughh!' Brogan feigned a fed-up expression making Anoushka and Gabe laugh. 'He's a stinky little rascal. Actually, I'm very pleased to say, he's not so stinky now, but he's still a little rascal. Took bloomin' ages to get rid of the smell. Which I think,' she took a hearty sniff of her sleeve, wrinkling her nose,' 'is still lingering on me even though I've got changed.'

'Well, I can't smell anything; it's probably just in your nose, if you know what I mean. Anyway, after your ordeal, sounds like you could do with one of these.' Anoushka poured a glass of Pinot Grigio, pushing it towards her friend. 'There, get that down you.'

'Mmm. Don't mind if I do.' Brogan took a sip, rounding it off with an appreciative sigh.

'Right, well, I'll leave you ladies to enjoy your evening.' Gabe went to stand up.

'There's no need to go on my account,' said Brogan. 'You're very welcome to join us, isn't he, Noushka?'

Before she could answer, Kristy bowled in, her nose red with the cold. 'Now then, lasses, sorry I'm late. Hiya, Gabe. Ooh, please tell me that radiator's on, I'm absolutely nithered. Anyone would think it was still winter out there.' She gave a shiver as if to prove her point. 'And hello, gorgeous Bob.' She bent to ruffle the Labrador's ears with both hands, which had him in raptures.

'Hi, Kristy. You can have my seat; I was just about to head over to the bar. And you'll be pleased to know the radiator is blisteringly hot.' Gabe pushed his chair back.

'Oh, there's really no need, Gabe, I was—'

'Honest, it's fine, I need to get back to Sim and Caro before they think I've deserted them.' He smiled warmly. 'I'll catch you later. Be sure to have a grand evening,' he said, his eyes lingering on Anoushka.

TWELVE

'He's got it *seriously* bad for you, Noushka,' said Kristy as she slipped her padded jacket off and hung it over the back of the seat vacated by Gabe. The three friends watched him make his way over to the bar where he joined Lady Caro and Sim.

Anoushka shook her head despairingly. 'You've *seriously* got the wrong end of the stick there, Kristy,' she said, feeling a swirl in her stomach.

'Oh, come on, you'd have to be blind not to notice; he so does have it bad for you,' said Brogan.

'You two are seeing what you want to see,' said Anoushka.

Brogan appeared to ignore her. 'And sticking to the serious theme, his butt looks *seriously* hot in those jeans.' She arched a suggestive eyebrow and flashed a mischievous look in Anoushka's direction. 'And I wish I could find a man who looked at me the way he looks at you.'

Anoushka sighed. 'Right, I think we need some ground rules for tonight before you two start getting carried away with yourselves.' She set her hands on the table, splaying her fingers and eyeing her friends intently. 'As you're both fully aware, I've only just got out of a relationship – and a difficult one, at that – so there's absolutely no way I'm looking to dive headfirst straight into another one. In fact, as I've said a million times already, I've completely and utterly sworn off relationships; they're more trouble than they're worth, I don't have the energy or the inclination for one. And, just in case you think I don't actually mean that, let me tell you, I absolutely, totally do. Right now, I just have the overwhelming urge to have some time on my own, getting all the crap out of my head, without the distraction of having a man in my life. Actually, scrap having "some" time on my own, that's how I see my long-term future.' She sat back in her chair. 'I'm going to up my mission to find a suitable premises for my dance school and getting it set up, which I've got more time to do now Damon's out of the picture. And being so focused on that will mean I won't have any spare time to dedicate to a relationship. Which suits me just fine. My dance school is my sole priority. I know you both mean well, but I really need you to listen. No more trying to fix me up with someone – Gabe, or otherwise. Okay?'

'Okay,' her friends said in unison, nodding contritely before Brogan said, 'He's still got it bad for you though, Noushka. And for what it's worth, I think you're being really cruel, not even giving him a tiny little kiss. It'd make his day, and keep him going while he's on tour.'

'Ughh! Broge!' Anoushka rolled her eyes good-naturedly. 'That would so give him the wrong impression; I'm not going to lead him on. *That* would be cruel.'

Kristy pursed her lips, as if preparing to say something, but Anoushka got in first. 'Right, much as I know your hearts are in the right place, there'll be no more talking about my love life tonight. End of – and I really mean it.' *How hard can it be to get the message across?* Got it?' She glanced between them.

'Yep, got it,' Brogan said reluctantly.

'Me too,' said Kristy, though the sideways look she cast Brogan didn't go unnoticed by Anoushka.

'Good.' Ignoring it, she heaved a sigh of relief and said, 'Right, so what's new with you two?' She reached for the bottle of wine and topped up their glasses.

Conversation flowed seamlessly. Had she heard about Hetty Johnson and how she'd been caught cheating on her husband of five minutes? Anoushka hadn't, so between them, Brogan and Kristy brought her up-to-speed. Brogan had gone on to share how she was getting fed up with her dog-walking business, grumbling that she seemed to spend most of the day traipsing over the moors, which was fine when the weather was good. 'But when it's tanking down, it's bloomin' miserable,' she said. 'I could do with someone to help, which Ella does when she's got time. And I'm getting so inundated, I'm having to turn folk away. I mean, I adore all the dogs I walk and I love working with animals, but... I don't know... my heart's just not in it anymore. I'm twenty-six and I'm not even settled in a career.'

'Broge, twenty-six is hardly old!' Anoushka said, laughing.

'Feels that way to me right now,' Brogan said despondently.

'Well, you might be interested to know I've heard a rumour there's a new vets' practice opening up on the outskirts of the village in another one of the old Danskelfe Estate buildings. You could maybe get a job there; you're a trained vet nurse,' Kristy said.

'Ooh, that would be perfect for you, Broge.' Anoushka smiled, though she was inwardly cursing on hearing of another property she'd missed out on.

That had piqued Brogan's interest. 'Sounds good; I'm definitely interested. Where did you hear that?'

'Ben told me; he heard it from one of his mates who's in the Young Farmers over at Middleton-le-Moors. I think one of the vets is Chris Crabtree from the surgery there – not sure about any other ones – but I can ask Ben to find out more, if you like?'

'Yeah, that would be great, Kristy, thanks.' Brogan beamed at her. 'Anyroad, what's new with you?'

Kristy outlined her and Ben's plans for the campsite at Withrin Hill. 'Molly's given us free rein with it, which is awesome, so we're looking at some purpose-built pods and wood-fired hot tubs.' Her blue eyes danced happily. She'd been in a relationship with Ben Pennock – one of Molly's twenty-three-year-old twin sons – since they'd been at agricultural college together, the couple moving into a converted stable block up at Withrin Hill Farm a few years ago. Like Anoushka, Kristy had an old head on her young shoulders.

Their conversation was brought to a halt by octogenarian couple, Big Mary and her artist husband, Gerald, who burst into the pub in a pop of their usual vibrant colours and enthusiastic babble. 'Eee, hello, Gabe, pet. It's good to see you, didn't know if you'd still be here.' Big Mary's sing-song Geordie accent boomed around the room as she made her way over to the bar. Turning to her husband, she said in a loud stage whisper, 'Gerry, have you remembered your gnashers or did you leave them in the dishwasher?'

'They're right here, pet.' He gave the pocket of his bright purple batik-print trousers a theatrical shake. 'Clean as a whistle they are, after their whizz around with the pots and pans.'

'Well, get them in your gob, pet, we can't have you flashing your gums to all and sundry, especially local celebrities.'

'Aye, righto, my sweet, anything for you.' Gerald flashed her a gummy smile as he had a quick rummage in his pocket, pulling out a pair of false teeth, bits of fluff stuck to them. 'Tada!' After giving them a cursory wipe on Big Marys scarf, he popped them into his mouth. 'Better?' he asked, grinning broadly.

'Aye, much. Now come on, let's get a drink.'

Anoushka felt a giggle rising in her chest, but didn't dare look at Kristy or Brogan who were spluttering beside her. She caught Gabe's eye, the pair struggling to hold in their amusement.

'You couldn't make it up, could you?' said Brogan, through her giggles.

'Ah, I love Big Mary and Gerald, the village has definitely been brighter since they moved here.' Anoushka looked fondly in the couple's direction.

'Jeez, you're not wrong there,' said Kristy. 'I'm just glad he's stopped painting pictures of her bits and bobs in the buff and moved on to landscapes. Those exhibitions he used to put on were absolutely terrifying.'

'They were different, that's for sure,' Anoushka said, chuckling.

'Don't go there.' Brogan held up her palm. 'Please, don't either of you utter another word on the subject. I don't even want to think about Big Mary's landscape, it'll risk conjuring up a mental image that could scar me for life. I'm very pleased to say all that nude business was before my time here.' She wrinkled her nose.

Kristy snorted. 'You had a lucky escape, Broge. And you've got the wrong end of the stick there; Gerald's moved onto painting *scenery* landscapes and not *Big Mary's* landscape.'

'Phew!' said Brogan, feigning mopping her brow as the three friends collapsed into a fit of the giggles.

'Ah, but they're such a kind-hearted couple; they'd do anything for anyone,' Anoushka said warmly.

'Aye, you're right there. And I don't know anyone else who can get away with out-there fashion like Big Mary. That jumper she's wearing would look like a multi-coloured furball on anyone else, but she's totally rocking it, what with her bold personality,' said Brogan. 'She's awesome.'

'She is,' said Anoushka.

'The shocking pink in it matches Gerald's beard,' said Kristy thoughtfully.

'It does actually.' Brogan gave a throaty giggle. 'They're definitely soulmates.'

It was fair to say the ebullient couple's arrival in the village had added a welcome splash of colour.

The evening seemed to fly by and before they knew it, Jonty was calling last orders. Anoushka sat back in her seat and gave a contented sigh, glad she'd decided to swap her plans of a night in front of the telly for an evening catching up with her friends. And she was pleased, and not a little surprised, that Damon hadn't crossed her mind once.

As she called her goodbyes and made her way home, she felt buoyed with enthusiasm, her heart light with happiness. She hadn't felt that way for quite some time and she welcomed it back wholeheartedly. And, she had to admit, it had been good to see Gabe again. The look in his eyes as she'd bid him goodnight had turned her knees to jelly. 'Ughh! If only...' she said softly to herself before the little voice of reason jumped in. *Steady on there, Noushka, don't forget what you've told yourself – and everyone else for that matter!* She was in danger of not taking heed of the promise she'd made to herself. And that would never do.

THIRTEEN

Anoushka was making her way along the bridle path that ran along Great Stangdale Rigg. Wednesday had dawned sunny and bright with barely a cloud in the sky, and the glorious panoramic view stretched for miles. Already, the cool air was doing a sterling job of clearing the headache that had been brewing since yet another disappointing viewing of a prospective building for her dance studio. Earlier that morning, she'd had a call from Dave Stonehouse who farmed at North View Farm over in Arkleby, saying he had a building he thought she might be interested in. When she'd got there, he'd guided her to an old stone barn, the roof of which looked ready to cave in. Her spirits had plummeted instantly. They plummeted further still when he opened the dilapidated door to the building revealing it was so full of junk, ranging from old tractor tyres, to rusting vehicles, it would take months to get it properly cleared. But it didn't matter anyway since the building was too small for her needs. And though Dave had said the renovations would be her responsibility, he'd had the brass neck to name an astronomical rent. She was glad when she climbed back into her little car and trundled off down the track.

She'd even considered something purpose-built – Kitty and Jimby had offered her the use of a piece of land they joint-owned in the Fairfax family trust – but that would involve obtaining the use of an architect, applying for planning permission and then getting the place built. Though it was an option, it wasn't ideal and would no doubt take forever, as well as being costly. She was champing at the bit, eager to get her dance school up-and-running, and the prospect of continuing to hold lessons at the village hall while she waited for the building to be finished was simply not appealing. She was beginning to think she'd never find anywhere, and that rankled for several reasons, one of which was Damon; she wanted to prove him wrong about making a success of herself, but at this rate, that wasn't going to happen any time soon. She puffed out her cheeks and ploughed on, watching the Campion's lambs gambolling around the field.

She was just about to take the track back down to Lytell Stang-dale when she heard the thunder of hooves behind her. She turned to see Lady Carolyn Hammondely bearing down on her. As she drew closer, Caro pulled on the reins of her chestnut mare, Delilah. 'Noushka, darling, I'm so glad to have seen you,' she said, smiling broadly from the lofty heights of the saddle. She looked every inch the toff in her highly-buffed thigh-length riding boots and fitted tweed jacket, her glossy, dark-brown ponytail snaking over her shoulder.

'Hi, Caro.' Anoushka returned Caro's smile, looking up at her quizzically.

'I'll cut to the chase. Gabe tells me you're looking for some-where to locate your dance studio and I was wondering if you'd found anywhere suitable?'

'No.' Anoushka's shoulders slumped. 'It's proving to be harder than I expected. I'm beginning to think I'm never going to find anywhere.'

Caro's smile grew wider. 'In that case, darling, I think I could be the bearer of some jolly good news.'

'Oh?'

'I'm sure you're aware – especially since your father and Jimby have been working on them – but my latest plans for the castle, and getting the old pile contributing towards her upkeep, involve converting that cluster of old estate offices on the Lytell Stangdale road. They've been standing empty for absolutely yonks which is a scandalous waste.'

'Yes, I know the ones you mean.' Anoushka had heard her dad and Jimby talking about them, singing their praises.

'Well, there's a large, detached unit – for want of a better word – that I think just might be perfect for you. It's just come free again since the person who was originally going to take it on has backed out. I wouldn't care but, like the other tenants, he's had his name on the list before the units were even started. But that's by-the-by. If you think it'd be any good for you, you're very welcome to take a gander.'

'Oh, wow!' Anoushka's interest had been well and truly piqued. These were the buildings Gabe had mentioned the previous week. Until recently, they'd been in a state of disrepair for as long as she could remember, with the roofs of some collapsing in, walls crumbling in places. Several months ago, work on renovating them had started in earnest – her dad had secured the contract to do the joinery work, and Jimby had been commissioned to make new cast iron fencing and a grand set of gates to the entrance. Memory of what Kristy had said about the new vets' taking over a Danskelfe Estate premises swirled in her mind; she wondered if it would be located at one of these buildings? If her memory served her right, their location was perfect and came with plenty of space for parking. That would certainly ease the problem of cars clogging up the village before and after her classes, which had been a cause for concern with her current set up. 'I'm intrigued,' she said, 'and very keen to take a look. Would I have sole use of the building?' With the increased interest in her dance classes, she was finding it difficult to fit everyone in the village hall. Booking extra sessions had proved tricky as it was already in great demand, what with Gerald's art classes, Vi's burlesque classes and flower arranging classes to name but a few.

'Oh, definitely; the building would be let to you alone; yours to do with whatever you will.'

'Right.' Anoushka nodded, rubbing her fingers across her chin as she processed the information, her hopes springing to life. 'The only thing is, I'd need to have the rooms soundproofed, that way I wouldn't run the risk of disturbing your other tenants, and I'd need to have special sprung flooring fitted too. Would that be a problem with them being old buildings?' She braced herself, hoping she hadn't talked herself into a deal-breaker.

Caro leaned forward and patted Delilah soundly on the withers. 'Not at all; none of those buildings are listed so there's no need to worry about that, which is a blessed relief. So, if you like what you see, you're welcome to crack on with whatever needs doing right away. The unit I've earmarked for you is detached and the walls are jolly thick, which should help stifle any noise before you even get started on the soundproofing.'

'Sounds perfect! When can I take a look at it?' Excitement was thrumming through her veins; from what Caro had described, the unit had the potential to be the answer to her prayers.

'Tomorrow morning too soon? Say, ten-thirty?'

'Perfect. Thank you, Caro,' she said, as a huge smile spread across her face.

'It's actually Gabe you have to thank; he's been badgering me to find something for you on the Danskelfe Estate. Sim and I wondered if he'd actually willed the chap to back out of the unit so you could have it.' She gave a hearty laugh.

Anoushka felt her cheeks grow warm. 'Well, I'm very grateful to you both.'

Caro gave her a loaded look. 'Yes, he's a good man is Gabe.' Just then, Delilah snorted and started pounding the ground impatiently, plumes of steam billowing from her nostrils. 'Okay, madam, bide your passion, we're heading off now.' She smiled at Anoushka. 'See you tomorrow, darling.'

'See you tomorrow.'

Anoushka couldn't help but do a happy dance as she watched

Caro trotting off along the path, Delilah's hooves drumming on the ground; she had a good feeling about this. 'At last!' she said, with a little squeal of joy. Brimming with happiness, she hurried home; she couldn't wait to share the news with her family.

That night Anoushka lay in bed, her mind way too busy to contemplate sleep. With excitement bubbling away inside her, she envisaged how she'd have the rooms of her new dance school, the colour schemes she'd use and the sign she'd have above the door, not forgetting the dancewear. Vi had already put her in touch with a brand designer and together they'd settled on a logo and font. It was contemporary and stylish in shades of midnight blue, dusky pink and antique gold featuring a pair of ballet shoes and a rose. All she'd been waiting for was an address so she could get her business cards printed. Anoushka wiggled her toes happily. *Ooh! This is so exciting!* Tomorrow morning couldn't come round soon enough.

As her mind gradually wound down, her thoughts turned to Gabe. She was grateful to him for mentioning her situation to Caro. If it wasn't for that, she was sure she wouldn't have had the chance of the unit; it would've been snapped up before she'd heard it was back up for let again. Caro was right, she thought with a sigh, he was a good man. She recalled the look in his eyes the last time she'd seen him. He'd stopped her as she was leaving the pub last Saturday. 'Bye, Noushka. I probably won't see you 'til I get back,' he'd said, giving her arm a squeeze. Her heart gave a little leap at the memory. *Don't go there, Noushka, you've got enough on your plate.*

FOURTEEN

Caro's fancy sports car was already parked up when Anoushka drove into the spacious courtyard, tyres crunching over the gravel. She pulled up outside the unit – the word really didn't do the building justice – her stomach fizzing with excitement; she couldn't wait to see inside.

'Morning, darling.' Beaming, Caro appeared in the doorway before striding over, her ponytail swinging jauntily. 'Mwah. Mwah,' she said, clasping her hands on Anoushka's shoulders, delivering a kiss to each cheek. 'Come on, let me show you the space, see if it suits your needs.'

'Morning, Caro, thanks so much for this. It looks fabulous from the outside,' Anoushka said, following her.

'As you can see, there's plenty of space for parking, and there's more either side and to the rear, too.'

'That's great.' Anoushka nodded, taking it all in. Already, this was looking so promising. It was the largest of the group of buildings, and set back on its own. Before even stepping over the threshold, she hoped with all her might it would be perfect.

Inside, she glanced around at the generous entrance area – it would make an ideal reception and waiting room. It had four doors leading off it. The two on the back wall opened onto two generous sized spaces that would be absolutely perfect for dance lessons. Another door gave way to a small, newly installed kitchenette, while the other led to a toilet and a room that could be fitted out as a changing room. Anoushka's mind was racing. Already, she could visualize how she'd have everything set out. 'This is fantastic!' she said, unable to rein in her enthusiasm.

Caro turned to her and grinned. 'I thought you'd like it, darling,' she said as she made her way up a set of narrow stairs that gave access to a space above. 'And there's plenty of room up here for storage.'

When they were back downstairs, Caro asked, 'So, what do you think?'

Anoushka gazed around her, a wide smile on her face. 'I think it's absolutely perfect.'

Caro clapped her hands together. 'Oh, that's wonderful!'

'And you're sure you don't mind me installing a sprung floor and soundproofing? Oh, and mirrors along the far walls in the two bigger rooms as well as ballet barres?' Her heart was thudding excitedly.

'Not at all, darling. I trust you; you're free to do whatever you need.'

'Thank you.' Anoushka thought she would burst with happiness. When she'd discussed Caro's proposition with her family the previous evening, her dad had told her if the building proved suitable, he'd crack on with the flooring and soundproofing straightaway, telling her Jimby had offered his services whenever they were needed too. They'd have the place done in no time. There was only one thing that could put the dampeners on the project.

'And how much would the rent be?" Anoushka asked. She held her breath, hoping with all her might Caro wouldn't come out with an extortionate amount that would be way out of her price range.

'Ah, well, as the initial idea behind renovating these buildings was to support local businesses, we decided early on to keep our rents reasonable.'

Anoushka's heart pinged with happiness when Caro named an

amount that would be easily affordable. 'That's great, and how soon could I have the key?' Anoushka asked, secretly hoping there wouldn't be months to wait.

'I'll get onto my solicitor right away; get the agreement drawn up. Could be all done by the end of next week.'

'Oh wow! That'd be brilliant.' Excitement bubbled up inside her, she didn't think her smile could get any wider.

Her dreams were about to become a reality.

They headed out into the sunshine. Caro reached into her bag for her sunglasses, glancing across at Anoushka, her face suddenly serious. 'Would you mind if I say something?'

'No, not at all.' Anoushka's brow creased into a frown. She wondered where this was going, hoping it wasn't going to be something that would affect her plans for the dance studio.

'Running the risk of sounding like I'm sticking my nose where it's not wanted, I'm going to dive right in and say that Gabe's a really decent guy.' She held Anoushka's gaze, smiling kindly.

'Oh... um... yes, I agree, he is.' *Not Lady Caro as well now! Please, spare me.*

'And you've utterly stolen his heart. Sim and I have never seen him like this before.' She held up her hands in a placatory gesture. 'I know it's none of my business, and I also know you've had a horrid time of it recently, but if I could just say one thing, it would be to ask that you, please, don't close off your heart to him forever. Maybe, when you're in a better place for a relationship, you might be able to think of Gabe in a romantic way.' Caro paused and rolled her eyes. She laughed and said, 'Sorry, that came out hideously cringe-worthy and not at all how I wanted it to sound. Ughh! What I meant to say was... well, Gabe's a decent guy who thinks the world of you... and maybe take with a pinch of salt everything you read about him in the media dating lots of women; it's really not true, but I suppose it's newsworthy.'

Anoushka was utterly mortified. Why did Caro have to go and do that? 'Oh, erm... I agree, Gabe's a really nice guy, but I'm not ready for another relationship and don't think I will be for foreseeable future. I want to give the dance school my full attention; I'd rather not have any distractions.' She could feel her cheeks blazing.

Caro gave her a small, albeit warm, smile. 'I totally understand – and my apologies again for mentioning it. I still think it's a shame though; you'd be perfect together.'

Just then, a delivery van pulled into the courtyard. Anoushka was grateful for the distraction, saving her from having to respond. They watched with interest as the driver heaved several large boxes onto a sack barrow, struggling over the gravel to get to one of the buildings.

'Righty-ho, darling,' said Caro, turning back to her. 'I'll head home and get on to my solicitor right away, set the ball rolling.'

'That's great, thank you. I really appreciate this.'

'Not at all. I hope it all works out fabulously for you.' She delivered a couple of kisses to Anoushka's cheeks. 'I'll be in touch.' With that, she strode off over to her gleaming sports car.

Anoushka watched it disappear through the huge, stone gateposts, her excitement mingling with the feelings Caro had stirred up about Gabe. Truth be told, if it hadn't been for him mentioning her plight to Caro, she wouldn't be in the position of having such a fantastic location for her dance school. For that she would be eternally grateful. But it didn't mean that she should feel obliged to go on a date with him. She needed to focus on getting the studio set up, and all that went with it, no matter how much of a great guy everyone seemed keen on telling her he was.

She turned and took another look at the building, its buttery yellow bricks glowing in the sunshine. A shiver of delight ran through her. She could hardly believe her dream was coming tangibly close to becoming a reality.

FIFTEEN

Sunday morning found Anoushka sitting in the kitchen of Oak Tree Farm, chatting away with Kitty and Molly and Vi who'd popped in for a catch up. Molly was in the middle of entertaining them with how she'd stopped Camm's snoring the previous evening using a method that sounded more akin to mediaeval torture.

'I'm scared to think where this is going. Sounds like he's in serious danger of losing body parts,' said Vi. She looked as glamorous as always in her trademark fifties-style dress and sculpted aubergine-coloured waves.

'You've no idea how close he came,' said Molly, feigning a sinister tone, making everyone laugh.

Just then, there was a sturdy knock at the door. Their laughter ceased and Ethel and Mabel jumped up and flew down the hallway, barking vociferously.

'Anyone would think those two were a pair of Rottweilers the way they go on,' Anoushka said with a chuckle.

'I know, they don't realise everyone round here knows they're as soft as washing,' said Kitty, as she headed off to answer the door.

'Well, whoever it is, I hope they're quick; I'm dying to know how Camm reacted to Moll's homemade instrument of torture.' Vi giggled. 'Come to think of it, you've got a bloomin' nerve, Moll, you snore like a right old pig, as Kitts and I can vouch... oh!' Her eyes settled on the door, growing wide with shock.

Everyone turned to see Kitty in the doorway, her face ashen and her eyes filled with anxiety. Anoushka frowned, trying to make sense of her step-mum's expression. Her gaze moved to the figure behind her, her face falling. 'Damon?' *No! This can't be happening!* Her heart lurched. She'd always known it was the risk she took by blocking his number. He was holding an extravagant bouquet of flowers and wearing a self-pitying expression which was more than a little annoying. He clearly had no intention of giving up easily.

Aware of all eyes on her, Anoushka took a moment to steady her nerves, drawing in a deep breath. 'Damon, what are you doing here?'

His eyes flickered at her chilly tone of voice. 'You haven't answered any of my messages.'

'Ever thought there was a reason for that?' asked Molly, which earned her an icy glare from him.

'I was addressing Anoushka actually,' he said. 'Coming here's the only way I can get to speak to you. Can we talk, Anoushka? Please? In private.' His pathetic pleading look only served to make her bristle even more.

'Molly's right, I've got nothing to say to you; we're finished. You've had a wasted journey.'

'Please, Anoushka, just give me five minutes of your time. I've come all this way.'

She looked across at Kitty, searching for reassurance. 'Why don't you take Damon into the living room? Let him have his five minutes there; get it over and done with. We'll be here if you need us.' The steely look in her step-mum's eyes was all she needed.

'Okay. Five minutes, Damon. That's all.' Anoushka nodded, wondering how she'd managed to magic up this feisty version of herself. She was glad she had; this last Damon-free fortnight had been bliss, and she had no intention of letting him back in her life again.

In the living room, she closed the door behind them and turned to face him.

'Can we sit down?' he asked, gesturing to the large squishy sofa that sat opposite the wood burner.

'I'd rather stand; what you've got to say shouldn't take long.'

He looked taken aback. 'Don't be like that.'

'I'm not being like anything, Damon. I just want to get this over and done with, then you can go.' *That's right, keep up the badass act. Don't let him in. Do not weaken.*

'Look, Anoushka, I'm sorry you got upset and felt you had to storm off. I've racked my brains since then but I can't think what can have happened to make you do it. But what I do know is that we're good together. I know I might come across as hard sometimes – you know, like the expression you've got to be cruel to be kind – but it's only because I want the best for you; want you to realise your full potential.'

'Oh, really?' Anoushka folded her arms across her chest. 'You hide it well. And I don't suppose it would even cross your mind how patronising that actually sounds.'

Damon's eyes flashed angrily. He pushed his shoulders back and drew himself up to his full five-feet-nine – at an inch shorter than Anoushka, he'd always insisted she must never wear heels in his presence. 'Someone should tell you it's time you acted your age. You've carried on like a silly little girl for long enough. I've let you have your hissy fit and now it's time to act like a grown up again. I've had the decency to go out of my way and come over here, bought you an expensive bouquet of flowers. I've even booked us a table for this evening at that fancy new restaurant in York.' He paused as if letting her absorb his words, waiting for her to rush towards him, gushing with apologies and gratitude.

She tipped her head to one side. That kind of spiel may have worked once, but not anymore. 'Is that right?'

Her response appeared to have wrong-footed him. Angrily, he threw the bouquet down on the floor and stepped towards her, his eyes cold and mean. 'Listen to me, you little country mouse. I don't know who you think you are to turn me down but it's high time you pulled yourself together. If you don't come back to York with me now, I'm warning you it's over between us. Finished! And you won't get another chance.'

She leaned away from him, his familiar overpowering cologne mixed with the strong mouthwash he used, suddenly repulsing her. 'You seem to be forgetting something, Damon. We're already finished; have been for exactly two weeks, so there's no way I'll be heading to York with you.' She hoped he couldn't hear the shake in her voice.

A muscle pulsed in his cheek as he glared at her. 'You little fool! I don't know why I expected any different from you. But I can assure you, breaking up with me will prove to be the worst decision you ever make. That pathetic country yokel family of yours will only hold you back – don't think I don't know it's their influence that's been the catalyst for this out-of-character behaviour of yours. There's no way they'll help you achieve your best like I could. They won't push you out of that small-minded little comfort zone you're always so keen to bury yourself in. You'll just plod on being an ambitionless nobody when my influence could've set your career on the path to success.'

Anoushka's anger was rising. She went to speak but he held up his hand, silencing her. He drew his top lip over his teeth and glowered. 'I don't know what I ever saw in you; you've been nothing but a waste of my valuable time. You can keep your sad little exist—'

Just then the door flew open. 'That's enough! Get out! Right now!'

Anoushka and Damon turned to see Kitty walking towards them, her face blazing with anger. 'Don't ever, ever talk to my daughter like that again. Do you hear me? I don't know who the bloody hell you think you are coming in here acting like an arrogant little prick, but let me tell you this, she's worth a hundred of you, you little weasel!' She prodded Damon hard on the shoulder, making him take a step back.

'What the...?' His eyes flashed angrily. 'I think you're forgetting something; she's not actually your daughter.' He shrugged his shoulders and gave an arrogant smirk.

'Anoushka may not be my flesh and blood, but I love her every bit as much as if she were. Make no mistake, matey, I'd lay down my life for her just as I would for my other children.' She narrowed her eyes, stepping closer to him until her face was inches away from his. 'And I'd kill for all four of them, too.'

Damon leaned back and gulped audibly.

Anoushka looked on, her mouth hanging open. She'd never seen her step-mum like this before; she'd hardly ever heard her raise her voice. But this version of Kitty was actually quite terrifying. Sensing movement behind her, she turned to see Molly and Vi coming into the room, stopping either side of her in a gesture of support. Vi reached across and rubbed Anoushka's arm, giving her a sympathetic smile.

'Rest assured, there's no way I'm going to stand back and let you speak to *my daughter* like that. Got it?' Kitty glared at him.

Damon gulped again, holding up his palms at her, adopting a softer tone to his voice. 'Hey, you've got it all wrong. I'm only trying to help Anoushka; my method of being cruel to be kind might not—'

'How dare you? Don't even think about trying that out on me. Cruel to be kind? Who the heck do you think you are? You're the worst sort of bully; a manipulative, gaslighting, nasty little shit. I know the signs; I used to be married to someone just like you. You're wasting your breath on me and on Noushka. Now get your sorry arse out of our house before I set the dogs on you.'

Anoushka took a sidelong-look at Ethel and Mabel who were watching events unfold with great interest. They appeared to be as surprised by this version of Kitty as everyone else. She caught Molly's eye, who was struggling not to laugh at Kitty bandying about the threat of the dogs as if they were savage killers, and bit down on her own smile.

'They may look soft and friendly, but I can assure you, they're highly trained; all it takes is one word from me,' said Kitty, pointing at Ethel and Mabel.

The pair blinked back at her.

'I'd do what she says,' said Molly, her tone deadly serious, no hint of the laughter that was ready to burst forth.

'I agree; you don't want to risk it,' said Vi.

Damon inhaled briskly, his nostrils flaring as he brushed an imaginary piece of fluff from the lapel of his jacket. 'Right, well, no one can say I didn't try.' He walked towards the door, giving Kitty a wide berth. 'Goodbye, Anoushka.'

The women held a collective breath, waiting for the sound of his car to fade as he disappeared out of the village. As soon as the coast was clear, Anoushka ran over to Kitty, throwing her arms around her. Ethel and Mabel trotted over to them, nudging at their legs and wagging their tails excitedly. 'Oh, my God! You were totally awesome, Mum! I can't believe you said all that to him.'

'Oh, Kitty, I do love it when you get angry, you're so utterly fearless,' Vi said, laughing.

'I know, our Kitts is a hoot when she loses her rag, and it's so hilarious when she swears; seems to have more impact 'cos she doesn't usually have a filthy mouth.' Molly gave a throaty chuckle.

'Unlike her cousin.' Vi arched her eyebrows at Molly who pulled a face at her in return.

'Mind, I'm not so sure threatening him with those two was that convincing; they're soft as muck, the pair of them.' Molly nodded towards the dogs as she strode across and wrapped her arms around Kitty and Anoushka.

Vi scrunched up her face as she made her way over to join the group hug, her kitten heels clickety-clacking over the flagstones. 'Yeah, I'm with you on that one, Moll. I think the biggest threat they pose is death by slobbering.'

'Ooh, that would be perfect for Damon, you know how fussy he is,' Anoushka said gleefully, releasing herself from the knot of arms. She looked down at Kitty, her hands resting on her shoulders. 'But seriously, Mum, thank you so much for being there for me; I thought he was never going to leave unless I backed down to him.'

'It's all right, lovey. There's no way I was going to stand back and let you go through what I did, you're too precious to your dad and me. We might not have Damon's grand plans for you, but we want you to follow *your* dreams, and we'll be here to support you in any way we can. And we know you'll be amazing at whatever you do.'

'Hear, hear,' said Vi, sniffing and wiping a rogue tear from her eye.

'Too right,' said Molly.

The affection shining in Kitty's eyes made Anoushka's throat constrict. She felt the sting of tears and swiped them away. 'Love you, Mum.' She wrapped her arms around Kitty once more, burying her face into her step-mum's neck. The glimpse of the tough core Anoushka had guessed at filled her with a new-found respect for her.

'Love you too, my darling.'

'Have we missed something?' The women turned to see Ollie standing in the doorway, a bemused expression on his face, his dark-blond hair ruffled by the breeze.

'Oh, nothing much; just your missus being a total badass.' Molly grinned at him, making the others laugh.

'What? Kitty's been a badass?' he said, glancing between them, his face a picture of disbelief.

'Ey up, you lot. Who's been a badass?' Jimby bowled into the kitchen, wearing his customary grin. 'And was that Damon's car we've just seen flying through the village like his backside was on fire?'

'In answer to your first question, it's your little sister who's been a badass,' said Molly, still laughing at Ollie's expression. 'And in reply to your second, yep, it'll have been Damon's car you saw.'

'Damon's been here?' asked Ollie, his face darkening.

'He turned up wanting to get back together. Got a bit unpleasant when I told him I didn't want to. But don't worry, Dad, he didn't stay long.' Anoushka noticed his body tense at the mention of her ex's name.

'Good.' Ollie nodded, his shoulders relaxing as relief washed over his face.

Jimby scratched his head. 'What? Are you saying his visit here and Kitty being a badass are connected?' Jimby glanced from Molly to Kitty then to Ollie.

'Yup. She just lost it on that little weasel– which is why he'll have been driving like a lunatic,' said Vi.

'Yeah, he'll have been terrified she was after him,' said Anoushka, making the women giggle.

'With the killer mutts,' said Molly.

'Shame you missed it, fellas; she was pretty spectacular.' Vi squeezed Kitty's shoulder, making her friend blush.

'That right, Kitts?' Ollie asked, a smile twitching at his mouth.

'I… well… um… I heard him talking to our Noushka in a really horrible way, and something inside me just flipped.' Kitty appeared to be as shocked by her reaction as everyone else.

'Mum was totally amazing. She flew in like a raging whirlwind. I'm in complete awe of her; Damon looked absolutely petrified!'

'I don't think that bullying waste of space will be troubling your daughter again, that's for sure.' Molly chuckled. 'Tell you what, why don't we have a cuppa and we can tell you fellas all about it?'

'Sounds like a plan. I'm intrigued to hear what happened. And I'm just glad you're all okay.' Ollie's eyes flicked between his daughter and his wife. 'Where are the rest of the kids, by the way?'

'Lottie's having a snooze, and Lucas and Lils are out with friends,' said Kitty, looking self-conscious.

'And I think Vi's mum and dad'll be okay to hang on to our Pippin for a bit longer while we hear all about this. I reckon it's not going to be suitable for the delicate ears of a two-year-old,' said Jimby, grinning as they all made their way into the kitchen. Pippin was the nickname given to Vi and Jimby's daughter before she was born owing to Vi's ferocious craving for apples while she was pregnant. And though her real name was Elspeth, Pippin had stuck.

Vi's eyes flicked to the clock on the wall. 'I expect she'll be in the middle of her afternoon nap too.'

'Right then, I'll stick the kettle on,' said Ollie.

'Go, Kitty,' said Jimby when they'd finished recounting the details of Damon's ill-fated visit.

'I reckon her words'll be ringing in Damon's ears for quite some time,' said Vi, looking at her friend fondly.

Jimby let out a hoot of laughter. 'She's fiercer than a lioness guarding her cubs is my little sis. Woe betide anyone who hurts her kids.'

'Aye, cross her at your peril,' Molly said with a giggle. 'I wouldn't have the balls, that's for sure.' She glanced across at Kitty whose blushes had been deepening by the minute.

'Well, seems Noushka's right, you are awesome, Kitts.' Ollie's eyes were shining with pride. He looked over at Anoushka and gave her a wink before throwing his arm around his wife, kissing her on the cheek. Anoushka didn't need him to say how it had warmed his heart that Kitty had stood up for her just as she would her own flesh and blood; it was written all over his face.

Kitty looked up at him. 'I only said what you would've said if you'd been here.'

He smiled down at her. 'That may be so, but I doubt it would've had the same impact as it did coming from you; I should imagine it'll have shocked him to the core.' He bent to kiss her full on the mouth.

'Ughh! Purlease! Would you two mind saving that mush for later.' Molly, who didn't have a romantic bone in her body, mimed being sick, making everyone laugh.

'Right then.' Jimby sat forward in his seat, rubbing his hands together. 'I can see our Kitty is getting a tad embarrassed about all this attention, so it's probably a good time to mention the idea I've got brewing for the next village fundraiser.'

SEVENTEEN

'Hells bells, brace yourselves.' Molly cast a worried glance around the group.

'Uh-oh, here we go,' said Vi. 'Careful what you volunteer yourselves for, folks.'

'Before, you get started, Jimby, I just want to put it out there, I'll be remaining fully clothed for whatever it is you've got planned. I don't give a monkey's what the fundraiser's for.' Ollie threw him a warning look.

'Don't blame you, Oll. If Jimby's past ventures are anything to go by, he'll have you posing in the buff for some photoshoot before you can say, "knack-naked",' Molly said dryly, as giggles ran around the kitchen. 'And from what I can gather, there's still some locals who haven't recovered from the shock of seeing him tearing down the street in nowt but his wellies and a pair of skimpy budgie smugglers.'

'I don't think anyone's recovered from that, Moll.' Ollie chuckled. 'I'm personally scarred for life.'

'I'll have you know, I got many, many admiring glances that day.' Jimby flashed them a haughty look.

'That right?' Vi could hardly keep herself from laughing. 'Even with those pasty chicken legs of yours?'

'Oh, yes indeedy,' he said jokingly, feigning a seductive pose.

'Jimby, what are you like?' Kitty giggled, shaking her head.

'I reckon the "admiring glances" he's referring to must've come from Maneater Matheson.' Molly giggled. 'And she dishes them out to old Hugh Heifer, so hers don't count. Anyway, I'd heard it was birds of the feathered variety that were showing an interest in Jimby... something about a "tiny worm".' She waggled her little finger and raucous laughter filled the room.

Jimby shot her a mock offended expression. 'Rude,' he said, before breaking into a wide smile and laughing along with the rest of them.

A few years earlier, Jimby had persuaded several men from Lytell Stangdale and the surrounding villages to take part in a photoshoot for a calendar he was having put together to raise funds for a village defibrillator. Everyone had happily volunteered, unaware he'd been frugal with the details that they'd have to pose naked but for a strategically placed prop that related to their profession. The calendar had gone down a storm, much to his delight, and had given him, Ollie and Zander Gillespie, the now local GP, a generous fifteen-minutes of fame – and several indecent proposals! – on social media.

'Anyroad, getting back to this fundraiser, I was thinking it would be a bit of a laugh to organise an auction of promises; we haven't had one round here before.'

'Well, as long as it involves you keeping your clothes on, I'm all for it, mate,' said Ollie.

'Same here,' said Vi, giggling and blowing her husband a kiss.

'I assume this is for the school,' said Kitty. 'In which case, I don't think anything involving the removal of clothes would be very appropriate.' Various sounds of agreement followed.

Jimby held up his hands. 'I can assure you, not a stitch of clothing will need to be removed for my latest idea.'

Molly put a hand to her ear. 'I could swear I just heard folks in the village heave a collective sigh of relief.'

'Funny,' said Jimby.

'I think an auction of promises is a fab idea. I'd be happy to offer a block of free dancing lessons.' Anoushka beamed, thoughts of her dancing school sending a surge of happiness through her. 'Lytell Stangdale Primary is a great school and I'm happy to support it.'

'Yeah, me too, especially now I know I can keep my kit on,' said Ollie.

Vi nodded. 'Mmm. Schools are the heart of a village. Without one, places like Lytell Stangdale, Danskelfe and Arkleby would just become full of second homes or holiday lets. I still want it to be there when it's time for Pippin to go to school.'

'And it'd be good to support it in any way we can to keep it attractive to the younger generation round here, stop them moving away when they decide to settle down and start their own families; keep pupil numbers up,' said Kitty.

'Like Noushka's age-group, you mean?' Molly flashed her a grin.

Anoushka threw her a knowing look, but didn't bite. She wasn't going to be drawn in on a conversation about her love life that would inevitably lead to Gabe.

'And your lads, Moll.' Kitty gave Anoushka a sympathetic smile. 'Ben and Kristy'll be parents before you know it.'

'Ughh! Don't remind me.' Molly pulled a face. 'Not so sure I'm ready to be a granny just yet, but I agree, we need to do all we can to keep the school open. It's not so bad that the older kids have to travel to secondary school in Middleton, but I think it wouldn't be ideal for the littlies. I mean some of them are only four years old.'

'I agree; I wouldn't fancy our little one having to traipse over there,' said Vi.

'Which is why I agreed to help,' said Jimby.

The local primary school was thriving, and had been awarded the status of "Outstanding" by Ofsted for three consecutive inspections. So popular was it, pupils travelled from out of the local area to attend. The school's forward-thinking headteacher, Mrs Prudom, was always working on ideas to safeguard its future. Her latest vision was the addition of a new two-storey extension to the Victorian sandstone building, creating extra space that would accommodate a separate computer room, library and dedicated room for the breakfast and afterschool clubs. Despite the Local Authority pledging a generous lump of money, it still wasn't enough to bring her plans to life. Knowing of Jimby's involvement in the village fundraising committee, Mrs Prudom had approached him with a view to organising an event that would help fill the coffers.

'We've been given funds for a batch of new computers – which comes from a separate pot of money that can't be put towards building work. It would be wonderful to create a new space for them,' Mrs Prudom had said.

'Leave it with me.' Jimby had smiled. He hadn't needed asking twice.

'So,' he said, rubbing his hands together and glancing around the table, 'if you lot could all get your thinking caps on, as well as spreading the word, it'd be good to get the event organised for the summer. I think the village hall would be the best venue, so we'll need to get a suitable Friday or Saturday night booked. Once that's done we can take things from there. Let's try to make this a fabulous night.'

'Don't know about you, mate, but I reckon this calls for a committee meeting at the pub.' Ollie grinned at Jimby.

'Couldn't agree more, Oll.' Jimby chuckled, patting his friend heartily on the back.

Anoushka glanced around her. Everyone was chatting away, chipping in with ideas and anecdotes, their eyes shining with enthusiasm. She hadn't realised how much she'd missed this sort of get-together, missed the feeling of being buoyed along by the banter of family and friends. The thought that she'd come close to losing it sent a shiver up her spine.

EIGHTEEN

JUNE

June had arrived in a burst of blazing sunshine, the cottage gardens in the village positively brimming with blousy flowers and the moors resplendent in lush, green foliage. Frothy swathes of cow parsley lined the roadside, hundreds of vivid yellow dandelion heads at their feet; they were out in force this year.

It had been two months since Gabe had left for London where his tour had kicked off. And while Anoushka's time had been jam-packed with the exciting preparations for the opening of her dance studio, she'd regularly found her mind wandering its way to him, each time, triggering a little surge of something indefinable; or maybe it was definable, she just didn't want to admit it to herself. Having said that, she still hadn't been able to stop herself from checking social media, scrolling through posts that contained images of him, poring over videos fans had taken at his gigs. By all accounts, this tour, at the smaller, more intimate venues, was going down a storm.

Golden sunshine spilled through the windows of Oak Tree Farm, the heady scent of the rose that scrambled up the wall outside filling the air. Anoushka was feeling happy; she'd stormed through her to-do list that morning.

She was engrossed in sorting through a batch of newly delivered T-shirts she'd ordered for the students of her dance school when she heard the latch on the front door rattle. Seconds later, Kristy's head appeared around the door.

'Knock, knock,' she said, a smile lighting up her pretty face.

'Kristy! It's good to see you. How's things?' Anoushka beamed at her friend as Mabel and Ethel rushed over to greet their visitor.

'Hi, Noushka. And now then, you two rascals.' She bent to fuss the dogs, peering up at Anoushka as she did so. 'Things are good, thanks. Broge and me were wondering how you were doing since we hadn't seen you for a while, but now I can see why.' She laughed as she took in the table piled high with dance school paraphernalia. 'You look snowed under.'

Anoushka flicked her plait over her shoulder and puffed out her cheeks. 'I've just been working flat-out getting everything ready for the dance school. Honestly, it's just been totally crazy-busy. I've barely had time to do anything else, which is why I haven't been in touch – sorry.'

'Hey, no worries. I can see just how bogged down you are. If you like, I can pop back later when you're not so busy.'

'No, not at all. Like I said, it's good to see you, and I could do with a break so it's the perfect time for a catch up.' Anoushka pushed the T-shirts to one side and flipped her laptop shut. The prospect of a minute or two away from her tasks was suddenly very welcome. 'Cuppa, or would you prefer something cold?'

'Tea's great, thanks, but only if you're really sure you've got time.'

'I've definitely got time.' Anoushka gave her friend's arm a squeeze as she headed for the Aga. 'Park your bum while I stick the kettle on.'

'Okay. I'm happy to give you a hand with anything you think I'll be able to help with, but I need to be back over at Withrin Hill no later than one o'clock; Ben and me are heading out to take a look at some hot tubs with wood-burning stoves that heat them; I think I've mentioned them before.' Kristy picked up a plastic bag containing a T-shirt. 'Wow, these look really cool.'

Anoushka smiled at her. 'Yeah, they look even better than I was expecting; the quality's really good. In fact, I've just been in touch with the company who supplies them, and they've agreed to print other dance stuff too, you know, hoodies, leotards, dance tights, gym bags, even water bottles.'

'Wow! You really do mean business, don't you, missus?' Kristy looked impressed.

'I sure do. It was always my intention to start as I mean to go on; create a professional impression right from the get-go.' Anoushka scooped up the kettle and made her way over to the Belfast sink.

'Well, you'll definitely do that with these, they're really stylish and the colours are gorgeous; the contrast's fab.'

'Thanks, Kristy; I'm super-chuffed with them.' Damon's snidey words about her ambitions for the dance school had been sneaking up on her today, setting her stomach jittering. *What if he's right? What if I'm just fooling myself? What if my business falls flat on its face before it even gets started?* Her friend's well-timed words of support pushed away the final toxic dregs of his influence. 'And I can't wait to get up to the new premises.'

'I bet you can't. When do you think it'll be ready?'

Setting the kettle on the Aga hotplate, Anoushka turned to her friend. 'Well, 'cos everyone's been working like mad – Dad and Jimby have been amazing – things have got finished way sooner than we expected. Everything should be done in a couple of days. Which means I can bring the move forward by a few weeks so the classes will officially start there a week on Saturday.' Saying it out loud sent a thrill wriggling up her spine. She gave a squeal of happiness, making both of them giggle.

'Oh, wow! Noushka, that's so exciting!'

'I know, it's taking some sinking in. Actually, Dad's up there now, fixing the sign above the door; I can't wait to see it – maybe I'll really actually believe it then. Anyway, I'm heading over there this afternoon to do all the final bits and bobs, like hang pictures, dot a few reed diffusers about the place – help get rid of the smell of paint – that kind of stuff. You and Broge are welcome to pop up and take a peek before the opening party when you've got a minute.'

'Ooh, we'd love to.'

Ollie and Jimby had worked hard at fitting the sprung flooring and soundproofing, staying late in the evening and working weekends, for which Anoushka would be eternally grateful. It had been a dream she'd nursed for so long, she could hardly believe the opening of her brand new dance studio was drawing near. She'd contacted all of her pupils, inviting them to the opening party she'd organised for a week on Friday; she really wanted to mark the beginning of this new chapter in her life by sharing an event with the pupils and parents who'd supported her since she'd started her dance classes in the village hall.

Leaning against the worktop with her back to the open window, mug of tea in hand, Kristy asked, 'So, now I've seen just how swamped you are with getting stuff ready, this is going to sound like a daft question, but I'm going to ask it on the off chance it's a yes; I don't suppose you've got time for a quick get-together with Broge and me sometime this week? Like I said, I can give you a hand with stuff for a couple of hours now if that would help at all.'

Anoushka took a moment to think over Kristy's invitation. 'You know what? Much as I've still got loads to do, the thought of having a catch-up over a glass or two of wine with you and Broge sounds very tempting. I reckon I could justify a break from it all for a couple of hours.'

'So is that a yes?' Kristy smiled hopefully.

'It's a yes.'

'Woohoo!' Kristy thrust her mug aloft, splashing tea down the front of her top. 'Bloomin' 'eck!' The two friends burst out laughing, attracting the attention of Ethel and Mabel who trotted over to see what all the excitement was about, tails swishing busily.

'So is this Friday evening any good?' asked Kristy, once she'd finished dabbing her top dry.

'This Friday's perfect. There's another four full days before then for me to get pretty much everything organised and set out ready for the big day, so the panic should be over; I intend to keep the week after free so I can go over everything, check for snags, make sure I haven't forgotten anything; I'm keen to avoid a last-minute panic.'

'Organised as ever, I see.'

'Doesn't feel much like it at the moment, but I'm hoping by the end of the week it will.'

Kristy nodded, pausing for a moment before she spoke. 'So, have you heard anything from Gabe?' Her attempt at nonchalance didn't fool Anoushka, who could feel her face growing pink at the mention of his name. She sincerely hoped her friend hadn't noticed.

Choosing to ignore the question, Anoushka thrust a plate of choc-chip cookies and custard creams in front of Kristy. 'Biscuit?' she asked, giving her a gentle warning look.

'I was only asking; it's a perfectly innocent question,' Kristy said, a hint of mischief dancing in her eyes.

'Hmm. Not so sure about that. And, no, I haven't heard anything from Gabe. Why would I?'

Kristy shrugged, taking a biscuit. 'Just wondered, that's all.'

'Well, you can stop wondering. As you can see, I've been too busy to think about anything else other than the dance studio; it's occupied my every waking thought for the last few weeks, as you well know. And I reckon Gabe will have been too busy with his tour to give me a second thought.' Though her tone was good-natured, Anoushka hoped it didn't disguise the hint she wanted their conversation to continue down a different route.

'Yeah, righto, Noushka, we all know he'll have given you way more than a second thought. The way he looks at you, I'd put money on you being his first waking thought and the last thing he thinks about before going to sleep.'

Anoushka shook her head, a smile tugging at the corners of her mouth. 'Kristy, can I just say, I think you're getting a little bit carried away with yourself there, chick.'

'I really don't think so.' Kristy gave her a knowing smile. 'It's not only me who's noticed the sparks flying when you're in his company.'

Anoushka rolled her eyes and sighed. 'Well, you and whoever else thinks that – Brogan, no doubt – have got very vivid imaginations and are seeing things that really aren't there! I like him as a friend, of course I do, he's a lovely guy, but that's as far as it goes. There are no sparks. In fact, he hasn't crossed my mind since he left.' *You little fibber!*

'Really?' Kristy didn't sound convinced. 'And you won't know anything about how his tour's been a roaring success.'

'Well... I... I suppose I have heard that, but I think it was Lils who told me.' She could feel her face growing hotter.

'Course she did,' said Kristy, smiling. 'And, of course, *you* wouldn't have been scrolling through social media, checking to see how he's doing.'

'No, I would not!' She turned, making a sweeping gesture with her arm towards the laden kitchen table. 'You can see how busy I've been; I've been too swamped with getting my dance school ready as I keep telling you.' She huffed indignantly.

'Oh, yeah? Well, if I didn't know any better, Anoushka Cartwright, I'd say you had the hots for our Irish singer.' Kristy giggled into her mug.

Anoushka was beginning to feel niggled by the turn their conversation had taken; Kristy didn't seem to be picking up any of Anoushka's subtle messages. *Ughh!* She wanted to focus on one thing, and one thing alone, and Anoushka was getting a bit tired of telling everyone that. It was beyond frustrating! In fact, she was getting tired of everyone trying to fix her up with Gabe. She drew in a deep breath. 'You're so way off the mark. And if this is what I'm going to be subjected to on Friday night, I'll be staying at home.' Her face was burning with annoyance now.

Kristy's smile fell. 'Hey, calm your jets, flower, I was only joshing.' She placed a placatory hand on Anoushka's arm. 'I'm really sorry if it didn't come across that way. I promise I won't do it anymore.'

'Good.' Embarrassed by her sudden outburst, Anoushka found she couldn't make eye contact with her friend.

Kristy set her mug down and wrapped her arms around Anoushka. 'I'm sorry if I've upset you; I hadn't realised it was bothering you so much. I really should try thinking before I open my great big trap. I get that you've had a crappy time of it with that dickhead Damon, and you want to be on your own for a while, I really do. It's just... well, I want you to be happy, that's all, but... anyway, I'll keep my beak out and I promise I won't mention Gabe any more today.' She released Anoushka, resting her hands on her friend's shoulders.

Anoushka suddenly felt guilty for being snappy; she really didn't want to fall out with Kristy over Gabe – or any man, for that matter – she was just getting her life back on track since Damon and she didn't want anything to scupper her friendship.

'Are we good?' Kristy asked, giving Anoushka's shoulders a quick squeeze.

'We're good.' Anoushka smiled, nodding. 'Sorry I was a ratty-pants.'

'Hey, no worries, you had every right to be; I'd be exactly the same in your shoes.'

As much as Anoushka was reluctant to admit it to herself, she'd found she was thinking about Gabe more and more, and her heart might have beat that little bit faster whenever she did so. *What's that they say about absence making the heart grow fonder?* asked a little voice? *Ughh! Don't you start!* she thought, quickly shooing it away.

'So, tell me how your plans for the new camping pods are coming along,' she said to Kristy, offering a discreet olive branch in the shape of a change of subject.

Her friend's face became suddenly animated. 'Well, Ben and me made a list of things we wanted to feature in them – something that would make them that bit more unique, stand out from the crowd, you know. Anyway, we decided to scribble down some designs and were showing them to Molly and Camm, and Moll suggested we talk to your dad about him making them for us, which actually made perfect sense.' Her eyes were shining with excitement.

And just like that, they were back on track, all traces of their recent difference evaporating into the air.

Later that afternoon, Anoushka's car was nosing its way through the entrance of the newly converted office buildings of the Danskelfe Castle estate, her heart thumping with excitement as she pulled up in front of the premises she'd leased. Ever since Lady Carolyn had offered it to her, she'd been waiting for this day to come with great anticipation. And if the way things were looking from the outside were anything to go by, she wasn't going to be disappointed. Today, the scaffolding had gone, revealing window frames painted a deep shade of midnight blue; it was the perfect contrast to the local stone from which the building was hewn.

She stilled the engine and climbed out of her car, her stomach performing a somersault as she spotted the new sign above the door declaring it to be "Danskelfe Dance Studio". Its background was painted the same shade as the building's door and windows, the curly font and pair of hand-drawn ballet shoes in a warm dusky pink, edged in antique gold. It looked just as she'd hoped it would. The colours matched the T-shirts she'd ordered, one of which she was wearing right now, knotted at the waist; she looked every inch the dance teacher in her leggings and trainers, her golden hair in a neat bun at the nape of her elegant neck.

Her gaze swept across to the other premises, each one

springing to life after so many years spent in varying states of dilapidation. Tinny music was seeping from the open window of one, it was accompanied by the rhythmic sound of someone hammering; she'd heard that particular unit was going to be occupied by a potter or ceramicist. Were they building a kiln? she wondered. Another one had been taken by a florist, another by a new bakery, and another by a beautician. The one at the far end was rumoured to be the new vets' practice. Exciting times for everyone.

Anoushka's face broke into a smile as she slotted the key into the lock. Pressing down on the sturdy antique-gold handle she pushed the door open, excitement rippling through her as she stepped over the threshold, the smell of fresh paint tickling her nostrils. The reception area looked smart and stylish. She'd kept the walls and woodwork a crisp white, the carpet a hardwearing sisal. She'd fitted it out with a small desk and chair, and two sofas that faced one other, a coffee table sitting between – Anoushka intended to have magazines set out for parents to flick through while they waited for their budding dancers. Her eyes alighted on the water-cooler in the corner; it must have been delivered that morning.

She wandered around, unable to stop her smile from growing wider, as she took in how neat and new and perfect it all looked. Her dad and Jimby had done a brilliant job of fitting the sound-proofing and the pale-wood sprung flooring – buying it in had taken a huge chunk of her savings but it would be so worth it; she was grateful to her dad and Jimby whose work had kindly helped keep costs down, offering their skills and time for free. Kitty and Lily had chipped in too, helping with the decorating. At the time it had felt like a mammoth task, but the three of them had cracked on, assisted by Lily's choice of "motivational" playlist that boomed from the brand-new speakers. It might have been hard work, but they'd had great fun, laughing and chatting away as they got stuck in – at times, they'd even burst into impromptu dance routines when a favourite song came on, singing at the top of their voices, using their paintbrushes as microphones. Anoushka felt a wave of gratitude wash over her; there was no way she would have been able to get to this point without their help. Already she'd decided she was going to treat them all to a slap-up meal at the Sunne.

Another thought crept in. If she hadn't stood her ground with Damon, if she'd still been with him, her dance school would be nothing more than a pipe dream. She shuddered as an image of his face filled her mind, the arrogant smirk he was wearing just before Kitty had burst into the room and torn through him. His smirk had fallen pretty quickly then. The memory made her chuckle. But now wasn't the time to think about him. Now was the time to feel happy and positive. It was time to look to the future.

Kicking off her outdoor shoes, she ventured into the first of the two designated dance studios. The large, airy rooms were almost identical. Like the reception area, the walls here were painted a crisp white. There was a run of floor-to-ceiling mirrors along the far wall with ballet barres fixed along the other three. And each space was flooded with natural light from the beautiful, large arched windows. All that remained to be done was to hang the black and white photos of dancers in action that were currently wrapped up in the back of her car, place a vase of flowers on the reception desk – she'd decided to always have fresh flowers – and pack the T-shirts away in the storage area upstairs. Then, Danskelfe Dance School was good to go. Well, it would be once they were on the other side of the opening party.

Standing in the middle of the room, Anoushka clasped her hands to her cheeks, a thrill whirling around her stomach. Her dream of starting her own dance school really had come true. 'Someone pinch me,' she said out loud, giggling.

'Not sure I'd be too happy about doing that,' said a familiar Southern Irish voice.

TWENTY

Anoushka spun round. 'Gabe! I didn't know you were back.' He looked handsome in his sky-blue T-shirt and battered jeans, his broad shoulders filling the doorframe he was leaning against. His easy smile made her heart speed up and she couldn't help but smile back.

'Ah, that's because I'm not supposed to be, but with the next leg of my tour being in Leeds and me having a few days off before I'm next performing, I figured it was the perfect excuse to head here for a break; I've actually just got here.'

'Oh, right.' Her mind ran over his words, a buzz of happiness filling her chest, pushing her smile wider. 'No Bob?'

'I haven't got as far as the castle yet, so I've not had chance to see the wee fella. I saw your mum as I was driving through the village and she said you were up here. Thought I'd drop by en route, take a look, see how you're getting on. Which reminds me, why, exactly, were you asking to be pinched?' Gabe pushed himself away from the door jamb and made his way over to her, grinning all the while.

'Ah, well...' She giggled as she looked around her, arms outstretched. 'All this, it's... well, it might not be much to some people, but it really is a dream come true for me. I've wanted to have my own dance school for so long, and now it's a reality. I'm just so unbelievably happy, which is why I need pinching, to make sure it's really happening.'

He looked at her, his eyes shining. 'I promise you, it's really happening, Noushka. And you've every right to be happy; it's a fabulous achievement, and I know you're going to make it a roaring success. I love your branding too, it's awesome.' He nodded to her T-shirt.

She felt her face prickle with the heat of a blush. 'Thank you,' she said shyly. His attitude couldn't be more different from Damon's if he tried. 'But I can't take credit for the branding, Vi sourced that for me; she's been amazing.' She looked into his soft brown eyes. 'And I wouldn't have this place if it hadn't been for you putting a word in with Caro for me. I know there were quite a few other people interested, so thank you for that.'

'Hey, it was nothing,' he said, holding her gaze. 'And it's great to see you've got your sparkle back. You'd lost it for a while, but now it's returned in full-on dazzle mode.' He laughed, making jazz hands.

'Thanks.' She giggled. She knew he was referring to her time with Damon.

A beat passed.

'Don't suppose I can tempt you to join me at the Sunne tonight, can I?' he asked hopefully.

'Oh, I... erm, it's just—' Gabe's question had knocked her off-balance.

'I don't mean as a date; you're perfectly safe on that score.' He held his hands up. 'Only Sim and Caro have suggested heading there this evening – he's sneaked back too; dropped him off in Middleton-le-Moors where he was meeting Caro – and much as I love those guys to pieces, playing third wheel is starting to wear a bit thin.'

His hopeful expression sent a wave of guilt crashing in her chest. She pulled an apologetic face. 'I can't, sorry, I've... I've got other commitments and I can't get out of them.' That wasn't strictly true. Molly, Camm and Emmie were joining her family for a meal at Oak Tree Farm that evening, and Anoushka knew full well if she'd told her parents Gabe had asked to meet her, they'd encourage her to go. But it was the last thing she wanted, especially after her earlier conversation with Kristy. If she went to the pub with Gabe, she'd only be adding fuel to the fire of speculation. There was no way she was going to encourage that.

'No worries, I understand.' Crestfallen, he still managed to muster up a smile.

As guilty as she felt, Anoushka was determined to stick to her resolution and resist his charms.

'So, what are your plans for the afternoon?' he asked.

Uh-oh. He doesn't give up easily. 'I want to have a thorough check round, make sure everything's perfect, then get all the final bits and bobs finished, and I've got a load of pictures to hang, T-shirts to put away. That sort of thing.'

'Okay, well, will you at least let me give you a hand with the pictures? I can hold them while you decide where they're best placed... you know, left a bit, right a bit, higher, lower. I'm told I'm very good at that kind of thing.' He chuckled good-naturedly, his disappointment apparently forgotten.

There was something about his smile that made her soften and she found herself saying, 'That'd be great, thanks; shouldn't take long.'

'Cool.' His smile spread, making his eyes crinkle at the corners. Her wayward heart gave a little flip.

With Gabe's help, the pair got the job done in no time, the black and white photos of dancers adding the perfect finishing touch to the rooms.

'There, all done,' he said, screwing the lid on the jar of picture hooks. 'I think we've earnt ourselves a mineral, wouldn't you agree?'

'A mineral?' Anoushka asked, her brow crinkling at the unfamiliar expression.

'It's what we call a soft drink back in Ireland.' He grinned at her. 'I've got a few cans in my car, might not be as chilled as we'd like, but they'll at least wet your whistle.'

'Mmm. Sounds good.' A thud from outside followed by the crunch of footsteps walking over gravel stole her attention. 'What was that?' she said, her face falling. She rushed over to the window to find whoever, or whatever, it had been was gone. A feeling of unease crept over her skin. Several times that afternoon she'd had the uncomfortable feeling that they were being watched but she'd pushed the notion out of her mind, telling herself her imagination was playing tricks on her. But now that uneasy feeling had returned. Was it Damon? Was it a fan of Gabe's who'd been following him? Or was she simply just blowing things out of proportion? She rubbed her hands up and down her arms and fixed a smile to her face before turning back to Gabe. 'There's no one there.'

'It was probably just something to do with one of the other tenants,' he said, giving her a reassuring smile.

'Yeah, I reckon you're right.' She smiled back, trying hard to ignore the little niggle that told her otherwise.

Five minutes later, they were sitting on the wall at the side of the studio, soaking up the sunshine and sipping from their cans as they gazed out over the view. The battlements of Danskelfe Castle, perched precipitously on its crag, were visible through a gap in the trees, its flag waving in the breeze. The sound of a woodpecker drumming away, echoing around the dale, triggered a laugh from Gabe. 'That's such an amazing sound. Poor bird must have a heck of a headache by the end of the day.'

Anoushka looked across at him and smiled. Much as she was reluctant to admit it to herself, she'd found herself glad that he'd turned up; she'd enjoyed these last few hours with him. And with his down-to-earth outlook on life, it was so easy to forget his celebrity status. She took a surreptitious glance at his arm that was inches away from her own, the sudden urge to run her finger over his sun-kissed skin taking her by surprise. She swallowed, quickly averting her gaze.

Oblivious, Gabe gave a contented sigh. 'Being a townie, I hadn't actually realised how noisy the countryside could be until I first came to stay up here with Sim and Caro. When I say *noisy*, I don't mean I think it's a bad noise. What I mean is, I was expecting the moors to be deathly quiet, which is exactly what it isn't.'

Anoushka turned to him, listening intently as he went on.

'The air's just brimming with the most joyful sounds, from lambs bleating, stags barking, birds calling in a whole host of fabulously different ways, to the gentle hum of a tractor in the distance. It's quite the cacophony.' He laughed again, his expression animated. 'I've grown to love all the sounds that make up the moors. I've never felt so inspired; I write my best music here. Just makes me want to keep on coming back. Well,' he said, his eyes dropping to the can in his hand, 'maybe it's not the only reason.'

As if on cue, a magpie flew by, the sun picking out the iridescent blue flash on its wings. It landed in a nearby rowan tree, its piercing squawk shattering the peace. 'And where do you stand on the racket our friend over there's making?' asked Anoushka, thankful of its sudden presence.

'Hmm, I think I'd have to say, it's a little harsh on the ears.' Gabe chuckled, changing position, causing his arm to brush against Anoushka's, the warmth of his skin sending a charge through her. He turned to her; he'd clearly felt it too.

The weight of his gaze made her feel suddenly self-conscious. Hurriedly searching for an escape from the situation, she looked at her watch. 'Oh... er, heck, is that the time? I really should be heading home; I've still got loads to do. Still need to update my social media pages; they're on today's to-do list.' Even to her own ears, her reason sounded flimsy.

'Oh, right, yeah, okay.' He smiled, giving a small shrug. 'I'd offer to give you a hand with that, but I'm afraid I'm pants at anything to do with social media.'

'No worries, but thanks anyway.' She flashed him a smile before jumping down from the wall. 'I need to make sure all my pupils and their parents know about the dance school's opening party. I've already sent a note out but a post or two on the dance school's social media pages are great for acting as a reminder; notes can have a nasty habit of getting lost, and emails unopened.'

'True. And it's always good to be organised.' He jumped down beside her, dusting lichen from his hands.

Feeling mean spirited at turning down his invitation to the Sunne, Anoushka found herself saying, 'You'd be very welcome to join us, if you're in the area again, that is. It's a week on Friday at the village hall; starts at six o'clock. I appreciate it's probably not your thing, but Caro's going to be there – she's offered to do a little bit of a speech, which is really kind of her. Sim's welcome too if he's back. My family, Vi and Jimby, Molly and Camm are going, and I dare say some of us will be finishing off at the Sunne then – though I won't be having a late night since I've got a dance class at nine the following morning. And it won't be anything like your showbiz kind of parties; it'll be very tame by comparison, so don't go building your hopes up.' She smiled at him, aware she was starting to gabble.

Hope flickered across his face. 'I'm in Nottingham the night before and after, but I'll see what I can do. Oh, and I should probably say, I hate showbiz parties. They're so not my thing, all that posing and preening. Ughh!' He gave a mock shudder, making Anoushka giggle. 'Right then, I'd best go and see what my wee fella Bob's been up to.' He bent and kissed her cheek, his skin soft against hers, the smell of his cologne triggering a quickening of her pulse. 'Been good to see you, Noushka.'

Their eyes locked and for a moment Anoushka found herself wishing he would kiss her on the mouth.

TWENTY-ONE

Anoushka had almost reached the pub when the distinctive rumble of a Land Rover made her ears prick up as it drowned out the evening song of the blackbird perched in the rowan tree of Sunshine Cottage. She watched as the vehicle pulled up on the opposite side of the road, and Kristy and Brogan spilled out, heralding a chorus of enthusiastic hellos. Anoushka smiled, feeling instantly glad she'd agreed to their Friday evening get together.

'Flippin' heck, look at the state of me. I knew we shouldn't have come in the Landie; my new jeans are covered in dust from that bag of sheep feed that'd split.' Kristy bent to brush dust from her black skinny jeans.

'Stop fussing, they're fine; you can't see anything,' said Brogan.

'Ey up, Noushka. How're you diddlin'?' Ben leaned out of the passenger window, a smile dancing over his friendly face.

'Hiya, Ben. I'm good, thanks. How about you?'

'Can't grumble. I gather from our lass you've been working your backside off, getting ready for your dance school, and could do with letting your hair down a bit.'

Anoushka laughed. 'Kristy's not wrong there.'

'I never need much of an excuse to let my hair down,' Brogan said with a giggle.

'Don't we know it, Broge,' said Kristy, shooting Anoushka a "tell us about it" look.

Ben laughed. 'Aye, well, there's nowt wrong with that. Anyroad, I'd best be off. There's a ewe and a couple of lambs broken free from the top field; I need to get 'em caught and the fence fixed before we have any more escapees. Have fun, lasses. Send me a text when you want picking up, Kriss.'

'Will do.'

'I can't tell you how much I've been looking forward to this. I've had a stinker of a week.' Brogan gave a sigh as she hooked her arms through her friends'.

'That doesn't sound good, Broge. Is everything all right?' Anoushka looked at her friend, concerned when she detected a hint of weariness on Brogan's face.

'It's just... oh, it's nothing really. I've just been feeling a bit "meh" about things. You know how it is sometimes? Our night out has come at a good time.'

Anoushka felt a pang of guilt; she'd been so wrapped up in her own dramas and plans, she hadn't picked up on how things hadn't been running so smoothly in Brogan's life.

'It sounds to me as if we need a round of Bea's delicious hot chocolate fudge cake while you tell us all about it,' said Kristy.

'Mmm. Now you're talking.' A smile brightened Brogan's face. 'With gallons of her amazing custard.'

'Oh, my days, we so do.' Anoushka's tastebuds sprang to attention at the thought.

Inside the pub, the friends found a table for three tucked in a corner beside a window through which a welcome breeze was drifting, the scent of the damask rose that sat beneath it wafting through every now and then. Kristy finished pouring the wine and held her glass aloft. 'Cheers, lasses. Here's to a good night.'

'Cheers,' Anoushka and Brogan echoed her.

'So, what's up, Broge?' Anoushka asked. She had a feeling it was going to be more than feeling weary of her dog-walking business.

'Yep, come on, chick, spill the beans.' Kristy took a sip of her wine.

Brogan sat back in her seat and puffed out her cheeks. 'Ughh, jeez. I feel a bit daft, to be honest, and you're going to think I'm blowing things way out of proportion when I tell you – and I don't really know why it's bothering me as much as it is – but yesterday, I got a call from a girl called Maisie who I used to work with when I lived over at Skeltwick.'

Kristy nodded. 'Oh yeah, you've mentioned her a few times; she seems nice from what you've said.'

'She is. Anyway, the reason she got in touch was to tell me my ex, Archie, has only gone and got married. Poor lass was tying herself up in knots when she was telling me.' Brogan glanced between her two friends.

'What?' said Kristy. 'I thought he was dead set against marriage. Are you sure Maisie's got that right?'

'You're kidding?' said Anoushka. From what she remembered, Brogan had been with Archie for about four years before they broke up. 'After all he said to you?'

'I know. And would you believe his new wife's a friend of mine? Karina Roberts; we went to school together.'

Anoushka and Kristy looked at her, confused.

'You mean Karina as in the girl who's been ignoring your texts?' asked Anoushka.

'Yep, the very one. And that's not the worst of it.' Brogan drew in a deep breath. 'She's expecting his baby.'

The two friends stared open-mouthed. 'What? He's suddenly decided he wants to be a dad now?' Kristy didn't hide her outrage.

Brogan nodded sadly. 'Getting married and starting a family were the two things he told me he could never see in his future, and the reason we broke up. Seems he's changed his mind.' There was no mistaking the hurt in her eyes.

'Oh, Broge. I'm so sorry.' Anoushka reached across and squeezed her friend's arm.

'What a horrible thing to do. Goes without saying you're better off without both of them in your life,' Kristy said vehemently.

'I honestly don't know why I'm so upset, I mean, I'm over him, really I am. I think I'm just shocked because of how strongly he felt about not settling down and having kids. Maisie was really sweet; said she didn't want me finding out through seeing their wedding photos on social media and getting a shock.' She released a wavery sigh. 'I suppose it explains why Karina ghosted me, which I could never understand; we were quite good friends at one time, until she stopped answering my texts. I honestly don't mind that they've got together; I mean, me and Archie split up ages ago. It's the fact that she ignored me and has actually blocked me on social media that hurts the most. Plus, I suppose it does feel kind of like he didn't love me enough to tempt him to get married and have kids; that hurts a bit too.' She gave a resigned shrug of her shoulders. 'Sounds daft, I know. I guess I'm feeling sorry for myself. Just ignore me.' She picked up her glass, swirled the wine around and pushed her mouth into a smile.

'We get we're you're coming from, Broge, and it doesn't sound daft at all. Karina hasn't treated you very nicely. Kristy's right, you're definitely better off without them. And Archie clearly wasn't right for you. You've got us now; we've got your back, hon.' Anoushka gave her a sympathetic smile.

'Too right we have.' Kristy nodded resolutely.

'Thanks, girls, that means a lot.'

'I think this calls for that hot chocolate fudge cake I mentioned earlier. Are you two lasses still up for some?' asked Kristy.

'Since when have you known us turn down one of Bea's puddings?' Anoushka looked at her in mock disbelief.

'Um, that'd be never.' Kristy chuckled as she went to place the order at the bar.

Before they knew it, Bea was at their table, her hands laden with a tray of chocolatey puddings and a large jug of custard. 'Here we are, my darlings. I've added a dash of orange liquor to this batch; I do hope you approve.'

'Mmmhm. They smell delicious, Bea. I think we'll most definitely approve.' Anoushka inhaled the intense aroma of chocolate, her eyes on the puddings that were dusted with icing sugar and garnished with a handful of jewel-coloured berries and a sprig of fresh mint.

'Oh, wow! And to think I was considering giving up chocolate,' said Kristy.

'I could never give up chocolate,' said Anoushka.

The friends were halfway through their puddings, chatting away, when a rasping voice interrupted them. 'I'm surprised to see you here, Kristy, and not with your Ben.'

They looked up to see Anita Matheson – known locally as Maneater on account of her predatory nature. She was looking down at them, a sneer of a smile on her lips. Anoushka's heart sank; there was something in the delivery of Anita's words that spelt trouble.

'Oh, and why's that?' asked Kristy, a challenging look in her eye.

'Oh, nothing.' Anita fluffed up her bouffant of over-processed hair. 'Only, if I had a man like him, I wouldn't let him out of my sight. He's quite a catch, what with those big muscles he's got on him and his "come to bed" eyes.'

'Really?' Kristy spoke through clenched teeth.

'Really.' Anita adjusted the plunging neckline of her clinging black dress, putting more of her cleavage on display, and thrusting out her chest as John Danks walked by. His eyes widened in alarm and he scuttled back to his seat at great speed.

Kristy drummed her fingers on the table. 'I'm really not sure what you're getting at here, Anita, but, just so you know, I trust Ben implicitly and am more than happy to "let him out of my sight" as you put it.'

Anita smirked. 'There's no need to be defensive, missy; I was only making conversation. And I was going to offer my services, being highly qualified in the art of massage. I'm sure I've got a few techniques I could use on him to help ease his aching muscles after a hard day slogging on the farm.' Before Kristy could reply, Anita turned to Anoushka. 'And it's such a shame about that Gabe Dublin, especially with you being so sweet on him. I mean, we all thought you two were going to get together, but I suppose you being a simple country lass, well, it would be a bit tricky for you, wouldn't it? At the end of the day, a man with his *celebrity* status needs someone with a profile and lifestyle that equals it. A little country bumpkin would hardly do that.' She laughed. 'I mean, he wouldn't want you to be out of your depth; he's considerate that way.'

Anoushka could feel her face burning with a mix of embarrassment and annoyance. Anita's passive-aggressive tone rankled with her but she did her best not to rise to it. She was trying to think up a suitable response when Brogan spoke.

'Anita, why do you think any of this is your business?'

'Gabe is a public figure; he's everybody's business. I mean, we've all seen the photos of him and that famous model Lilith Dean that are plastered all over; they looked very cosy and loved-up from what I could see. The gossip columns are rife with rumours they'll be announcing their engagement any time soon.'

Anoushka's stomached lurched. Could this be true? Surely not. But then again, she had no right to feel this way; she'd made it perfectly clear to Gabe she wasn't interested in a relationship, she couldn't expect him to live the life of a monk, and he was perfectly entitled to date anyone he chose. It still didn't stop this new information feeling weird though. Lilith Dean was stunning, successful and uber glamorous. It was easy to see why he would have fallen for her; they'd make the perfect celebrity couple; their photos together would help sell shedloads of magazines. But announcing their engagement? Really? She'd never even heard Gabe mention her name before. Surely Anita had got it wrong? Then again, there was no smoke without fire...

TWENTY-TWO

Though Anoushka was trying to hide it, Anita's news had knocked the wind out of her sails. Not only that, but she was also taken aback by her own reaction to it; it was totally out of proportion to her feelings for him. Or at least that's what she told herself. Her heart was pounding and a lump of hurt sat heavy in her stomach. She tried to swallow, but her throat felt tight and the threat of tears was gaining pace. She clenched her teeth in a bid to stop them, hoping no one had noticed.

'Thanks for sharing that with us, Anita, but if you don't mind, we'd like to get back to enjoying our night out.' Brogan shot the woman a piercing look.

'Yeah, unlike some people, we're not keen on gossip.' Kristy's stony glare matched Brogan's.

'I just thought you'd like to know.' A smirk still hovered on Anita's mouth. 'Ooh, there's Dr Gillespie; I need to have a word with him about something of a personal nature. Enjoy your evening, ladies.'

Anoushka watched as Anita flounced off in the direction of an unsuspecting Zander and Livvie Gillespie.

'Ughh! Good riddance.' Brogan practically spat her words out.

'My thoughts exactly,' said Kristy. 'She's got some brass neck on her, that's for sure. And why does she always have to make every-thing sound so sleazy? "A few techniques", my eye!'

Anoushka steadied herself before she spoke, hoping her friends wouldn't detect how she was feeling. 'She's unbelievable.'

Kristy nodded. 'She is. There's no wonder she's got no female friends, the way she goes on. She's no woman's woman, that's for sure.' She started fishing in her bag, pulling out her mobile phone, and proceeded to scroll through it.

'I don't think she's bothered about that.' Brogan's top lip curled into a snarl as she watched Anita simpering over Zander, pointing to her chest. Zander looked distinctly uncomfortable. She turned back to Anoushka, quickly softening her expression. 'I know the subject of Gabe's supposed to be off-limits tonight, flower, but seeing as I'm not the one who's brought him up, all I'll say is, take no notice of Anita. I'm sure she's talking rot, don't you, Kristy?'

'Oh!' Kristy's hand went to her mouth. 'Um... yeah, course.' She glanced up from her mobile, the uncertainty in her eyes betraying her true feelings.

Anoushka's pulse started galloping.

'What's up? Why are you looking like that?' asked Brogan.

'I'm sure there's a perfectly innocent explanation and that it really isn't what it looks like.'

'Not what it looks like?' asked Anoushka. But she'd already guessed. 'Is it Gabe?'

'Um, yes, but it's nothing, Noushka; it's not worth looking at.' Kristy went to put her phone back in her bag. Brogan's eyebrows knitted together.

'It's okay, I know what it's going to be.' Anoushka shrugged resignedly. 'If I wanted to, I could easily find it myself, and I'm actually okay about it, so you might as well let me see. After all, he's entitled to date whoever he wants.' She didn't even sound convincing to her own ears.

'I think we should leave it for tonight.' Brogan flashed Kristy a warning look.

'No, I want to see,' said Anoushka. 'Honest, please believe me,

I'm fine; it was just a shock hearing it from Anita Matheson, that's all, you know... what with the way she said it.'

'If you're sure.' Kristy was worrying her bottom lip as she tapped the screen of her phone, holding it out to Anoushka.

She took it, scrolling through the images looking back at her. They were all of Gabe and Lilith Dean in various poses and venues – including the showbiz parties he'd only recently told her he hated – their wide smiles radiating happiness. One of him dressed in a smart suit, holding Lilith's hand as he led her to the door of a swanky restaurant, another of them laughing over the meal. Anoushka's heart went into freefall. There were hundreds more, all with captions declaring Gabe and Lilith Dean to be "head-over-heels in love" and to "expect wedding bells soon". "Perfect match", said one, "Gabe's Girl", said another. The final one featured the pair in a passionate clinch.

Anoushka felt her eyes burn with tears. She blinked quickly, her throat constricting even tighter. Why were the photos of Gabe and Lilith Dean eliciting such pain? She had no room in her life for him or any other man. She had no reason to feel like this.

'Noushka?'

'Uhh?' She tore her gaze away from the photo to see Brogan and Kristy looking at her, both wearing concerned expressions. She realised they must have been talking to her, but her mind was in such turmoil she hadn't heard them.

'Are you okay, chick?' Kristy asked, resting her hand on Anoushka's shoulder.

Anoushka nodded, drawing in a fortifying breath. 'Yeah, I'm fine. It's just a bit of a surprise, that's all. He's never mentioned her before.'

'I'm getting a feeling of déjà vu here.' Brogan raised her eyebrows. 'Seems it isn't just Archie who likes dropping big news.' Kristy caught her eye and frowned. Brogan picked up her non-verbal message straight away. 'And like we said, it's probably not what it seems. You know what these gossipy rags are like, they're full of exaggerated nonsense.'

'Broge's right. And my mum always says you should only believe half what you read in the papers and on social media.' Kristy gave her a smile.

But even half of what Anoushka had just seen was still enough to take the edge off her happiness. Much as she hated to admit it, Gabe and Lilith Dean made an attractive couple. Anita Matheson was right – though she could have put it more sensitively – Gabe was a celebrity and needed to be with someone who moved in the same social circles as him; a "country bumpkin" – it wasn't wasted on her that Damon had described her as exactly that – just wouldn't cut muster. She needed to forget about him and focus on her dance school, which, she told herself, had been her plan all along. And tonight was all about having a fun evening with her friends, which is what she intended to do.

Though she'd done her best to put the photos of Gabe and Lilith Dean out of her mind, it hadn't stopped her thoughts from drifting back to them, but Kristy and Brogan were good company and the conversation had flowed with plenty of laughter thrown into the mix. She was feeling brighter and was pleased to see that Brogan appeared to have put her sorrows behind her too.

Before they knew it, Jonty was calling for last orders.

'Don't know about you two, but I reckon we should finish the night off with a glass of something fizzy?' Anoushka pushed her hair back over her shoulders and sat up straight.

'Ah, you're a woman after my own heart,' said Kristy, beaming at her.

'Mine too; I'm totally on for that.' Brogan knocked back the dregs of her Pinot Grigio.

'Right, two ticks and I'll just go and grab us something suitable.' Anoushka hurried over to the bar.

Five minutes later she returned with a tray set with three glasses of Prosecco, their bubbles sparkling in the soft light of the pub.

'Tell you what, tonight had the potential to go rapidly down-hill,' said Brogan. 'What with Archie-the-Arse and the info Anita dumped, but you two awesome women have pulled it back and it's turned out to be a brilliant night. I don't know what I'd do without you, honest I don't.'

'Right back at you, Broge,' said Anoushka, smiling at her.

'Couldn't agree more,' said Kristy.

'Right then, lasses, I reckon that calls for a toast.' Brogan raised her glass and the others followed suit.

'To friendship,' said Anoushka.

'To friendship,' the other two echoed as they clinked glasses and beamed broadly at one another.

Family and friends, Anoushka said to herself, were all she needed; what she'd learnt tonight was certainly proof of that.

TWENTY-THREE

Anoushka made her way along the trod from Oak Tree Farm to the village shop, the sunshine warm on her back. Birds were chatting away in the hedgerows, their exuberance making her smile. The village green had been recently mown and the sweet scent of freshly cut grass filled the air. She breathed in a generous lungful, savouring it; there was nothing like the smell of summer.

She'd been up since just after six and had had a busy morning, dealing with her final preparations for this evening's opening party and her first day of dance lessons at the new venue the following morning – she was keen to ensure everything would go smoothly – and had jumped at the chance of running an errand to pick up a few bits and bobs for Kitty, welcoming the break and breath of fresh air it would offer.

It had been a week since Anita had dropped her bombshell and the following day, Anoushka had given herself a stern talking to. Getting upset about Gabe dating another woman was ridiculous. She'd made it perfectly plain to him she wasn't interested in him so it made no sense to get upset if he was photographed with Lilith Dean. And if he wanted to get engaged, then that was fine too. Anoushka had no claims on him. Yes, she had to admit to herself that she liked Gabe, but the feelings she had were no more than rebound emotions – surely anyone would seem attractive after Damon? She needed to push Gabe right out of her mind and focus on her dance school and its future. She'd forbidden herself from checking any form of social media for mentions of him, reasoning that would make the situation easier for her. And to a degree, it had worked. The sharp edges of hurt may have been smoothed, but it still hadn't stopped her wondering.

'Morning, pet.' Big Mary's voice boomed out from the little garden of the heavily thatched Damson Cottage as Anoushka walked by. Shielding her eyes with her hand, she looked over to see the older woman sitting in a deck chair, waving, and flashing her gap-toothed smile. In her summer get-up, Big Mary was a bold splash of colour, topped off by a broad-brimmed hat, trimmed with sunflowers. She had her gypsy skirt pulled up, revealing a pair of sturdy, milk-bottle-white legs and a flash of bright yellow knickers.

'Oh!' Anoushka quickly averted her eyes. 'Morning, Mary. Looks like your garden's a right little suntrap.'

'Eee, you're right there. Mind, much as I think this weather's absolutely glorious, if it gets any hotter, I think I'll have to head indoors. Phew! I'm in a right old lather.' She flapped her loose-fitting T-shirt, treating the village to a display of her generous bra-encased bosom. Anoushka didn't know where to look.

'Morning, Noushka.' Gerald emerged from the cottage, two mugs of tea in his hands. He was dressed as brightly as his wife, though he'd swapped his usual roomy trousers for a voluminous pair of tie-dye shorts, teaming them with a pair of multi-coloured striped socks and shocking-pink sliders.

Only a character like Gerald could get away with such a statement look, thought Anoushka. 'Hi there, Gerald.' She couldn't help but smile at the cheerful-looking pair.

'How's the plans for the party going, pet?' he asked, lisping on account of him not wearing his false teeth. He passed his wife one of the mugs. 'Don't suppose you've got time to join us for a cuppa? There's plenty more tea in the pot.'

'Gerry man, pop your choppers in. Noushka won't be able to understand a word you're saying.'

'Oh, aye, sorry, pet. I've got them here, in my pocket.'

'Everything seems to be running smoothly – touch wood.' Anoushka tapped her head with her fingers, fighting the giggle that was rising inside her as Gerald pulled a selection of faces as he pushed his false teeth into his mouth, adjusting them with his tongue. 'And much as I'd love to join you for a cuppa, I'm afraid I've just popped out quickly; I need to get back, finish my list of things to do for tonight.'

'Well, Gerry and me are looking forward to it enormously, aren't we, pet?' She glanced over at her husband, frowning as his struggle continued.

'Aye, we are that,' he said, just as his bottom set of dentures shot out, landing on the grass. Before Gerald could reach for them, a ginger tom cat leapt down from the wall and pounced. It proceeded to give the false teeth a thorough investigation, sniffing and licking away at them. 'Oy, you little rascal, give over. They'll be too big for your cakehole,' he said as he and Big Mary roared with laughter. Anoushka looked on with morbid fascination.

'Anyroad, we can't wait for you to start them ballroom classes so we can trip the light fannydingo, or whatever it is you call it. Me and Gerald have been doing some exercises to limber up in readiness, like. Supple as a couple of whippets, we are now, aren't we, Gerry?' Big Mary gave a throaty chuckle as she kicked her leg in the air, flashing yet more of her yellow knickers.

'Aye, that we are, pet,' he said as he tried to wrestle his false teeth off the cat who was having none of it. 'Ouch, you little... there was no need for that.' He pulled his hand away as the ginger tom's paw shot out to scratch him again.

Anoushka did her best to suppress a giggle. 'I'm looking forward to them too; loads of locals have signed up for them.' It would definitely make for a fun night with Big Mary and Gerald as students.

The sound of a cockerel crowing nearby rang around the

village. It was Jimby's infamously cantankerous leghorn, Reg. The cat ceased licking the false teeth and glanced around warily before shooting off.

Big Mary rolled her eyes. 'Uh-oh. He's been making his presence very felt this morning, that little menace.'

'Hasn't he just?' Gerald quickly scooped up his denture and popped it into his mouth, making Anoushka's stomach curdle. 'He might be cracking on for a bird, but the little so-and-so's been strutting up and down the street like he owns the place; he's showing no sign of hanging up his spurs, that's for sure. And he's looking for trouble today, mark my words.'

Anoushka pulled a concerned face; Reg's bad temper was legendary and woe betide anyone who got on the wrong side of him. 'In that case, I'd better skedaddle before he sees me and decides I'm the one he's going to vent his anger on. I'll see you folks later.'

'Aye, bye, pet,' they chorused in their lilting Geordie accent.

As she crossed the road to the shop, the thought of what she'd just witnessed with Gerald's teeth running through her mind, she spotted Little Mary making her way along the trod, her familiar huge shopping bag over her arm; it was almost as big as her. It was fair to say, you couldn't go far in the village without seeing a whole host of locals. When she'd just broken up with Damon, she'd been thankful she lived on the edge of the village, so she could sneak out and go for a walk without having to encounter anyone. But that feeling was well and truly in the past and now she relished bumping into her fellow villagers.

'Morning.' Anoushka beamed at the petite, older woman.

'Good morning, lovey. What a glorious day. Are you looking forward to tonight?' Little Mary smiled up at Anoushka, her cheeks pink from the heat.

'I am, yes. And I have to say, you're looking very smart, Mary.'

Little Mary patted her neat rows of snow-white curls and smiled shyly. 'Thank you, sweetheart, I've just had my hair done, specially for your party.'

'Well, you look lovely.'

'Thank you, that's very kind of you. Thought I'd pop to the Post Office to send a parcel and get some more stamps before it closes for lunch. Then I'm going to sit in the garden and read my book.'

Before they could say anything more, they were joined by Rhoda and Freda from Fern Cottage. Rhoda negotiated the small pram she was pushing onto the trod.

'Hello, ladies,' Anoushka said, squinting in the bright sunlight.

'Morning,' the pair said in unison, wearing matching happy smiles.

'We're just heading over to the teashop; we're meeting Livvie there for her lunchbreak. We're hoping Len can join us at some point.' Rhoda seemed to be in particularly high spirits. Both she and her stepdaughter, Livvie, had only lived in the village for a couple of years but both had settled in quickly and were regarded warmly. Livvie had secured herself a job designing and making wedding dresses for Kitty and Vi at Romantique Designs, and it hadn't taken long for a gentle romance to bloom between Rhoda and local cycling enthusiast, Len.

Anoushka peered into the pram to see a chubby-cheeked baby Holly sleeping contentedly, plump arms thrown above her head, rosebud lips pouting, and a shock of dark auburn hair, so like her mum's, bright in the sunshine. 'Ah, she's beautiful.'

'She is,' said Little Mary softly. 'And she's growing so fast.'

'You're not wrong there,' said Rhoda proudly. 'She's having a real growing spurt, and has a hearty appetite on her, I can tell you.'

'Aye, she's a right little gannet, but she's lovely to cuddle,' said Freda, chuckling. The older lady had been staying with Rhoda ever since she'd been poorly a year-and-a-half ago, and the two had become firm friends.

'Ooh, she certainly is.' Rhoda's eye's shone happily as she gently jigged the pram up and down. 'She's just had a feed so we're hoping she'll have a good sleep while we have our lunch and some cake before she wakes up,' she said with a giggle. 'I've got my heart set on a huge slice of Lucy's chocolate-fudge traybake.'

'Aye, me too.' Freda chuckled, patting her stomach. 'We can't resist the cakes in there; it's a bit too handy the tearoom just being over the road.'

The village shop – whose shelves were stocked with everything you could imagine and more – had a busy tearoom attached to it. It was famous for owner Lucy's mouth-watering cakes, particularly her moreish chocolate-dipped flapjacks.

'Seems we're all heading in the same direction,' said Anoushka as they made their way down the street, reaching the shop first. 'Right, ladies, I'll see you tonight.'

'That you will,' said Freda.

'Bye, flower,' said Rhoda.

The bell above the shop door jangled as Anoushka pushed it open, the scent of freshly baked scones filtering through from the teashop and making her mouth water. She clocked Livvie at the counter, talking to Lucy and her husband, Freddie. 'Oh hi, Livvie. I've just this minute been talking to Rhoda and Freda before they headed to the tearoom with little Holly – who's looking absolutely gorgeous, by the way.'

'Hi there, Noushka.' Livvie flashed a wide smile. 'Thank you; I think so too, but then I'm biased. I can't tell you how I'm looking forward to catching up on some baby cuddles. Actually, I was just sharing my news with Lucy and Freddie here before I joined them.'

'Your news?'

Livvie's eyes twinkled happily. 'I'm expecting again.' She placed her hand on the small round of her stomach. 'I popped in to stock up on pickled onions; I've got the wildest craving for them at the moment. Honestly, it's *serious*, I've just bought the last two jars, but thankfully, Lucy and Freddie are getting more in.'

So, that would explain why Rhoda was looking extra happy; she was going to be a step-grandma again, Anoushka thought.

'Wow! Congratulations – I mean about the baby, not the pickled onion craving,' she said, and they all giggled.

'Thank you. Zander and me are over the moon.' From the size of the smile she was wearing, their happiness was evident.

'We were just saying how the pair of them didn't hang around on the baby production line,' Freddie said with a chuckle.

'I know.' Livvie beamed. 'We plan on having quite a big brood so we thought, "what the heck, we might as well go for it".'

Anoushka nodded as she tried to remember how old baby Holly was. If her reckoning was right, she must be no more than six months old. 'So when's baby number two due?'

'It's actually baby number two *and* three; I'm expecting twins, and they're due in November; Holly will almost be a year old when they arrive.' She shook her head, her thick, auburn waves bouncing. 'We must be mad! I have to admit, I did actually think that when I had horrendous morning sickness, but thankfully that's eased loads and now I couldn't be happier.'

'Might be an idea to avoid snow drifts this time, Liv,' Freddie said, smiling as he placed her shopping in a bag.

'Oh, my goodness, yes.' Anoushka recalled how Livvie had been stranded up on the moors when she was heavily pregnant last year.

'Ughh! Don't even joke about it,' Livvie said, her eyes wide. 'Trust me, after coming a cropper two winters on the trot, I've learnt my lesson big time; it's definitely not going to happen again.'

'You heard it here first, folks,' Lucy said jokingly.

Anoushka left the shop armed with the items on Kitty's list, her heart feeling light, a spring in her step. She loved village life, loved how you could pop into the local shop for a catch-up, or have a quick drink at the Sunne, everyone welcoming you in. It made you feel you belonged, that folk looked out for one another. It was days like this that made her inexorably glad she hadn't stuck it out with Damon and turned her back on the village. And it was days like this that helped keep her mind off a certain Irish singer.

As she crossed the road, swinging her bag of shopping, she caught a glimpse of a shiny red car, shockwaves rushing through her. *No?* Her breath caught in her throat and her stomach squeezed. *It couldn't be? She was imagining things!*

TWENTY-FOUR

Before she could give the car any further thought, Reg's squawks pierced the tranquillity of the village. Anoushka turned in the direction of the unholy sound, craning her neck to locate the bird. She didn't have long to wait; his vocal outrage was quickly followed by a man's pompous, angry voice. A pompous, angry voice that sounded uncannily like Damon's. *Please let it not be him.* Anxiety prickled over her skin and her heart started thumping. He was the last person she'd expected to see in the village, today of all todays. It was so typical of him to want to take the shine off anything good that happened in her life, his disapproval always having to leave its mark. She was sure it couldn't be a coincidence he'd decided to show his face on the day of her opening party; he was too calculating for that.

Frustrated, she rubbed her hand across her forehead as she struggled to marshal her thoughts. In the next moment, Reg flew onto the roof of the shiny red car, screeching and flapping his wings in a blatant display of aggression. Damon would be livid! Anoushka wondered if it was wrong that it gave her a tiny sliver of pleasure. Well, more than a tiny bit if the truth be told.

'Get off there right now! Get off! Get off! Get off before I ring your flaming neck!' Damon lunged towards his precious car, his arms flailing as he tried to knock Reg off his perch. But the bird was having none of it and delivered a succession of vicious pecks to Damon's hands. 'Ow! Bloody ow! You cantankerous little...'

Anoushka felt a giggle bubble up inside her; it really was becoming quite a spectacle.

Soon, people spilled out on the street to see what the commotion was about.

Gerald let out a loud guffaw that seemed to come from the depths of his stomach. 'Serves the pompous prat right,' he said. 'Never liked the lad; he was too arrogant for his own good. You were right to ditch him, pet.' He gave Anoushka a sympathetic smile which made her wonder just how much he knew about her relationship with Damon.

'Aye, Reg couldn't have picked a more deserving person to take his temper out on.' Big Mary chortled as she peered over the garden hedge. 'Eee, this is entertaining, mind.'

The stampeding of feet made everyone turn to see Jimby hurtling along the middle of the road. 'Reg! Wait 'til I get my hands on you, you little basta... oh...' He slowed his speed when he saw the identity of Reg's sparring partner. Gradually, he came to a halt, his chest heaving as he tried to catch his breath, his brow furrowed in puzzlement. 'Is that who I think it is?'

'It's Damon,' said Anoushka.

'What the fu... I mean, what the heck's he doing in the village?' he asked.

'That's just what we were thinking, bonny lad. I reckon he'll be wishing he stayed at home after your Reg has finished giving him what fettle.' Gerald grinned, his eyes gleaming with mischief.

Jimby turned to Anoushka. 'You okay, Noushka? I mean about *him* being here.' He nodded towards Damon.

'Yeah, I'm fine, thanks. I haven't spoken to him, I just spotted his car, then, well... Reg appeared and this happened.' She gestured in the direction of the disturbance.

The squawking and shouting increased as Reg flew at Damon, landing on his shoulder and pecking angrily at his head. Damon was waving his arms around wildly. 'Arghh! Get off me! Leave me alone! Get off!'

'Right.' Jimby looked on, his mouth twitching with a smile. 'Much as I'm tempted to leave things a bit longer, I suppose I'd better go and rescue Reg.'

'Hah! Rescue Reg! I love it!' Gerald said, as he and Big Mary dissolved into peals of raucous laughter.

Reg's squawking continued until Jimby managed to grab him by his scraggy yellow ankles, his wings flapping in consternation. 'Gotcha, you little menace!'

'That creature's a liability. It should be shot. Have you seen the state of my car? I've just had it cleaned and valeted.' Damon straightened his jacket, pushed his shoulders back and ran his fingers through his hair as Jimby took in the dollops of bird muck that covered the roof of Damon's once gleaming car. 'I'll be sending you the bill to get rid of the scratches the damn thing's claws have made.' Damon sniffed, eyeing Reg with distaste. 'And look at the state of my jacket; you'll be getting the dry-cleaning bill for that too, make no mistake. Or an invoice for a new one, and it won't be cheap.'

'If I were you, lad, I'd get my backside out of this village before I set Reg free again.' Jimby's usual smile had been replaced by a thunderous expression. 'And what the heck are you doing here anyway? You've no reason to be back; unless you're intent on making trouble.'

Anoushka watched as Damon's face turned puce. 'I've come to see Anoushka actually – not that it's any of your business – to wish her well on the opening of her new dance studio; I always knew she could do it. The months' of support I invested in her are the reason she's been able to realise her dream.'

'He *what?*' she said under her breath. Damon caught her eye, his gaze cold and sinister.

Ignoring Reg's vociferous protestations, Jimby said, 'That right?' Anoushka had never seen him look so angry.

Damon slid his eyes back to Jimby, looking at him haughtily. 'I can assure you, if it wasn't for my encouragement, she wouldn't have got to this stage. Without me, she'd still be working part-time for another dance school.'

'What a load of old bollocks,' said Gerald, spitting out the words. 'We've got the measure of you, laddo.'

Damon turned sharply. 'And who are you?' He looked Gerald up and down distastefully.

Anoushka felt her blood begin to boil. She moved forward, anger burning in her stomach. 'You've got no right to be here, Damon, and you've got no right to talk to my friends that way. Gerald's right; what you've said is a load of bollocks. If I'd taken the advice you were always ramming down my neck, I wouldn't be in the position I am. It might not seem much to you, but it's every-thing to me and I couldn't be happier.'

'You tell him, chick,' said Little Mary, looking as fierce as genteel Little Mary ever could.

'And if I'd listened to you, I'd have turned my back on this village and everyone I love here; my family, my friends...' Anoushka paused a moment, her courage building. 'And you know what? I would've been absolutely miserable. Being with you made me more unhappy than I've ever been in my life. I felt isolated and useless and unbearably sad. But not anymore.'

Damon looked daggers at her, his chest heaving with rage. 'You're nothing but a fool. You're clinging on to some pipe dream that's doomed to amount to nothing! I'll give it a year before you fall flat on your face. Less; six months if you're lucky! Like I said, you're a fool.'

Usually, Anoushka would have felt intimidated by his behaviour, but not today. It hadn't taken long for his influence to loosen its grip, for her old confidence to emerge. And, boy, was it empowering. 'I was a fool while I was with you, but not in the way you mean. I was a fool for staying with you for so long, but now I'm free of you, I can see how good my life is here. I'm surrounded by people who love me and who I love back, I'm about to start a career I've been dreaming of and it looks as though it's going to be a success – despite what you say. As far as I can see, there's nothing foolish about that.'

'Go, Noushka.' Brogan's voice rang out. She'd been dropping old Mavis Breen's poodle, Fifi, off when she'd heard the kerfuffle and come to investigate. She started clapping her hands and soon a ripple of applause ran around the crowd.

Damon's top lip pulled over his teeth in a snarl – an expression Anoushka had been on the receiving end of so many times before. 'Don't worry, I'm leaving; you're all a bunch of half-wit, farm yakkers. I don't know why I thought *you'd* be any different,' he said, throwing a disapproving look over his shoulder at Anoushka as he swaggered over to his car. 'You've had your chance; you won't be getting any more from me.' He climbed into the vehicle and a resounding cheer went up as he drove off out of the village, revving his engine in a pitiful display of machismo.

Anoushka looked around her, taking in the smiling faces. Her still-thudding heart lifted at their show of support – even if it did feel slightly surreal.

When everyone had dispersed, she walked home feeling not a little punch-drunk by events. Damon was the last person she'd expected to see when she left the house for her innocuous trip to the shop, but the adrenalin it had triggered and the bolstering she'd received thanks to the support of her friends and neighbours meant an odd mix of emotions were currently swirling around inside her.

Reaching the peace and quiet of Oak Tree Farm, she headed into the sanctuary of the kitchen, absently glancing over at a huge bunch of flowers that filled the sink.

Kitty looked up from the list she was writing. 'Oh, hi, lovey. You okay?' she asked.

Anoushka puffed out her cheeks. She felt suddenly shaken as the impact of coming face-to-face with Damon caught up with her, sending thoughts of the bouquet right out of her mind. 'I think so. I could do with a cuppa; fancy one?' She shook the kettle and set it down on the Aga hotplate.

'I'd love one, thanks.' Kitty's forehead was crumpled with a frown as she studied her stepdaughter. 'I'm sure I could hear Reg making a racket not long ago. Did you see anything on your trip to the shop? Our Jimby's going to have to stop him from getting out before he causes someone a real injury.'

'You might not say that once you've heard this, but...' Anoushka went on to tell Kitty all about her trip to the shop and the ensuing debacle.

Kitty clapped her hand to her mouth on hearing about the cockerel's assault on Damon, her giggles spluttering between her fingers. 'Good old Reg, just when you think he's pushed his luck, he does something to redeem himself. And you're right, I take back what I said.' Her face turned serious for a moment. 'Mind, I hope you're not going to let that lad spoil your day, lovey. It was no coincidence he turned up today, you know. He's the sort that has to be the centre of attention; in control of everything. It'll have been eating him up to know you've been moving on with your life, making a success of it without him having a hand in it.'

'Don't worry, I intend to push him right out of my mind; there are too many lovely things happening in this village, and there's no place in my thoughts for him.'

'You're absolutely right there. What with your new dance school and Livvie and Zander's baby news, it's all very exciting.' She smiled fondly at Anoushka.

'And I wish you could've seen how supportive everyone was; it was so touching.'

'Ah, well, that's because everyone thinks fondly of you round here, chick,' Kitty said warmly.

Anoushka smiled. 'I think it's probably more to do with them all being really decent people.'

'Aye, you're not wrong there. Ooh, I almost forgot.' Kitty's eyes grew large. 'Flowers!'

Anoushka's gaze flicked to the bouquet in the sink. 'Did Dad send you them?' Her dad wasn't known for being big on sending flowers, usually saving the gesture for birthdays and his and Kitty's wedding anniversary and other such special occasions, none of which were today.

'They're not for me, lovey, they're for you. They arrived ten minutes ago. I just popped them in there 'til you had a chance to arrange them.'

'They're for *me*?' Anoushka never got flowers. A thought raced through her mind; could he have sent them before he set off for the village? *Please, please don't let them be from Damon.* It was just the sort of thing he'd do.

'Yes, for you. There's a card tucked in amongst them.'

Anoushka's stomach started churning as she headed over to the bouquet, chewing at her bottom lip. Half of her felt thrilled at being sent flowers, the other half felt trepidation 'They're gorgeous.' Her eyes skimmed over the roses in scrumptious shades of dusky pink and pale purple. They were interspersed with frothy gypsophila and other stunning flowers in complementary shades. Feeling Kitty's eyes on her she nervously slipped the card from the envelope, quickly scanning the words. Overwhelming relief was quickly followed by confusion.

'They're from Gabe. For the new dance studio.' She fixed a smile to her face, not really knowing how she should react. Talk about mixed messages. Why was he sending her flowers when he was supposed to be madly in love with Lilith Dean?

'Oh, how thoughtful of him.' There was an uncertain tone in Kitty's voice. Anoushka had given her a brief version of what Anita Matheson had told her in the pub and the photos she'd seen on Kristy's phone. Though her step-mum had sounded surprised by it all, she'd warned that things might not be as they seemed. 'I just get the feeling those pictures aren't telling the full story,' she'd said. But Anoushka hadn't been convinced.

'Mmm. He says he's sorry he won't be able to get up here in time for the party but wishes me the best of luck. Says he knows the dance school is going to be an amazing success.' A ripple of sadness ran through her, and she pushed her smile as high as she was able, handing Kitty the card to read for herself.

He would hardly want to rush up here for the opening of a little rural dance school when he could be spending time with Lilith Dean in some swanky restaurant she reasoned. A thought flashed through her mind: at least he wasn't going to turn up with the model; that was something, she supposed. Anoushka cringed at how excruciatingly awkward that would be.

Since seeing the photos, every time she'd found her mind wandering to Gabe, she'd quickly remonstrated with herself, focusing her mind on something else. Anything else. She repeatedly reminded herself she wasn't at all bothered by his new relationship; she couldn't expect him to wait around for her to change her mind about dating him. And it had worked. Until today. Reading his note and the strength of the disappointment it had triggered had taken her completely by surprise; she really didn't want to be feeling this way. He'd sent her flowers as a friend, nothing more; he was a kind-hearted man making a kind-hearted gesture. She'd be a fool to read anything more into it than that. *Just focus on your dance school and forget about Gabe.*

'Right then, I'll just grab a vase to pop the flowers in rather than them taking up the sink,' she said with faux breeziness. Kitty could read her like a book and Anoushka hoped her step-mum hadn't detected the disappointment she was feeling. The last thing she needed was sympathy and soothing words; they'd only make her blub. Today was all about moving forward, taking her business to the next level. Without a man in her life. She was an empowered woman, she told herself firmly, and that's how she intended to stay.

She ignored the ache in her heart and the little voice that told her she was fooling no one.

TWENTY-FIVE

'Right then,' Jimby clapped his hands together and glanced around the table, 'as you all know, the village hall is booked for Saturday the ninth of July; I'm told we can have the keys from two o'clock that afternoon – apparently the knitting club are using it until twelve-thirty; they've had to switch from the usual time for some reason.'

In his capacity as chairman of the Village Fundraising Committee, Jimby had called a meeting at his favourite venue for such things: the pub. And, as it was a Friday evening, nobody needed much convincing to attend which meant there was a good turnout.

'Can't imagine the knitting club leaving it in a mess,' said Molly, lifting an amused eyebrow. 'Mind you, Granny Aggie's a member; I suppose anything's possible.'

Granny Aggie was the grandmother of Molly's late husband, Pip. Molly kept a watchful eye on the old lady, and though she regularly grumbled about her, it was done with fondness, despite the fact she was Granny Aggie's first port of call to get her out of the mischief she was locally infamous for, particularly with Rev Nev, the long-suffering vicar.

'Too right,' said Vi with a giggle. 'Hey, maybe she could

promise not to hassle Rev Nev for a day. I reckon he'd pay generously for that.'

'I bet he would, poor soul,' said Molly.

'Well, I think she's really sweet,' said Noushka. Only last week
she'd seen her sitting in her garden with Little Mary, chuckling as
they read from one of the books they'd borrowed from the mobile
library that called at the village every week. The pair were known
for their fondness for racy novels. Little Mary swore blind she
skimmed over the more salacious pages, but no one believed her for
a minute.

'You wouldn't think that if you had to make excuses to poor old
Rev Nev for the horrendous text messages she sends him.
Honestly, they're something else.' Though Molly rolled her eyes, a
smile was playing over her mouth. 'In her latest one, would you
believe she asked him if he'd enjoyed dogging with Mrs Richardson
– you know, she's the new woman who's renting Sycamore Cottage
with her husband; sniffy madam by all accounts. Anyroad, I'm not
so sure she'd see the funny side if she heard about that one.'

'Bloomin' 'eck!' Jimby almost sprayed his mouthful of beer over
the table as everyone fell about laughing. 'Not so sure Mr
Richardson would either!'

'How the heck can Granny Aggie blame that on predictive
text?' Ollie asked through his laughter.

'Or arthritic fingers.' Jimby chuckled, wiping beer from his
chin.

'I daren't ask what she meant,' said Anoushka, looking horrified. She'd offered to babysit that evening so Kitty could attend the
"meeting" but her step-mum had declined, citing a brewing
headache as her reason. Anoushka suspected Kitty had invented it
to encourage her to go out. It had been a week since the dance
school's opening party – which had been a roaring success – and a
week since Damon's visit which had shaken the young woman
more than she'd let on, though she'd guessed Kitty had sensed it.
Apart from heading up to the studio for her dance classes,
Anoushka had been reluctant to go out for fear of finding him

lurking somewhere. Much as she was loath to admit it, he still had some kind of hold over her.

'She said she'd seen Rev Nev and Mrs Richardson going past her house, both walking their dogs. Reckons she thought "dogging" was the same as "dog walking" so couldn't see what was wrong with the text. It's a load of rot; we've had the dogging one before and I explained it to her then,' said Molly.

'And when Moll went round to ask her about it, she acted all innocent and said she couldn't see what the problem was,' said Camm, chuckling.

'Yeah, right,' said Jimby.

'Innocent, my eye; she knows exactly what she's doing.' Molly grinned, shaking her head.

'You certainly get plenty of laughs out of the old stick,' said Vi.

'Which is exactly why I love her so much,' said Molly fondly.

'Right, back to the matter in hand; I'm not sure I'm strong enough to hear of anymore of Granny Aggie's misdemeanours,' Jimby said. 'So we've got a couple of weeks to get all the last-minute things organised, make sure everything runs smoothly. Any idea how we're doing with ticket sales?'

'We've sold out,' said Lucy. 'Did ages ago.'

'That's brilliant.' Anoushka beamed.

'Aye, everyone's up for a night out round here.' Jimby took a swift glug of his pint. 'Look at Noushka's opening party; that had a great turn out and was really good do.'

'Well, it was a great night 'til you started to strut your stuff, Jimby,' said Molly. 'You take up a heck of a lot of room on the dance floor, that's for sure.'

'Always love a chance to shake my booty,' he said.

'You should try dancing with him, Moll; you get flung around all over the place. I've still got whiplash to prove it,' Vi said dryly.

'I think I'll leave that pleasure to you, hon. I'll stick with Mr Dad-Dancer, here.' Molly nudged Camm who smiled and shook his head as a flurry of laughter ran around the table.

'The trouble with you lot is don't know raw talent when you

see it,' said Jimby, adopting a look of feigned offence. 'Anyroad, back to Noushka's night; it was a cracking example of a fabulous family event. Makes me think we should do more things like that.'

Anoushka had managed to put the events of earlier that day out of her mind and throw herself into enjoying her opening party. The atmosphere had been upbeat, it had been well attended and she'd been inundated with "Good Luck" cards and gifts which was something she hadn't expected. It had been a wonderful start to her new venture.

'Yeah, thanks for supporting it, everyone,' said Anoushka.

'No probs, chick.' Vi smiled warmly at her.

'Remind me, what do folks get with their ticket price for the Auction of Promises, apart from entry?' Ollie asked.

Molly looked at her list. 'Well, as we're keen to keep the cost of the tickets down to encourage folk to spend on the auction, we're just going to set nibbles out on the tables – Lucy's very kindly offered to make some bitesize pieces of her chocolate-dipped flap-jacks and Bea said she'd make some mini caramelized onion sausage rolls and pizza bites; the rest of us can rustle up some other bits and bobs.'

'Fabulous.' Jimby patted his stomach, grinning.

'And people are bringing their own drinks,' Molly said.

'Let's hope they bring plenty of booze to encourage them to spend,' said Vi.

'Well, with the items people have promised, I don't think anyone'll take much convincing to splash their cash. Folk have been very generous, and promises are still coming in,' said Freddie. 'I'm liking the sound of the hour's drive of a racing car, very kindly donated by Flash-By Finlay.'

'Yeah, and Lord Hammondely called in this morning to say he'd donate a couple of bottles of vintage port from the Danskelfe Castle cellar,' said Lucy.

Camm gave a low whistle. 'Wow! They'll be worth a fortune.'

'And Caro's promised a weekend stay at one of the new lodges on the Danskelfe estate,' said Vi. 'Shame it's so close to home; I quite fancy that myself.'

The impressive list of promises and donations included everything from pledges to wash cars and windows or cut the grass, to treats such as a trip in a hot air balloon, a three-course meal at the Sunne with a bottle of wine thrown in, a ten-week course of dance lessons from Anoushka, a voucher from Hair by Stefan – the popular hairdressers at Middleton-le-Moors – and a week's free dog-walking from Brogan to name but a few.

'Ey up, watch out folks, Maneater's heading this way. Time to be on high alert, fellas; get your family jewels covered, you never know where those wandering hands'll get to.' Jimby pulled a worried face, sending a flurry of laughter and snorts around the table. The only person who didn't smile was Anoushka; she felt her heart sink. She hoped the woman wasn't going to drag up the topic of their last conversation.

Everyone watched as Anita Matheson slinked her way towards them in a clingy dress. She took a swig from the large glass of wine in her hand; judging by the way she was swaying, it clearly wasn't her first of the evening. 'Well, bonsoir all.' She cast a squiffy glance around the table. 'I thought I'd better let you know I've got a promise I'd like to add to your auction list. Her eyes settled on Jimby as she licked her lips. He visibly paled. Vi bit down on a smile.

'No wonder our Jimby's quaking in his boots; I'm scared to hear what she's going to say,' Molly said sotto voce, making Vi's giggle burst out. She quickly tried to disguise it as a cough.

Anita continued, Anoushka resisting making eye contact with her. 'I'd like to offer a couple of hours over at my place, complete with a massage using the skills I've honed to perfection, using only the most sensual of massage oils. It's specifically tailored to men and their muscular needs; I go deep,' she said, pouting suggestively.

Ollie gave an audible gulp.

'Flippin' 'eck!' Molly shot Vi a look of outrage.

'Did she really just say that?' Vi said quietly, wearing an expression of disbelief.

'Righto, Anita. Thanks very much for that, we'll add it to the list,' said Jimby nervously.

Anita leaned forward, flashing an eyeful of cleavage. 'And I'm expecting all of you men to bid generously.' She gave a saucy wink before wobbling off in the direction of the bar.

Anoushka released the breath she'd been holding, relieved the woman hadn't touched on Gabe and Lilith Dean.

'Phew! You've had a lucky escape there, Jimby. I thought she was going to offer you a quick demo.' Camm chuckled.

'You say that in jest, mate, but I thought she was too. I'm shaking here. Look,' he said, holding out his hand that was trembling theatrically. 'Anyroad, has anyone got any ideas of how I can put her promise into words without making it sound indecent?'

'Nope,' said Vi.

'You haven't got a cat in hell's chance,' said Molly.

'Helpful as ever, Moll,' Jimby said with a chuckle.

'I don't know about you fellas, but I'd be too terrified to bid for that promise,' said Camm.

'You're not alone there, mate,' said Ollie.

'Maybe we could buy it as a gift for someone.' Molly was wearing a wicked expression.

'Like who?' Jimby looked at her in disbelief. 'And don't you dare go looking at me!'

'And please don't say Rev Nev; I think the poor bloke's suffered enough with what Granny Aggie puts him through,' said Vi, making everyone fall about laughing.

Walking home later that evening, Anoushka slipped her arm through her dad's. The air had cooled and it still wasn't properly dark, though the moon was sneaking its way into the sky and early stars were twinkling away. Lights shone from the cottages, creating a cosy atmosphere in the village. 'That was a great night; thanks for talking me into joining the committee.'

'No problem; it actually takes some believing, my little girl on a village committee with me.' He laughed. 'Takes even more to believe my little girl's all grown up and is now a successful businesswoman who's gone and got herself a dance studio up and running. Seems like only yesterday when it was all a dream and you were ten years old, dancing about everywhere, teaching dance routines to your friends in the back garden. Where've those years gone?' Ollie looked down at her and smiled, squeezing her arm. 'You haven't turned out too badly, lass.'

She hugged him close and smiled back. 'Thanks, Dad, that means a lot. Couldn't have done it without you and Mum.'

'Aye, we make a good team, us Cartwrights.' He winked at her as they headed through the gate to home.

TWENTY-SIX

JULY

'Can I have your attention please?' Jimby's voice boomed around the village hall, cutting through the excited chatter that filled the air. Everyone obeyed, turning their attention to him. He was standing on the small stage at the back of the room a wide smile on his face, Lady Carolyn beside him in her capacity as co-host for the evening. She was poised at the auction block, gavel in hand – the equipment had been supplied on loan by one of her contacts at the auction house in Middleton-le-Moors. Mrs Prudom, headteacher of Lytell Stangdale Primary School, was standing to her right, smiling happily. She was the was the first to speak, taking the proffered microphone from Jimby.

'Good evening, everyone, and a very warm welcome to what I believe is the village's first Auction of Promises. It's incredibly heart-warming to see so many of you here, and on behalf of myself and all of the staff and pupils of Lytell Stangdale Primary School, I'd like to say a huge thank you to you all for giving up your Friday evening in support of this event, which I'm sure you're all aware is to raise funds for the school's exciting new extension.' She beamed around at everyone. 'And, I'd like to extend that thank you to Jimby and everyone on the Village Committee for organising this event, and for the many wonderful "promises" that have been so generously donated. When I approached Jimby to see if the committee would be interested in organising a fundraiser for school, I had no idea that he'd come up with something as thrilling as this.' She turned to Jimby. 'In light of this, I'm very happy to tell you, you've been awarded Star Student of the Week, and have earned yourself ten house points, Mr Fairfax.' Laughter ran around the audience, accompanied by a quick burst of applause.

Jimby chuckled. 'Makes a change from doing lines and having to stay in at playtime. Come to think of it, I don't think I was ever given any house points when I was a pupil. Can't think why.' He feigned an innocent expression.

'That's 'cos you were a mischievous little rascal and used to torment the living daylights out of the teachers,' called a voice from the audience.

'Aye, some things never change,' said another, making everyone laugh.

Jimby scratched his head. 'Aye, I suppose I can't argue with that, but I'll promise to be on my best behaviour tonight; specially seeing as though the headteacher's here.'

Still smiling broadly, Mrs Prudom continued. 'That's good to hear, Jimby. But before I hand over to you and Lady Carolyn, all that's left for me to say is I hope you all have a wonderful evening, and thank you once again.'

Jimby waited for the applause to die down. 'Thank you for that, Mrs Prudom, let's hope we can get you close to your target.' He cast his eyes over the sea of faces looking back at him. 'So, folks, as you know, when you arrived, in exchange for your tickets, you were handed a small wooden paddle with a number unique to you – actually, now would be a good time to share our gratitude to local woodworker, Ollie Cartwright, who very kindly made the paddles specially for the occasion. Thank you very much for that, Oll.' He nodded in the direction of his best friend who was sharing a table with Kitty, Vi, Molly and Camm. A cheer went up followed by yet more applause, making Ollie blush.

Jimby continued. 'Right then, you'll need to keep those paddles handy so you can give them a good old wave when you want to bid on one of our fabulous promises. The number of the winning bids will be noted down by Lady Caro or myself and you can collect the vouchers for your promises at the end of the evening, or even the actual promise itself since some of them have already been dropped off.'

The place was buzzing with anticipation, the room crowded with people eager to enjoy their night out. Anoushka felt a fizz of excitement. She and Kristy had joined Kitty, Molly and Vi earlier to help decorate the hall in readiness for tonight. Jimby, Ollie and Camm had arrived later and help set out tables and chairs. Crisp white tablecloths were thrown over the tables and set with jam jars brimming with country cottage flowers, ribbons tied around them. Plates were piled with delicious-looking nibbles, while a trestle-table ran along the side of the room, a mixture of glasses set out for people to grab. Granted, the decor might not be the height of sophistication, but it looked pretty and would serve its purpose.

Popping a crisp into her mouth, Anoushka's gaze ran around the friends sharing her table. Though Brogan, Kristy and Ben had arrived in the Land Rover with Molly and Camm, the younger ones had broken off and had opted to sit together; they'd been quickly joined by a loved-up Ella Welford and Joss Campion. The friends were all poring over a pamphlet containing the list of promises that had been left on the table, putting a tick beside the ones that caught their attention. Anoushka had her eye on a voucher for a pamper session at the new beautician's that had just opened up in one of the buildings near her dance studio. It looked stylish and welcoming and Rachel, the beautician, had a friendly face. She'd pop over when she next got chance, and introduce herself properly. She'd already decided, if her bid won, she was going to give the treatment voucher to Kitty. Since Rosie and Robbie had disappeared so suddenly a few months earlier to go and care for Robbie's sick mother somewhere near Barnsley, their monthly pamper sessions, courtesy of Rosie –who had her beauty rooms at her home, The Manor House in the village – had been put on hold and Anoushka knew how much her step-mum missed them.

Jimby was still in full swing. 'As you can see from the ones we've already been given, there's a whole array of fabulous-looking things to bid for, like hampers of wine, for example – quite like the look of that myself.' He chuckled. 'As I've already said these can be collected at the end of proceedings. You just need to bring your paddle and your wallet, and Lady Caro and I will sort out the rest for you. So, with all of that out of the way, there's nothing more for me to say but have an awesome evening and please, please bid generously, folks, it's for a great cause. Now here's Lady Caro with a final word.'

'Thank you ever so much for that, Jimby.' Caro's cut-glass voice was in stark contrast to his broad moorland accent. 'So, without further ado, it's time to kick-off proceedings and dive into Lytell Stangdale Primary School's Auction of Promises!'

A huge wave of applause followed, accompanied by cheers and whistles. Spirits were high.

'So, who'd like to bid for this fabulous chocolate hamper very kindly donated by The Chocolate Cherub over in Middleton-le-Moors?' Caro looked around, smiling broadly, gavel poised. Jimby picked up a wicker basket wrapped in cellophane and came to the front of the stage to show it around.

'Mmm-hm. It smells absolutely amazing,' he said.

'Becca, who owns The Chocolate Cherub, tells us it includes over sixty pounds-worth of chocolate, from bars containing salted caramel, to boxes containing violet creams. I'm sure we're all familiar with The Chocolate Cherub's products and we can all agree they're absolutely scrumptious,' Caro said.

The villagers were hesitant at first, but it didn't take long for them to get into their stride and dive into bidding wars with great enthusiasm. Caro and Jimby proved to be a great team, their rapport reminiscent of a comedy double-act. They used all of their powers of persuasion throughout the evening, entertaining everyone as they did so and keeping the mood buoyant. At one point, Jimby modelled a jaunty leather hat donated by the country store in Middleton-le- Moors, strutting about like a model on a catwalk, earning himself hoots of laughter and even the odd wolf-whistle, which only encouraged him to ham things up even more.

'Come on, folks, who's going to start the bidding for this? It's amazing quality and perfect for stylish walks in the countryside,' he said.

'Yes, you too could look as fetching as Jimby in this.' Lady Caro pulled a jokey face before saying, 'Seriously, though, folks, it really is excellent quality.'

After a brief bidding war, it was snapped up by local cyclist Len, gentleman friend of Rhoda, who bid way more than it was worth. 'Thank you for your generosity, darling,' said Caro when the bidding for it had finished.

'Aye, not so sure I'll be parading around like Jimby when I'm wearing it, mind,' he said dryly. 'But it's nice to support such a worthy cause.'

'Now, this next promise is a real goodie and we've got our very own GP, Zander Gillespie, to thank for it – or should I say, it's his parents we should be thanking. They've offered the use of their newly restored chateau in Carcassonne for a week. It looks absolutely amazing. I'm told it's kept its original features but still has all mod cons which have been added sympathetically. It's got a gener-ous-sized pool too, and a wonderful garden. Quite fancy it for myself and the missus, actually,' he said.

'Me too,' Vi said from the audience, triggering a ripple of laughter.

Unsurprisingly, the chateau attracted a lot of attention and bidding for it was vigorous, with it getting down to Lord Danskelfe and someone from out of town who no one recognised. Everyone looked on, holding a collective breath as the bidding heated up. The stranger wore a determined look, each time out bidding Lord Danskelfe. But Lord Danskelfe wasn't to be beaten and his wildly generous bid secured him his week there. The stranger looked daggers at him before storming out.

The winning bid for Anoushka's one-to-one dance lessons belonged to Lady Caro who seemed inordinately thrilled at her success. Her enthusiasm surprised Anoushka; she'd never expressed an interest in learning to dance before now. 'Oh, darling, I'm absolutely delighted, and I can't wait to put it to use,' she said, her eyes glittering.

The evening passed in a blur, with all of the promises being bid on and paid for – including Anita's which had been won by an unsuspecting soul from out of the area.

'Well, that was a resounding success.' Molly was sitting at a table with Vi as the pair totted up the money. 'There's an absolute fortune here.'

'And some folks who didn't manage to win any bids have actually made donations. Look, here's a cheque for three hundred quid from Hugh Heifer.'

'Wow, that's amazing,' said Anoushka who'd sat down to help them. She wondered why he didn't spend some of his money on a new pair of wellies instead of cobbling his old ones together with bits from others. It would seem he took the spirit of "make-do-and-mend" to the extreme. Her thoughts on Hugh aside, she'd thoroughly enjoyed the evening; neither Damon nor Gabe had crossed her mind once.

'I really can't thank you enough. You've all been amazing, organising this for our school; it's very touching.' Mrs Prudom looked almost tearful. 'And your enthusiasm is so infectious, Jimby; who couldn't help but have a marvellous time with you and Caro at the helm?'

'It was no bother at all. It's a great little school; we want to make sure it's still here generations from now.' Leaning on the brush he was using to sweep the floor, he flashed her one of his trademark beams.

Anoushka was heading towards the door, chatting animatedly with Brogan, when Caro stopped her. 'Noushka, darling, I'm terribly eager to book the first dancing lesson; I'd like to do it as soon as possible if that's okay? Strike while the iron's hot and all that.'

'Course, no problem. It's probably best if you call me and we can work out a suitable time between us. Or an email would do just as well; whichever suits.'

'Perfect! I think you're going to have lots of fun.' Caro gave an enigmatic smile before shooting off, calling after her father. 'Oh, there you are, Daddy. I was beginning to think you'd got lost.'

Anoushka looked after her, a puzzled expression on her face.

'What d'you think she meant by that?' asked Brogan.

'I really haven't a clue.' Anoushka's mind was a little woozy from the four glasses of Prosecco she'd polished off earlier. 'Maybe she's going to show me some dance skills she's been keeping hidden.' Though, somehow, Anoushka doubted that was what she meant; she'd give it more thought later, when her head was clear.

TWENTY-SEVEN

It wasn't until she was having breakfast the next morning, nibbling on a slice of thick, buttery toast, that it crossed Anoushka's mind Gabe hadn't donated anything to the Auction of Promises. It struck her as odd; there were any number of things he could have offered: tour T-shirts, tour merchandise, T-shirts worn by him... it didn't have to be him offering to *do* anything, like be a slave for a day as someone from Arkleby had put themselves forward for. An item would have sufficed and attracted a lot of interest. This lack of thought – for want of a better expression – didn't match the man she was familiar with. He was usually the first to jump in and get involved with village activities or to offer help if anyone needed it. Carrying Little Mary's shopping sprang to mind. Adopting Bob, the rescue Labrador, rather than having some fashionably expensive statement breed, quickly followed. Gabe had always been keen to blend in with the village, but his lack of a donation puzzled her. Maybe he'd been so busy it had simply slipped his mind? Even so, that really wasn't like him, and with Lady Caro as a friend, there's no chance he would have been able to forget about it; when she was on a mission, everyone knew about it – in the kindest possible way.

Though his tour had finished, Anoushka hadn't expected Gabe

to turn up at last night's fundraiser; according to Caro, other commitments had taken him to London. Lilith Dean, no doubt. If she was being honest, him not being at the auction had actually come as a relief; relief at not having to have people's eyes on her, of being the subject of whispers as people tried to guess how she was feeling. But she couldn't deny she'd been dreading the awkwardness of her first meeting with Gabe after *those* photographs had exploded onto social media; she wasn't so sure she'd be able to smile without revealing how she really felt.

'Now then, sleepyhead.' Ollie ambled into the kitchen and tousled her hair. 'Good kip?'

'Mmm. Not bad thanks, Dad.' The pressure of the last few weeks, getting her dance studio ready, helping with the auction and not forgetting the stress of Damon, had finally caught up with her, resulting in her sleeping soundly 'til gone eleven.

'You must've needed it, flower,' said Kitty, quickly flicking her eyes over to Anoushka as she lifted the huge joint of roast beef from the Aga. She proceeded to tip a pan of potatoes in, basting them in meat juices. The kitchen was suddenly filled with the delicious aroma of Sunday dinner.

'I did; I haven't slept that late for yonks. But I'm all refreshed now. I'll just have a quick shower then I'll be free to give you a hand. That smells gorgeous, by the way.'

'Thanks, chick. Lucas has offered to do the Yorkshire puds; Bea's been teaching him how to make them and he's keen to put his newly acquired skills to good use.' Kitty smiled affectionately. Lucas had a job waiting on the tables at the Sunne but had recently been taking a close interest in what went on in the kitchen; particularly Bea's cooking. He'd been coming home with all sorts of tips after his shifts, and had been particularly thrilled when Bea had told him he showed lots of promise and had the potential to be an excellent chef.

'Sounds good.' Anoushka drained her tea and sauntered over to the sink, rinsing her mug. 'What time's everyone due?' Molly, Camm and Lottie were joining them for Sunday dinner, together with Jimby, Vi and Pippin. Kristy and Ben, together with Molly's other twin son, Tom, and his partner, Adam, wouldn't be joining them. Instead, they were heading over to Ellerby Farm in Arkleby where they'd arranged a meeting with Titch Ventress to pick his brains about goat farming. They'd planned to travel over to Middleton-le-Moors and have lunch in one of the pubs there.

'Half-twelve,' said her dad, looking at the clock on the wall. 'Which doesn't give me too much time to get things set out in the garden.'

'I don't know where this morning's gone,' said Kitty, her face flushed from the warmth of the stove. She slid the roasting tray back in the Aga and glanced over at Anoushka. 'When your dad's got the gazebo up, you could fix the bunting to it, if you wouldn't mind, lovey? You being nice and tall will make a better job of it than me.'

'No probs; I'm happy to help.'

'Right then, I'd best get cracking.' With a smile, Ollie headed in the direction of the back garden.

Anoushka stood back, admiring her work on transforming the gazebo, the grass tickling her bare feet, the blazing sun hot on her shoulders. She was glad she'd opted for her cotton maxi dress, it being cool and crisp, but its thin straps meant she'd have to slap on some more sunblock before she did anything else; her fair skin burnt easily. Her wavy blonde hair shone like spun gold as it hung loose down her back, fastened off her face by thin plaits at either side which were tied loosely at the back of her head. Beneath the gazebo – she'd trimmed with bunting in shades of pinks and greens and cream – Ollie had placed two trestle tables end-to-end which Anoushka had set with pretty floral tablecloths, rustic water hyacinth placemats, crisp white napkins – tied round the middle with green ribbon – and chunky wine glasses. The finishing touch was courtesy of squat vases filled with country cottage flowers that had been freshly picked from the garden and placed at intervals along the table.

Birds were twittering happily from the trees accompanied by the background chirping of grasshoppers. The mouth-watering aroma of Sunday dinner floated through the open kitchen window, mingling with the smell of a barbecue from a garden further down the village. Anoushka felt a wave of contentment wash over her. She relished days like these, sunny and balmy; just perfect for lazy afternoons with her family. She released a gentle sigh and an image of Gabe unexpectedly popped into her mind. Her pulse quickened in response. What was going on with her? How many times had she told herself in no uncertain terms, she wanted to be nothing more than friends with him? Yet something inside her would have her believe otherwise. It obviously hadn't got the memo he was head-over-heels in love with someone else. *Ughh!* It was all so confusing, not to mention unsettling.

'That looks lovely.'

More than happy to be pulled from her thoughts, Anoushka turned to see Vi smiling at her, her glossy aubergine hair shining in the sunshine. As usual, her mum's friend looked glamorous in her designer cat-eye sunglasses and full-skirted dress covered in blousy lilac flowers. She couldn't help but smile back. 'Oh, Vi. Thanks; I've just finished. You been here long?'

'Only five minutes.' Just then the sound of Jimby's laughter spilled out into the garden and Vi smiled again, rolling her eyes. 'Honestly, he's like a foghorn.'

'Which was perfect in his capacity as auctioneer last night.' Anoushka laughed. 'It was an absolutely brilliant event.'

'It so was. I'm super-chuffed mine was the winning bid for the voucher from the new shoe shop in York; I can't wait to get that little beauty spent.' Vi's green eyes sparkled happily.

'Oh, I bet you can't,' Anoushka said with a chuckle. 'Mum was over the moon with the voucher I bought, you know, for a pamper session at the new beauty salon up at the old Danskelfe Estate offices.'

Before Vi could answer, Molly joined them, glass of wine in hand. 'Now then, lasses, so this is where you're hiding, is it? By, that looks gorgeous, Noushka.' She nodded in the direction of the newly decorated gazebo.

'Thanks.' Anoushka beamed back at her.

She was toying with the idea of asking if either of the two women knew if Gabe had contributed anything to the auction – the more she thought about it, the more she realised it wasn't like him not to – but didn't quite know how to put it into words without sounding nosy, when Kitty called out that dinner was five minutes off being ready. And why does it matter so much to you? she asked herself. You need to forget about it.

Everyone busied themselves, helping carry things to the table, Ethel and Mabel weaving in and out of them, in raptures at the smell of food in the air. Soon everyone was at their seat, serving themselves and passing around dishes piled high with jewel-coloured vegetables and mashed potato.

'Wow! Look at those Yorkshires; they look amazing,' said Camm, helping himself to one.

'Aye, I gather our Lukes is to thank for them. They don't look half bad for the efforts of a little squirt.' Jimby aimed a playful wink at his nephew.

'Oy, Uncle Jimby, I'm not such a little squirt anymore; I'll soon be as tall as you. And I should warn you, you'll pay dearly for that comment. I'll get you back when you're not expecting it.' Lucas flashed him a mischievous grin.

'Aye, well, you'd be very wise to think twice about taking on the infamous assassin here.' Jimby couldn't hold onto his serious expression for long and his face broke out into a wide smile. 'But if you choose to ignore my warning, I'll look forward to seeing what you come up with.'

Vi shook her head. 'Honestly, Jimby, I swear the teenage version of you is still trapped inside that man's body of yours.'

'Aye, but what a body it is.' He waggled his eyebrows, triggering a mix of groans and giggles.

'Do you have to, Jimby? We're just about to get stuck into our food.' Molly shot him a look of distaste before giving in to her chuckles.

The family's laughter was interrupted by the dogs who suddenly shot off into the house, barking noisily.

'Ey up, I wonder what's up with them?' Ollie said, getting to his feet.

Moments later, Ethel and Mabel bounded back into the garden, Bob hot on their heels. The three proceeded to tear around, thrilled to be reunited.

Ollie stepped back into the garden, a shadowy figure behind him.

'Wayhay, look who's here,' said Jimby.

Anoushka looked up, her heart leaping at the sight of Gabe standing in the doorway. He looked devastatingly handsome in an aquamarine T-shirt, battered jeans and aviator sunglasses, his fringe flopping over his forehead.

TWENTY-EIGHT

Welcoming voices filled the air. 'Now then, Gabe, it's great to see you. How're you diddlin', mate?' said Jimby, his voice warm.

'Hi there, everyone.' Gabe took off his sunglasses and glanced around at the sea of faces, his eyes finally resting on Anoushka. A smile broke out, lighting up his face.

In an instant, butterflies took flight in Anoushka's stomach as she tried to keep her emotions under control.

'Gaybublin!' From her seat piled high with cushions between Jimby and Vi, little Pippin gave a shriek of delight, kicking her legs and waving both hands at Gabe, apparently overjoyed at his arrival. Emmie and Lottie glanced at one another, clamping their hands over their mouths, giggling at their young cousin's unbridled enthusiasm.

'Well hello, little lady.' Gabe chuckled before turning to Kitty. 'I'm really sorry, I had no idea you were eating. Will I come back later when you've finished your meal? I don't want to intrude on your family time.'

Oh, that voice is just so delicious! Anoushka swallowed, still battling to get her emotions under control. She quickly reminded herself of his relationship with Lilith Dean, which had the desired effect, making her happiness slump in a flash.

'Hey, it was me who told you it was okay to drop in. Kitts and Oll don't mind, do you?' said Jimby.

'Definitely not.' Ollie gave their new guest a friendly pat on the back. 'S'good to see you.'

'Oll's right. Have you eaten? You're very welcome to join us,' said Kitty, smiling at Gabe. She put down the bowl of maple roasted parsnips and headed over to him, squinting in the sunshine.

'Aye, our Kitts has done loads; there's more than enough to go round,' said Molly.

'There is, and there's space next to Noushka down at the end of the table; we just need to grab you a seat,' said Kitty. Ollie obliged by fetching a chair and placing it next to his daughter while Kitty hurried off to seek out another mat and some cutlery.

Anoushka's stomach was in knots at the prospect of making conversation with him. Why did she have to go and sit herself here and not in between anyone else? And more importantly, how could they possibly avoid touching on *those* photos?

'Well, thank you, if you're sure?' Gabe said, watching as a place for him was set in a flurry of activity. He looked decidedly happy at the prospect of joining them.

'Of course we're sure; the more the merrier,' said Kitty as she handed him a plate. 'Just tuck in and help yourself.'

Anoushka felt her cheeks blaze as he headed over to her, aware of the surreptitious glances her family were throwing her way. *Oh my days! I really wasn't prepared for this.*

Settling himself in his seat, Gabe turned to her, his dark eyes gentle. 'So, how're you doing, Noushka?'

Her heart rate upped its speed, the scent of his cologne sending a thrill through her. 'Fine, thanks. You?' She pushed her mouth into a smile, wishing her body would listen to her brain and calm its bloomin' jets.

'I'm good, thanks.' He nodded, smiling. A few moments passed as he loaded up his plate with thick slices of roast beef. 'You look very pretty; you suit your hair like that.'

She felt her blushes deepen. 'Thank you.' *Why was he talking to her like this? He'd be better off saving his compliments for his girlfriend.* She searched her brain for something to say. 'How's the song writing going?' She sliced into a roast potato and pushed half onto her fork.

'Not bad, thanks. Though I'm hoping it'll be better now I'm back here. Back home; I just got back this morning.'

'Oh, right.' *Home? Surely he wouldn't be settling up here with Lilith Dean? How would that work with their careers?* Anoushka couldn't see that happening in a million years. From what she'd gathered, Lilith Dean favoured the bright lights and buzz of city life, something that was in short supply in the middle of the North Yorkshire Moors where the nearest nightclub was a good thirty miles away.

An air of awkwardness settled between them and Anoushka found her mind going frustratingly blank.

'Tell you what, you missed a cracking night last night, Gabe.' Jimby's voice travelled down the table, piercing their uncomfortable bubble for which Anoushka was inexorably relieved. 'It was loads of fun and raised thousands for the school's extension funds.'

'Yeah, I was disappointed I couldn't get to it, but it's exactly the reason I wanted to speak to you today.' Gabe reached for his glass of water and took a sip. 'I'd like to make a donation; I'd have put something into the auction but I didn't think it would raise that much, so I thought giving you a cheque or making a bank transfer would be better.'

Didn't think it would raise that much? Didn't he realise just how popular he was? Anoushka listened in disbelief.

'Gabe, mate, you could've put a pair of socks you'd worn for a week and they'd have raised a shedload of money.' Camm grinned at him.

'I'm not too sure about that.' Gabe laughed. 'You can't know what my feet are like after a day in these trainers, never mind a week.' He jabbed his fork in the direction of his feet. 'The horrors that lie within would shock you to your very core.'

'I reckon I've seen worse in my days as a district nurse; my core was well-and-truly shocked many times then,' said Molly, shaking her head at the memory. 'The horror stories I could tell you. I can remember going to see old Mr—'

'Stop!' Vi held up her hand. 'We don't want to hear any more stories about the scary body parts you had to dress or tend to, thanks, Moll. We're enjoying a civilized *family* afternoon and would rather not know about anything gory or inappropriate.'

'I would,' said Lucas, grinning broadly as he chewed on a mouthful of beef. 'The gorier, the better.'

'Well, I wouldn't, Lukes!' Lily said, pulling a horrified face.

'Pfft! I wasn't going to mention any of my testicle stories, just the ones about grotty trotters.'

'Not sure they're much better,' said Vi.

Lucas spluttered a guffaw.

Gabe's eyes grew wide. 'Testicle stories?' he said quietly, looking at Anoushka for clarification, his expression making her laugh.

'From what I can gather, Molly's got a whole repertoire of testicle-themed stories about her experiences as a nurse. Apparently some of them are real toe-curlers for the men.'

'Jaysus, I can feel my own toes curling at the mere thought. Remind me never to ask her about them.' Their eyes locked as they shared a giggle, the uncomfortable air rising up and drifting away.

'I think it's probably a good time to change the subject,' said Jimby, giving a theatrical shudder.

'I think you're right there.' Gabe grinned.

'As long as it's not for tups, Landies, or the price of sheep feed,' said Vi shooting her husband a warning look. 'We don't want to be sent to sleep.'

'How about the fact that The Manor House is in the process of being put on the market?' Jimby had got everyone's attention with that bombshell.

'Wow, that's a big old property,' said Gabe.

'What? No!' Kitty looked crestfallen.

'You're joking?' said Molly, her expression matching Kitty's.

'I'm not, you know.' Jimby went on to explain how he'd been delivering a set of gates he'd made for Alan Moss, owner of the estate agents in Middleton-le-Moors, and been told of it then.

'Apparently Robbie and Rosie are getting divorced and don't intend to move back to the area,' Jimby said.

'Oh, that's so sad, but I have to be honest, I did wonder after the last text I got from Rosie,' said Kitty. 'I've suspected things haven't been right there for a while.'

'Mm. Me too,' Molly said.

'Same here.' Vi nodded before turning to her husband. 'And how come you never mentioned about the house going on the market to me, Jimby? It's major news; they were good friends of ours.'

'What with all the preparations for the auction it slipped my mind. Sorry.' Jimby shrugged sheepishly.

'Typical man.' Vi gave a roll of her eyes.

'We'd guessed it was on the cards though, Vi,' said Molly.

'I know, but we'd only assumed; didn't know it was a fact,' Vi said.

'Well, I'm sorry to say it is. And according to Alan Moss, they're completely turning their back on Lytell Stangdale and what he said Rosie had referred to as her "unhappy memories". They both want a completely fresh start.'

'What a shame,' Kitty said sadly.

'It is,' said Molly, her expression grave.

'So it's been more than Robbie's mum being poorly that's kept them away,' said Vi. 'Just goes to show, you don't know what goes on behind closed doors.'

'True. Maybe that's the reason for the radio silence from them. Lils hasn't heard from Abbie for ages – poor lass, I wonder how she's doing. They've been having quite a time of it.'

'Aye, Kitts, they have that,' said Ollie.

'I think I'll message Rosie later, just to let her know we're thinking of her.' Kitty glanced up at her husband who nodded his agreement.

'You'll have a job. According to Alan Moss, she's got rid of all her social media, and she's apparently changed her phone number too.' Jimby gave his sister a regretful look.

'Well, they'll be a real loss to the village, and to us as friends. I wish them all the best, whatever their future holds,' said Camm. They all made sounds of agreement.

With the meal over and done with and sunblock slathered over bare skin, the adults sat back in their seats while Lottie, Emmie and Pippin scurried off to splash about in the small paddling pool Lucas and Ollie had filled earlier. Lily was happy to keep a watchful eye on them, videoing their antics on her mobile phone. Their squeals of delight made everyone laugh while little Pippin's deliciously chubby legs earned lots of "ahhs" as she kicked them about in the water.

A phone pinged on the table next to Kitty. 'Ooh, is this yours, Moll?' she asked, picking the phone up.

Molly was busy unravelling a knot in her necklace. 'Aye, it is. I wondered where I'd put it. It's probably a text from our Ben giving us an update on the goat situation over in Arkleby. Would you mind reading it out for me, Kitts?'

'No probs.' Kitty tapped in the password Molly gave her and looked at the screen, frowning.

'Ey up, something wrong?' asked Camm.

'It's from Granny Aggie.'

'Uh-oh,' said Ollie.

'This'll be good.' Molly rolled her eyes theatrically. 'What does she say?'

'Fart,' said Kitty.

Gabe caught Anoushka's eye, his expression making her laugh.

'You what?' Molly asked, perplexed.

'I've heard worse from Granny Aggie,' Jimby said, chuckling.

'Tell me again, Kitts,' said Molly.

'Fart.' Kitty repeated the message.

'Fart?' Molly said. 'Is that an order? I can't just rustle them up on demand, you know.'

'Oh, I think we know you can,' said Vi, arching a sculpted eyebrow.

'Cheeky.' Molly poked her tongue out at her friend.

'No, *I'm* not telling you to do that,' Kitty said between her giggles. 'It's what Granny Aggie's message says.'

'And that's it? She doesn't say anything else?' asked Molly.

'Nope, that's it. Look.' She took the phone over to her cousin.

'Hmm. What's the old minx up to now?' Molly pushed a dark curl off her face. 'As far as I was aware, she was supposed to be going to Little Mary's for some afternoon tea and the pair were going to watch an old movie, never mind sending messages like that. I reckon they've been knocking the sherry back.'

'I think she's just keeping you on your toes, Moll.' Camm smiled at her affectionately.

'Well she does that all right.'

'At least she's leaving poor old Rev Nev alone,' said Jimby.

'Good point,' said Molly.

The banter flowed as the sun beat down, hoots of laughter drifting around the cottage garden at Oak Tree Farm. Ethel, Mabel and Bob sat in the shade beneath the old, gnarled apple tree, panting away in the heat. Being in Gabe's company hadn't been anywhere near as difficult as Anoushka had anticipated. In fact, she'd found she was actually enjoying it. Reminding herself that they were friends –nothing more – seemed to go some way to settling her anxiety about being around him.

He was sitting beside her on the swing seat, rocking it gently back and forth with his feet. They'd been enjoying a few moments of quiet reflection under the shade of the canopy. 'Your family are awesome; I'll bet there's never a dull moment with them,' he said. 'They remind me of my own.'

'Yeah, they're not bad.' She glanced over at them, her eyes settling on Jimby who was sitting at the table with Pippin laid out on his chest where she was sleeping contentedly, his hand rhythmically patting his little daughter's back. He bent his head and absently dropped a kiss onto her dark curls. 'And there's definitely never a dull moment when Jimby's around; the only time he's quiet is when Pippin's asleep.' She smiled affectionately.

Gabe gave a quiet chuckle. 'He's a really cool guy; so's your dad; quieter though.'

'Mm-hm. Though from the stories I've heard, they were a right mischievous pair when they were little boys, always up to something – nothing bad, they were just full of high-spirits; inseparable too.'

He smiled. 'Yeah, I can believe that. And it's great your mum and dad finally got together after being teenage sweethearts; they're well suited. I still get a buzz at having played a part in that.' His smile widened. Gabe and his band had been performing at Lady Caro's first venture of Music in the Wood and Caro and her husband, Sim, had arranged with Gabe for Ollie to go up on stage half-way through the gig to propose to Kitty who'd be in the audience, totally oblivious to his intentions.

Anoushka met his gaze. 'Oh, me too. That was such an *amazing* day. Dad was so nervous but he just wanted everyone to know how much he loved Kitty.'

'I think that was kind of obvious from the way he looked at her; still is.' He smiled.

'Yeah, they're definitely loved up, and it's great to see Dad looking so happy. Being with Kitty's really changed him; she's so good for him, and him for her.' Her eyes lingered on her dad and her step-mum. They were sitting side-by-side on the rattan sofa, Ollie's arm draped around his wife's shoulders, absently rubbing the top of her arm. They were listening to something Vi was saying, nodding and smiling. Kitty tucked her feet beneath her, leaning into Ollie who pressed a kiss to her cheek. Anoushka felt a yearning inside her; a sudden need making itself known. She wanted something like that. She stole a glance at Gabe, overwhelming feelings for him creeping up on her.

'I can't wait to have my own family; have my own wee wains running around the place,' he said wistfully.

An image of Gabe and Lilith Dean mid-passionate embrace filled her mind, sending her happiness trickling away.

Gabe sat forward, his arm brushing against hers, his skin warm and soft, sending an ache through her. 'Noushka, can we talk?' His voice sounded serious.

'Talk?' She turned to look at him, seeing the earnest expression in his eyes. 'Yes, of course.' *Oh, heck, what was he going to say?*

'I mean... um... it's just, there's something I'd like to explain to you and I've been waiting to do it face-to-face, only I'd rather not do it here with everyone around, I'd prefer somewhere more private. Would you go for a walk with me, Rose?'

'Oh, right... yeah, a walk would be good actually.' Her heart started hammering in her chest, not helped by the way he way he said her middle name. She didn't know what else to say. She knew exactly what he wanted to talk to her about: Lilith Dean. But was there really any need? And did she really want to hear it? *Oh jeez, no, she didn't; it would be too excruciating.* 'Listen, Gabe, if it's about the—'

'I just need to set things straight with you, Noushka, that's all. I won't be able to settle until I do.'

TWENTY-NINE

Anoushka slipped her feet into a pair of plimsolls, popped a bucket hat trimmed with daisies on her head and she and Gabe set off, taking the three dogs with them.

They made their way up the track towards Great Stangdale Rigg, making small talk, their footsteps kicking up the scents of warm earth and crushed grass. The bracken had grown tall, its fronds shoulder high in places, reaching out over the path. Up above, the sun sat in a cloudless blue sky. July was really outdoing itself. Before long, they reached a bench with spectacular views that swept right over the dale. 'Phew! That was some pull up the track in this heat.' His chest heaving, Gabe wiped beads of perspiration from his brow. 'Fancy a sit down?'

'Sounds good to me.' Anoushka flopped down beside him, the dogs at their feet, panting heavily. She took off her hat and started fanning herself, watching as a fly started to torment Bob, hovering around his face. He snapped at it frantically; they couldn't help but laugh.

'Such a beautiful place,' said Gabe, taking off his sunglasses and casting his gaze over the view. In the distance, local farm contractors Paddy and Ant Ford were busily gathering the silage in the fields over at Tinkel Bottom Farm, the gentle hum of their tractors drifting along the deep cut of the valley. Gabe drew in a deep breath, pausing before he spoke.

Anoushka braced herself. *Here goes...*

'So, the reason I wanted to talk to you is... well, I'm sure you've seen the photos that were splashed all over social media; the ones of me and Lilith Dean.'

'Yes, I did. She's very pretty; you make a good couple.' Anoushka frowned, hoping that didn't sound snipey, but she couldn't think what else to say.

His eyes darted to her. 'Oh, right.' He seemed wrong-footed for a moment. 'See, the thing is, we're not actually a couple...' He rubbed his hand over the back of his neck.

'You're not? But in the photographs you were... you seemed...' She didn't know how he was going to explain this one; they looked pretty damned close for not being a couple.

'I know.' He pushed his fingers into his hair, frustrated. 'But they're honestly not what they look like.'

His obvious discomfort tugged at her conscience. 'Hey, it's really none of my business, Gabe. You don't have to answer to me; you're free to live your life as you see fit, with whoever you want.'

'I'd still feel better telling you about it.' He looked at her beseechingly.

'Okay; if that's what you want.' She shrugged, her heart slowly sinking.

Gabe went on to tell her how Lilith Dean's manager had been in touch with his. It would seem Lilith's star was rising and she was finding herself much-in-demand with the big name fashion houses and brands. Her manager had thought it would be an excellent publicity stunt to get the couple seen out and about together, hoping it would generate a flurry of strategically-taken photos, thus giving their profiles an extra boost. With Gabe's new album due for release in the autumn, and the first single from it coming out in late August, it would be perfect timing. Photos of them looking loved up would be like rocket fuel to their popularity and, consequently, their earning potential – which had been the real driving force behind the respective management teams. Unbeknown to Gabe, the two managers had arranged a meal for the pair of them and had tipped off the paparazzi with the name of restaurant they'd be at. Lilith Dean's had gone one further and dropped hints about the imminent announcement of their engagement. Both Gabe and Lilith had been shocked at this, as had the model's boyfriend of three years. Lilith had been as oblivious to their scheme as Gabe. Though, thanks to downing a bottle of expensive champagne, she hadn't taken much encouragement to pucker up and pull Gabe into a clinch in front of the flashing cameras. As predicted, it had been gold dust with the photos selling for a small fortune; the pair's profiles had gone stratospheric.

'They've even arranged with my record company for her to star in my next video. Part of it's being filmed up here at the end of this month, on the moors and fields belonging to the Danskelfe Estate.'

'Oh, wow. You couldn't get a more beautiful location,' Anoushka said quietly, her eyes focusing on the blade of grass she was twisting in her fingers as she slowly absorbed his words. It would seem Kitty had been right when she'd warned her that the photos of Gabe and Lilith Dean might not have been what they seemed.

'True.' He reached out, his hand touching her chin, turning her face to him. His dark eyes looked deep into hers. 'Noushka, I know you've made it clear to me you don't want us to be anything more than friends, and I totally respect that – I'm no fool, I know I can't make you love me; I've definitely got the message – but I couldn't walk this earth thinking your opinion of me was that I was nothing more than a shallow eejit who was turned down by you one minute, and then went and proposed to the very next girl I bumped into, who also, incidentally, happened to have a long-term boyfriend.' His eyes locked onto hers. 'I'm not that kind of man.'

Anoushka's heart was beating faster than ever, relief coming in a huge wave. It was impossible not to feel the charge that sparked between them. She felt her resolve waver, its foundations slowly crumbling. The urge to feel his lips against hers was suddenly overwhelming and she found herself willing him to kiss her with all her might.

'Sweet Rose.' His voice was no more than a whisper.

Just as he was inching closer, a rabbit shot out of the bracken and the dogs leapt to attention. Bob gave a howling bark before darting after the rabbit, only to be pulled back by his lead that had been tied to the arm of the bench.

And just like that, the spell was broken.

Back at Oak Tree Farm, they found everyone still chilling in the garden, the rich aroma of coffee circulating from the mugs set out on the table. The three dogs raced off to the utility room to quench their thirst at the water bowls.

'Ooh, that was good timing,' said Kitty, her eyes searching Anoushka's face. 'We all thought we needed a bit of caffeine to pep ourselves up; the heat's making everyone drowsy.'

'Yeah, Moll's been snoring like a pig,' Jimby said with a chuckle.

'I have not, have I, Camm?' Molly shot Jimby a filthy look.

'Hmm...' Camm pressed his lips together. 'Let's just say, we all knew you were asleep,' he said diplomatically.

Molly gave him a sideways look and huffed. 'Thanks for the support; I'll remember that next time you're letting rip.' Her mouth twitched with a smile.

'Coffee, Gabe?' Ollie asked.

'I'd best be heading back, but thanks for the offer. I just need to get the bank details for the Village Committee so I can transfer a donation across.'

'Don't worry about that, I'll text it ove—' Before Jimby could finish, Lucas shot out of the kitchen, his eyes dancing mischievously. In his hands was a water-filled balloon. Before anyone could speak, he reached his arm back and lobbed it at Jimby with all his might.

It exploded on Jimby's chest, water covering his face. 'Warghh!' He spluttered. 'You little... you'll pay for that!'

'Told you I'd get you back for calling me a little squirt.' Lucas roared with laughter as he shot off down the garden, Jimby in hot pursuit. Shrieks of laughter from the younger children filled the air. A moment later, Bob, Ethel and Mabel joined in the fun, charging around after them.

'Come here and take your punishment, you little squirt!' Jimby raced after Lucas who was heading towards the house, effortlessly clearing the paddling pool as he went. Jimby wasn't quite so agile and landed with one foot in the water. He slid across the base, his arms waving frantically as he tried to right himself, before shooting backwards with an almighty sploosh. The dogs didn't waste a moment and joined him, Bob leaping about and kicking water everywhere. Everyone looked on, rendered helpless with fits of laughter.

'Arghh! Get off me you stinky hounds!' Jimby tried to climb out of the pool but the dogs, who thought it was a wonderful game, were having none of it and continued to leap all over him; they were having a whale of a time, with Mabel tugging at his T-shirt.

Finally he managed to break free, rolling away from the danger zone, leaving the dogs splashing about in the pool. Bob was on his back, kicking his legs in the air, his eyes wild with happiness. 'Thanks for your help, everyone,' Jimby said as he pulled himself upright, water dripping from him.

'Like I said, your family are awesome.' Grinning, Gabe looked across at Anoushka who'd been laughing so hard, her eyes were watering.

'Well, you're certainly right about there never being a dull moment,' she said, her mind going back to their unfinished moment up on the rigg. What would've happened if they hadn't been interrupted? Would they have kissed? And if they had, how would she be feeling about that now? Her heart started racing at the thought.

'Noushka?' Gabe's voice brought her back to the present.

'Hmm?'

'I was just saying I'm heading off; I'll see you later.' He slid his sunglasses on. Bob nudged her leg, and she bent to give his soggy head a pat as she marshalled her thoughts.

'Oh, right, yes. See you later.' She mustered what she hoped was a nonchalant smile that would give no hint at the turmoil currently swirling around inside her.

She followed him out, Lily close behind, taking away the chance to pick up where they left off high up on the rigg.

'Sorry about my daft brother, Gabe. Him and Uncle Jimby are always larking about like that.' Lily grinned. Her blonde corkscrew curls had escaped their ponytail and stood out around her face that was glowing pink from an afternoon in the sun. 'Uncle Jimby's a big kid.'

'Hey, no need to apologise, it's been cool spending time with you all.' He smiled.

Lily caught Anoushka's eye, her beam growing wider.

'I'll see you later.' Gabe pressed his fingers lightly on Anoushka's arm, sending a buzz of electricity shooting through her. 'And thanks for coming for a walk with me.' His mouth lifted with a smile, though the feelings in his eyes were hidden by his his aviator shades.

'See you later.' Anoushka smiled back. She and Lily watched him head down the path, Bob in tow.

'Gabe's a special kind of person, isn't he?' Lily looked up at her big sister.

'Mmm, he is,' said Anoushka, as myriad emotions bombarded her. She drew in a deep breath; it was time to put her thoughts and her feelings in order. If only she knew where to start.

THIRTY

'There, all done,' Anoushka said to herself as she flipped her laptop lid down. It was Thursday morning and she was at the studio, updating the dance school's social media page, adding an extra Street Dance class. Since Vi had relocated her burlesque classes to the studio from the village hall she'd gained some extra pupils – Anoushka being one of them – which had given Anoushka something else to think about for the future: the prospect of taking on another dance teacher. A thrill rushed through her. Her dance school was proving to be a bigger success than she'd anticipated; the move to her own premises adding kudos to it, not to mention the stylish branding. It looked professional, told potential students she had the ability to get them through all the necessary exams.

A sound from outside made her head shoot round. She felt the squeeze of anxiety in her stomach. *Please, not this again.* She went to check the window but, as usual, there was nothing there. 'Get a grip, Anoushka! Stop letting Damon get to you,' she said aloud, telling herself the sound was probably made by the deer she'd seen earlier, roaming around nearby. But would a deer really give her the uneasy feeling that had hovered in the background since she'd arrived? She blew out a sigh and checked the clock on the wall. Ten-forty-five, she had fifteen minutes before

Caro arrived for the first of the one-to-one-dance lessons she'd won at the auction; at least she wouldn't be on her own for much longer. She recalled how Caro had been evasive when Anoushka had asked her what type of dance she wanted to learn, 'Oh, I'll leave that up to you, darling,' she'd said somewhat vaguely. Which meant, today, Anoushka didn't know what to expect. She didn't even know if Caro would be bringing Sim as a dance partner.

She slipped her laptop into the drawer of her desk and was heading towards the stairs when the door to the studio opened. She looked across, her mouth falling open. 'Gabe?'

'Hi.' He gave a heart-melting smile, taking in her flared jazz pants and dance school T-shirt. 'You look ready for business.'

She glanced at the clock again. 'Is everything okay? I'm expecting Lady Caro any minute.'

'You are?' He returned her puzzled gaze. 'Only, I don't think she'll be showing up.'

'You don't?'

'No.' He shook his head. 'She shot off early this morning saying she had a meeting over at York and wouldn't be back 'til late this afternoon.'

'Oh, but...' Anoushka's brain played catch-up. 'I don't suppose she mentioned anything about a dance lesson, did she?'

'Not a word, was a bit vague really. She just said I was needed here. So here I am.' He shrugged and scratched his head, looking suddenly awkward.

'Right,' Anoushka said; it was slowly dawning on her what Caro was up to.

'Are you thinking what I'm thinking?' he asked, raising an eyebrow.

'That we've been set up?'

'It's looking that way.' He nodded, smiling.

'Honestly! What's she like?' Anoushka said, her voice sounding more annoyed than she intended.

Gabe's face fell. 'Hey, Noushka, I'm really sorry, I honestly didn't know anything about it. I feel such an eejit. I can go, if you like... I mean, there's no real reason for me to be here.'

His expression triggered a spike of guilt in her chest. She pushed her mouth into a smile. 'No, I'm sorry, I didn't mean to sound snappy, it's just...' A thought sprang into her mind and before she knew it she found herself saying, 'We might as well use the lesson – if you fancy it, that is?' *What the heck are you thinking? Talk about cringe: "Use the lesson" indeed! Why would Gabe Dublin want you to teach him to dance? Jeez!*

'Are you saying you'd actually be willing to give me a dance lesson?' He gave a lopsided grin.

'Why not?' She grinned back. *Why not? Are you bonkers? There's a million reasons why not!*

'Hmm.' He rubbed his hand over his chin. 'Tell you what, I'm actually quite liking that idea. Though I think it's only fair to warn you, I've two left feet.' His smile widened, making his eyes crinkle at the corners in that appealing way that made her heart skip a beat.

'Oh, I'm sure you're not that bad.'

'Oh, I'm pretty sure I am, as your fraught nerves and bruised toes will testify when we're done.' He followed as she made her way to the studio she'd prepared for her lesson with Caro.

'I don't suppose you've any idea what style of dance you'd like to learn?'

'What do you teach? I'm open to suggestions.' He rested his hands on hips, amusement dancing in his eyes which Anoushka found a little disconcerting.

'Ballet, street dance, hip-hop.' She struggled to keep her face straight.

He gave a hearty laugh. 'Can't really see myself as a ballet man – I'm told these old legs of mine look terrifying in tights – don't ask; something to do with a stag night in Temple Bar. I'm told people are still having nightmares about it.'

'Okay.' Anoushka couldn't help but giggle. 'Maybe you fancy

going a bit more old school. How about ballroom, or maybe a jive? That's fun.'

He hooked his thumbs into the pockets of his jeans. 'Tell you what,' he said, looking suddenly enlightened. 'I've always fancied learning a bit of salsa; I love the music. Don't suppose you could teach me a few Latin moves?'

'No problem.' She beamed at him, tucking her loose hair behind her ears. 'I love salsa; it's one of my favourite dances.'

Anoushka selected a suitable piece of music then slipped on a pair of heeled dance shoes, the up-tempo beat of the music filling the room, giving her the urge to dance.

'Fabulous!' Happiness lit up Gabe's face as he tapped his foot to the rhythm.

After a few minutes' warm up she said, 'Right then, let's get started. I'm going to show you the forward and backwards basics.'

'Okay. I'm liking the sound of basics. Think I can manage that.'

They stood side-by-side in front of the mirrors, the salsa beat pounding through them. Gabe listened intently as she ran him through the basic steps, calling out instructions as he copied her moves. 'Left foot forward, right foot back, one, two, three, don't step on four, five, six, seven. And repeat. Let's go! Left foot forward, right back, one, two, three, don't stop on four.' He found it difficult to follow at first, tripping over his own feet several times, but didn't seem to mind and had roared with laughter at his clumsy attempts.

'I did warn you I have the coordination of a herd of charging elephants after a night on the sauce,' he said, attempting the steps again, counting quietly to himself.

'You're doing really well; it can be tricky to get the steps right but once they click, you'll be fine; it'll come naturally. Come on, let's try again. Then we can speed them up a bit.'

'Speed them up? Hells bells! Has anyone ever told you you're a slave driver?' he asked, grinning.

'Many times, but no one's ever grumbled when they've passed their dance exams with flying colours.'

'I'll be doing an exam?'

His worried expression made her laugh. 'Not unless you want to; this is just for fun.'

'Well, it's definitely fun.'

'There, you've cracked it! I told you you would,' she said, jumping up and down, clapping her hands when he'd finally managed to get the knack of the steps.

'Woohoo! I did it!' he said, punching the air. 'Jaysus, I never thought I'd get there.' He looked as thrilled as a child on Christmas morning.

Anoushka couldn't help but think how good it felt to be around him.

A flash of something in the corner of her eye drew her attention to the window. She glanced across, but as usual there was no one to be seen. An image of Damon forced its way into her mind. Unnerved, her pulse started to race and goosebumps prickled over her skin.

'You okay?' Gabe asked, concern in his eyes.

'Fine.' She hoped she sounded more convincing to him than she did to herself.

Moments later, there was the rev of an engine and the sound of a car speeding off, making her heart leap. *Please don't let it be Damon.* Anoushka swallowed; she was letting her imagination run away with itself. There was no way he would trouble himself to come up here, especially after his last ill-fated visit to the village when he was pretty much chased out. There's no way his arrogant pride would risk something like that happening again. She needed to release the grip *she* was letting him have on her life.

Brushing her doubts away, she took a calming breath, forced a wide smile and turned back to Gabe. 'Okay, now it's time to move on to what we call open and closed holds; we'll start with open.' She took his hands in hers, her eyes flicking shyly up to meet his gaze before quickly looking away. 'So, this is what we do...'

Getting into his stride, Gabe didn't hide how thrilled he was to have mastered the open hold so easily and was eager to learn more. 'Sorry about your toes though; I've lost count of how many times I stood on them there; they'll be black and blue by the time we're done.'

'It's fine, don't worry; you're doing great,' she said, smiling, his buoyant mood brushing off onto her and chasing away her worries about Damon. 'We'll try the closed hold now.' Anoushka struggled to make eye contact with him as she demonstrated how he should place his hand on her shoulder blade. The heat of his touch burnt through her T-shirt making her skin tingle and her pulse rate soar. They were standing so close she was suddenly aware of how broad his shoulders were, of his breathing. Oh, the warmth of his body so close to hers, the aroma of his cologne... It was intoxicating. She blinked several times, taking a moment to regain her focus. As she rested her hand on the firm muscle of his arm a ripple of something indefinable ran through her, the sudden intimacy distracting. She could feel the weight of his eyes on her. Her newly recovered focus was in pieces. *Oh my days. This is intense! You need to calm your jets, woman! Think of something to take your mind off it! Emptying the bin, washing Mabel after she's rolled in fox poo. Anything!* She drew in a deep breath, pushed her shoulders back and said, 'Okay, you need to lead, but I'll show you how first.'

They tried the manoeuvre several times before Gabe cracked it. 'That's great! You seem to have got the hang of that one pretty quickly, and you hardly stepped on my toes at all that time.' She smiled, hoping nothing about her behaviour would betray the feelings she was currently battling inside. She gathered the courage to look up at him, her heart fluttering at the dark pools gazing back at her. She couldn't stop the gasp that escaped her lips. His chest was heaving; there was no doubting his feelings for her. The jaunty salsa beat, bouncing away in the background seemed incongruous set against the electricity that crackled between them. 'I... I think you're ready to move on to what we call the "New York Walk" now.' She added a breeziness to her voice she didn't feel as she went to step away from him.

'Rose,' he said huskily, stopping her in her tracks.

The music came to an abrupt halt, breaking the spell.

Anoushka released herself from his arms and cleared her throat as she walked over to where she'd left her water bottle. She took a quick glug, glancing up at the clock on the wall as she did so. 'Right, well, we've been going for over an hour; I reckon you've worked hard enough for today. You've been a great student; you picked it up really quickly.' She looked across at him and smiled, hoping she didn't sound too abrupt.

He took the cue without question. 'Thanks. I've had a great time; I've no idea where that last hour's gone.' Sounding disappointed, he pushed his hands into his pockets. 'I suppose I'd best go and relieve Sim of that wee rascal Bob, make sure he hasn't demolished anyone's shoes – I mean Bob not Sim; I don't think Sim's known for his love of chewing shoes, but then again, you never know...' He gave a chuckle, his humour relieving the tension.

When he'd gone, Anoushka flopped down at her desk and put her head in her hands. 'What the heck is going on with me? Why do I keep finding myself in situations like that with Gabe? Bloomin' Caro, pushing us together! Bloomin' everyone pushing us together!' How many times did she have to tell them she didn't want a man in her life right now? Why were they struggling to get the message? 'Arghh!' Their almost kiss popped up in her mind and she felt a flutter in her heart. Just because she found him attractive didn't mean she had to act on it, she reasoned with herself. She wasn't ready to commit to anyone else after her claustrophobic time with Damon. What did she have to do to get everyone else to accept that? Come to think of it, what did she have to do to get herself to accept it?

THIRTY-ONE

'So, have I got this right? You've been teaching Gabe how to salsa dance?' asked Brogan.

'Mm-hm.' Anoushka rolled her eyes as she took a sip of her Pinot Grigio.

'And how did that go?' asked Kristy, shooting Brogan a loaded look.

It was Friday evening, the day after her dance lesson with Gabe, and the three friends were sitting at their usual table at the Sunne. Anoushka had told them earlier in the week how he'd explained about the photos of him and Lilith Dean.

'The whole dance lesson thing was a blatant set up. Lady Caro organised it with the voucher I'd donated to the auction; led me to believe she'd be the one coming.'

'Sneaky,' said Brogan, unable to suppress a smile.

'Sneaky but genius. I like it,' said Kristy, grinning across at Brogan.

'Hmm. Not so sure I do.' Anoushka looked at them warily. 'I mean, I like him, and he's a good laugh, but that's it. My feelings don't run any deeper than that. I just wish he and everyone else would get the message instead of trying to push us together. I don't know how many times I have to say I'm not interested in him like that, and never will be.'

'Noushka,' said Kristy quietly, her eyes growing so wide Anoushka thought they'd pop out of her head if she wasn't careful, while Brogan started glaring at her intently as if trying to convey some non-verbal message.

She frowned at them. 'What?' she asked, just as Bob shot over and pushed his head into her lap, his tail thudding against the table leg. 'Bob!' Anoushka's heart sank as realisation dawned. 'Oh...' She bit down on her bottom lip and closed her eyes before turning to see Gabe standing close behind her. Though his face was set stern, the hurt in his eyes was unmistakable.

'Bob! Heel!' he said. 'Sorry, Anoushka, I hope he isn't bothering you.' His cool tone, so unfamiliar, made her cringe inside.

'Hi, Gabe, er... no, he's fine, it's good to see him.' How she wished the ground would open up and swallow her whole.

'Unlike some other folk I expect.' He reached for Bob's collar and pulled him back, clipping his lead on. 'Come on, fella, we don't want to make a nuisance of ourselves.'

Brogan and Kristy looked on in awkward silence as Anoushka scrambled through her mind for something to say. 'Gabe, I—'

'Change of plan; we're just leaving.' He turned and strode out of the pub.

Anoushka covered her face with her hands, tears stinging her eyes. 'Oh, my God. What have I done?'

Kristy and Brogan looked on sympathetically. There was nothing they could say to help her.

'I've hurt him, which is the last thing I want to do. It's just... ughh!' She pushed her hair back off her face and looked at her friends despairingly. 'What should I do? Do you think he heard?' She rolled her eyes. 'Of course he heard, he never normally acts like that. Oh, flippin' 'eck!'

'You could always go after him,' said Brogan. 'Explain what you meant.'

'I'm not sure that's going to make things any better, Broge,' said Kristy, wearing a regretful expression.

Anoushka blew out her cheeks and hissed out a noisy breath. The thought of hurting his feelings was unbearable. Why did she have to go and say something like that? The pain in his eyes was tearing her apart. She bit back her tears. 'What can I do? I can't just leave it like that.'

'You could always try being honest with yourself, Noushka.' Kristy looked at her pointedly, reaching for her glass of wine.

'What do you mean by that?' Anoushka could feel her pulse whooshing in her ears.

Kristy glanced at Brogan, taking a moment before she replied. 'Well, we can all see how you feel about him; the only person who seems to be struggling to see it is you.'

'I agree with Kristy; which is why we can't understand why you seem so intent on pushing him away. He's nothing like Damon.'

'Ughh! You've got it so wrong.' Anoushka flopped back in her seat, scrubbing her hands over her face. 'Why does it have to be so complicated? Why can't everyone just accept that he's a friend? Him included!'

'Noushka, flower, don't you think it's unfair to expect that of him? I mean, if we can see it, your parents can see it, bloomin' 'eck, even Lady Caro can see it, don't you think he might be able to sense you have feelings for him? He's already laid his cards on the table; it's blatantly obvious he's crazy in love with you. Jeez, I wish someone looked at me the way he looks at you.' Brogan shook her head in despair. 'And you do seem to be happy to spend time in his company. It kind of looks like you're sending out mixed messages.' She looked at Kristy for support.

'Broge's right. And we can all see how you come alive when you're around him; you positively sparkle. You shouldn't let what happened with Damon or what you promised yourself about having time on your own, stop you from falling in love with someone who's so perfect for you and who absolutely adores you.

There's no right or wrong time, and he's a really decent guy, Noushka.'

The reference to her sending out mixed messages rankled. 'Oh, my God, this is way, *way* too heavy. When will you all realise I'm not interested in being a relationship and won't be for...' she threw her hands up in the air, '...forever!' Feeling an unpleasant mix of frustration, guilt and annoyance churning her insides, Anoushka scooped up her leather jacket and grabbed her bag, her nostrils flaring. 'I'm sorry, I can't do this tonight. I'll see you later.' With that she flounced out of the pub, her friends staring after her.

'Noushka! Don't go,' Brogan called after her, but her words fell on stony ground.

Outside, Anoushka looked up and down the road, but there was no sign of Gabe which was probably just as well; she wouldn't even know what to say to him if he had been there. She closed her eyes and shook her head, her heart aching for the hurt she'd caused him. How was she ever going to put this right?

THIRTY-TWO

Anoushka woke the following morning, a feeling of dread pooling in her stomach as events of the previous night came flooding back. She clapped her hand to her forehead, wishing she could turn back the clock. She should have kept her thoughts to herself, or at least kept her voice down in the pub, then she wouldn't be awash with regret, and Gabe's feelings wouldn't be hurt.

She hadn't mentioned anything to her parents when she'd got home, despite their enquiring looks at her early return. Instead, she'd headed upstairs and run a bath, mulling her options over in her mind until the water had gone cold. Her thoughts of how to make things better with Gabe continued to torture her into the early hours where she'd talked herself in and out of going to speak to him, to face up to what she'd said and apologise. Granted, she couldn't take her words back, but offering an apology was the least she could do, and give her reasons. And, in truth, she'd only been strong in expressing her opinion to her friends to stop them from getting carried away with their matchmaking. Despite her best endeavours to convince herself otherwise – never mind everyone else! – she knew she should acknowledge that her feelings for Gabe went way deeper than just friendship. Not that anyone else needed to know that. But she wasn't ready to tackle them right now, nor their potential implications. It was way, way too complex for her to get her head around. She had an inkling – more than an inkling if she was honest with herself – that if she allowed herself to fall for him, she'd fall hard. He stirred feelings inside her no man ever had before – definitely not Damon! – and that scared her. Really scared her. And what if she took the risk and opened her heart to Gabe, only for him to decide he didn't want to be with her anymore? That thought was just too painful to consider. Being abandoned once in her life was bad enough; there was no way she was going to let that happen to her again. She had a plan for her future and that didn't include a romantic relationship. The more she thought about it, the more she decided she'd be wise to stick to those plans and keep her heart safe out of harm's way.

Still, the hurt her words had caused Gabe tugged at her conscience and she resolved to go and see him after her last dance class was over that afternoon. She wouldn't be able to settle until things were right between them.

As hard as she'd tried, Anoushka had struggled to give her classes her full attention. She was relieved when three o'clock came round and the last of her students had trickled away. After a quick tidy round, she was awaiting a parent who'd messaged her earlier and asked if she could bring her daughter to look round the studio with a view to taking lessons there. Despite Anoushka explaining it wasn't really convenient and suggesting several alternative dates, the woman was surprisingly insistent that today would suit her better. Fed up of negotiating, Anoushka had eventually backed down and agreed. From experience, she knew it didn't bode well for a parent to be so inflexible and pushy, and part of her hoped the woman would decide the dance studio wasn't suitable. She envisaged a slew of future complaints if the prospective student wasn't given the starring role in whatever productions the school would put on; she'd witnessed that several times at the dance school in

York where she'd worked. Plus, it delayed the time she could speak to Gabe.

Anoushka glanced at the clock; she was itching to close up and head off to find him – he hadn't replied to her text asking if they could meet up – which made it annoying that the woman was already fifteen minutes late. Maybe she was struggling to find the school? Anoushka wondered. Sat Nav had a habit of dumping drivers a good half-a-mile further down the lane.

By three-thirty, and after texting the woman and getting no reply, Anoushka decided she wasn't going to wait any longer. She gathered her stuff together, slung her bag over her shoulder and headed for the door.

Outside, the courtyard was a blazing suntrap, with heat bouncing back from the ground and the sandstone walls. The hum of bees buzzing around the lavender in the stone planters that were dotted about filled the air. She popped her sunglasses on and walked around the low wall to get to her car, her mobile and keys in her hand.

'Hi there, Anoushka.' She turned to see Zander Gillespie raising his hand in a wave. He was heading towards the newly opened beauty salon, Danskelfe Beauty Rooms. 'Good day?'

'Oh hi, Zander. Yes, you?' She smiled at him.

'Great, thanks.' He beamed. Tall and broad-shouldered, it was easy to see how the GP set so many hearts a-flutter with his film-star good looks and friendly manner.

'How's Livvie doing? Is she still craving pickled onions?' It had been a good few days since Anoushka had seen her friend.

'She fine, a bit hot and bothered in this heat; I'm just on my way to pick up some relaxing bubble bath and book her a special expectant mum's massage as a treat.' He nodded towards the salon. 'And did you know the pickled onion craving's been joined by one for cheese and onion crisps?'

'Wow! No, I didn't; it all sounds very tangy.' Anoushka laughed. 'And I'm sure she'll love her massage.' She surveyed him a moment; he was a man who was so very obviously in love with his wife and she him. The pair exuded undeniable contentedness whenever she saw them together with their little daughter. The thought that she could have such a life with Gabe flashed through her mind. She felt a sudden longing wash over her, but sent it scurrying off a moment later. No, she told herself, a life like that would be unattainable for them, what with his high profile and music keeping him in the public eye. Such an idyllic existence would be well out of their reach; she couldn't live like that. No way. The thought of her picture – and that of any of their potential children – appearing in the gossip columns sent a shiver up her. The very idea was abhorrent!

'You finished for the afternoon?' he asked, pulling her out of her musings.

'Yep, all done.'

'Well, enjoy the rest of your day.' He smiled, pushing his hands into the pockets of his jeans and sauntering in the direction of The Beauty Rooms.

A ping from her mobile phone sent her heart racing. Gabe! She looked down at the screen, her brows knitting together at the unfamiliar number. The word, "CHEAT" glared back at her accusingly. 'What?' she said under her breath, her thoughts heading in one direction.

'You just can't help yourself, can you?'

At hearing the familiar voice, her head shot round, the hairs on the back of her neck stood on end, her heart started thumping hard against her ribcage. 'Damon!' He must have got a new phone, or an extra one.

'You've always got to be throwing yourself at other men, don't you? You should've seen yourself just then, flicking your stupid hair around, flirting with that bloke.' His eyes looked wild. 'You don't even realise you're doing it.'

She swallowed, aware of her pulse thrumming in her ears. 'I wasn't flirting or throwing myself at anyone, Damon. The man I was just talking to is the local GP, his wife's a friend of mine.' She glanced around, hoping to see someone, anyone, but the courtyard was deserted. She prayed that Zander would make an appearance soon.

'Since when has that stopped you?' he said, a cruel sneer spreading over his face. 'And that crap singer with the ridiculous name who's so full of himself. What's he called? Gabe something or other? Don't think I haven't seen how you go on with him.'

Realisation dawned. The feeling she'd had over the last week about being watched was because she *had* been. Damon must have been creeping about while she was teaching and, worse, when she'd been giving Gabe his salsa lesson. Goosebumps erupted over her skin. 'You've been spying on me?'

'Ah, so you don't deny it then?'

'I don't have to answer to you anymore, Damon, we broke up quite a while ago, remember? You've got no right to be here, stalking me.' She felt her anger rising.

'Stalking? I'm not stalking!' His eyes took on a sinister glare and his top lip curled into its familiar snarl. 'I've got every right to come up here to see what's been going on.'

Fear gripped Anoushka but she did her best to keep her voice calm. 'No you don't; you've got no right to be creeping about spying on me, and if you don't leave right now, I'm calling the police.' Though it was harder than she could ever have imagined, she held eye contact with him and was surprised when his snarl faltered and he appeared to back down.

'You're not worth wasting my time on; you're nothing. I don't know why I bothered with you in the first place.' He turned and strode angrily away, disappearing around the corner of the end building.

Shaking, she let go a juddery sigh, squeezing her eyes tight shut as she did so. She needed to get away from here as soon as she could. Away from Damon.

As she was heading over to her car, a surge of anger suddenly nudged her feeling of anxiety out of the way; this was so typical of Damon to make her feel like this. How dare he make her feel threatened at her dance studio? He had no right! He had no claims on her.

She was almost at her car when another text messaged pinged through, it was from the woman she'd stayed back for. She stopped to read it; the woman was apologising for being late, saying she'd got lost but was now on her way. Anoushka became suddenly aware of the roar of an engine followed by Zander's voice shouting her name. In the next moment, she felt herself being catapulted across the gravel, her own scream loud in her ears.

THIRTY-THREE

'Anoushka? Anoushka? Anoushka, are you okay?'

Dazed, she gradually realised Zander was talking to her. Somewhere in the distance, she was half-aware of a red car shooting off, sending a shower of gravel into the air. She blinked and looked up at the concerned face peering down at her, her brain struggling to process his words. 'Um... I... yes, I think so...' She tried to move and winced. 'Ouch! My arm...' It was alive with a burning sensation. 'My leg...'

'Did you bump your head?'

'No, I don't think so.' She sensed her head was resting on something soft and lumpy: her bag; it must've saved her from hitting her head against the ground. What had just happened?

'Good, that's something. Do you think you can stand up?' Though Zander's voice was calm, his eyes were filled with concern.

She nodded, too stunned to cry despite the pain she was in. 'I'll try.'

'What's been goin—?' Rachel, the beautician, came rushing out of her salon, stopping stock still. 'Oh, my God! Are you all right?' She hurried over to them, her pretty face wrought with disbelief.

'Yeah, I think so.' Anoushka nodded again. She caught sight of her sunglasses on the floor; they'd shot off with the impact and now one of the lenses was shattered into tiny pieces.

'Here, let me help you,' said Zander. Gingerly, he helped her to her feet, Rachel on the other side of her, and she limped her way over to the wall where he sat her down. She noticed the sleeve on his shirt had been ripped, blood was seeping through the pale blue fabric.

'Your arm,' she said, her voice barely a whisper.

'It's fine; it's just a graze.' He gently lifted the sleeve of her T-shirt to get a better look at her injury. 'I'm sorry I came flying at you, it's just, well... he seemed to veer away at the last moment, but there was no time to risk it.'

'It's okay, I understand... I'm grateful.' She was still trying to process what had happened, her mind too much of a jumble to form a full sentence.

He pressed his lips together and nodded. 'I'll just nip to my car and get my medical bag so I can get this cleaned up; I'll be two ticks.'

'Okay.' She sat, taking in her skinned right arm and leg, her ripped trousers, pieces of gravel embedded in the wound.

'What happened?' asked Rachel. 'I just heard the sound of an engine revving like crazy, then heard a load of shouting before the driver shot off. I came out to see you on the floor.'

'I don't... I'm not really sure,' Anoushka said, her voice wavery. What would have happened if Zander hadn't been there? Panic lurched inside her, setting nausea churning in her stomach. Before she knew it, shock had kicked in and she started shaking, tears streaming down her cheeks.

'Oh, chick, don't cry,' said Rachel, rubbing Anoushka's good arm. 'You're going to be okay. Doctor Gillespie'll get you cleaned up.'

'Sorry, I'm just... I can't believe what's just happened.' Anoushka leant her head on Rachel's shoulder and sobbed as the beautician stroked her hair.

'Hey, I'm not surprised; and you don't need to apologise.'

Zander reached into his pocket for a tissue, handing it to her. 'It's okay, Noushka, you've had an awful shock.'

'Thanks.' She took it and dabbed her eyes.

'So have you any idea who was behind the wheel?' he asked.

She nodded, her stomach clenching. 'I'm pretty certain it'll have been Damon.'

'You mean your ex, Damon?'

She nodded again. 'I can't believe he'd do something like that. Would he have swerved if you hadn't been there? If he hadn't, he would've... his car would've hit me and I would be...' She couldn't bring herself to put her fears into words.

'He was probably only trying to scare you, rather than injure you,' said Zander.

'Well, he's certainly succeeded in that,' said Anoushka.

Rachel looked on, her mouth hanging open in disbelief.

'Making someone fearful is all part and parcel of coercive controlling behaviour. It'll have been his way of taking back an element of control over you, of your feelings,' Zander said.

'Blimey. I didn't think things like that happened round here,' said Rachel.

'They don't, as a rule.' Zander sat down beside Anoushka, carefully lifting the sleeve of her T-shirt. 'Do you mind if I treat this?' he asked.

'No.' She shook her head and sniffed, watching as he rifled through his medical bag.

After cutting away the tattered parts of her sleeve, he set about removing the ripped leg of her trousers. 'Sorry about this, but needs must.' Working swiftly, he doused her injuries with antiseptic wound spray before carefully removing the gravel with tweezers, explaining what he was doing as he worked. His soothing tone helped to calm her. And though he was concentrating on treating his patient, the expression on his face said he was more than a little concerned by the turn of events.

'There, done. It might be a good idea to pop over to the surgery on Monday, and get Jill, the practice nurse, to change the dressings and give them a quick check over.' He sat back on his haunches. 'Again, I'm sorry I had to hack at your trousers.'

Anoushka looked down at her tattered clothing, the padded dressings on her injuries. 'That's okay. But what about your arm? That looks like it needs some attention.'

'I'll be fine, it's nothing compared to yours; my legs weren't skinned like yours; my thick jeans took the brunt of my fall. Like your bag saved you from a nasty bump to the head.' His face turned serious. 'So, have you any idea why Damon would behave the way he did?'

Anoushka nodded. Taking a fortifying breath, she shared what had happened before the car had come flying towards her.

Rachel's hand flew to her mouth. 'Oh, my God! Seriously? He shouldn't be walking the streets; he's a psychopath.'

'Rachel's right, and he's clearly dangerous – or at the very least, reckless – we don't know what he might do next.' Zander paused a moment, his expression serious. 'You do realise we need to report this to the police, don't you, Anoushka?'

His words sent a spike of fear through her, but she knew he was right. 'Yes. I always knew he had a temper on him, but nothing like—'

She was cut off by a car driving into the courtyard. It appeared to be heading in the direction of the dance school, sending her heart rate rocketing once more. 'Who's this?' she said, panic in her voice as her body tensed.

'I don't know; I don't recognise the car,' said Zander. 'But they're driving calmly so there's nothing to worry about.' He rested a reassuring hand gently on her shoulder.

The three of them watched as a woman stepped out of the vehicle, her eyes searching the facades of the buildings, finally alighting on the dance school's sign. She had a kind face and, from what Anoushka could gather, her body language didn't appear to be hostile.

The woman walked towards them, taking in Anoushka's T-shirt, her brows knitting together. 'Anoushka Cartwright?' she asked.

'Who's asking?' Zander got to his feet, pulling himself up to his full height of well over six feet.

'I'm, er, I'm Gina. I had an appointment to look around the dance studio, only I'm late. Sorry...' She glanced across at Anoushka, her expression uncertain. 'I had trouble getting away and then I got a bit lost.'

A feeling of relief was quickly followed by one of dread; with all the drama, Anoushka had forgotten about the meeting and the last thing she needed right now was to play hostess and dance teacher when what she wanted more than anything was to get to the safety of home and have a soothing cup of tea. She couldn't even face seeing Gabe; she'd have to find another time for that conversation.

'I'm Anoushka. And I hope you don't mind, but I think it might be better if we re-arrange it,' she said, the bright sunshine making her squint. Though she hadn't bumped her head, a dull ache had crept in, squeezing at her temples.

'Like I said, I'm really sorry I'm late.' Gina bit down on her bottom lip.

Just as well you didn't come sooner and have to witness what had happened not fifteen minutes ago. 'That's okay, but if you don't mind, I'll contact you to rearrange a suitable time; now's a bit... difficult.' If Anoushka didn't know better, she'd think the woman looked awkward, anxious even. She glanced across at the car; there was no sign of the daughter Gina had referred to. Something about this "meeting" didn't feel quite right.

Gina's gaze shifted between the three of them. 'Oh... um, right.' She hesitated, her expression suddenly changing. 'Has something happened? You look as though you've been involved in an accident.'

'Yeah, you could say, but we're fine now, just a bit dazed.' Anoushka didn't want to go into detail with a stranger.

'Actually, if you wouldn't mind, I think Anoushka needs to get home.' Zander had clearly picked up on the odd vibe too.

Gina swallowed, her eyes bearing a hint of what looked – if Anoushka wasn't mistaken – like fear. 'Listen, I didn't really come here to look around the studio; I don't have a daughter who wants lessons. I'm here to warn you about someone.' She licked her lips nervously, glancing around her. 'I'd have preferred to talk to you alone, Anoushka, but I understand that you probably wouldn't feel comfortable doing that. Only, it would be safer if we could go somewhere... private, out of view.' She glanced around her again, like a frightened animal. 'I'm just, well, I'm scared someone might hear.'

Anoushka felt fear spiralling inside her. What on earth could she have to say?

'I'd be happy to stay with you, if that would help, Noushka?' said Zander.

'I'm afraid I have to get back, I've a client due any minute,' said Rachel, glancing at her watch. 'But let me know if you need anything, or if there's anything I can do, okay?' She reached out and squeezed Anoushka's hand.

'Thanks, Rachel. And thanks for helping me.'

'No problem.' She gave a kind smile.

Inside the dance studio, Anoushka led Zander and Gina to the seating area, ensuring the blinds were closed. It appeared to make Gina more relaxed, the tension in her shoulders easing a little.

'So what is it you wanted to speak to me about?' Anoushka asked as Zander handed her some painkillers then got busy making tea for the three of them. She took a moment to study Gina's face, her instinct telling her she was genuine, decent.

Gina sucked in a deep breath. 'I've battled with whether or not I should say anything to you for ages. Ever since I first heard you were linked to...' She paused, apparently considering her words. 'My sister, Stevie, was married to someone you know; someone who's nasty and vindictive...'

Anoushka's stomach lurched. She had a horrible feeling she knew where this was going.

THIRTY-FOUR

'He doesn't happen to be called Damon Swales does he?'
Anoushka asked, her eyes flicking to Zander who was looking trou-
bled as he headed over with the tea. 'Thanks.' With a shaking
hand, she took the mug he held out to her.

'Yes, I'm afraid he does,' said Gina, fear returning to her eyes.
'But, before I go any further, Damon must never find out I've been
speaking to you.' She looked at Anoushka pleadingly. 'I've taken a
big risk coming here; I didn't want to commit anything to a text or a
written message for fear of him somehow finding out. And I didn't
want to tell you over the phone. I thought you'd think I was mad;
that I was making it up or exaggerating. I needed to tell you face-to-
face.'

'I promise you, I won't mention a word to Damon,' Anoushka
said earnestly

Gina released a juddery sigh. 'Good.'

Content with Anoushka's assurances, Gina began telling how
her sister, Stevie, had met Damon when she was seventeen. 'At the
time, she was bright and bubbly – looked quite like you actually –
pretty, with long blonde hair,' she said. Like Anoushka, Damon
had been Stevie's first serious boyfriend, and in the early days, he'd
been all charm and romance, sweeping her off her feet with grand

gestures. Stevie hadn't noticed when things had started to change, when his controlling behaviour had begun to creep in like a pernicious weed, infiltrating every part of her life. Before she'd realised what was happening, he'd managed to isolate her from her family and friends and had talked her into giving up her college place in favour of staying at his apartment, looking after him.

Anxiety curdled in Anoushka's stomach; it all sounded scarily familiar.

Gina went on to say how, at eighteen – despite her family's warnings – Stevie had married him, with just his brother and sister-in-law in attendance as witnesses. Needless to say, her family had been frantic with worry.

'Stevie ended up having a breakdown, which was when we managed to get her back; bring her home.' Tears fell from Gina's eyes, running in rivulets down her cheeks. She dashed them away with her fingers. 'She was in a terrible state, but it was such a relief to have her back, away from him. But even then, he wouldn't leave her alone, kept hounding her. He'd watch the house, wait for us to leave, then start hammering on the door, calling through the letter box. He even had the nerve to start sending huge bouquets of flowers, and letters, telling her how much he loved her, that they belonged together.' She shook her head at the memory. 'He had a funny way of showing it. That was three years ago.'

'How's Stevie now?' Anoushka asked, her heart going out to the young woman and her family.

Gina gave a watery smile. 'She's much better since the divorce, thanks; she's finally been able to move on. It's taken a while for her to be able to trust again, but she's just started dating someone new. Baby steps...'

'That's good to hear.' Anoushka paused, thoughtful for a moment. 'So what made him stop hounding her?'

'Stevie took out a restraining order; he started seeing you pretty much straight after; your presence in his life seemed to take his mind off her which was a huge relief.' Gina looked almost apologetic.

'Oh, right.' Anoushka let the young woman's words sink in. 'You know we've split up?'

Gina nodded. 'I'd heard, which is why I'm here. A friend of mine had overheard him talking to someone in a pub in York. Apparently Damon had been drinking heavily and had started saying how he'd been treated badly by his latest girlfriend, went on to say he wasn't going to let her get away with it. We knew who you were 'cos we'd been keeping an eye on his social media posts. We felt we had to warn you.'

Anoushka pressed her hand to her mouth, glancing over at Zander who'd been listening quietly throughout. 'He was here today; not long before you arrived,' she said.

Gina visibly tensed. 'Oh my God. He was here?' She glanced fearfully between Anoushka and Zander.

'Don't worry, he shot off like a bat out of hell; he'll have been long gone before you got here,' said Zander. 'And I dare say you'd have noticed a red car flying along the country lanes at break-neck speed.'

'I didn't spot anything like that,' she said, visibly relieved. She turned to Anoushka. 'So what was he doing here?' Her eyes widened as realisation slowly dawned. 'Your accident? Don't tell me he was involved.'

'He was.'

'No!' Gina clapped her hands to her mouth.

'You're really going to have to contact the police, Noushka,' said Zander, his tone grave. 'Maybe take out some kind of restraining order on him. I'll provide a statement if one's needed. He's already proved he can be reckless; he needs stopping before he goes too far.'

A feeling of unease ran through Anoushka. She knew Zander was right. 'I'll get in touch with PC Snaith right away and make an appointment with a solicitor if necessary.' She hoped she wouldn't have another encounter with Damon before anything got put in place. She rested her hand on Gina's arm. 'Thank you so much for coming here today, and for warning me. I appreciate it can't have been easy. Poor Stevie's been through a horrible time; I'm just glad I got away from him when I did. Please would you tell her I wish her every happiness for her future.'

'I will.' Gina got to her feet and smiled. 'I'd best be off but I'm glad I told you; it feels like a weight off my shoulders. I'd never have forgiven myself if anything had happened to you.'

'It's been good to meet you, Gina; I'm just sorry it wasn't in better circumstances.' Anoushka went to hug the other woman, being careful of her sore arm.

Once Gina had left, Zander said, 'Don't forget to talk to PC Snaith as soon as possible.' He reached for his bag.

'I won't. I'll contact him as soon as I get home; I don't want to risk Damon coming back.' She gave him a quick smile. 'And thank you for everything, for getting me out of the way and for sorting out my injuries.'

'Hey, no worries. Pop into the surgery on Monday, get your dressings changed. I'll mention it to the practice nurse, tell her to expect you. She'll be able to check it's healing okay too.' He smiled kindly. 'Would you like me to stick around until you're ready to leave?'

She released a slow breath. How on earth had it come to this?

'I'll head off now,' she said, the thought of what she'd say to her parents spinning around her mind.

THIRTY-FIVE

Much as she hadn't wanted to concern them, Anoushka had reluctantly told her parents what had happened with Damon, and the subsequent conversation with Gina. She'd added that she didn't want Lucas and Lily to know about it; she didn't want them upset or worse, scared – and she most definitely didn't want a fuss. Kitty and Ollie had listened with ashen faces, with Kitty rushing over to her, carefully hugging her close. 'Oh, lovey, that must've been terrifying for you.'

'The cowardly little worm isn't going to get away with this!' her dad had said through clenched teeth, his chest heaving as he leapt to his feet and started heading for the door.

'Ollie! Don't! You can't do anything.' Kitty's eyes had been filled with fear as she'd pulled on his arm.

Barely able to contain his anger, Ollie had shoved his fingers into his hair, pushing out air between his teeth. 'At least let me call PC Snaith.'

'Okay.' Kitty had looked visibly relieved.

An hour later, the local bobby called round and took a statement.

'Your ex has put you in fear, using his car as a weapon; he could be prosecuted if you want to go down the criminal proceedings route,' PC Snaith, who never seemed to look a day over fourteen, had said. 'You could potentially have a non-molestation or restraining order taken out against him; he'd be in bother if he breached either of those. Or if you'd prefer not to proceed that way, I could ask one of my colleagues in York to call round at your ex's and have a word with him? Do you think he's the sort of person who'd take notice of that?'

Anoushka nodded, she thought Damon would hate being effectively "told off" by the police. And, fearful of antagonising him any further, it felt more palatable than going down the courts and prosecution route right now; she didn't want something like that hanging over her. 'I think I'd prefer it if your colleagues just had a word with him for now; he won't like that at all,' she'd said. 'And if he turns up round here again, then I'll think about taking legal proceedings.'

'Fair enough.' Uttering assurances that Damon would receive a visit from a York police officer that day, PC Snaith had left to take a statement from Zander.

After he'd gone, Anoushka had headed up to her bedroom and stretched out on her bed, her head thumping. The whole thing had left a horrible taste in her mouth. She'd texted Brogan and Kristy and shared what had happened with them, swearing them to secrecy. She'd been too tired to tell them everything in great detail, promising to do that later when she felt a bit more with it, but the pair turned up on Sunday morning armed with flowers and chocolates and words of concern.

'Bloomin' 'eck, Noushka, you had a lucky escape there. Imagine if you'd moved in with him then found out all that. Makes my skin crawl just thinking about it,' said Brogan, giving a theatrical shudder after hearing about his ex-wife.

'Damon *always* made my skin crawl; there was something just too smooth, too perfect about him,' said Kristy, her nose scrunching with distaste. 'I'm just so glad you came to your senses when you did, chick.' She wrapped her arm around Anoushka's neck and hugged her gently. 'Flaming heck, Noushka, to think you could've ended up like that poor lass, Stevie; doesn't bear thinking about.'

'You've got to promise that if he shows up again, you'll call someone. Me and Kristy will be with you quick as a flash if ever you need us.' Brogan looked serious.

'Too right. I'd love an excuse to kick the little worm's backside right out of the village.' Kristy's eyes flashed angrily.

'Same here; I'll be right behind you with my great, hefty biker boots,' said Brogan.

Anoushka couldn't help but smile. 'Thanks, lasses, I appreciate that. And I promise I'll call someone if he turns up round here, but like I said, not a word to anyone, okay?'

'Okay,' they both said.

Anoushka had woken on Monday morning, relieved she didn't have to face any dance lessons that day – Sunday and Monday were her days off, the dance school closed. As Zander had instructed, she popped over to the surgery at Danskelfe where Jill the practice nurse checked over her wounds. 'Ooh, they're healing nicely,' she said. 'I'm going to put another dressing on for now. And, I know it's tricky and you'll feel like you've got to be a contortionist when you're in the bath or the shower, but if you can carry on keeping them nice and dry just like you have been doing, they should be able to come off next time I see you; it'll be good to let the air get to them by then. Just pop in again on Wednesday; I'm here 'til five o'clock, so any time before then'll be fine.' Her sympathetic smile suggested Zander had explained how Anoushka had sustained her injuries.

As she made her way home, Anoushka's thoughts turned back to Gabe, a pang of guilt filling her chest.

Her mind had been too full of everything that had happened on Saturday for her to even start thinking about getting in touch with him. But as she headed down the country lanes towards Lytell Stangdale, seeing the flags fluttering at Danskelfe Castle, she made up her mind to seek him out that very afternoon. She'd already decided she wasn't going to let Damon get to her, which she knew would be easier said than done, but his aim was to direct her attention towards him and she wasn't going to give him the satisfaction. She was going to leave him to the police.

Once home, she changed out of the loose jersey T-shirt dress she'd worn to make it easy for Jill to change her dressings, and pulled on a pair of khaki combat trousers and a long-sleeved T-shirt that covered her injured arm – she'd already made up her mind she didn't want Gabe to know about what had happened with Damon. Not just because she couldn't face another round of questions about her ex, but she didn't want the topic of conversation to revolve around that. Finally, she released her hair from its messy up-do and wove it into two plaits.

She checked her phone, disappointed to see there was nothing from the person she'd hoped most to hear from. Despite texting him twice that morning, Gabe still hadn't replied though she could see her messages had been delivered. *He's still ignoring me; he must still be hurting.* The radio silence spurred her on to head up to the castle right away, see if she could track him down.

'What are your plans for the afternoon?' Ollie asked as he took a bite from his sandwich.

'I'm going to head out for a bit.' Anoushka was reluctant to say where she was going, not wanting to encourage any speculation about her and Gabe, especially considering the conversation she wanted to have with him. It was the last thing she needed. She could see from the look in her parents' eyes they were desperate to know, their worry for her being so great after what she'd imparted yesterday. She could completely understand; she'd feel the same if it had happened to Lily. But, much as she didn't want to give them a reason to worry, she remained resolute not to share her reason for going out. 'Don't worry, I'll be careful.'

'Make sure you are, chick,' said Kitty. 'Though I'm sure you'll be absolutely fine.' She mustered up a smile.

'Aye, I get that you don't want to stay cooped up, but just keep your wits about you, Noushka, 'til we know that maniac's properly under control. And if anything, anything at all, gives you cause for concern, no matter how small, get in touch with me or your mum and we'll be with you like a shot,' her dad said, his voice laced with concern.

'Of course I will.' Their warnings, though well meant, set anxiety squirming in her stomach but she did her best to quash it. She kissed them both goodbye, popped on her bucket hat and stepped out into the sunshine.

Fifteen minutes later, Anoushka's car nosed its way into the castle courtyard, the building's vast sandstone walls looming over her, sunlight glinting off them. Being this close up gave a greater sense of its size and presence; perched high on its craggy plinth, it seemed to grow out of the rocks. She was disappointed to see there was no sign of Gabe's car so she reversed out and drove away, suddenly recalling him mentioning something about moving out of the castle and into one of the new lodges. With this in mind, she headed down the private track that wove its way to them.

After driving by a couple of newly constructed timber buildings with unfamiliar cars parked outside, she spotted one with Gabe's four-wheel drive beside it. Her heart rate picked up and she felt a flurry of nerves in her stomach. She'd rehearsed what she wanted to say to him all the way here, but now her mind had gone utterly blank. 'Oh, jeez,' she said under her breath as she pulled on the handbrake. It would have been so easy to turn back, but the thought of him being hurt by her words had been eating away at her, and she was determined to smooth things over with him.

Knocking at the door several times, it was obvious Gabe wasn't home. She stood for a moment, gazing around her, the heady scent of the rose in the pot by the door lingering on the warm air, butterflies dancing over its petals. Anoushka sighed. Maybe he'd taken Bob for a walk, she thought. She turned and set off down the track that led to the moors high up on Danskelfe Rigg, hoping with all her might she'd find him.

She did her best to ignore the sting in her injured leg as she followed the dusty path. The cry of a buzzard echoed around the dale and she glanced up to see it soaring high up in the clear blue sky. A couple of ewes with their lambs from Finn Tindall's flock of sheep from Castlegate Farm were chewing their cud, watching her with interest as she headed past them. One of them gave a plaintive bleat which set off a chorus as the others joined in.

The sun was blazing down relentlessly and a trickle of sweat ran down her back, making her wish she hadn't had to wear a long-sleeved top, but needs must; it was the only way she could hide the dressing on her arm.

Before long, the gentle strum of a guitar reached her ears, a familiar voice singing along softly. Gabe! Her heart fluttered in her chest. She followed the sound, noting the tune had a slightly melancholy feel to it, and before long, she spotted a figure sitting on a weather-smoothed rock, hunched over an acoustic guitar. Bob was stretched out on the grass beside him, his head on his paws, looking out over the view.

Here goes, she thought as she headed towards them, her stomach performing somersaults.

She was halfway there when Bob jumped up and turned to look at her, his tail wagging frantically. Gabe followed his gaze, a smile lighting up his face when he spotted her. 'Rose!' he said, his smile suddenly falling, memory of her words no doubt creeping in and wiping it away.

As she got closer she forced herself to ignore her jittery insides and the little voice that was telling her coming here was a mistake. 'Hi, Gabe.' She smiled back, raising her hand in a small wave. Bob whimpered and shot over to her, his lead trailing behind him. 'And hello, Bob, this is a lovely welcome,' she said as she bent to ruffle his ears.

Gabe had set his guitar down and got to his feet by the time she'd reached him. His skin had been kissed by the sun, she noticed, and the tips of his hair bleached golden-blond. A bolt of attraction shot through her, making her feel wrong-footed, leaving the words she'd planned to say scrambled in her mind.

'What are you doing here? Is everything all right?' he asked, taking his sunglasses off. The rich tone of his voice and the soft look in his eyes made her heart ache.

She cleared her throat and smiled up at him, her nerve wavering. 'Yeah, it's fine.' *Go for it! Don't back out now!* 'I just wanted to clear something up with you, if that's okay? Something I said in the pub the other night that I think you might have overheard.' She swallowed, blimey, this was hard. 'It's just I didn't really mean—'

He raised his palms. 'Hey, it's okay, there's really no need.' He returned her smile, though it didn't quite reach his eyes. She felt another tug at her heart.

THIRTY-SIX

Undeterred, she continued. 'It's just, when Kristy and Brogan get started on that topic of conversation, there's no stopping them and I really needed them to ease up with it that night. I love them to bits, and I know they mean well, but, it gets too much sometimes. And since Damon, well, you know.' Mentioning his name sent a burst of anxiety shooting through her, putting a stop to her gabbling.

'I get it. Stop beating yourself up about it; we're cool.'

She heaved a sigh of relief. 'We are?'

'We are.' He nodded and smiled again, this time it crinkled his eyes, making her heart do its familiar leap.

'Oh, thank goodness. I'd hate for you to—'

'Like I said, just forget about it.'

Bob nudged her leg with his head, catching where it was sore. Her face crumpled with pain. She went to stroke the Labrador's velvety head again, hoping Gabe hadn't noticed her reaction. 'I heard you singing, it sounded lovely. Is it something new?' She peered up at him.

'It's my next single; the first one from my new album. It's due for release at the end of August,' he said, a puzzled expression on his face.

'Oh, right.' Anoushka hated how this felt so awkward. 'What's it called? I'll be sure to download it.'

He paused a moment. 'My Rose-Shaped Heart.' His eyes sought hers.

'Oh.' She felt colour flood her cheeks. He'd called her Rose a few times since she'd told him it was her middle name. Why did she get the feeling it was a reference to that? Or was she simply over-thinking things?

His gaze forced her mind to search for something to take the conversation in a different direction. 'So, the weather's been gorgeous.' *The weather? Are you serious?* She groaned inwardly at her pathetic choice of topic.

'It has; not sure how long it can last like this.' He smiled, brushing his fringe back off his forehead.

'Who can tell on the North Yorkshire Moors? It can be blazing sunshine one week and freak hailstorms the next,' she said. They both gave an awkward laugh.

Anoushka glanced around her, feeling suddenly self-conscious. 'So, how long are you here for?'

''Til mid-August; we're shooting the video for my new song here on the moors of the Danskelfe Estate in a couple of weeks' time. Then, a couple of days after that I'll be heading down to London to tie up a few loose ends, and do an interview on *The Tina Stone Show*.'

'Oh, wow! *The Tina Stone Show*? That's awesome.' The host of the chat show had been taking the country by storm with her friendly, yet disarming conversational manner that managed to make her guests believe she was their best friend and confide in her over a cup of tea poured from a china teapot. She was like a cool big sister, and had a happy knack of winkling information out of her guests without them even realising. Even big-name stars had found themselves quite happily spilling their guts, seemingly unaware that they were doing so.

'I'm not so sure about that.' Gabe pulled a regretful face. 'But my manager and my record label seemed to think it was a good idea

– *another one* – to help promote the new the album. I, however, can think of way better things to be doing with my time, that's for sure. As soon as I'm done, I'll be heading back here as fast as my legs – or, rather, the train – can carry me.'

'I'm sure you'll have a great time; Tina always seems really friendly and her guests always look like they're enjoying her banter.'

Gabe heaved a sigh. 'Yeah, I suppose they do,' he said, though he didn't look convinced.

They stood in companionable silence for a while, Bob between them, his ears twitching at the sounds of the countryside that filled the air. Anoushka's gaze roamed over the view of the dale. It was a picture of bucolic perfection, yet somehow incongruous set against the storm that was currently raging in her heart. The patchwork of fields set out before them were a vibrant mixture of lush greens interspersed with rectangles of pale golds where stubble remained after the silaging had been done. Large, round bales of hay were set out in neat rows, ready for collection and storage, while in others, cows or sheep grazed idly under the heat of the afternoon sun.

Anoushka drew in a lungful of sultry air, hints of Gabe's cologne threaded through it. She was suddenly conscious that no further communication would be forthcoming from him and she felt a pang of regret. This new awkwardness between them didn't sit right with her, but after what he'd overheard last week, what could she expect? 'Well, I suppose I'd best head back home,' she said, giving him a small smile.

He turned to face her. 'It's been good to see you, Noushka; I appreciate you coming to talk to me.' He reached out, pressing his fingertips gently against her arm, pulling back sharply when she flinched. 'What's wrong? Are you okay? Have I hurt you?' His brow creased with concern as his eyes went to her arm.

'I... it's just... sorry. It's nothing; just me being silly.' She cursed herself for reacting in such a way.

Bob, sensing something was amiss, parked himself in front of

Anoushka, resting his paw on her foot and whimpering as he gazed up at her.

'It's okay, Bob.' She gave him a quick scratch between the ears.

'That reaction didn't suggest it was nothing. What's happened to your arm? Have you hurt it?' Gabe asked. 'It felt like there was some sort of padding under your T-shirt.'

Anoushka rubbed her hand over the back of her neck, struggling to meet his eyes. She really didn't want to have to explain about Damon. 'Like I said, it's nothing; just me being clumsy. I fell over, skinned it. Luckily Zander was there when it happened so he was able to dress it for me.'

'Right,' Gabe said slowly. She could feel the intensity of his gaze on her. When she eventually made eye contact with him, the look she met told her he didn't quite believe her.

'I'm fine.' She flashed him a smile. 'Honest, I am. I got a fresh dressing put on it this morning and it's healing really well. It'll be good as new in no time.'

'Okay, if you're sure,' he said slowly, his eyes still locked on hers.

She felt a flutter in her stomach as her emotions took off. *No way! Don't go there!* She took a moment to steady her thoughts. 'Right, well, it's been good to see you, Gabe, and you too, Bob.' She smoothed the Labrador's silky head and he nudged her hand, giving it a quick lick. 'I'll see you later.' She smiled again before turning away.

'See you, Rose.' Gabe's voice floated after her, accompanied by another whimper from Bob.

Why did walking away from him like this feel so wrong? she wondered. An image of herself sitting beside him on the rock, his arm flung around her, her head resting on his shoulder, filled her mind. *Why are you fighting these feelings?* a little voice asked her.

Wrong time, she replied. We're just not meant to be. Simple as that.

THIRTY-SEVEN

Two weeks had passed since the incident with Damon. Gradually, the unsettling feeling that he could appear at any moment had trickled away and Anoushka had allowed herself to relax again. An officer from the police station over at York had paid Damon a visit the evening he'd driven at her and laid down the law in no uncertain terms. Damon had been mortified at the threat of yet another restraining order being taken out against him, apparently objecting vociferously, saying Anoushka had "imagined it all" and how she had asked him to call round and hadn't been looking where she was going and had "stepped out in front of him as he drove away". But the police officer was having none of it and Damon had eventually backed down.

Anoushka hoped it would mean he'd leave her alone.

It was the last Sunday in July and Anoushka was sitting on the swing seat in the garden, her nose in a book when her mobile started ringing. She picked it up to see Gabe's number, a thrill shooting through her that set her heart galloping.

'Gabe?'

'Noushka, thank God you picked up! Are you busy?' His voice sounded urgent.

'No, I'm just sitting in the garden. Why? Is everything okay?'

'Ughh! Jaysus, no, it's so not! We're shooting the video for my new single and we've run into one hell of a problem.'

'Oh, no.' Her brows drew together. Why was he calling her about it?

'I honestly can't believe this is feckin' happening. The model, you know Lilith Dean? She's sick. She's picked up some bug and has been puking up all over the place; she's too ill to work, poor woman. And I wouldn't ask this unless... I mean, if we don't get the filming done today we're going to lose a shedload of money, never mind not know when we can reschedule it; it's impossible... we've left it so late...' He released an exasperated sigh. 'So, I wondered, well, 'cos I know you did drama as well as dance at uni, I wondered if you'd maybe help out?' Anticipation hung heavy in his voice.

'*Me?*' What could she do? she wondered.

'Yeah, you; you'd be awesome.'

'What? You mean you want me to—' Her eyes widened as what he was asking dawned on her.

'Yeah, yeah. Please, Noushka, we're desperate. I mean... ughh! Sorry, I'm a clumsy eejit; I didn't mean it to sound that way, but it'd be great if you'd stand in for Lilith. I just know you'd be brilliant,' he said. 'It's very straightforward, I'll explain all when you get here. In fact, why don't I come and get you? If you'll do it, that is? Please say you will; we're completely knackered if you don't.'

'No pressure then,' she said with a nervous laugh as she tried to process the implications of what he was asking of her.

'Yeah, I know. I'm sorry.'

She scratched her head, feeling utterly torn. 'Gabe, I really don't know...'

'I know you hate the thought of being in the limelight but I give you my word, your identity will remain a secret.' He sighed heavily. 'Please, Noushka, you'd be helping out a mate. We've already had to cancel it once before; we're running out of time. The deadline's tight.'

Before her brain knew what was happening the words, 'Okay,

I'll do it,' were out of her mouth and Gabe was whooping down the phone. *Oh, jeez, what have I done?*

'Ah, my lovely Rose, thank you. Thank you! You'll be absolutely, fantastic! The director will love you! Everyone will!'

'What about clothes? My hair?' She fingered one of her plaits, eyeing it doubtfully. 'My makeup?'

'Don't worry about that, we've got loads of stuff and people here who can organise all of that.' His voice sounded giddy with happiness. 'Thanks again, Noushka; I'll be with you in a flash.'

'Gabe, and what about—' Her voiced tailed off as she realised he'd gone, doubts sending her insides into a frenzy of nerves. She clapped her hand to her forehead. 'What have I just agreed to?'

THIRTY-EIGHT

Fifteen minutes later, hearing the sound of a car coming to a halt outside Oak Tree Farm, Anoushka opened the front door to see Gabe hurtling up the path. He came to an abrupt halt as he set eyes on her. 'Noushka,' he said softly. He smiled, clearly knocked off kilter for a moment as he took in her skin, made golden by the sun, against the white of her broderie anglaise dress with loose-fitting bodice and lace straps, one of which had slipped off her shoulder.

'Hi, Gabe.' She smiled back. Despite the anxiety that was twisting in her stomach, a bolt of attraction shot through her. *Oh my days!* She didn't need that right now!

'Thanks for doing this; you're a real life-saver,' he said. 'We'd best get going before Jake blows a gasket – he's the director, by the way.'

'Oh, no. I hope he doesn't do that.' Gabe's comment did nothing to ease her nerves as an image of a red-faced man, barking out instructions, loomed in her mind.

Gabe flashed her a grin, his teeth extra white in his sun-kissed face. 'Don't worry, as soon as he sees you he'll be a pussycat.'

'But what about my arm? That won't look good in the video.' She glanced down. It was healing well, but there was no getting away from the large area where it had scabbed over. It was the same for her leg, but that was currently covered by her dress.

'Honestly, it won't be a problem. I've already mentioned it to Jake and he's cool with it. Any shots with it in can be cut out.'

'Okay.' She felt relieved at that.

They whizzed along the roads to the castle, by-passing its vast walls and heading down a track where a clutch of cars, a couple of large white vans, and a straggle of people soon came into view. It looked to be a hive of activity. Gabe pulled up behind one of the vans and climbed out of his four-wheel drive. With her heart pounding, Anoushka followed him. After a few hurried words with who she assumed was Jake the director, Gabe stood back, revealing a tousled-haired man in his late thirties. Beads of perspiration peppered his face and he was wearing an expression of utter irritation. Her heart sank.

He managed a smile before he spoke. 'Hi, Anoushka, I'm Jake. Thanks for this. Gabe tells me you've studied drama?'

'Mm-hm, that's right.' He elicited the same feelings in her as a rather strict headmaster she once had at secondary school.

'Okay, well, I don't mean to sound rude, but I need to see how you get on with the camera before we get started, so if you could just head over there and follow my directions, that'd be great.'

'Okay.' She knew he'd want to see if she looked natural rather than awkward, make sure she didn't over-exaggerate her gestures.

Once Dave the cameraman had finished shooting her from various angles, she hovered by Bob who was sitting in the shade, panting heavily. She looked on as Gabe was busy chatting to Jake. Both men were nodding their heads enthusiastically and smiling broadly.

'Oh, thank you, God,' Jake said, a broad smile spreading across his face. He turned to Gabe. 'You're right, she's perfect. She looks like an angel.'

'That's exactly what I said when I first set eyes on her.' Gabe released a wistful sigh.

'And I don't want her to change out of that dress she's wearing;

it's exactly the look I'm after.' Jake was beaming like he'd won the lottery.

Gabe headed over to her, thrilled to be sharing the news that Jake was a happy man once more. 'You've really saved the day, Noushka.' He smiled at her. 'I just need to go and get tidied up, before the band and me are filmed, then it'll be your turn.'

With his hair and make-up fixed, Gabe joined the rest of his band and the chords to his new single struck up, his rich, smoky voice filling the air. Anoushka was suddenly struck by the familiarity of the tune. It was the one she'd heard him strumming along to when she'd found him sitting on the rock that day. "My Rose-Shaped Heart." A small gasp escaped her lips. Up to now, she'd been too frantic with nerves to even think about which song Gabe had asked her to perform to, but now her nerves were frantic for a different reason. *Why did it have to be this one?*

She watched the band playing along with the recorded track, the cameraman moving around them, filming from a variety of angles. This was the first chance she'd had to listen to all of the words, having only caught a snippet of the song that day. It appeared to be about a girl he called "his rose" who'd stolen his heart the very moment he'd first set eyes on her.

Anoushka felt a squirm of discomfort as her face grew hot; he'd told her that's how he'd felt the first time he'd seen her at Livvie and Zander's wedding. And he'd called her "Rose" several times since she'd shared her middle name with him. *Oh, no! This was going to be excruciatingly embarrassing.* She cringed inwardly.

Before she could dwell any further, Anoushka had been swooped on by Saskia the hairstylist and Meena the makeup artist. They ushered her into the stone building where tables were piled high with hair and beauty equipment, sending her thoughts scurrying. 'Ooh, I'm in love with your hair, babes,' said Saskia as she released Anoushka's golden waves from her plaits and teased it out. 'And I don't need to do much to it, just give it a quick tousle, let it hang loose. It'll be perfect.'

'Oh, your eyes, honey. Have you ever considered modelling?'

asked Meena, who'd pounced, wielding her makeup kit, as soon as Saskia had finished fixing Anoushka's hair with spray. She had the thickest eyelashes Anoushka had ever seen.

'No,' she said, feeling self-conscious. 'I'm not really keen on being the centre of attention.'

'Bit late for that now.' Meena smiled kindly at her. 'Anyway, I'm just going to give you a natural look; enhance those gorgeous features God gave you.'

'Oh, right, thank you,' said Anoushka.

Once Meena was done, Saskia appeared, holding a circle of wild flowers in her hands. 'Right, lovely, here's the pièce de resistance,' she said as she carefully placed them on top of Anoushka's head. 'Gorgeous! Now, go knock 'em dead.'

Anoushka stepped out into the bright sunshine, squinting as she gazed around the "set" where a handful of people stood about, waiting. Gabe's band were set up on a flat area of the moor where, despite their unusual venue, they looked perfectly at ease.

'Ah, man, you look beautiful, Noushka.' Gabe appeared beside her, smiling broadly. 'And I'm so grateful for you agreeing to help.'

She smiled back at him, feeling more self-conscious than she could ever have imagined. 'Thank you.'

'Right, everyone.' Jake's voice got their attention. 'Let's see if we can get things back on track. There's no time to lose.'

He headed over to Anoushka, and gave her a brief rundown of what she was to do. She was inordinately relieved to hear it was straightforward and just seemed to involve her wandering around while being filmed with the moors as a backdrop. She could do that! Gabe would be playing with his band for part of the time, at others, he'd be walking over the moortop, holding her hand. 'Just act natural, Anoushka. For the purposes of the video, he's your boyfriend; act like you're in love with him.'

She felt her face flame at his words. She suddenly wished she was still sitting in her garden at home, reading her book, minding her own business. *Why did I agree to this?*

Doing her best to put the awkwardness out of her mind, she

dug into the resources she'd learnt at uni and soon found herself relaxing. And, she told herself, it wasn't exactly taxing to look happy while you were wandering around such a beautiful place as Danskelfe High Moor. *With Gabe Dublin*, said a little voice which she tried to ignore.

Anoushka followed Jake's instructions, her hands trailing through tall grass. 'Look up at the sky, spin around with your arms outstretched... hold the rose up to your nose, take a sniff... smile... throw your head back and laugh...' Jake's voice called out. 'You're doing brilliantly, Anoushka... Right, you need to stand still now and look right into the camera... oh, man, that's beautiful. I love that smile... that's perfect. Now cut! Phew!'

After several takes – one thanks to the sound of whirring of blades as a helicopter made an untimely appearance – Jake seemed more than happy with how things were going. 'Thanks for that, Anoushka, you were amazing,' he said, smiling broadly. 'You can go and take a break, get freshened up.'

The sun was blisteringly hot and her mouth was dry. She welcomed the opportunity to grab a drink. She stood in the shade of the stone building sipping from a bottle of water, looking on as Gabe and Jake pored over the newly shot footage with Dave. The two men appeared to be inordinately happy, Gabe giving the director a friendly slap on the back.

It seemed only moments before she was heading back out on the set, after having her make-up and hair re-touched. Now was the part she'd been worrying about the most: she had to get close to Gabe. She gulped; she felt more nervous than ever.

'Come on, fella. It's your time to shine. And no rolling now you've been groomed. We don't want you covered in dust and bits of grass like yesterday.' She followed Gabe's voice to see him walking towards her with Bob in tow. The Labrador raced towards her and nuzzled her hand.

'You've been such a good boy, Bob,' she said, smiling down at him, her nerves evident in her voice.

'He has. He's almost forgiven for demolishing two pairs of

Lady Davinia's shoes. Almost, but not quite.' He pulled a regretful face while trying not to laugh.

'Oh, dear.'

'Bet you're not surprised to hear she wasn't exactly gutted when myself and "Bob the Shoe-Shredder" here moved out of the Castle.'

'No, I can't say I am,' she said, the hint of a laugh in her voice.

'Anyway, I'm hoping he'll redeem himself in her eyes when she sees his star performance in the video.' He looked down at Bob who was blinking up at him, his tail swishing over the grass.

'Oh, I'm sure she will. He'll be awesome; a real superstar.'

'Yeah, superstar's the word. But, I tell you, I'm already a bit worried about his diva behaviour. You should see his list of riders: pure white lilies in his room, a crystal bowl of doggy biscuits, milk, cooled to perfection and poured from a china jug, half-a-dozen lady Labradors, and, perish the thought, a four-poster dog bed... the list's endless. To be sure, looks like fame's already going to your head, young man.' He looked down at Bob whose tail wagged some more. Anoushka couldn't help but giggle.

The reprieve was brought to an abrupt end when Toby the runner hurried over to them, pulling their attention away from Bob. 'Gabe, Anoushka, Jake wants you in your places.'

'Right, here we go. You okay?' Gabe looked across at Anoushka.

'I'm fine.' She nodded, not wanting to share how nerves had started wriggling like crazy inside her.

Gabe's song boomed out again, and he took her hand, leading her along the path, turning to her, singing along to the words. Bob was bounding around them happily, his black coat glossy in the sunshine. The moors looked stunning in the background, bathed in the mellow afternoon sun. Anoushka smiled shyly back at him, reminding herself of Jake's words: "act like you're in love with him". She suddenly realised that wouldn't be so hard to do.

Before she knew it, she was in Gabe's arms, her hands pressed against his chest, him gazing down at her. Butterflies took flight in her stomach. She could feel his heart beating hard beneath the fabric of his shirt, feel the warmth radiating from his skin. It took her breath away.

'Look into Gabe's eyes, Anoushka,' said Jake. She did as she was bid, peering up at him beneath her lashes. The look that met her left her in no doubt of his feelings. 'Fantastic. Right, bend your head and kiss her now, Gabe.'

Jake's voice seemed to fade into the distance as Gabe brushed her hair back, cupping her face in his hands, rubbing his thumbs over her cheeks. Her heart was thumping. His eyes had become dark pools as his lips meet hers, soft and gentle, sending invisible sparks of electricity flying in the air around them. She closed her eyes and allowed herself to fall into his kiss. *Oh, my days!* It felt like a million fireworks were going off in her stomach! She'd never been kissed like this before. Never felt this way before. It was overwhelming. Dizzying. She couldn't stop herself from kissing him back with equal ardour, pushing her hands into his hair, pressing her body against his.

'That's absolutely brilliant, guys!' said Jake. 'That's a wrap.' But neither of them seemed to hear him.

THIRTY-NINE

It took a succession of loud barks from Bob for them to finally pull apart. Dazed, Anoushka reached a hand to her lips; they were still burning from Gabe's kiss. She was tingling all over and her knees felt like they could buckle at any moment. She was vaguely aware of Gabe looking down at her, his breath coming in short bursts. What had just happened? Where had these feelings come from?

'Seriously, that was fantastic, you guys. You were on fire!' Jake strode over to them, clapping Gabe soundly on the back. 'The chemistry between the pair of you is amazing; anyone would think you genuinely had feelings for each other.'

'Oh,' was the only word Anoushka could say, not knowing where to look as a round of applause broke out and ran around a relieved-looking crew.

Realising Gabe was uncharacteristically quiet, she stole a look at him. A gasp escaped her mouth as her eyes met his. He knew! He knew how she felt! *Of course he does!* said a pesky little voice. *He's not stupid. After that kiss, everyone will know!*

She gulped, not knowing how to deal with this new state of play between them. She felt suddenly overwhelmed by it all. She needed to get away from here; needed to get her head straight. This... this new *thing* that had suddenly happened between them had rocked her equilibrium to its very core. Anoushka found she suddenly didn't know how to be around him. 'Right, well, if that's it, I'd best head home; I've got lots to do.' Her words spilled out in a rush. It was glaringly obvious that was a fib; she'd intended to take the full day off before Gabe had rung her.

Meena and Saskia rushed over to her, hugging her tightly. 'It's been great meeting you, babes,' said Saskia.

'It so has, and you're a natural in front of the camera. You've been a joy to work with.' Meena kissed her noisily on the cheek. 'Not like some of the prima donnas we have to tiptoe around,' she said, lowering her voice.

'Yeah, you should seriously consider a career change. Maybe you'd get another chance to lock lips with...' Saskia flicked her eyes Gabe's way and gave Anoushka a wide grin.

'Oh, well, I don't—'

'Yep, sure, that's fine, we've taken up your afternoon,' said Jake before Anoushka could finish. 'Though I might need to get in touch if we need to do any further close-up shots, but from what I've seen so far, everything's looking good.' He looked triumphant. 'And thanks for coming to the rescue, Anoushka, I'll be sure to see you get paid for your time.'

'Oh, goodness, I don't want anything for it; I was happy to help out.' She smiled back at him, trying with all her might to quieten the riot of emotions currently hurling themselves around inside her. She glanced quickly over to Gabe, not quite meeting his eyes. 'I'll see you later.' She went to walk away, suddenly realising her car was parked up at Oak Tree Farm; Gabe had brought her. 'Oh.'

'Noushka, wait up.' In a moment, Gabe was next to her. 'I'll run you home.'

'It's okay, I'll walk; it'll do me good.' *What are you talking about? It'll do you good?* Keeping her eyes fixed to the path, she continued along.

He fell into step beside her. 'But it's miles, and it's scorching. A walk in this heat will do you anything but good; you'll get heatstroke.'

Realising she sounded silly, she backed down. 'Okay, good point, thanks.' Her lips were still tingling from his kiss; she had no idea how she was going to manage being in such close proximity to him, especially when the urge to repeat what they'd just done was all she could think about. At least the journey was only a short one, she thought thankfully.

For the first few minutes they drove along in silence, a new frisson crackling between them. Anoushka could almost hear Gabe's mind turning over beside her. He was fidgeting, rubbing his hand over his face, scratching his head, drumming his fingers on the steering wheel. She could sense he was bursting to say something. Eventually, he could hold it in no longer.

'Noushka, you can't tell me you didn't feel it too. That kiss! I mean, I've never experienced anything like it in my life.' He pushed his fingers into his hair. 'It... it rocked my world. You rock my world.' He glanced across at her. 'And you felt it too. I know you did. I mean, the way you kissed me back... it was... it just... the look in your eyes... I saw what you were feeling. Man, I *felt* it. You can't seriously expect me to believe you don't feel the same as me.' He paused for a moment, his voice sounding suddenly despondent. 'Unless you're a good actress, of course.'

Anoushka's heart was thudding hard, her chest heaving as she gazed out of the window as the moors passed by. He was right; she couldn't deny it. How could she? The feelings she'd been trying her hardest to suppress had suddenly burst free and now infiltrated every part of her being. This was like nothing she'd experienced before: powerful and utterly overwhelming. And it scared her. Really scared her. But somehow, she was going to have tell him she hadn't felt what he was so sure of. It was too much. Her heart wasn't ready to open up and expose itself to something that felt as big and all-encompassing as this. And there were other things to consider too. There were certain implications of being in a relationship with Gabe that terrified her. Being in the media spotlight, for one; having their relationship under close scrutiny. The thought of that made her shudder. Then there was the fact that he'd have to be away for months on end, then there'd be times she'd have to join him in far off places. How would that affect her dance school? She couldn't just drop everything. But then again, she'd never felt anything like this before. She couldn't deny she'd fallen utterly head-over-heels in love with Gabe. It made her acutely aware that what she'd had with Damon was a pale imitation of love; if it had been love at all. But the thing she was most fearful of was what was really holding her back. What if she gave her heart to him and he walked away? Decided he didn't want to be with her anymore? Rejected her love. Abandoned her, just as her birth mother had.

Her throat tightened; the thought was utterly, utterly unbearable.

She was relieved when they approached the village sign for Lytell Stangdale. The opportunity to escape to the sanctuary of her bedroom and give her head the clarity it very much needed right now was at last within reach.

'So, here we are.' Gabe stilled the engine and turned to face her. 'When can I see you again, Rose?'

'Gabe, I...' Oh, God, this was so hard. She needed to think. Needed to get her head around this. Was she ready to take the next step with Gabe? Once she did, there'd be no going back. 'Gabe, I need to think about this. I don't want us to get it wrong.' She took a deep breath. 'I don't know if I'm ready for a relationship. I've promised myself the dance school has to be my priority for the fore-seeable future. What if I can't be the person you need me to be?' Her gaze was fixed on her hands twisting in her lap.

'Noushka, I don't need you to be anyone other than the person you are. You, exactly as you are, that's who I've fallen in love with. And I totally understand what you say about the dance school; I wouldn't expect you to give it anything less than your full atten-tion.' He reached across and put his finger under her chin, turning her face to him. 'But surely that still leaves a little bit of space for love?'

Their eyes met and the frisson sparked up once more. Her breath caught in her throat and she quickly tore her gaze away as myriad emotions hurled themselves around her body. She couldn't deny the power of her feelings for Gabe, but it was their very strength that made it impossible for her to give her heart to him. It was just too big a risk.

'I'm sorry, Gabe. You're a really amazing guy, but I don't want to mess you about. I just don't think... I... I'd better go.' Biting down on her bottom lip, she opened the door and climbed out of the car. Her heart was squeezing in her chest and she felt tears burn at the back of her eyes. There was no way she could look back. She knew what would happen if she did.

FORTY

AUGUST

It had been a battle to play down her role in Gabe's video to her family and friends. Lily and Lucas had been bouncing with excitement when she'd told them. 'Why didn't you tell me, then I could've been in it too?' Lily had said.

'Because you were out at Go Ape with your friends, Lils,' Anoushka had said, doing her best to act nonchalant. 'And anyway, it was no biggie really. I was just helping a friend out.'

'Course you were, Noushka,' Lucas had said with a smirk.

Her parents had exchanged knowing looks, the happy smiles that had danced over their mouths had made her roll her eyes inwardly. 'It doesn't mean anything, you two, so don't go getting yourselves carried away.' If only they knew of the torment raging inside her.

'Course we won't, lovey,' Kitty had said unconvincingly.

Anoushka had been in the pub, sharing a drink and a bowl of chips with Brogan and Kristy the following Friday when she'd told them. Fiddling with the base of her wine glass, she'd used the speech she'd spent hours preparing, playing everything down, adopting a casual tone in the hope of keeping their match-making impulses in check. Their giddy reaction told her she'd failed miserably. 'Flippin' 'eck, Noushka, this is serious news!' Kristy had said, her voice shrill, while Brogan had squealed excitedly. Anoushka had groaned as heads had turned with interest.

'Honestly, would you keep it down?'

'Never mind that, you little dark horse, you'd better spill,' Brogan had said.

'Yeah, come on, tell all, and don't even think about missing anything out 'cos we'll be able to tell if you have.' Kristy's eyes had twinkled knowingly.

Despite her friend's warning, Anoushka relayed a heavily edited version of the afternoon. She dreaded to think what the pair would have done if she'd told them about the kiss and how it had turned her world upside down. That didn't bear thinking about; she'd definitely be keeping it to herself for the time being. She was still struggling to get her head around it herself. She'd deal with what they had to say once they'd seen the video – which they'd told her they'd make a point of doing – when the time came.

'You know he's a guest on *The Tina Stone Show* tomorrow, don't you?' Brogan had said, popping a chip into her mouth.

'Oh, yeah. I wonder if he'll mention anything?' Kristy's eyes slid to Anoushka who'd felt her face grow warm.

'We'll have to make sure we watch it just in case.' Brogan had shot Kristy a loaded look.

Anoushka had groaned inwardly. She hadn't even wanted to start thinking about that.

'Surely you're going to watch it with us, Noushka lovey?' asked Kitty. They were in the kitchen and she was setting nibbles out on plates in readiness to take through to the living room. It was quarter-to-nine, fifteen minutes before *The Tina Stone Show* was due to air.

Anoushka, who'd been poring over her laptop at the table for the last hour, scrunched up her face. 'I'm not sure. I'd like to get these orders finished.' She didn't notice the look that passed between her parents.

'Come on, Noushka, it's not every day you see someone you know on *The Tina Stone Show*; everyone in the villages round here'll be tuned in. It's big news,' said Ollie, his eyes shining happily as he poured hot water into the teapot.

Which is exactly why she didn't want to watch it with anyone else. 'I might watch it on catch-up.'

'What? And miss out on sharing a pot of tea and some mighty fine nibbles with your old folks? Anyone would think you don't appreciate how rock 'n' roll we are.' Ollie chuckled.

She got to her feet and walked round to him. 'Well, Dad, when you put it like that...' She rested her arm on his shoulder and kissed his bristly cheek. 'How can I miss out on a cup of "rock 'n' roll" tea and nibbles with you and Mum?'

'Hey, don't forget about me. I'll be there too.' Lily bowled into the kitchen, grinning broadly, grabbing a handful of crisps from one of the bowls.

'Don't worry, Lils, I hadn't forgotten about you.' Anoushka smiled at her stepsister. She was thankful it was only their little family unit who'd be watching the interview together; she'd half-expected Jimby, Vi, and Molly and Camm to rock up and make an event of it. That would've had the potential to be excruciating.

Anoushka was nestled in her favourite squishy chair, legs tucked underneath her, hugging her mug of tea when the familiar theme tune of *The Tina Stone Show* struck up and the opening credits began to roll on the pre-recorded episode. She felt a flutter of nerves in her chest and scolded herself inwardly. There'd be nothing to worry about; Gabe was hardly likely to share his innermost feelings on national TV.

After the first two guests had been on, it was finally Gabe's turn. Tina gave him a glowing introduction and he walked onto the set to rapturous applause, his new single, "My Rose-Shaped Heart", playing in the background. The flutter in Anoushka's chest had become a full-on thud and her stomach gave an accompanying flip. Conscious of her family taking surreptitious glances, she lifted her mug, hiding her face behind it. Gabe looked heart-stoppingly handsome in his dark suit and light blue shirt, open at the collar. He'd had his hair cut since Anoushka had seen him last, lending him a boyish air.

The set – designed to make guests feel instantly at ease, which it successfully did – exuded a trendy loft apartment vibe. Gabe took a seat on the large, midnight-blue velvet sofa opposite Tina. A coffee table made of rustic metal and salvaged scaffolding planks, set with a teapot and two mugs, sat between them. The applause finally died down and Tina was able to speak. 'So, Gabe, that was quite a welcome.' Her friendly grin flashed whitened teeth.

'Ah, it's amazing what a bit of bribery can do,' he said, smiling broadly and turning to look at the audience. 'Thanks for that; you can collect your drinks at half-time.' They replied with a ripple of laughter.

'Well, thank you so much for being here. Tea?' she asked, the teapot poised.

'Thanks so much for inviting me, and yes, I'd love some tea. Splash of milk, no sugar, if that's okay.'

'There you go, a good old mug of builder's brew.' Tina handed him the drink. 'And can I just say, you're looking very dapper in your snappy suit.'

Gabe gave a throaty laugh, resting one leg over the other. 'Ah, well, you wouldn't be saying that if you'd seen me this morning. I tell you, it wasn't pretty. I swear my jeans were that grubby, they could've walked off on their own. It's surprising what a change of clothes and a trip to the barbers can do.' He ruffled his newly shorn locks with his hand.

After a few questions asking about his early days, and how he'd got started in the music industry, Gabe seemed to relax, reaching for his tea. 'And am I right in thinking "Dublin" isn't your real surname?' Tina asked. Gabe chuckled and went on to explain how when he'd moved to London there were two of them with the name Gabe in his group of friends. Gabe had gone from being referred to as "Gabe from Dublin", to "Gabe D" – the "D" standing for the first letter in his real surname, Donoghue – and eventually morphing to Gabe Dublin.

'It stuck and I quite liked it, so decided to keep it as my professional name.'

'What a charming story,' said Tina.

Anoushka watched intently but all she could think about was that kiss and how it had turned her world upside down, replaying it over and over in her mind.

'So, Gabe, you've got a new single coming out in a few weeks' time – "My Rose-Shaped Heart" – gorgeous title by the way. Can you tell us about the inspiration behind it?'

The artwork for the song appeared on a screen in the background; it was a heart shape filled with pink roses, overlayed with a filigree pattern and accompanied by Gabe's name and the song title in his familiar font. Simple but striking.

Anoushka's own heart jumped.

'Ah, well, to put it in its simplest terms, it's about unrequited love.' Gabe gave a smile as he set his tea back on the table.

'Really? Well, it's certainly got a haunting melody that gets right under your skin; I haven't been able to stop singing it since I first heard it.' Tina segued smoothly into her next question. 'You've mentioned before how you write from your own experiences, is that still the case?'

'It is, yes.' Gabe nodded.

Uh-oh! Anoushka tensed.

'Surely that can't be so with "My Rose-Shaped Heart"? Are you expecting us to believe you've been in love with someone who doesn't love you back? I mean, most of the audience here are in love with you, heck, I'm in love with you – sorry Mr Stone, I still love you too,' Tina said playfully, keeping the atmosphere light.

'Well...' Gabe scratched his head, clearly struggling with how to answer her.

Tina deftly stepped in, filling the gap. 'So, I'm guessing you've used an experience from way back in those heady days when you were just a young lad at school and had an enormous crush on a girl who didn't love you back as your inspiration?' Tina took a sip of her tea, peering at him over her cup, anticipating the delivery of a delicious scoop.

Gabe paused, not meeting her gaze. He puffed up a cushion beside him on the sofa. 'Er, yeah, something like that.'

'Oh?' Tina's interest was piqued.

'Yeah.' It hadn't escaped Anoushka's attention that Gabe's smile had faltered a little.

Sensing his reluctance to elaborate any further, the presenter picked up the conversation and calmly changed tack. 'Now, Gabe, everyone knows I'm a huge fan of your music, and the way you sing with that hint of your Southern Irish accent adds a gorgeous richness to your songs; it's enough to turn my knees to jelly.' A cheer went up from the audience, accompanied by a slew of wolf-whistles. 'See, they agree with me.' Tina laughed, continuing with her questions. 'So, can you share with us how you start writing a song? What's the process? What comes first? Is it the tune? The words? What is it that inspires you to take that first step in creating a brand new song?'

Gabe cleared his throat, looking thoughtful. 'Well, it can be a line that pops up in my head, or a melody, but it's life that inspires me really. I wouldn't be able to write about something I've no experience of; it wouldn't be authentic. I can't write without being truthful. I'd feel a fraud.'

'Well, that's obvious from the depth of your wonderful songs, which I've noticed are predominately about love.'

'That's right, yeah.' He scratched his head again. 'Though, I've just got myself a dog, so you never know, I might start writing songs about him now.' Gabe gave a disarming grin. Was he trying to steer the conversation in a different direction? Anoushka wondered.

'A dog, eh? And what sort is he?'

'He's a black Labrador called Bob and he's a grand fella. Mind, he's partial to chewing the odd shoe which has got him into a spot of bother recently, but I wouldn't be without him now; he's my songwriting buddy.' The audience gave a collective 'Ahh,' making

Gabe laugh. 'You wouldn't have found it so funny if you'd been there when the owner of the shoe found it, I can tell you.' He scrunched up his eyes and sucked air over his teeth at the memory. 'They went ape.'

'Bob sounds loads of fun, despite his penchant for footwear.' Tina chuckled and moved swiftly on. 'So, from what you've just told us, you've obviously been in love before.' She was clearly trying to guide the conversation back to matters of the heart.

'I have, yeah.' He shuffled in his seat.

Tina bent to top up his tea, leaving a deliberate pause for him to fill.

'But I've only genuinely been in love once.'

'Oh, really?'

'Mm-hm.'

'And can I ask if you're in love at the moment?'

Anoushka's heart took off with a gallop. The atmosphere in the living room was suddenly alive with expectation and she held her breath as she anticipated his reply, not daring to look at anyone else in the room.

Gabe rubbed his hand across his chin, taking a moment before he answered. 'Now that would be telling.' He gave an embarrassed laugh.

Slowly releasing her breath, Anoushka felt herself relax a little.

Tina beamed. 'Ah, yes, we all saw the photos of Lilith Dean. Is this the genuine love you alluded to just now?'

'No, it's not. And I've to be truthful here, Lilith and me are just friends; she's got a boyfriend. That's not to say I don't love her to bits. I do, but purely as a friend. She's awesome though and the craic's always good when we meet up, but her man Jonno's got her heart and rightly so. He's a great guy; they're a good match.'

'Oh, right, just as well you cleared that one up or we'd all be having the pair of you married off,' Tina said jokingly. 'So then, Gabe, do we know this person who captured your heart? Are they in your line of work? And do they – or did they – love you back?'

Gabe paused, his chest heaving with a sigh. He mustered up a smile. 'Erm, no, you won't know them, and they're not in my line of work; they don't like the whole being in the limelight thing.'

'Oh.' Tina took a moment. 'So am I right in assuming "My Rose-Shaped Heart" is about this person you are, or were, in love with?'

'Jeez, Tina, you certainly know how to ask them, don't you?' he said with a good-natured laugh. 'But if you don't mind, all I'm going to say is I'm not in a relationship at the moment, and leave it at that. I've got no one waiting at home who loves me. And yes, I'm no stranger to unrequited love, though, to be honest, I don't think any of us is.'

A chorus of, 'Ahh,' filled the studio, followed by a voice shouting, 'We love you, Gabe!'

'Thank you. I love you all too.' He laughed again, though his smile didn't quite reach his eyes.

'Oh, poor Gabe. I think he looks sad,' said Lily.

Anoushka gulped, shuffling uncomfortably in her seat, aware of Kitty and her dad exchanging a look as an air of awkwardness descended in the living room at Oak Tree Farm.

'Well, hopefully there'll soon be someone waiting for you at home and you'll be able to write more of your gorgeous love songs,' Tina said, picking up on his unspoken message of not wanting to share any further. More cheering from the audience followed.

'That'd be nice,' Gabe gave a half-hearted smile.

Anoushka felt a twinge of guilt, not liking herself for the hurt she'd caused him. Her reasons suddenly seemed flimsy.

'Oh, Gabe, I wish we could continue this conversation but I've got the director in my ear telling me we need to show a clip of the video of your new single. So without further ado, here it is, everyone. It's what you've all been dying to see; here's the first glimpse of "My Rose-Shaped Heart" by the fabulous Gabe Dublin.'

'Ey up, Noushka, here we go, lass,' said her dad, rubbing his hands together, grinning.

'Oh my God, Noushka, you're going to be famous,' said Lily, bouncing up and down on her seat.

'I sincerely hope not.' Anoushka wished the ground would open up and swallow her as the video started to play. She'd never felt more uncomfortable in her life. Why hadn't she stuck with her decision to watch this on catch-up?

'Oh, lovey, just look at you up on that screen,' said Kitty proudly.

'Oh, no!' It was the first time Anoushka had seen it. She cringed and clapped her hand over her eyes, peering through her fingers. 'Oh, jeez!' As if the close-up of her face wasn't embarrassing enough, she hadn't realised just how much the cameraman had zoomed in, lingering as she looked directly down the lens, her plump lips slightly parted, her eyes bright, gazing back shyly, the barely-there breeze lifting tendrils of golden hair. It had even picked out the smattering of freckles that covered her sun-kissed skin.

In the next moment her heart froze as right there in front of her, for all the world to see – and *worse*, her parents, not to mention all of Lytell Stangdale, including Kristy and Brogan – was her sharing a passionate kiss with Gabe Dublin. She'd been hoping with all her might they wouldn't play that part. Anoushka shrank into her seat as she recalled the feelings that had surged through her that day, her face glowing scarlet. There was no getting away from the on-screen chemistry that was exploding between them. And there was no getting away from how urgently she was kissing him back. She heard her dad give an embarrassed cough. Why, oh why, had she agreed to appear in it? She was never going to live it down.

The video over, Tina turned back to Gabe as the audience erupted into applause. 'Wow! That was some kiss, Gabe. So convincing, anyone would think she was your real girlfriend. Maybe you should ask the young actress there out on a date, she certainly seems to like you.'

Reluctantly, Gabe pulled his eyes away from the screen. 'Yeah, maybe I should.'

'Well, thank you for joining us tonight...' Tina's voice faded into the background as the family turned to face Anoushka.

'Noushka,' Lily turned to face her stepsister, her eyes sparkling, 'I think you're the girl Gabe's talking about when he says he's only been in love once. And I think he's still in love with you. And you know what else? I think you love him too.'

'You've got it completely wrong, Lils.' Anoushka was trembling. If her younger sister thought that, then other people would too. Damon sprang to mind, sending an icy ripple over her skin.

'Oh, sweetheart, that video was just beautiful,' Kitty said, resting her hand on her chest.

'Aye, it was, you were fantastic, Noushka.' Ollie looked across at his daughter. 'But poor old Gabe and his unrequited love he says the song's about. I can remember feeling the same about your mum here, thinking I'd never get the chance to be with her. Gave me the most awful ache in my heart. I knew I'd never be able to love anyone as much as I loved her.'

Kitty rested her head on her husband's shoulder and he pressed his lips against her short crop of curls. 'I'd had a crush on your dad for ages and it was when he kissed me I knew we were meant to be together, we just took the long way round and got us some gorgeous kids on the way.'

'Bleurgh!' said Lily, miming throwing up. 'Will you two quit with the puke-worthy stuff?'

'There's nowt puke-worthy about falling in love, Lils. As you'll find out when you get yourself a boyfriend.' Ollie laughed, throwing a rolled-up paper napkin at her.

'Arghh!' she said as it bounced off her nose. 'I'm never getting a boyfriend. Boys are so stupid and smelly.' She scooped up the balled napkin and hurled it back, but aimed badly and it landed on Mabel who was curled up by Ollie's feet. The little cocker spaniel jumped up, giving a startled bark, making everyone but Anoushka giggle.

She was only vaguely aware of the conversation going on around her, too churned up to speak, emotions charging around her body. There wasn't a cat in hell's chance she could wriggle out of the chemistry she'd just witnessed on the screen, of the feelings she very clearly had for Gabe and he for her. And it had been captured on film for all to see. *Oh, no!* A feeling of dread landed heavily in her stomach at the prospect of facing Brogan and Kristy. How on earth was she going to explain this to them? And, more worryingly, how was she going to face Gabe?

FORTY-ONE

The following morning, Anoushka was sitting at the kitchen table, working on her laptop, dealing with the last of the orders that had come in. It had been a hard slog and she was struggling to focus. She'd barely slept the night before and was glad there were no dance classes today, for more than one reason; she didn't relish the comments that would no doubt ensue from some of the parents after last night's interview. The room was warm from the languid sunshine that poured in through the open windows along with the song of a blackbird perched in the apple tree. Kitty wandered in from the garden, her hands filled with freshly cut flowers. 'These smell wonderful, especially the stocks,' she said, setting them down on the draining board and heading to a cupboard to fetch a vase. She was a keen gardener, just like her mum had been, and spent hours tending their large garden.

Anoushka glanced up. 'Mm, they look really pretty too.'

'Fancy a cuppa when I've finished arranging these? Or there's some homemade lemonade in the fridge if you'd prefer a cool drink.'

'Yeah, lemonade sounds good. I'll get it though. How about you? Tea or lemonade?' She closed her laptop down, glancing across at her step-mum, whose cheeks were pink with the heat.

'Mmm. I think I'll have a lemonade too.'

With the flowers arranged in a vase and placed on the windowsill, Kitty joined Anoushka at the table. 'So, how are you feeling, chick?' Kitty reached for the jug, ice cubes rattling as she poured the lemonade into her glass.

Anoushka gazed into her drink; she didn't need to ask what her step-mum meant. 'Ughh! I can't believe I'm in this mess.' Her shoulders sagged as she sat back in her chair.

'Mess?'

'Yeah, mess. I'm, just... I think...' She huffed out a sigh. 'I don't actually know what to think. It's all so confusing.' She rubbed her hands briskly up and down her face. 'What am I going to do, Mum?'

'Well, that all depends, lovey.'

'On what?'

'On you.'

'What d'you mean?'

Kitty sat back in her chair, her kind eyes looking at Anoushka. She took a moment before she spoke. 'Would you like me to be completely honest with you?'

Anoushka knew what her step-mum was about to say would come from a place of love and good intention, but all the same, it didn't mean she was going to like it. Still, she valued Kitty's opinion, so she nodded. 'Yes,' she said in a small voice.

'Well, before I go any further, I just want to stress that I don't want you to think that I'm interfering or being a busy-body, but having been in your shoes, I kind of know what you're going through. I love you to bits, chick, and just want you to be happy. So,' she said, getting comfy in her seat, 'now we've got that out of the way, the first thing I would say is, it might be a good idea if you think about whether or not you're being completely honest with yourself as far as your feelings for Gabe are concerned.'

Anoushka drew in a deep breath and gave a small shrug of her shoulders. 'It's complicated.'

'It's only complicated if you make it so. And, I hope you don't mind me saying, but you seem to have set yourself a load of rules – for want of a better word – and from where I'm standing, they just seem to be making your life difficult. They look like they're actually getting in the way of your happiness. I'd go as far as to say it's almost like a kind of self-sabotage.'

'Self-sabotage? And what rules do you mean?' Anoushka's forehead crumpled with a frown. She'd never considered that her promises to herself could be having the opposite effect she'd hoped they would.

'Well, for starters, there's the one where you can't think about getting emotionally involved with anyone because you just need to focus on the dance school; that it needs your full attention.'

'But it does.'

'Are you sure about that?' Kitty looked at her, smiling gently.

'And then there's Gabe and you.'

Anoushka's eyes dropped from Kitty's gaze. 'There's no Gabe and me. He's a friend, nothing more.'

Kitty reached across and squeezed Anoushka's hand. 'Oh, sweetheart, when are you going to stop fighting it? What happened with Damon doesn't mean you can't find happiness with Gabe. I know exactly how you feel. When I left Dan, I couldn't imagine ever being free to love your dad, but I'm glad to say, after an almighty internal battle with myself, I soon realised that I wasn't going to be happy unless I opened my heart to him. And I don't regret it for a single moment; it's the best thing I ever did. I look back now and can't believe I held off the way I did, but I was cautious after what had happened with Dan, didn't want to unsettle Lucas and Lily. But I know I'd never have been properly happy if I wasn't with your dad – and you, too.'

'I'm so glad you let yourself love Dad.' Kitty's words resonated with Anoushka. She was inexorably glad Kitty had come to her senses too. 'But you and he were childhood sweethearts, you had a history together.' Before Kitty could reply, Lucas charged into the room, his face covered in beads of perspiration, his damp sandy-blond hair pushed up at the front. He'd been playing football with his friends on the local playing fields. Ethel and Mabel, who were stretched out in the cool of the utility room, briefly opened their eyes, closing them again with a groan; it was too hot to move.

'Flippin' 'eck, I'm absolutely parched. It's boiling out there. Ooh, man that lemonade looks good.' He grabbed a glass and poured himself a drink, gulping it down noisily.

'Lukes, you'll give yourself stomach ache, drinking like that,' said Kitty.

'I won't you know.' He grinned and released a loud belch. 'See.'

'Lucas! That's awful!' Kitty couldn't help but giggle as she shook her head despairingly.

'Charming, Lukes.' Anoushka chuckled.

'Could've been worse, I could've farte—'

'Thank you, Lucas,' Kitty said, the corners of her mouth twitching.

'Well, it's true.' He wiped the back of his hand across his mouth and flashed her an impish smile. 'Anyroad, all my mates are talking about you, Noushka. Saying how hot you were in Gabe's video. Chester's asked me if you'd go out on a date with him, but I told him he had no chance.' He took another generous glug of his lemonade, eyes peering over at his mum who was giving him a warning look.

Anoushka shook her head, her smile fading. She didn't like the thought of being talked about. 'You're right there, Lukes. Chester has no chance. I'm not in the habit of dating seventeen-year-olds.'

'That's what I told him. I mean, you're not exactly gonna date him if you won't date Gabe, are you?' With that he polished off his drink and headed out of the room, calling, 'See ya,' over his shoulder. His words were followed by another loud belch that rattled down the hall.

Anoushka and Kitty looked at each other in disbelief before falling into a fit of the giggles.

'He's shocking,' said Kitty affectionately. She took a sip of her lemonade. 'But, getting back to you and Gabe, I would really urge you to have a think about your decision to avoid getting involved in a relationship with him, and the reasons behind it.' Kitty paused, taking a deep breath. 'And I hope you don't think I'm over-stepping the mark here, lovey, but I've got a bit of a suspicion it might have something to do with your mum leaving the way she did too. I think it's left a scar, made you wary, and that's nothing to be ashamed of, it's perfectly understandable. But if you let her actions define you, or define your future, then you'll run the risk of denying yourself the opportunity to be properly happy. Don't let her, or your experience with Damon, ruin your chance of a potentially wonderful relationship with Gabe, because it's pretty obvious to me, flower, you're as in love with him as he is with you.' Kitty lowered her head, peering into Anoushka's eyes. 'Am I right?'

Anoushka's head dropped, knowing when she was beat. Kitty had seen right through her. When she'd started her relationship with Damon, Anoushka had always been subconsciously aware that her attachment to him didn't run deep; that if they split up, it was never going to break her heart. But with Gabe there'd always been something different, something more, and she knew it was powerful. In moments of quiet, she'd begun to allow her thoughts to wander to what being in a relationship with him might be like. Something told her that they were right for each other, just as her parents were. But each time, she'd quickly dismiss the idea, telling herself she needed to prioritise her dance school, that there was no room for love in her life. And each time, she'd ignored her deepening feelings for him.

But the time had arrived to be honest with herself and with her step-mum.

Anoushka sighed and nodded slowly. 'Yeah, you're right. I'm in love with him.' She felt suddenly overwhelmed with tiredness, her bad night's sleep catching up with her. Before she could stop them, tears started streaming down her cheeks. She covered her face with her hands and let them flow.

'Oh, lovey, come here.' Kitty rushed to Anoushka, wrapping her arms around her and sweeping her up in a hug.

'I've been such a cow to him,' Anoushka said, sobbing into her step-mum's shoulder.

'No, you haven't, you've just been cautious. He knows that,' Kitty said, smoothing Anoushka's hair. 'And he'll respect you for it.'

'You think?'

'I do.'

Ten minutes later, her tears finished, Anoushka was dabbing her eyes with a paper tissue when Brogan and Kristy burst through the door, the pair of them out of breath. Kitty and Anoushka turned, startled while Ethel and Mabel jumped to their feet, barking at the sudden rumpus.

'What on earth's the matter?' asked Kitty.

'Noushka, have you heard?' Brogan asked.

'Heard what?' Her pulse started racing.

Kristy sucked in a deep breath. 'Molly just bumped into Lady Caro who said she's been trying to call you, but your phone keeps going to voicemail.'

'It does; we tried it too,' said Brogan.

'It's turned off.' Anoushka had turned it off after *The Tina Stone Show* yesterday evening, not strong enough to face the inevitable barrage of phone calls that would ensue.

'Anyway, Lady Caro was going to tell you that Gabe's been in an accident,' said Kristy.

'An accident?' Panic flooded her veins.

'Yeah, he's in hospital,' said Brogan.

FORTY-TWO

Kitty gasped, her hand flying to her mouth while Anoushka's face drained of colour, her heart going into freefall. 'What... what do you mean, he's in hospital? What's happened? Is he okay?' *Please let him be okay.*

'We don't know all the details, but from what Caro told Molly, he was riding a motorbike and came off it. Happened yesterday. He's in hospital over at York. Molly was going to ring your landline but we said we'd come and tell you and take you there, if you want?'

Stunned, Anoushka nodded, nausea burning in her stomach. She felt suddenly dizzy. 'Yes, yes, I want to go, I want to see him.' The horrible thought that Damon could somehow be involved swirled around in her mind.

'Do you know if he's allowed visitors?' asked Kitty.

'We think so,' said Brogan.

'He was in the critical care unit but Caro thinks he's been moved,' said Kristy.

'Critical care?' Anoushka's voice wavered and she felt her tears rising again. 'I've got to see him.' She grabbed her bag from the coat hooks by the door, panic squeezing her chest. 'I've got to tell him, Mum. I've got to.'

'I know, sweetheart. Would you like me to come with you?' Kitty asked.

'No, it's fine, you stay here. I'll keep in touch.'

'We'll look after her,' said Kristy, giving Kitty's arm a reassuring squeeze.

The journey to York seemed to take forever, with the A64 being bumper-to-bumper for a frustratingly huge chunk of time. All the while, Anoushka was willing the traffic to clear, praying Gabe would be okay. She'd texted Caro, who'd updated her with the ward he'd been moved to following an MRI scan. There'd been no mention of Damon, but it still hadn't stopped her from worrying about him being involved. *Please tell me Gabe's life hasn't been put at risk because of me.* She felt sick to her stomach at the thought.

When they finally arrived at the hospital, Kristy pulled up at the entrance and Anoushka jumped out. 'Don't worry about us, we'll find you,' said Brogan.

The lingering scent of bleach hung in the corridors that were bustling with a mix of medical staff, patients and visitors. Finally, Anoushka arrived at Gabe's ward, stopping at the reception desk where a nurse with a kind face was working at a computer. 'Can I help you?' she asked, glancing up from the screen.

Anoushka drew in a steadying breath. 'I'm here to see Gabe Dublin. Can you tell me if he's still on this ward, please?' Her stomach was churning and she battled to keep herself from crumbling.

The nurse smiled. 'Can I ask who you are, flower?'

'Anoushka, Anoushka Cartwright.'

'Anoushka, eh? He's mentioned your name a few times, that and someone called Rose.' She smiled again.

Relief flooded through her. 'He has?'

'He has.'

'Is he going to be okay?'

'He's a bit tired, but he's going to be fine. He's had a bit of a bump to his head; it's nothing serious but we're keeping him for another night for observation, just to be on the safe side.'

'Can I see him, please? I've come all the way from Lytell Stangdale over on the moors; I came as soon as I heard what had happened.'

'Course you can, flower, follow me.'

The nurse headed to a bay, Anoushka close behind. 'He's just in here. I'll leave you to it.'

Tentatively, Anoushka stepped into the room, her eyes going to the solitary bed where Gabe lay propped up on crisp white pillows, a drip leading from his arm. He appeared to be sleeping. She rushed over, pulling up a chair by the bed, her eyes roving over his face. He had a bruise to his cheek, he was pale and dark shadows hung beneath his eyes. 'Gabe,' she said softly, but there was no response. She took his hand in hers. 'Oh, Gabe, I'm so sorry for how I've behaved.' She rested her head beside his, tears spilling from her eyes and running onto the sheet. 'I've been a fool; I don't know why I acted that way but I'm so glad you're going to be okay. I'd never have forgiven myself if... if... oh God.' She sniffed and dashed her tears away. She glanced over at him; even asleep he looked so handsome. Her heart squeezed and she felt an overwhelming compulsion to kiss him. Unable to resist the urge, she got to her feet and gently pressed her lips against his. 'I love you, Gabe. I love you with all my heart. Please wake up so you can hear me. Please.'

Before she knew what was happening, his eyelashes fluttered and two dark pools gazed up at her. 'Noushka?' he said, his voice wavery, a smile tugging at the corners of his mouth. 'Am I dreaming or did you just tell me you love me?'

A smile broke out on her face. 'Oh, Gabe.' Her voice caught in her throat and she flopped back into her seat. 'You scared the life out of me. I'm so relieved you're okay.'

'I'm fine. Think I'll be avoiding motorbikes for a while though.' He gave a small laugh.

'Good.'

'You didn't answer my question; the one where I thought I might be dreaming.' His eyes twinkled at her.

'You weren't dreaming, I definitely said it.' She felt suddenly self-conscious.

'Say it again, my beautiful Rose,' he said softly.

Anoushka felt a flutter in her heart as she gazed down at him. 'I love you, Gabe Dublin. I love you with all my heart.' God, it felt good to say that out loud. To finally admit her feelings to him.

'Oh, man, I can't tell you how good that sounds.' He gave one of his lopsided smiles. 'And you already know I lost my heart the moment I set eyes on you, but I'm going to say it anyway. I love you too, Anoushka Cartwright.'

All at once she was laughing, unstoppable tears pouring down her face.

'You're crying,' he said.

'Happy tears.' She smiled, swiping them away.

'The best sort.' He reached his hand up to her cheek.

She covered his hand with hers.

'Don't suppose there's a chance of another one of those kisses? I was half-dozing when I felt your lips touch mine. I knew it was you though; only your kisses feel that way, and, well, I suppose the nurses aren't in the habit of kissing their patients, so it wasn't going to be one of them. But that's beside the point, I wouldn't mind another one of yours so I can appreciate it while I'm fully awake.' He gave her a cheeky smile.

'You can have as many as you want,' she said, laughing. She hadn't the heart to ask him if anyone else had been involved in the accident; part of her didn't want to hear if they had. It would save for later.

'As many as I want, eh? I'll hold you to that, so I will.'

Anoushka had just gently pressed her lips against his when a female voice with a rich Southern Irish accent made her jump up with a start. 'Well now, it's good to see you're well on the road to recovery, Gabriel.'

Anoushka turned to see a young woman wearing blue and

white striped dungarees smiling at her; she had dark hair that was cut in a blunt bob, a familiar pair of twinkling brown eyes and bore a striking resemblance to Gabe.

'Hi, erm, Gabe woke up.'

'So I see.' Amusement hovered over the young woman's mouth.

'Ah, Noushka, this is my big sister, Clodagh, she's come up from London to boss me about, I mean, visit me,' he said jokingly, shooting his sister a cheeky grin. 'Anoushka's just been making me feel better.'

'You don't say.' Clodagh walked over to them, her eyes dancing just like Gabe's. 'Hi there, Anoushka, it's good to finally meet you. Gabe's told us lots about you.' She held out her hand.

'Hi there. He has?' asked Anoushka as she took Clodagh's hand, her eyes flicking over to Gabe.

'That he has. Though he hadn't quite got round to sharing that you two are a now an item.' She hitched an enquiring eyebrow at her brother.

Two dots of colour bloomed on Anoushka's cheeks. 'Ah, well, we haven't—'

'It's only recent; we haven't had the chance to tell anyone,' said Gabe, quickly coming to the rescue, his eyes locking on hers.

'Oh, really? Well, all I can say is that the family are going to be jumping over the moon when they find out.' Clodagh gave them both a wide smile.

Anoushka looked between brother and sister, wondering what conversations had gone on between them. She knew from what Gabe had previously said that he was closest to Clodagh out of all of his sisters, and from the brief interaction of sibling banter she'd just witnessed, the strong bond between them was evident.

'So, little brother, I've just been talking to the nurse and she tells me it looks as though you'll be able to go home tomorrow.' She sat down on the side of the bed, smoothing the cover with her hand.

'Well, isn't that good news?' He beamed.

'It is, but you'll have to decide where you want to go; we've been having a family conflab and decided you can either come and stay with Genevieve and me, or you can head back over to Dublin with the parents and stay with them. Mind, I appreciate all that travelling's not ideal, but Saoirse, Sean and the kids'll be back from Italy the day after tomorrow, so Mam'll have to head home in time for that. Roisin's out of the question; she can't get time away from work, and it's the same for Grainne and Mairead.'

Gabe went to speak but Clodagh held up her hand, silencing him. 'No point in arguing, little brother; you shouldn't be on your own after a head injury.'

'I'll be fine in the lodge at Danskelfe, there's plenty of people around,' he said.

'That's not an option, Gabriel. State o' you; you need someone with you for a good few days. I'd stay myself, but I've got to get back to work and with Gen being due next week; the baby could arrive anytime soon. I mean, staying with us wouldn't exactly be ideal, but it's doable at a push I suppose – please excuse the pun – push, Gen, baby, get it?'

Gabe groaned and rolled his eyes.

Anoushka recalled him telling her that Clodagh's wife, Genevieve, was expecting their first child. She couldn't imagine it would be an ideal set up, him staying there when the couple would be distracted by the imminent birth. She felt a wave of sympathy for him wash over her, an idea springing into her mind. But before she could give it any proper consideration, she was pulled back into the conversation by Clodagh's voice.

'Oh, and while I remember, Mam asked me to tell you she and Dad'll be back to visit this evening. She's asked if you need anything?' Clodagh bent to puff up his pillows. 'But if you could let us know which one of us you'd like to stay with as soon as possible, then we can get everything sorted out for you.'

Anoushka looked on as Gabe closed his eyes and sighed. It was clear Clodagh was used to bossing him around. 'Like I said, Clo, I'll be fine, you should get back to Gen, she needs you more than me. I've got Sim and Caro nearby if I need help.'

'Yes, but it's not the same as—'

'I'll stay with you. If you'd like me to, that is, Gabe?' Anoushka turned to Clodagh. 'I'm not at work tomorrow, and I could cancel my classes for a couple of days after that.' It felt so natural for Anoushka to offer; she knew instantly it was the right thing to do, what she *wanted* to do. Which is why it didn't surprise that her offer wasn't immediately followed by a pulse of regret on her part, of wishing she'd kept her mouth shut. She and Gabe had turned a corner in their relationship and it felt good.

Clodagh opened her mouth to argue but stopped when she saw Gabe's expression.

'You'd really do that for me, Noushka?' he said, a mix of happiness, disbelief and not a little relief creeping across his face.

'I would. In fact, I'd invite you to stay at Oak Tree Farm, but it's not exactly peaceful with Lucas, Lils and Lottie tearing around the place,' she said with an apologetic smile. 'The racket they make would be enough to give you a headache without having a bump to the head.'

'Well, in that case, I'd love you to stay, but it's on one condition,' he said.

'Which is?' Anoushka couldn't begin to think what it would be, but she hoped it wouldn't be something that would incur Clodagh's disapproval.

'Uh-oh, I just knew it couldn't be straightforward with our Gabriel.' Clodagh pursed her lips, eyeing her brother warily.

Ignoring his sister's comment, he said, 'That you don't cancel your lessons; I'll be fine on my own, really I will, and it's not as if you'll be out for the whole day. All of this stuff,' he nodded towards the drip, 'makes everything look way worse than it is. Like I said, I'll be fine. And I promise I'll take it easy.'

Anoushka glanced over at Clodagh who released a noisy sigh and shook her head.

'What have I just been saying, Gabriel?' his sister asked.

'I can ask my family and friends to pop in and check on him while I'm working if Gabe's dead-set on me not cancelling my classes, and I'm certain Sim and Caro will be happy to as well; I'll make sure he won't be on his own. And there's an excellent GP surgery in Danskelfe, with access to some brilliant district nurses.' Anoushka hoped she'd covered all bases and would satisfy Clodagh's high standards. She'd picked up on the weary look that had briefly flitted across Gabe's pale face; she got the impression his older sister was no stranger to putting up a rock-solid fight to win her arguments, whether they be big or small.

Clodagh thought for a moment. 'Okay, I'm happy with that.' She turned to Anoushka. 'And you'd give us regular updates on how he's doing?'

'Goes without saying.'

'Well, that's settled then. And you'd better promise to behave yourself, fella. I don't want any reports of how you're ignoring the doctor's advice.' Clodagh wagged a warning finger at her brother.

'Jaysus, what have I done to be surrounded by such bossy bleedin' women?' Gabe rolled his eyes good-naturedly. But there was no mistaking his joy at the prospect of spending time with Anoushka.

'Ah, don't tell me you don't love it.' Clodagh leaned across and picked up the water jug on Gabe's over-bed table, topping up his glass. 'And the minute I hear from Anoushka that you've not been behaving yourself, I'll be sending oul' Granny Donoghue to come and look after you; she'll soon have you whipped into shape, young fella.' She threw a wink in Anoushka's direction, apparently pleased at having found an ally in her.

Gabe raised his hands in defeat. 'Sure, there'll be no need for that now, Clo. I'll be in perfectly good hands with Noushka here.'

'Don't worry, I'll make sure he does as he's told.' Anoushka caught Clodagh's eye and the pair of them giggled.

'And I stand by what I was saying about being surrounded by bossy women.' He gave them a wide grin.

The three of them sat chatting for a while, Gabe filling Anoushka in on the details of his accident which, it turned out, hadn't been as bad as she'd initially feared. He and Sim had been riding along a country road near Skeltwick. They'd been heading towards York when Gabe had been overtaken by a car that had got too close. He'd been forced to swerve, clipping some object in the grass verge which had up-skittled him and sent him flying in one direction while his bike had gone in the other. Finding his friend unconscious in the road, Sim had called an ambulance which had, thankfully, arrived quickly and blue-lighted him to York hospital. While they'd been waiting, the driver of the car had returned, full of apologies. A wave of relief washed over Anoushka when she heard it hadn't been Damon but a young lad who'd only recently passed his driving test.

'Thank the Lord you were wearing a helmet and your leathers, otherwise it could've been a very different story,' said Clodagh. 'And from what I've heard from Sim, I don't think the young driver of the car will be getting behind the wheel again any time soon.'

Despite her relief at Damon not being involved, it didn't stop Clodagh's words sending a chill running over Anoushka's skin. She reached for Gabe's hand, giving it a squeeze, thankful that he'd escaped with mild concussion and minor grazes. He squeezed her hand back, treating her to a sleepy smile.

'Fancy grabbing a coffee in the café; your man's looking a wee bit bored of our scintillating conversation.' Clodagh nodded in her brother's direction.

'Sounds like a plan. I need to find my friends who brought me here, and I need to text my family too, let them know he's okay; they'll be worried about him.'

Downstairs in the coffee shop, Anoushka found Brogan and Kristy sitting at a table sipping tea. As she approached them, they looked up, two eager faces, keen for news.

'How is he?' asked Brogan.

'He's going to be fine, thank goodness,' she said before turning to Clodagh. 'This is Gabe's sister; she's come up from London to visit him.'

After exchanging greetings, Clodagh offered to go and grab them a drink while Anoushka updated her friends.

'Thank God he's okay,' said Kristy afterwards. 'Ben's been threatening to get a motorbike, but I'm hoping this might make him think twice.'

'Can't see Molly letting him get one,' said Brogan before turning her attention to Anoushka. 'So, you little dark horse, you're going to be living with Gabe, eh? Well, that's a turn up.'

'Yeah, talk about a fast mover,' said Kristy, giggling and flashing Anoushka a cheeky smile.

'It's not like that, you two, as well you know.' Anoushka quickly glanced around her and leaned towards them. She lowered her voice. 'Clodagh's really lovely and means well, but I get the impression she's quite bossy; still treats Gabe like he's a little boy – in a loving way. I could see the potential for a lot of little arguments and niggles, which he doesn't need right now, and that's the reason I offered to stay with him. And just so you know, if there's only one bedroom, I'll be sleeping on the sofa.' She looked pointedly at her friends who were prevented from saying anything further by the return of Clodagh with their drinks.

'Here we go.' Smiling, Clodagh set the tray down on the table before pulling out a chair. 'Sure, I didn't think it would be in a hospital where I'd finally get to meet the girl who's stolen my little brother's heart. Seems we've got quite a bit of catching up to do.' She stirred her tea. 'So, when did you two finally get it together?'

Anoushka felt Brogan and Kristy's eyes swivel in her direction.

'Good question,' said Kristy.

FORTY-THREE

'Sure, it's good to be back home, though it seems strange without the presence of young Bob and his waggy tail.' Gabe wandered into the lounge area of the lodge, Anoushka following behind with his bag that she'd insisted on carrying for him.

'Oh, it's gorgeous in here,' she said, her eyes taking in the stylish-but-comfortable space that was deceptively roomy, the colour-scheme echoing the palette of the countryside in deliciously muted shades of purples, greens and browns. The heavy tweed curtains at the large bi-fold windows were the perfect frame for the view out over the moors that offered a glimpse of Danskelfe Castle. A collection of Gerald's landscape paintings looked striking on the walls, while a large, comfortable-looking L-shaped sofa and matching chair sat around a wood-burning stove which had a large basket of logs beside it. She noted Gabe's acoustic guitar propped up against the wall next to a well-stocked bookcase. At the other end of the room was a state-of-the-art kitchen painted a rich shade of pea-green, a dining table and four chairs set out in the corner. Portia had captured countryside chic – with a heavy emphasis on comfort – perfectly. 'I'd heard Portia had done a really good job of the lodges, but I hadn't expected them to be as fabulous as this. She's very talented.'

'Aye, she is that. Just wait 'til you see the bathroom. The bath's enormous; big enough for two.' He gave a comedic waggle of his eyebrows, making her laugh.

'I'll take your word for it.' She set his bag down on the floor by the door, feeling suddenly awkward, the prospect of them spending several days together under the same roof suddenly feeling very real. 'I'll just go back to the car and get my stuff.' She smiled up at him, tucking her hair behind her ear.

'Oh, course, yeah. I'll give you a hand.'

'It's okay, you stay put; I can manage.'

'I won't hear of it. Despite what Clodagh might think, I'm not an invalid; don't let her convince you otherwise.'

'Okay, I won't, but—'

'No buts. My headache's gone and I'm only left with a few aches and pains, nothing major. Clo's just fussing, which sometimes winds my parents up and gets them worried. You being here has stopped that, for which I'm very grateful. And, it goes without saying, it's not the only reason I'm glad you're here.' He smiled happily back at her. 'Anyway, come on, let's get you settled in before Caro gets here with the Bobmeister and all hell breaks loose.'

She didn't mention how she'd seen him grimace as he climbed in and out of her little car for fear of niggling him, but she resolved to make sure he avoided lifting anything heavy.

Anoushka had just finished hanging her things in the wardrobe of the smaller bedroom when Caro arrived. Gabe opened the door and Bob flew in on a wave of unbridled enthusiasm, bounding about his dad and whimpering excitedly.

'Hey there, fella, it's grand to see you but you might need to calm your jets a wee bit or you'll trash the place. Then what would Lady Davinia have to say, eh? She's not exactly your biggest fan right now.' Gabe laughed and ruffled Bob's ears.

'Welcome home, darling.' Caro pulled him into a gentle hug. 'Mwah, mwah.' She air kissed each cheek, doing the same with Anoushka. 'And don't worry about my mother, those shoes Bob chewed were hideous; he did her a favour.' She gave a wicked laugh.

'Well, thanks for bringing this young man over, I hope he's behaved himself,' said Gabe, easing himself down on the sofa. Bob parked himself in front of him, his eyes closed in happiness as Gabe stroked his head. 'Take a pew, Caro. Got time for a cuppa?'

'Just a quickie, darling. Sim should be here any minute; he had to nip over to the Sunne before he came here.'

'And how's Sim doing? It must've been a horrible shock, him seeing Gabe come off his bike,' said Anoushka as she made her way over to the kitchen to make a pot of tea.

'Yes, he was jolly shaken by it. Says it's put him off going out on his bike for a while. Can't say I'm devastated about that; my heart's always in my mouth when he goes out for a ride on that thing.'

A knock at the door made their heads turn. Bob gave a half-hearted bark but was reluctant to leave Gabe's side.

Caro strode over to the door, opening it to see Sim standing on the porch, a large cool bag in his hand which Caro immediately relieved him of. 'That was quick,' she said as he followed her in.

'All right, mate. S'good to see you up and about. Flippin' 'eck, you frightened the life out of me when you were lying unconscious on the road.' Sim headed over to him, resting his hand gently on Gabe's arm. He plonked himself down on the chair, concern in his eyes as he appraised his best mate.

'Hey, it's all good now. Thanks for looking after me, pal.'

Sim rubbed his hand across his forehead, puffing out his cheeks. 'I didn't do anything; it was the paramedics who were amazing. They were so calm, worked fast. I just stood there in total shock.'

'At least you were with me and I hadn't come off the bike on my own.'

Anoushka shuddered at Sim's words, catching Caro's eye.

'Well, it could've been so much worse, but thankfully you're here to tell the tale,' Caro said before heading over to the kitchen. She set the cool bag down on the countertop. 'Bea and Jonty have sent over some yummy supplies, which is why Sim had to pop over to the pub.'

'Oh, wow! That's very good of them. Bea's food's amazing.' A beam lit up Gabe's face.

'Ooh, it is,' said Anoushka, her smiles returning.

Caro leaned towards her, speaking softly. 'We're so glad you're staying with him. At least some good has come out of his accident; you two finally getting together.' She gave a small smile, happiness shining in her eyes.

Anoushka was about to say something but thought better of it. Tongues would inevitably wag eventually. What was the point of keeping quiet about it? Of delaying the onslaught of questions?

With Caro and Sim gone, Anoushka sensed Gabe's eyes on her. She glanced up to see him smiling softly. 'How about I open the bi-fold doors? Let some fresh air in?' she asked.

'Sounds like a plan,' he said.

With the doors pushed back, the sound of the moors flooded the lodge – the cackle of a nearby pheasant, the cry of a buzzard that circled above mingling with the low thrum of the tractor across at Castlegate Farm. Anoushka stepped out into the garden area, her eyes alighting on the all-weather rattan furniture, comprising of a sofa and two chairs, a glass-topped table in between. Yet more wood for the fire was neatly stacked in a log store. She spotted a built-in barbecue located in the corner – with strict instructions not to use in hot weather for fear of the tinder-dry moorland catching fire. Solar-powered fairy lights were festooned around the yew hedge that separated the seating area, while the borders were filled with colourful plants that were hardy enough to survive the savage moorland winters. There was even a slouchy hammock. It was all set to a stunning backdrop of the moors in all their summer finery, plump swathes of purple heather punctuated by clusters of woodland. It was breathtaking; Anoushka would never tire of its beauty.

'Wow! It's just gorgeous out here. And they really have thought of everything,' she said, looking around in delight.

'Yeah, they've created something really special. Caro's got great vision and employs the best people to make it a reality.' Gabe appeared beside her. 'And talking of something really special...' He moved round so he was standing in front of her, gently pushing her hair back off her face. He drew in a deep breath. 'Anoushka, I still can't believe it,' he said, his voice soft. 'It still doesn't feel real.'

She looked up to see his eyes were filled with emotion. Her heart began to race. 'Gabe, I'm sorry I took so long, I feel...' She sighed, her fingers gently touching the bruise on his cheek. How could she even begin to explain how she'd been feeling? Explain why she'd battled so hard with her feelings? 'I'm just—'

'Shh. There's no need to apologise.' He cupped her face in his hands, his eyes looking deep into hers as if waiting for permission to kiss her.

A deep yearning surged inside her, making her breathing grow rapid. With her chest heaving, she pushed her fingers into his hair and pressed her lips against his, releasing every ounce of the pent-up passion that had been growing ever since the first kiss they'd shared on the moors. There was no stopping her; no way she could hold back even if she wanted to. Her feelings for him had been well and truly unleashed.

'Wow! Talk about fireworks and thunderbolts,' Gabe said when they finally pulled apart.

Gasping, Anoushka pressed her lips together, savouring his taste and the heat of their kiss. 'It was the same for me. I've never felt this way.'

He smiled, his face glowing with happiness. He kissed her again, this time soft and gentle. Then he rested his forehead against hers. 'You've made me the happiest man in the world, my sweet Rose.'

'I'm feeling pretty happy myself.' She couldn't stop the smile that was pulling at her mouth.

Gabe went to speak but a sudden bark from Bob, reminding

them he was there, silenced him. They both glanced over to see the young Labrador sitting, looking up at them, his tail wagging happily and what appeared to be a smile on his face.

Gabe's eyes met Anoushka's and they both burst out laughing. Bob, eager to join in the hilarity, trotted over, dancing around them like a show pony. 'Oh, Bob, you're such a great little guy,' Gabe said, giving him a sound pat. 'I'm so glad to have you in my life.'

'I think he feels the same about you. He certainly gives off a happy vibe,' said Anoushka.

Bob took that as his cue and flipped onto his back, wriggling around, his eyes wild with happiness.

'What makes you say that?' Gabe laughed, as he watched the Labrador leap up and race around the garden, ears flapping.

'He's like a Jimby of the dog world.' Anoushka pressed her hand to her mouth and giggled.

'I'll tell Jimby you said that.' Gabe looked at her, his eyes shining.

FORTY-FOUR

Anoushka and Gabe were enjoying the afternoon, sitting on the rattan sofa, basking in the sunshine. The air was imbued with a blissful sense of tranquillity, the soundtrack of moorland life humming away gently in the background.

'Ah, man, this is the life,' Gabe said, almost drowsily. He gave a contented sigh.

'Mmm.' Anoushka's head was resting on his chest, listening to the rhythmic beat of his heart while he lazily traced his fingers up and down her arm which had healed well since her accident. It had been a long time since she'd felt this happy, this carefree, this utterly content.

'I'm amazed – and enormously relieved – there haven't been any repercussions because of you being in my video,' he said. After much persuasion from Gabe on their journey home from the hospital, Anoushka had confessed to the real reason behind the injuries she'd sustained to her arm and leg. She'd gone on to tell him about her conversations with Gina. And though he'd already guessed that Damon had somehow been involved, Gabe had tensed with anger, his already pale face blanching even more. It had taken some considerable effort on Anoushka's part to calm him down.

'Yeah, I have to say, it crossed my mind too. Got me a bit

worried actually, but Gina said he'd left Stevie alone after she'd taken out the restraining order. Like I said before, I reckon the police having a word with him, threatening him with another one, has been enough of a deterrent, which is a huge relief.'

'You're not wrong there.'

'Hmm. I heard a whisper he was dating someone new so it looks like he's switched his attention well away from me. I can't help but feel sorry for the poor lass, whoever she is. I hope she'll be okay.'

'Well, it's reassuring to hear he's turned his attention away from you, though the new girl has my sympathy. Hopefully, he's had time to think about his controlling behaviour.'

'I'm not so sure; I think it's pretty ingrained.'

They sat in silence for a while, watching a couple of roe deer make their way cautiously across a nearby field before disappearing into the depths of the wood. Anoushka felt suddenly conscious that Gabe was about to say something.

'You know, Noushka, much as I'm over the moon about us...' He paused a moment, sending a prickle of panic over her.

Uh-oh. I hope I'm going to like this. She tensed, bracing herself for what he was about to deliver.

'I think we should take things slowly. I don't want to rush you into anything; don't want you to have second thoughts. I'm happy for us to take our time. I know we've been friends for a good while, but this... this is different. This is special and I want to savour every moment of getting to know you as my girl.' He squeezed her close to him. 'And I actually need it to sink in properly; still doesn't feel real.'

Anoushka sat up, relief flooding her. She looked him directly in the eye. 'I'm not going to have second thoughts, Gabe,' she said earnestly, taking his hand in hers, weaving her fingers through his. 'I know it took me a long time to admit it to myself but I know right here,' she patted her heart, 'that being with you is what I want more than anything else in the world. I've never had these feelings for anyone before, and, yes, if I'm being honest, the strength of them scared me at first – a heck of a lot actually. But when I'd heard you'd been in an accident, that put everything into perspective, made me realise just how much you mean to me – how much I *love* you – the thought of not having you in my life was too much to bear. And now I've allowed myself to get used to the idea of us, well... I don't know how to put it into words.'

He pressed his hand against her cheek and looked deep into her eyes. 'Words aren't always necessary, my sweet Rose,' he said before kissing her tenderly, stirring the butterflies in her stomach and making them flutter about in a frenzy.

'That was delicious,' said Gabe, sitting back and patting his stomach. They were sitting at the table outside, and had just devoured the lemon chicken salad with fragrant, jewelled couscous and crusty bread followed by the rhubarb cranachan and cream Bea and Jonty had sent. A large citronella candle was helping keep the midges at bay. Bob was stretched out on the grass, his eyes firmly glued to the plates, ready to leap for any rich pickings that might come his way.

'Mmm. She's an awesome cook; Lucas is learning loads from her.' Anoushka dabbed her mouth with a paper napkin, savouring the delicious flavours that were still dancing over her tastebuds. 'Don't know about you, but I wouldn't mind a cup of tea?'

'Well, much as I'd prefer a cooling bottle of beer, I'm happy to follow the doctor's advice and avoid alcohol for the time being. So tea it is; I'll do the honours.'

Ten minutes later, they were back outside, sipping tea on the sofa. The sun had slipped away and darkness was creeping in, early stars twinkling in the sky. Brooding clouds were inching closer, encroaching on the remaining light. The atmosphere had become heavy and close.

'Phew, it isn't half muggy now,' said Anoushka, her short-sleeved shirt sticking to her.

'Yeah, feels like the weather's about to break.'

The moors had enjoyed uninterrupted weeks of blazing sunshine and, wonderful as it had been, it had left the land dusty and bone-dry. The farmers could be regularly heard airing their concerns and now the threat of a hosepipe ban was looming for the parched area.

Just as Gabe spoke, a flash of lightening streaked across the sky above the wood. It was followed several seconds later by a rumble of thunder.

Bob, who'd been sitting on the ground beside them, scrambled to his feet, looking around, puzzled, before rushing over to Gabe, pushing his head onto his dad's lap.

'I think it heard you,' said Anoushka as the sky suddenly darkened and was now glowering at them. The wind picked up pace, scurrying across the moor, lifting strands of her hair, its touch cool as it brushed over her skin. She looked on as the trees began to sway.

'I think it did,' said Gabe, giving Bob a reassuring pat. 'It's all right, fella.'

A moment later, huge splodges of rain started to fall. Before they knew it, the heavens properly opened and rain was cascading from the sky in a torrent; the wind took this as a signal to up its game and was now rocking the trees back and forth with all its might.

'Warghh!' said Anoushka as the pair leapt up. 'The cushions'll get soaked!' She grabbed the one from the sofa while Gabe reached for the two on the chairs, leaving his cup of tea on the table as they rushed indoors.

'Jaysus, I thought the rain was bad in Ireland.' Gabe's dark hair was now plastered to his head. He pulled at his saturated T-shirt that was clinging to his stomach. 'Ughh!'

'Yep, it really knows how to chuck it down, here.' Anoushka giggled as she closed the bi-fold doors, rainwater trickling down her face.

'You don't say.' Gabe grinned, turning his attention to Bob. He wrinkled his nose. 'Oh, man, there's nothing like the smell of wet

Labrador, is there? And, Bob, you may be a grand wee fella, but you smell like a pile of rotting cabbage. I think we need to get you dried off before you start steaming.'

Bob wagged his tail, his eyes shining happily as if he'd just been told some wonderful news, making Gabe and Anoushka laugh.

FORTY-FIVE

After being given a brisk rub over with a towel, Bob settled down in front of the newly-lit wood-burner, his ears twitching as the storm raged overhead.

Anoushka had swapped her soggy clothes for her light cotton pyjamas and a snuggly dressing gown she'd found hanging on the hook behind her bedroom door. As she headed into the living room, towel-drying her hair, she found Gabe in the kitchen, making a fresh pot of tea. Her stomach performed a somersault at the sight of him. His damp hair was ruffled and he was wearing nothing but a pair of pyjama bottoms that sat low on his hips. He looked unbelievably sexy. She couldn't stop her eyes from roving over his broad shoulders, sliding onto the smattering of dark hair on his chest, making their way down to his taut abs. She padded over to him in her bare feet, her eyes settling on his left upper arm. She reached out, her fingers hovering over the array of bruises, a reminder of his accident. Her heart leapt; God, he'd been lucky.

Before she had chance to think, his lips were on hers, kissing her hard, his fingers knotted in her hair. Lightening lit up the room followed by a deafening crash of thunder, so loud Anoushka felt it vibrate in her chest. Bob yelped and shot up, scooting over to them.

'It's okay, fella. You're safe in here with us,' said Gabe, getting down to Bob's level and smoothing his head reassuringly.

'Sounds like the storm's right overhead. I'll close the curtains and put some music on,' said Anoushka, her insides still molten from Gabe's kiss. She was just reaching for the curtain at the bi-fold doors when the lights went out, plunging them into darkness.

'Bugger,' said Gabe.

An hour later, the storm had all-but burnt itself out, leaving the air fresh and the sky clear. Anoushka was curled up on the sofa beside Gabe. She'd remembered seeing a collection of candles and tealights in one of the cupboards and had used the torch on her mobile to seek them out. Now, the room was filled with their delicious scent and a gentle, flickering glow.

Gabe yawned and went to stretch, his breath catching in his throat. Bob opened his eyes from his place curled up in front of the wood-burner.

'You okay?' Anoushka sat up to look at Gabe, seeing the pain in his eyes.

'Mmm-hmm.' He nodded. 'I just forget that it hurts if I do too much with my left arm; that took the brunt of the impact.'

'You're lucky you didn't break anything,' she said.

'Ah, tough as oul boots, me.' He gave her his lopsided grin that made her heart flutter then pulled her back into a hug. She rested her head on his shoulder and he dropped a kiss on it. 'So, I've been doing a lot of thinking recently.'

'Oh?'

'Yeah, I've been thinking about the future, about you and me, about where I see my career going.' He wrapped a strand of her flaxen hair around his finger.

Anoushka felt ripple of nerves in her stomach. She'd deliberately avoided thinking about how Gabe's career would impact on their relationship. But since she'd fallen hard for him, she'd found herself trying to quell the turmoil it instilled in her.

'I've realised my heart isn't in singing anymore, and, man, it *definitely* isn't in touring, it just doesn't give me that buzz; I'm weary of it. It's been creeping up on me gradually and now the feeling's got so strong, I just can't ignore it.'

A candle guttered, its light flickering around the room.

'Oh.' Anoushka hadn't expected this.

'The part I love the most, what gives me the biggest kick, is song writing. I've always loved that; scribbled down lyrics ever since I was a wee boy. Then, there's being up here in North Yorkshire, on the moors. I love it here; I feel more settled than I have anywhere else. And then there's you.' He tilted her head up to him, kissing her gently on the lips. 'I don't want to be anywhere else but here, with you.'

Anoushka pulled back, hoping to read his expression, her mind playing catch-up with his words. 'You don't?'

'I don't.' His eyes locked on hers.

She sat up straight, feeling utterly torn. It was one thing not to want to be in the limelight herself but she couldn't expect the same of Gabe; it wouldn't be right.

'Please don't tell me you're thinking this way because of me, because of what I've said about being in the public eye, and you being away for long stretches of time.' Concern filled her eyes.

He gently brushed her face with his thumb, looking at her tenderly. 'It's not as black and white as that, Noushka. Being here with you means more to me than all of that.'

'But... I mean... you can't give up your career because of me. You're so successful; it's been your dream, what you've worked so hard for. There's no way I'd expect you to do that.'

'I've achieved everything I set out to do as far as my career is concerned – and I don't mean that in a conceited way – but the bigger picture has always been very different.'

'It has?'

'It has. Being a singer was always a short-term dream for me. And, like you, family, and all it stands for, is right up there as far as what's important in my life. I've always wanted what my parents have; that bond, that love. They're soulmates, meant to be together, two halves of a whole. Jaysus, I'm sounding cheesy.' He gave a small laugh, catching her eye.

She smiled back. 'It's not cheesy; you could be describing my mum and dad, they're definitely soulmates.' It didn't escape her attention his goals for love and family life matched hers.

'That's plain enough to see.' He reached for her hand. 'I never thought I'd find that for myself, until I met you. Sorry, more cheese.' He smiled, his eyes twinkling. 'Then, when I was on tour, I found myself feeling so homesick for the moors – and you, even though I thought there was no hope of us getting together. The thought of just seeing you, of just being friends with you, kept me going. I felt tired to my stomach at the prospect of going on stage, night after night. I was counting down the days 'til I'd be back here from pretty much the first day. Hmm. Saying it out loud makes me sound like a right sad loser.' He pulled an apologetic face.

'Oh, Gabe, it doesn't.' Anoushka smiled up at him. 'I saw you on *The Tina Stone Show*,' she said softly, recalling the sadness in his eyes as he'd chatted away with the TV host.

'Ah, you did, did you? She's a one all right; almost managed to winkle all my inner-most thoughts outta me that day!' His smile fell and he heaved a deep sigh. 'So, after much soul-searching, I told my manager and my record company that I'd fulfil my contractual obligations, but after that, I won't be making any more records, won't be touring, won't be making any more television appearances. I'll be writing songs for other people to sing instead. And I'll be doing it from here; out of the limelight.'

Anoushka took a moment for his words to sink in, a huge smile spreading across her face as it did so. 'Are you absolutely sure about this?'

'Couldn't be surer if I tried.'

'And you're definitely not doing it because of me? I mean, I wouldn't want you to give up a career you love because you think it's what I want. It's important that you're happy too.' A little niggle reared its head. The last thing Anoushka wanted was for Gabe to make such a drastic decision that he'd regret a few years down the line. That sort of thing could breed resentment and wreck a relationship. There was no way she wanted to risk that.

'Doing this will make me happy. Being with you makes me happy. Happier than I've ever been. And I've more news.' He kissed the tip of her nose.

'You have?'

'I've recently put in an offer on The Manor House in Lytell Stangdale which has been accepted; should be completed within the next six weeks, all going to plan.'

'The Manor House? Six weeks? Wow! As long as you're certain...' She looked into his eyes, trying to read his expression, searching for any little thing that would signal a doubt in his mind.

'Noushka, I'm absolutely certain. I've lost track of how much thought I've put into this; I'm not acting on a whim. That's not my style. I've always followed my instinct and it's never let me down yet. I want to write songs, here on the moors, with you.'

'Oh, Gabe.' She flung her arms around him, her heart surging with happiness. 'I didn't dare let myself dream about this.'

Bob shot over and pushed his wet nose between them, his tail wagging furiously, making his whole body wiggle.

'See, even the Bobster's pleased for us.' Gabe laughed as they both fussed over the exuberant Labrador.

They sat a while, Anoushka listening as Gabe told her his plans for The Manor House, of how he'd still use the Danskelfe Castle recording studio in his song-writing process. He went on to explain his remaining contractual commitments with his record label; he'd need to make guest appearances and promote the songs on his new album, several singles from which would be released in the future. 'Much as I'm dreading doing it – more so since I made up my mind to quit – it doesn't seem so bad knowing it'll be for the last time.' She noted how he seemed so much brighter at the prospect of it all coming to an end, which helped chase away her doubts about his reasons behind it.

'And I don't want you to think I'm going to rush you or put

pressure on you to move fast with our relationship. I know we've been friends for a long time, but I'll take my cue from you; you can lead the pace. After all, there's no rush, we've got all the time in the world. Though I wouldn't mind sampling some more of those rather delicious kisses of yours.'

'Hold that thought.' Anoushka jumped up and headed out of the room, leaving a puzzled-looking Gabe in her wake.

She returned shortly and reached for his hand, pulling him up and leading him to the bathroom. The seductive scent of neroli lingered on the steam that filled the room, the large bath filled with bubbles. Candles were dotted about, their gentle light casting a romantic glow.

'What's all this?' Gabe asked.

'Well, you did say the bath was big enough for two...' A sultry smile lingered on Anoushka's lips.

'Are you propositioning me, Miss Cartwright?'

'I might be.'

'You'd best be careful or you'll have young Bob blushing.' He looked around for his Labrador.

'I think you'll find Bob's in the kitchen getting stuck into the dog chew I've just given him. He'll be too busy to think about us.'

'In that case...' Gabe closed the door and turned to Anoushka.

The following morning Anoushka woke to find herself nestled in Gabe's arms, her head moving with the gentle rise and fall of his chest. Sunlight was sneaking in through the gap in the curtains, the song of a blackbird trilling away outside. A wave of contentment washed over her and she savoured every second; she'd come a long way since her time with Damon. She'd never thought she'd feel this way. She raised her head, her eyes drinking in Gabe's features; what she'd give to have such thick, dark lashes. Her gaze travelled from the faint smattering of freckles that were dotted over his nose and cheeks down to his full lips. She found herself unable to resist the temptation to kiss him, lightly brushing her mouth against his.

His lips were warm and soft, sending a frisson shooting through her. Before she knew it, his eyes pinged open and he was kissing her back.

'Hmm. That's a mighty fine way to be woken up,' he said, with a lazy smile.

'I thought so too.' She smiled back.

'But you can't just leave it there.' His eyes were dancing, full of promise.

Before she could say anything further, he'd rolled her over and was gazing down at her. 'My beautiful Rose. Is it really possible to be this happy? Someone pinch me.'

For a second, his words sent her travelling back to the day he'd caught her in her new dance studio, saying the very same thing. They'd come a long way since then.

With a mischievous glint in her eye, Anoushka reached down to his backside and gave it a quick pinch.

'Ouch! What was that for?'

'I was just doing what you told me.'

'Oh, it's like that is it?' He grinned at her.

'It is.' She grinned back, her heart dancing with happiness.

'Well, let me tell you, that's going to cost you at least a hundred kisses.'

'In that case, we'd best get started.' She hitched a suggestive eyebrow at him.

'Mmm. I think we'd better had,' he said, pressing a soft kiss to her lips. 'But just so you know, I intend to take my time.'

A LETTER FROM THE AUTHOR

Huge thanks for choosing to pick up *Sunny Skies and Summer Kisses*. I hope you were hooked on this, the seventh instalment in the Life on the Moors series, and enjoyed getting to know Anoushka and Gabe – and all their moorland friends. If you'd like to join other readers in hearing all about my new releases and bonus content, you can sign up for my newsletter!

www.stormpublishing.co/eliza-j-scott

We won't share your email address, and you can unsubscribe any time.

If you enjoyed this book and could spare a few moments to leave a review, that would be hugely appreciated. It doesn't have to be long, just a few words would do, but for us authors it can make all the difference in encouraging a reader to discover our books for the first time. Thank you so much.

I've been looking forward to telling Anoushka and Gabe's story ever since they first met at Livvie and Zander's wedding. If you've read that book, you'll know Gabe was blown away when he first set eyes on the beautiful young woman with her cascading golden hair. It took him a while to win her round, but I'm so glad she finally gave in to her feelings and allowed herself fall in love with him. I don't know about you, but I think they're well suited.

On a more serious note, I thought the element of gaslighting Anoushka experienced at Damon's hands would add an interesting dynamic to her relationship with her stepmother, Kitty, whose first marriage had been blighted by her ex-husband's mind games and controlling, coercive behaviour. Kitty's love for her stepdaughter meant that there was no way she was going to let her head down that path without a good fight! It felt good to let Kitty have the opportunity to show her rarely seen tough side. Mess with Kitty's kids – blood related or not – at your peril!

www.elizajscott.com

ACKNOWLEDGEMENTS

So, here's where I get to say thank you to everyone who's helped in one way or another in the process of getting *Sunny Skies and Summer Kisses* ready for publication. And since this book, as with all of the Life on the Moors series, has been taken on and republished by the fabulous Storm Publishing, I think thanking the team there is a good place to start.

I'm going to begin by saying a massive thank you to Kate Smith, my wonderful, supportive editor. Kate's positivity and enthusiasm is infectious and her edits are always insightful. I truly love working with her.

Next up is the man at the top, managing director Oliver Rhodes. Thank you for setting up Storm, Oliver, and for gathering such a fabulous team together. Chris Lucraft needs a mention, too. He's Storm's digital operations director. Thank you for all you've done for my getting my books in all the right places, Chris! Storm's editorial operations director Alexandra Begley also deserves a huge thank you, as does newly appointed editorial operations assistant Maheen Mehmood in her role offering production support and file formatting. I do hope I haven't scared you off with all of my tweaking, Maheen! Thank you so much for all you do in getting my books shipshape for publication day, Alex and Naomi. Thanks are also owed to Elke Desanghere, who is Storm's head of digital marketing. Big thanks for all your hard work on the marketing side of things and for creating such beautiful social media graphics, Elke. And thanks also to publicity manager Anna McKerrow for her fab social media posts. Rose Cooper needs a mention, too, for the beautiful new cover she designed for *Sunny Skies and Summer Kisses*.

I must also send out a warm thank you to three fabulous people for their input in getting this book ready when I self-published it. They are: editor Alison Williams – thank you so much, Alison; I learnt a huge amount from you. Berni Stevens for the beautiful cover she designed for when *Sunny Skies* was first published, and to Rachel Gilbey of Rachel's Random Resources for organising a fab blog tour for that time.

I'd also like to send out an enormous thank you to the book community. Your kindness and support over social media is heartwarming and humbling. I truly appreciate it. Thank you.

Thanks is also owed to my lawyer friend for their advice on criminal proceedings and Anoushka's options regarding Damon's behaviour in the scene involving the car. I owe you yet another pint!

My fabulous author friends Jessica Redland and Sharon Booth both deserve a mention here, too. We have regular catch-ups involving lots of cake and cheese scones where we put the world to right, and I always look forward to our get-togethers.

Thanks as ever to my family for keeping me going with lots of tea and biscuits. I don't know what I'd do without you! Much love to you all!

My final thanks goes to you, the reader, for choosing my book and taking the trouble to read it. Thank you so much for being a part of this exciting journey with me; I really am most grateful. I do hope you'll stay in touch and keep following the adventures of the friends in the Life on the Moors series – it's *A Cosy Christmas with the Village Vet* next!

Wishing you all a merry Christmas and every good wish for the new year.

Much love,
Eliza xxx

www.ingramcontent.com/pod-product-compliance
Lightning Source LLC
Chambersburg PA
CBHW010432170726
48283CB00011B/3175